'As Soferman pick... in his right hand and ~~~~ ... ... the other, he was reminded of the arenas of ancient Rome. The gallery was baying for blood and the supreme arbitrator, the black patrician of the Small Fortress, sat on his haunches, arms crossed and resting on his knees, watching impassively. Schreiber was not satisfied with simply killing Jews. He demanded the ultimate indignity: that Jew should kill Jew for sport.

The Berliner turned to face his opponent. He felt Schreiber's beady eyes boring into his neck. He was the patrician's favourite. He was expected to uphold the honour of the dark empire. He was expected to satisfy his master's whim with the blood of an innocent.

"Wait!" ordered Schreiber. "Oberscharführer, where's my camera?" It was his favourite pastime. He focused the Leica and then smiled the most evil of smiles. "Okay, fight!"

"I shall live to testify, Schreiber, you bastard," Soferman muttered, at the same time raising the cudgel. "I shall never rest until you are brought to justice."'

I dedicate this book to
the memory of the victims of the Holocaust
and to the generations that will never be.

Also by ROGER RADFORD

The Winds of Kedem

ROGER RADFORD

Schreiber's Secret

PARADOS BOOKS

SCHREIBER'S SECRET

© Roger Radford 1995

ISBN 0-9518998-1-3

The right of Roger Radford to be identified as author of
this work has been asserted in accordance with sections
77 and 78 of the Copyright Designs and Patents Act 1988.

All rights reserved

Published by Parados Books
72 Redbridge Lane East, Ilford, Essex

Printed and bound in Great Britain
by BPC Paperbacks Ltd, Aylesbury, Buckinghamshire

For my wife, Yael.

ROGER RADFORD was born in London in 1946 and for most of his career has been a journalist. He spent almost ten years based in Tel Aviv working for various news organisation including the Associated Press and the Jerusalem Post. He also worked for the Press Association and Reuters. His first novel, THE WINDS OF KEDEM, became the most successful self-published thriller in recent years in the United Kingdom.

The author would like to thank that fine barrister, Nigel Lithman, Detective Inspector Frank Wetherley, Michael Gold, Vernon Futerman and Stephen O'Hara for their assistance.

'War criminals deserve the fullest retribution for their crimes. They should be shot on sight without trial...'

WINSTON S. CHURCHILL, 1943.

'There must be an end to retribution. We must turn our backs upon the horrors of the past, and we must look to the future.'

WINSTON S. CHURCHILL, 1946.

CHAPTER ONE

Theresienstadt, winter 1943

"Welcome to Paradise."

Herschel Soferman, hungry and exhausted after his long and arduous journey from Berlin, dropped his worldly possessions on the dirt-caked floor. The bundle of old clothes stared at him mournfully as his tired eyes lifted towards the source of the greeting. He did not possess the strength even to smile at the outrageousness of it.

"Where are you from?" came the scratchy voice again, penetrating the half-light of dusk struggling to filter through the grimy windows of the barracks.

"I'm a Berliner and I'm hungry."

"Let me see," the voice continued, "what day is it today? Friday. You're unlucky, I'm afraid. Friday is soup. Mondays are best. That's when we get a small loaf of mouldy bread. The rest of the week it's soup. If you find a piece of potato in it, you're a rich man. Otherwise it tastes like dishwater. In fact, we're all pretty sure it is dishwater."

The voice took shape and form as its owner stepped forward. "I'm Oskar Springer. I'm from Frankfurt."

Soferman, unprepared for such verbosity, shook the man's outstretched hand weakly. It had the consistency of a chicken's foot. In fact, the Frankfurter appeared to him to resemble a scrawny cockerel. The head, seemingly too large to be

1

supported safely by the emaciated structure upon which it bobbed, was framed by large, fleshy, almost succulent ears. For a fleeting moment Soferman imagined slicing them off and consuming them in cannibalistic fervour. A dry cackle forced its way from his throat.

"I'm Herschel Soferman," he rasped almost apologetically. "I'm twenty-two. How old are you?"

"I'm twenty-one, Herschel," Springer sighed, the deep-set eyes belying their age. "I know I look much older," he added quickly. "Tell me a Jew who doesn't age nowadays. Especially here. Come, let me show you our room upstairs. It's paradise compared to the filth here." The elfin-faced man giggled. "There I go using that word again."

Soferman smiled weakly. He had been ordered to report to Room 189 of Block 4 of the "Hanover" barracks, and now he was about to find out how luxurious his new accommodation would be. He picked up his rucksack and followed his diminutive host up two flights of stone steps to the first floor and then turned left into a corridor. Springer scampered through the first door on the right. There were twelve bunks arranged closely and in orderly fashion around the room. Upon each was a mattress and one folded blanket. The residents must all be fellow countrymen, thought the new arrival. The room was so tidy that only a bunch of German Jews could have been responsible.

"You can have the bed next to mine if you like," said Springer. "We lost Pavel yesterday. TB. It's a wonder I haven't caught it yet. Anyway, the one good thing about our barracks being so overcrowded is that we manage to keep warm in winter, although we put on as many clothes as we can."

The mere mention of the season caused Soferman to shudder. It was freezing. He stepped over to the room's solitary window and peered out at the courtyard below. Hundreds of people were milling to and fro, cowed not only by the inclement weather. They were *Untermenschen*, the lowest of the low, and they knew it. Soferman stood mesmerized by them. A procession of pregnant snowflakes began to fall. Everything would be white by the evening.

"I take it you've already been to the low barrack to get your identity card stamped," said Springer, breaking the spell.

Soferman fumbled in the right pocket of his overcoat. He and his travelling companions had been herded from the railway station to the collection centre. There, tired and hungry, they had been searched for forbidden goods and had had their identity cards stamped with the date of arrival and the inscription "ghettoized".

"You don't have to show me that, my friend," said Springer kindly.

Soferman felt foolish as he held up the card. It had been an automatic reaction.

"Come, I'll show you the washroom. The water's freezing, but then you don't exactly smell like a bed of roses."

As Herschel Soferman followed the smaller man out of the barracks, little did he realize how much he would come to rely on Oskar Springer for his very survival, and how much he would grow to love him for his selflessness and ingenuity.

Furthest from the Berliner's mind was the notion that he could be forced to act out a drama equal to the most brutal excesses of ancient Rome.

The two young men learned quickly that they had many interests in common. Both had a passion for the works of Schiller, Goethe and Kant. This was all the more remarkable in Soferman's case since he had worked in Berlin as a humble presser and was largely self-taught. Springer had enjoyed the benefit of a university education. They differed also in that the Berliner had spent most of his formative years in an

3

orphanage, while Springer was the second son of a family of eight. The Frankfurter had lost contact with them when the Nazis had decided finally to solve the problem of their own Jews. Every transport was "to the East" and fear of the unknown was not helped by the occasional rumour of mass slaughter, although most people had developed a finely tuned mechanism for denial.

For the first few weeks following his arrival, Herschel Soferman played the willing pupil to Springer's tutoring. He learnt that Theresienstadt was a transit ghetto set up in the old fortified Czech town of Terezin and that thousands of Jews from Bohemia and Moravia had already passed through on their way to "resettlement" further east. Now it was the turn of Jews from Germany and Austria to flood the ghetto.

"Never volunteer for anything," Springer told his young ward. "Always keep a low profile and learn to survive by your wits. The longer we stay in the ghetto, the better. And whatever you do, don't make yourself a candidate for resettlement. The Nazis are word jugglers. They've even produced a film. One of the Germans who comes to the cookhouse told me they called it 'Beautiful Theresienstadt'. It was made by Kurt Gerron. You know, the famous actor and director. Poor bastard. He must have done a wonderful job. They sent him on a transport to Auschwitz and ..."

"Auschwitz?" Soferman cut in.

"Oh, I forgot. You're fresh meat. You probably haven't heard of it yet. They say it's a death camp where they gas and murder Jews. Nobody wants to go there to find out if the rumours are true. Most people think it's a big ghetto with self-administration like here. I actually once got a postcard from my uncle Mordechai. It was a put-up job, of course. The first few lines extolled the virtues of the place. But then he wrote that he had met Yaacov Weiss, his closest friend."

"Well, that seems quite positive."

"Not quite. His friend Weiss was killed years ago. On Kristallnacht. But you can't tell anyone here that everything's a sham. They just don't want to believe it."

Soferman shivered in the chill air.

"Anyway," Springer went on, "one day not so long ago I saw the director crouching on his knees, pleading with the SS that he had made a magnificent film for them. 'That's just the trouble, Jew-swine,' the SS officer shrieked, 'it was so good that no one must ever know how you got the shits to act so well.' He then smashed Gerron over the head with a stick and threw him on the transport."

With that, Springer danced a sort of macabre jig.

"An actor. Who cares?" he continued as he bobbed up and down. "A painter, a scientist, a candlestick-maker. They all end up the same way. Most of them are German Jews like us. You know, those who were more German than German, who'd lost all their _Yiddishkeit_."

The jig continued.

"Look at this," he enthused, pulling a wad of banknotes from the pocket of his grubby and torn trousers. "Nice, aren't they? They've all got a portrait of Moses on them. Everyone has a bankbook and receives a monthly salary from our very own bank. There are bills in all denominations. Ten kronen, fifty, a hundred. Whoever comes here for a day or even a few hours is really impressed with the lot of the Jews. But you can't buy anything with this money. It's worthless. The whole thing's a farce."

Soferman soon learned the significance of Springer's first words to him when he arrived at Theresienstadt. In a frenzy of activity, signs were being erected outside various buildings. The banner at the entrance to the ghetto read "Welcome to Theresienbad" as if the place were indeed a spa. In other locations were other placards, some proclaiming "Ghetto Paradise", "Buy Your Own Homes", "District for Jewish Settlement and Jewish Self-Administration".

"What's happening, Oskar?" asked Soferman, his small brown eyes bright with curiosity.

"We're about to have another visit, my friend," Springer chuckled hoarsely. "Let's see if we can wangle a bit-part in the farce. At least we might get some decent food in our bellies."

"But you said never to volunteer for anything," the Berliner protested.

"It's okay, Herschel," the elf replied excitedly. "I've acted in one of these tragi-comedies before. You're about to become a film star."

And thus it was that Herschel Soferman from Berlin, by dint of his friend's connections with the Judenaltester, the head of the Jewish self-governing body in the ghetto, discarded his ragged garments for a reasonably well-fitting grey flannel suit and a seat in Theresienstadt's most luxuriously furnished "coffee house".

The coffee and cake had tasted real enough as the cameras whirred and members of the visiting delegation of the International Red Cross passed through the café on their way to the hurriedly decorated children's homes and other sterile sections of the "model Jewish settlement".

Soferman and Springer had smiled at the guests as the camp orchestra struck up a promenade concert. Food was the name of the game and nobody cared what the _Volk_ back home thought.

The visiting foreign delegates were accompanied by their Nazi hosts, and Soferman realized with a shock that they were the first SS men he had seen since his arrival at the camp. Springer had informed him that, but for the occasional German check-ups, the illusion of Jewish self-government was allowed to run its course.

The little Frankfurter had proven to be a mine of information, thanks mainly to his contacts in the Jewish Council, though how these were made and maintained remained a closely guarded secret. Through Springer, Soferman learned of the various illusions the Germans employed to create an air of normality in the ghetto, the greatest of these being the apparent non-existence of SS men. Discipline and punitive punishment were meted out by the Jewish kapos, while the Czech gendarmes remained onlookers.

"But there are more SS men running this place than you can imagine," the wiry man had told his friend. "That is why they carry out so many extensive registrations. They justify their existence by gathering detailed statistics, graphs, surveys and reports. It's efficiency gone mad. And those pen-pushers eat and breathe efficiency only because they don't want to get sent to the front. It makes our life difficult but at least it keeps us alive. As long as we can avoid ending up on a transport to the east, we too have a better chance of survival."

And thus the two men become willing and silent accomplices as the fat cats from Sweden and Switzerland passed their table, laden as it was with the sort of food the prisoners could normally only dream about. Obeying orders, Soferman and Springer kept their eyes averted from the guests lest they betray the true nature of the farce. It was all part of the game, and none of the inmates selected for the show was about to trade good food for posthumous glory.

"You certainly treat these people very well," said one of the Swiss. Soferman imagined the Nazi host smiling in smug satisfaction.

The delegation came and went and the actors returned to the vicissitudes of life in the barracks. Their room became so overcrowded that beds had to be shared. Good food became scarce, although Springer managed occasionally to procure the odd delicacy, a complete loaf of bread here, a whole potato there. He had not hesitated to share the treasure with his new bunkmate.

"How are you going to keep me warm in winter if you're all skin and bone?" he would joke. There was never a hint of sexual ambivalence. It was just that there was nothing more vital to survival than true comradeship. Loners did not last long in the ghetto.

By normal standards, Soferman and Springer starved. But by the parameters existing in Theresienstadt, the two men could count themselves among the privileged few. Springer was an expert in stealth and seemed to have contacts everywhere, especially in the kitchens and clothing stores.

"It's all done by what the Czechs call *slojs*," Springer explained. "We call it *schleuse*. It's the ghetto word for pilfering."

He reminded his friend that, upon arrival, each new transport had had to pass through the outbuildings where searches for valuables were carried out.

"The Nazis called it the *schleuse*", Springer went on, "because it's like a sluice-gate, a kind of dividing line between the place where the transport came in and the ghetto itself. Everybody passes through there and is robbed of most of his possessions. They rob. We pilfer."

Soferman learned that most of the pinching was carried out by the children of the ghetto, their morals corrupted speedily by the need to fill their empty bellies and those of their families.

"I have an aunt who works in the kitchens," Springer beamed. "She's checked every time she leaves her work. But she has a son and she always gives him four helpings instead of one. They never check the children. It keeps them, and us, alive. My friend, the children here see everything and know everything. Nothing in our lives remains secret from them.

They will look into your eyes and know whether you are a cheat or a pervert or, God forbid, whether you steal from your comrade. *Kameradschaftsdiebstahl* is the worst of our crimes here."

"What happens if somebody gets caught?"

"Stealing from your comrade or from the *schleuse*?"

"Both."

Springer shrugged. "If you steal from your comrade, the others will make sure you suffer more than you gained. I once saw a thief forced to lie on the ground. A small plank of wood was placed on his neck. Then another man jumped on it. *Fertig!* He was finished. The Nazis usually don't get to know about what's happening in the *schleuse* unless somebody squeals."

"And if they do get to know about it?"

Springer's eyes widened like black inkspots on parchment. "If they're lucky they get shot," he said matter-of-factly.

"And if they're unlucky?"

The little man shuddered, whether from the cold or from a vision of some terrible fate Soferman was unable to tell.

"Then", the Frankfurter replied hoarsely, "they get sent to the Small Fortress."

There was a pregnant silence. One man sought the words to express the horrors that had been related to him while the other waited for his curiosity to be satisfied.

"There was this priest, a Catholic priest," Springer began at length. "He was being sent from the Small Fortress on a transport to the east. I was on a clothing detail at the weir and managed to snatch a few words with him."

Again there was silence.

"What did he tell you, Oskar?" Soferman asked quietly. Springer looked at his friend sadly, the inkspots deepening. "He told me that no Jew ever left there alive. He told me to try to imagine the most bestial of acts that man could perpetrate

9

against man. He said that my imagination would pale in comparison with the truth."

"Did he elaborate?"

"No, not much. There was not enough time. He said all the SS there were sadists. He mentioned the commander's name, Jockl, his underling Storch and, especially, Obersturmführer Hans Schreiber. Apparently, Schreiber's favourite pastime is carving or branding a swastika on a victim's forehead after dispatching him with a bullet through the nape of the neck. It's a macabre ritual with him."

Oskar Springer fell silent once again. It was clear to Soferman that there had been no more time for his friend and the priest to continue their dialogue.

"What further horrors can possibly await us, Oskar?"

Springer stared ahead resignedly. Then quietly he said, "As we parted, I told him that if he ever lived to tell the story, he should let the whole world know what is happening to us."

Tears began to trickle down the desiccated husks of the little man's cheeks. Soferman, towering over him, gently pulled his friend's head to his chest and stroked the matted black hair gently. "I'll never leave you, my friend," he whispered. "Whatever happens, we shall remain together until the end."

Soferman and Springer survived the ghetto of Theresienstadt a further six months before an incident at the *schleuse* sealed their fate. Six months in which the population of the ghetto had been decimated by further transports, with fewer victims arriving to replace them. Six months in which Oskar Springer had used every ounce of ingenuity within his slender frame to ensure that he and his friend were not loaded like cattle onto one of the transports.

It was the dreaded commander of the ghetto himself, Obersturmbannführer Karl Rahm, who proved the catalyst.

Rahm, a choleric brute who was rumoured to have personally strangled two devout Czech Jews, was visiting the *schleuse* after welcoming a group of Dutch Jews from Westerbork. The Dutch had arrived looking relatively prosperous and laden with food, tobacco, valuables and money.

"The Dutch transports are best," Springer had told Soferman eagerly the day before. "I'll arrange for us to get on the *schleuse* detail. Little Emil will see to it."

Little Emil was a waif who was fifteen but looked half his age. He was lupine, a Springer in miniature, as Soferman once commented. Emil was a Czech Jew whose parents and sister had disappeared into the unknown two years earlier. To have survived so long in the ghetto needed more than luck. It needed resourcefulness of almost heroic proportions. Every risk Emil took was calculated. With no family to care for or be cared for by, he survived by wits alone, organizing small gangs of children to pilfer from the *schleuse* and then distribute the items, mainly food, to the starving longer-term inmates of the ghetto. The survivors from the old transports eagerly awaited the new. But now they were becoming fewer and their precious bounty was even more coveted. Thus the inmates had good cause to revere Emil, the Waif, as he was called.

"Come, Soferman, Springer!" the high-pitched voice had called urgently one morning as a shaft of warm summer sunlight pierced the barrack room, empty now save for the two forms lying on adjacent beds at the far end. "Wake up! The Dutch have arrived."

Soferman raised himself on one arm and rubbed his eyes. "Is that you, Emil?" he asked wearily.

"Quickly, Soferman. Wake Springer and be at the *schleuse* in no more than five minutes. I'll be in trouble with the gendarme Novotny if you aren't."

Springer and Soferman did not need to be told twice.

11

Thanks to the Waif they had eaten better than most for a long time. But there had not been a transport for over a month and now even they were suffering the compassionless pangs of chronic hunger.

Upon their arrival at the *schleuse* the scene was of the usual pandemonium. The Dutch were incredulous at being ordered to divest themselves of all of their most treasured possessions.

The detail, under the morose eyes of the Czech gendarmes, busily collected whatever came to hand, including food. Jewellery was of infinitely less importance to the old hands. One simply could not eat a gold ring. But valuable trinkets were of great interest to the Nazis and the new arrivals were warned that discovery of anything undivulged would render unto the owner the ultimate punishment.

"You!" barked Novotny. The plump red-faced gendarme pointed at Emil, Soferman and Springer. "Join the food collection detail."

The three needed no second invitation. Novotny always put on an act of severity at the *schleuse* in order to impress the new arrivals and any Nazis who might be around. But the Czech had a heart of gold and had endangered his life on many occasions in order that some ghetto Jews might have a little extra to eat.

Soferman stood behind one of the counters, which were scratched and pitted from the countless possessions that had scraped across them. The owners of the goods were jetsam too, he thought. They too had been tossed by fate into this maelstrom of iniquity. He could not bear to look at them squarely, for their eyes spoke eloquently of their indignation that it was now men wearing yellow stars who were robbing them. But those that had the good fortune to remain in the ghetto would learn quickly that this was the way of things and that anything was preferable to transport to the east.

The Berliner began collecting the parcels of food. The array was mouthwatering, from blocks of Gouda and Edam, some still encased in their chessels, to Bratwurst and Knackwurst, resplendent in length and aroma. The Nazis would take their fill, but there remained much that would be shared among the veteran prisoners of the ghetto.

Soferman passed the food to Springer who, in turn, handed the items to little Emil for stacking and packing. It was the Waif who organized the shortfall. Empty wooden crates were brought forward and quickly filled. But some had false bottoms and no one paid much attention to a prisoner labouring under a load of ostensibly empty crates. The bottom crate of each stack contained the lifeblood of the ghetto.

It was about half an hour after the arrival of the transport that cries of *"Achtung! Achtung!"* rent the dank air of the sluice. Jewish kapos and Czech gendarmes pushed the throng back as a lone figure stood silhouetted in the main entrance directly to the right of the counters.

Soferman peered intently at the form. It was the Waif who revealed the identity of the spectre in the doorway.

"It's Rahm," he whispered.

As Obersturmbannführer Karl Rahm continued to linger in the sunlit entrance, a passing cloud reduced the halo effect. The new arrivals would soon find out that here was indeed an icon; that the stubby apparition before them held sway over all life and death in the ghetto.

Rahm, hands clasped behind his back, strutted forward. The unlit cigar projecting from his mouth seemed to act as a pointer. He stopped at the first stall and leaned against it. Standing to his left were two SS guards armed with submachine-guns. There was absolute silence, save for the inevitable rustling and stifled coughing of a room packed with people.

Soferman had seen Rahm only twice before, and each time the Kommandant had made one or two prisoners suffer his ire.

It was unwise to look the Nazi in the eye, for the riding crop in his right hand did not brook insolence kindly.

At last the brute spoke.

"It has come to my notice", he said calmly, his eyes directed at the veteran prisoners behind the counters, "that some of our long-term guests have been abusing their privileges." The cigar, a large Havana, meandered around Rahm's mouth menacingly as he waited for his words to have the desired effect. He then withdrew it and crushed it beneath his jackboot.

Soferman glanced nervously at Novotny. The gendarme reddened but shook his head in protestation of his innocence. The Berliner then felt a rustling at his feet. Out of sight of the Nazis, Emil Lustig was squeezing himself into one of the green wooden crates.

"Food, gentlemen," Rahm sneered. "You swine have been pilfering good, honest Dutch food."

Soferman felt the icy tentacles of panic grip his stomach, but not on his own account. The Waif must be protected at all costs. Without him, hundreds would starve to death.

"I need a volunteer," Rahm screamed suddenly, bringing his crop violently down on the counter with a crack. There must have been at least a hundred people in the room and every one of them, prisoners, gendarmes and even the two SS hatchet-men, flinched.

Rahm again spoke in a quiet yet menacing voice. "I am not asking much. Just one lousy Jew-pig to set an example to our new guests here. But let me warn you. Should there be no volunteer, I will take fifty of these clog-dancers and have them shot." The Kommandant chuckled malevolently. "We will plant tulips on their graves."

This was a signal for the gendarmes and even the Jewish kapos to laugh conspiratorially. The crate by Soferman's feet creaked. To the Berliner, it sounded like the crack of a pistol.

Thankfully, Rahm appeared not to have heard it.

"Well," the pumpkin face blurted, "my patience is wearing thin."

Soferman felt a movement to his right. "No, Springer," he cried inwardly, "don't do it. The Dutch will die anyway."

Oskar Springer, a lone lemming in a colony dedicated to self-preservation, shuffled from behind the counter and stood in front of the portly Rahm, head bowed. The peacock and the sparrow, thought Soferman. One vain and the other humble. But the sparrow would have his day, one day.

"*Schwein!*" Rahm exploded, slashing the whip fiercely across the lupine face. "You Jew-pigs would steal from your own children."

Springer collapsed on one knee, blood pouring from the wound on his cheek.

Soferman did not fully understand why he did it, but Oskar Springer represented to him the only family he had left. He had vowed never to leave him, and certainly not in this, his hour of greatest need. The tall Berliner stepped out from behind the counter.

"I am guilty too, Obersturmbannführer," he said firmly.

Rahm glared at the man before him. The Jew was fair-haired. He could even have passed for an Aryan. He reminded him of someone, but he could not place who.

"Take them away," he ordered, his lips pursing in a rictus of hatred.

A feeling of emptiness gripped Soferman as one of the guards pulled him roughly by the arm. The Berliner did not look, but he felt Springer's quicker steps padding behind him. There was no doubting their destination. Rahm felt unfulfilled unless he sent at least two Jews a day to the Small Fortress.

The fort was sited a few hundred metres away on the other side of the river Ohre. The eyes of fellow prisoners turned away as they left the *schleuse* on the short journey to Hades.

Soferman asked himself whether their furtive glances were of pity or relief, or perhaps both.

The Berliner felt a moment of sublime giddiness as he relished the smells of the river. He had never been a country lad at heart. But after the confines of the ghetto, he found himself savouring the intoxicating fresh air. The morning was cool and pleasant, and the sound of birdsong was at once both strange and familiar. He sighed wearily, wishing at that moment that he were as free as the swallows.

"*Schnell! Schnell!*" cried the guard, angry at his ward's faltering step.

Soferman's brief interlude of exultation was cut short by a stinging blow to the back of the head. The Berliner quickened his pace as they neared the fortress. It was surrounded by trenches, and standing sentinel within its walls of ashlar and burnt brick was a row of barred windows.

The two prisoners were hustled into a small room to the right of the entrance. The guards stood either side of the door as they ordered Soferman and Springer to attention in the middle of the room. For what seemed an eternity they waited, not daring to move. The Berliner tried to organize his emotions. He had not looked directly at Springer since their arrest. He did not think he could bear the eyes that he knew were beseeching him. He had made his decision and to regret it was futile. He convinced himself that they were doomed anyway. The Germans would lose the war and they would probably slaughter all the Jews in order to leave no witnesses. It was simply a matter of time.

The sun was by now a little higher, and its warming rays shone through the room's solitary barred window to their right. They were facing away from the guards and did not hear the entrance of a tall, blond man dressed in the crisp black uniform of an SS Obersturmführer.

Suddenly Soferman sensed a presence behind him. He dared

not move. He felt the breath of the man on his right ear. It was scented, reminding him of the sprigs of lavender he used to bring to his mother on his way home from school.

"Pig-eaters," a voice whispered venomously. "You sons of bitches from Jerusalem. You world criminals. You arseholes." Hans Schreiber lingered a moment longer by Soferman's ear before stepping forward to face the two men. Soferman looked the Beast of the Small Fortress directly in the eye but kept his face expressionless. So this was Schreiber, he thought. The Nazi must have been about the same age as himself. He was blond and handsome in the sort of way revered by National Socialist ideology. The sole physical blemish was the pair of small hazel eyes. Where was the azure of Aryan mythology?

The epitome of evil stood about a metre from them, hands clasped firmly behind back and legs apart. The expression on the clean-shaven and perfumed face was a mixture of vanity and contempt.

"You have been brought here to die, Jews," he said at length. "The manner in which you die will be decided by me, Hans Schreiber. If you please me, it will be quick. But if you displease me ..."

Schreiber crossed his arms and waited for the imaginations of the prisoners to reach their own conclusions. He enjoyed sporting with these degenerates. They would find out soon enough what he had in store for them.

"Your identity cards," he barked, thrusting out a perfectly manicured hand.

Soferman stared in fascination at the long, slender fingers as Schreiber read aloud.

"HER-schel Soferman and OS-kar Springer," he enunciated with heavy and deliberate emphasis. "Both Germans."

Schreiber's eyes narrowed. "Where are you from?" he said to Springer.

"Frankfurt, Herr Obersturmführer," the little man said

shakily.

"And you?"

"Berlin, Obersturmführer," said Soferman, his eyes unwavering.

"Ah, good. My home town, SOFER-man." Schreiber's tone became threatening. "You know that if it wasn't for you Jew-pigs there would be no war. Back home they tell me that my city is being bombed by the Allies. You must answer for your sins, SOFER-man." He pocketed the identity cards. "You won't be needing these any more."

Suddenly, something quite extraordinary happened. The dust in the room caused Springer to sneeze. Schreiber sprung backwards, raising his hands to protect his face. He reddened and for a moment clasped one hand over his mouth. Then he leapt forward and dealt Springer a vicious blow to the face.

"Don't you ever spread your Jew-germs in my presence again," he shrieked. "Fritz, take them to the Jew-cell. Make sure they get a good night's sleep. I want them fresh in the morning."

With this, Schreiber turned on his heels and strode out of the room.

"I'm sorry, Herschel," Springer croaked. His eyes, hollow and helpless, sought forgiveness.

"Shut up, you pig's arse," cursed the guard named Fritz, moving threateningly towards them. "Follow me."

Springer shuffled into line behind Soferman as they made their way out of the room and into a cold, unwelcoming corridor. After some twenty metres, they turned into another room. It was a cell about six metres by six. In one corner were two buckets for excrement. The prisoners gagged on the stench.

"This is where you will eat and sleep," said the guard, backing away. "Don't worry, it won't be for long. Wait here until you are collected for the work detail."

The absence of any guards gave Soferman and Springer the opportunity to share their feelings. Both struggled to shake off the fear that had clamped their minds.

"So that is Hans Schreiber," Soferman whispered. "The devil incarnate."

Springer turned to face his friend. "It's strange, but ..."

Soferman looked down at the elfin eyes which were staring at him with a mixture of wonder and apprehension. "Go on, Oskar."

"It's stupid, but you and he are so alike physically. If you just had a few more kilos on you ..."

Just then a man appeared in the doorway. He was emaciated, his striped prison garb filthy and tattered. The yellow star was barely discernible through the grime.

"Come," he croaked.

They followed the angular figure out of the block and into a large courtyard. At the far end they could see two groups of prisoners working by the fortification walls. Soferman could make out the symbol that denoted politicals on the garb of those in one corner. The other group, to the right, were Jews.

"These are the old fortification walls," said their guide in a resigned monotone. "We have to pull them down. Take these." The man pointed to two pickaxes which were lying on the ground.

As he stooped to pick one up, Soferman noticed Schreiber standing about fifteen metres away. The Nazi, a riding crop held diagonally across his chest, seemed to be staring at him intently.

"You two, Soferman and Springer, join the gang on top of the wall," he called out. "And be quick about it."

The man who had led them to the wall was working with a group in a pit running along its base. "Quickly, do as he says," he gasped in Yiddish.

Soferman grabbed his friend's hand and began climbing a

mound that brought them to the top of the six-metre-high wall. The rampart was about a metre thick. Several other Jews were chipping away at the coping.

The two friends had hardly begun working at the top before there was a loud explosion. They screamed as the wall gave way beneath their feet. Soferman felt himself sliding towards the ground amid an avalanche of masonry. His body, engulfed in brick dust, was racked with pain as it thudded into the rubble. For a few moments the Berliner was stunned, unable to heed the terrible cries of men crushed and suffocating beneath him. "Oskar, Oskar, are you all right?" he called out desperately.

"I think so, Herschel," came the hoarse reply. "Just a bit bruised."

As the dust cleared, the two men saw that they were only a couple of metres apart, cradled in the debris of death.

The wretched cries of the entombed were soon drowned by a combination of laughter and shouting from the SS men who had raced into the courtyard on hearing the blast.

"Save the pickaxes and spades!" came a familiar voice. "Those of you Yids still alive dig the others out."

Soferman, Springer and the other survivors began clawing desperately at the rubble. Soferman, shrugging aside the pain, worked as a man possessed, the hatred he felt for Schreiber coursing through his veins. The politicals, too, joined the rescue, and the anguished cries of the buried became louder as more and more broken masonry was removed.

Soferman saw a hand projecting through the rubble. It turned and twisted like a defrocked glove-puppet. The Berliner clasped the hand gently and called out, "Are you okay?"

"I think my ribs are busted and both my legs are broken," gasped the hand's owner. "Water, for God's sake, water."

"Oskar!" screamed Soferman. "Come and help me with this poor bastard."

Springer scrambled over the rubble and they began dragging the heavy blocks from around the hand. After what seemed an eternity, the two had managed to remove enough for a couple of politicals to drag the unfortunate man clear.

Although the face was caked in dust, Soferman could see that it was the man who had led them to the wall. The Jew with no name groaned. He was semi-conscious, his body lying atop the debris like an abandoned marionette.

"Wheelbarrows!" screamed a voice with the authority of one who had experienced such scenes before.

Soferman, totally exhausted, sat and watched as a group of politicals brought the wheelbarrows. They loaded the dead and the dying crosswise and carted them away, among them the Jew with no name. In any other circumstances he would have been rushed to hospital and his injuries would have been treated. He would have survived. But the Jew with no name was at the bottom of the heap, his broken body draped over the edge, his head bobbing on the ground until coma and death relieved him of his torment.

Soferman sat watching the head in macabre fascination as the wheelbarrow passed out of sight. He too wished to die. He was twenty-two, alone in a cesspit of humanity with only one friend with whom to share his agony. He knew he would die. But not like this. And not without taking revenge.

"SOFER-man, stop loafing and follow me."

The voice, coated in venom, dissolved the Berliner's daydream. He hauled himself to his feet, glanced apprehensively at Springer, and fell in behind the straight black back.

"How old are you, Soferman?" asked Schreiber without turning round.

"Twenty-two, Obersturmführer."

"Ah, same as me, SOFER-man. Same as me."

The Nazi must have known that already from the identity card, thought the Jew. "Well, SOFER-man," the voice went on, "if you want to celebrate your twenty-third birthday, you will remain silent during the events I want to show you. I like you. We Berliners must stick together."

And with this the Nazi's head turned and the small brown eyes looked askance at the Jew. "But not too closely, eh?" he chuckled. "With that blond hair you may not look like a typical Yid, but you're Yid enough for me."

Soferman followed Schreiber into one of the many rooms leading from the courtyard. In the centre of the bare stone floor was what looked like a horse-trough. Leading into it was a hosepipe. The sound of gushing water made Soferman realize how terribly thirsty he was, for the brick dust had left his mouth parched and raw.

"Look inside," beckoned Schreiber.

Soferman peered into the trough. There were two blocks of white lying on the bottom.

"Ice, my friend," said Schreiber menacingly, glancing at his watch. "You may drink from it, but not now. In a few minutes, maybe."

The sound of shuffling feet combined with the ring of jackboots could be heard coming from the corridor. Seconds later, an elderly Jew was pushed into the room by a guard.

"Ah, grandfather Moses," said Schreiber, the rows of perfect white teeth gleaming in sentinel splendour. Lavender permeated the coolness of the room.

"*Shema Yisroel*," croaked the white-bearded Jew in a biblical affirmation of his faith. He knew he was going to die.

"Take off your clothes, Yid," said Schreiber with the contempt of a man who knew he held ultimate power.

Soferman watched as the old man, probably a rabbi, shed his prison uniform and stood naked and shivering before them. His frail body was like yellow parchment, his genitalia massive in comparison with the frame supporting them.

"Stand next to the trough, Jew-pig!"

22

The old man, paralysed with fear, did not move. His rheumy eyes beseeched the only person in the room from whom he might gain succour. But Herschel Soferman's stare was vacant, the small hazel eyes unable to bear witness to the rabbi's torment.

The guard, a huge brute, stepped forward and in one swift movement lifted the old rabbi by his ankles and hoisted him headlong into the trough. The rabbi's shriek was pathetic. Drained of strength by lack of food and his advancing years, the old man did not possess the will to struggle for life. He bobbed to the surface once before Schreiber turned him over with his riding crop and pushed down on the chest.

Soferman could not look away, his gaze transfixed by the bloodless visage staring out from beneath the surface. It appeared to him that the death grimace was a smile, the last desperate defiance of a stiff-necked Hebrew. Although he was far from being religious, he would say *kaddish* for the old man.

After a few more moments, Schreiber ceased holding the man down. He then turned to Soferman. "Now you may drink," he said simply.

Soferman, any vestige of resistance drained from him by the experiences of the day, stepped forward as would an automaton and drank from the trough. He was oblivious to the icy mixture of water and urine. "That's enough," said Schreiber quickly. "You don't pay the water bill."

Soferman stood up and wiped his grime-caked face with his hands.

"You know, Soferman, as I said before, I quite like you. I'd like to know more about you. Your background. Your family. I may be able to find out where they are. It pays to be one of Hans Schreiber's favourites, you know."

The Jew's eyes opened wide. The incongruity of Schreiber's request was grotesque. Here they were, the tortured and the

23

torturer, about to have a conversation about old times to which a third man, lying beneath icy waters, would for ever bear silent witness.

Yet, almost despite himself, Herschel Soferman began to talk. The very mention of his family brought back a flood of memories of the good and bad times in Berlin's Charlottenburg district.

Hans Schreiber suddenly became all charm, drawing from his prisoner intimate details of his life and family. The Nazi knew the weakness of every man who had been starved of love and warmth; the compulsion to grab hold of every opportunity to reminisce about the good old days, even if it was with their inquisitor. Not for nothing had he become one of the youngest junior officers in the SS. He saw himself as a beacon in a mire of mediocrity.

"That's enough, Soferman," said the Nazi, suddenly tiring of the largely one-way conversation. "Guard, take him back to his cell."

Schreiber's abruptness caught the Jew off guard, making him suddenly aware that he had just shared his most intimate secrets with the epitome of evil.

"Don't let me down tomorrow," was Schreiber's parting shot, the words failing to register in the mind of a young man now denuded totally of the only thing that had remained a bulwark against the desperation of his present. His past.

If the day had been torment for Herschel Soferman, then the night brought an anguish and misery the likes of which he had never experienced. On being returned to the cell, he was given some tasteless gruel and left to nurse his aches and pains alone until the return of his fellow inmates. It was then, after sundown, that the torture began.

The prisoners shuffled silently into the cell one by one, each man plumbing the depths of his personal misery. None had been in the cell for more than a month and the veterans were already bordering on insanity. By the time the twentieth man had entered, Soferman was beginning to feel the first stirrings of claustrophobia. He had still not spotted Springer among the sweating and grimy bodies. The man next to him sank on his heels and held his head in his hands in total exhaustion. No one spoke as still more inmates packed into the cell. The air became fetid and the odours of sweat and urine were suffocating. Soferman found that the only way he too could rest was by sinking onto his heels.

There must have been more than sixty men in the room by the time the door was bolted. Men without hope and dignity. Men caged like chickens in a coop, their wings clipped, wallowing in their own excrement. How they wished they were animals, dumb and ignorant. Suffering was universal but only Man could attach the label.

And thus did Herschel Soferman spend the worst night of his life, a night during which his aching joints, yearning to be stretched, fought with his mind, yearning to sleep. Some actually managed to sleep sitting on their heels, but never on the first night. On the first night in the Jew-cell of the Small Fortress of Theresienstadt, the mind exhausted itself rejecting the pain, leaving its owner utterly drained.

As the dawn sun streamed through the cell window, Herschel Soferman was surprised to find himself still alive. He could hardly move, the stiffness in his joints setting his muscles afire. Others stirred, their soft moans testament to shared torment. It was then that Soferman felt the coldness at his side. One more Jew with no name had been granted eternal release, never again to fear the rising of the sun. A sudden pang of envy gripped the Berliner.

Suddenly the bolts on the cell door were drawn and one of

the guards stood menacingly before them.

"Out, you shits!" he bellowed. "Leave the dead where they are until after roll-call."

As the men without hope filed into the courtyard, Soferman caught sight of Springer shuffling between two larger figures. It was obvious that his friend was in great pain. The Berliner shrugged aside his own torment and moved forward quickly to fall in behind him. He knew that any sign of weakness would be punished mercilessly by the guards.

"Oskar," he whispered. "It's me. Don't turn around. For God's sake pick up your step. Don't show them you're beaten. Do you hear me, Oskar?"

Springer was mute. He had neither the strength nor the will to communicate. He had become an automaton, unfeeling and remote. Insanity was but a hair's breadth away.

The two friends stood next to one another in the first of six rows of bedraggled prisoners. In the half-light of dawn their bodies craved the warmth of the sun's virgin rays.

"Stand to attention, you Jew-pigs!" barked a familiar voice to their right.

Hans Schreiber marched ramrod erect into the courtyard, beating the riding stick against his thigh in a metronomic beat. Scuttling behind him was one of the politicals. The man was labouring with a bucket and spade.

"Put them down and wait by the bucket," the Nazi ordered, then turned to the pitiful parade before him. "Now, you swine. Call out your names and don't forget the prefixes."

"*Stinkjude* Goldstein," called out the man at the end of Soferman's line.

"*Saujude* Feinberg," came the next.

"*Stinkjude* Schwenk," said a voice in a Czech accent.

It was obvious to Soferman that he was meant to call out his name with the appropriate prefix. But the Berliner was more concerned about the man to his left, who was last in line.

"*Stinkjude* Soferman," he cried out automatically when his turn came.

Then silence.

Soferman, not daring to move or speak, prayed that Springer would answer roll-call. For a few moments, even Hans Schreiber seemed lost for words. But he knew that there would always be one bastard who would not be a good little Jew-boy. That was why he had brought the bucket.

"Ach, so," he said at length, the small brown eyes narrowing to slits. "This little Yid seems to have forgotten his name. Perhaps a little food might help him remember. Step forward."

As Springer shuffled forward, the political, a stubby man who looked relatively well fed, took his cue and thrust the spade into the bucket. The smell left the prisoners in no doubt as to its contents.

"Best pig-shit for you, my little friend," spat Schreiber. "A true delicacy in the best tradition of *kashrut*."

Soferman was surprised by the Nazi's use of the word for Jewish dietary law. Most *goyim* knew only the word *kosher*.

But his musing was cut short when the spade was thrust under his friend's nose by the political. The sight and smell of the turd made him want to retch. The spade rose higher until the faeces, still steaming, brushed Springer's aquiline nose. And still the little man did not move.

"Eat!" barked Schreiber irritably, at the same time wiping his sweaty palms with a handkerchief.

Oskar Springer opened his mouth slowly, and with the first mouthful of the purest *treyfe* passed from the real world, awful though it was, into the hinterland of the psychotic.

Soferman stood rooted, a single tear etching its way down a face old before its time.

"The Jew seems to be enjoying it," laughed Schreiber. "That's it. Lap it up. Lap it up."

Springer showed no emotion as he swallowed the excrement. It was only after the third mouthful that Schreiber relented and ordered the wretched man to return to the line. The psychotic trance had prevented the prisoner from throwing up and the Nazi was visibly annoyed.

Roll-call took a further few minutes, after which the prisoners in the first two lines were ordered to march to a muddy inundation canal near the morgue. With each step, the dilemma tormenting Herschel Soferman burned fiercely within him. On the one hand, he planned to kill Schreiber and face the inevitable consequences. On the other, he reasoned that he must survive at all costs in order to bear witness to the atrocities of the Small Fortress. Oskar Springer, he knew, was no longer part of the equation. Oskar was already a member of the living dead. The black inkspots of his eyes were deep wells of total incomprehension. In its own way, a kind of freedom.

The ditch was about one hundred metres long, and the twenty men were separated into two equal groups. Soferman and Springer stood in the group at the near end. The Berliner peered into the trench. About half a metre down was murky water.

"All right," said one of the guards, "get in the ditch and start digging."

Soferman picked up one of the spades that were lying nearby and dropped down into the trench. The water, foul-smelling through rotting vegetation, was cold, and he gasped as it reached his thigh. He glanced at Springer. The little man had sunk to his waist. Digging would be virtually impossible for him.

"Try to pretend you're working, Oskar," he whispered with little conviction. The two Nazi guards sitting on a grassy bank overlooking them appeared to be dozing in the warmth of the sun's rays. Soferman knew that, by midday, the heat would be intense and he would be grateful for the cool of the ditchwater.

He toiled as diligently as he could under the circumstances and, wrapped in his own thoughts, gave scant attention to those around him. The sheer exertion created a barrier between him and reality. Herschel Soferman, the "farmer", was digging a drainage ditch around his wheatfield with the single-minded purpose of a man possessed.

No one in or out of the trench seemed to notice the pathetic figure of Oskar Springer sink beneath the surface of the ditchwater. To the other prisoners, death was a release that they might envy. Anyone who attempted suicide was to be applauded, not saved, for compassion was no longer in their lexicon. The prisoner, dehumanized, had become the willing accomplice of his captor. Moral right was no longer an issue.

It was the voice of one of the guards which first alerted Herschel Soferman to the demise of his friend.

"Hey, you. Big guy," the voice, in thick Bavarian brogue, called out. "Lift that stuck Jew-pig out of the ditch."

The Berliner, trapped within his own fantasies, carried on digging.

"I mean you, you arsehole!" shrieked the guard.

The prisoner to his right dug Soferman in the ribs, breaking the spell. The tall man looked up at the guard sitting on the bank.

"Yes, you. Get that carcass out of there."

Soferman's blond head swivelled slowly to the left. For a few moments, he stared in disbelief at the body hunched face down beside him.

"Don't just stand there, you great oaf. Lift him out of there."

"Oskar," gasped Soferman. "Oskar."

The body bobbed as the Berliner waded the couple of metres between them. He turned it over and lifted, cradling the slight form in his arms. The eyes were open. The inkspots that once used to sparkle in defiance of adversity were now opaque, impervious to the perfidy of man.

Soferman, showing no emotion, lifted the lifeless form onto the bank. He would not say *kaddish* for his friend, for now he believed that God was dead.

"Leave him there," the guard called out, "and get on with your work. Schreiber will be here in a few minutes and you lot will wish you were also corpses."

Soferman returned to his digging, but not before he had closed Springer's eyes. Even in death, he did not want them to bear testimony to whatever new horror Schreiber was planning. The little man-boy lay like a discarded rag doll. Iniquity's jetsam.

Schreiber was soon on the scene, accompanied by a bevy of guards and two wheelbarrows filled with sharpened sticks and pitchforks.

"Time for some sport, Jew-pigs," he cried out from high on the mound. "I see that one of you has already succumbed." The Nazi chuckled. "He's the lucky one."

Schreiber's entourage burst into laughter. They knew what was coming and eagerly took up their positions. Soferman counted up to a dozen guards perched on the parapet of the bridge overlooking the trench.

"You and you," Schreiber called out, pointing to the two smaller men alongside Soferman. "Each take a pitchfork and stick. The winner will get extra rations tonight ... the loser's."

Again there was hearty laughter from the gallery.

The two men, both in their thirties and both of about the same build, climbed out of the trench and reluctantly took their weapons from the wheelbarrows. They stood about a metre apart and for a few moments stared at each other in desperation and fear.

"Well," Schreiber called out ominously, "we're waiting."

"They're brothers," a voice cried out from the end of the line of prisoners. "For God's sake have mercy."

Schreiber laughed satanically. "Even better. Let's keep it in the family."

The gallery once more applauded. The Obersturmführer could always be guaranteed to put on an excellent show.

One of the brothers suddenly dropped to his knees and bowed his head. It was obvious that neither man was prepared to bear arms against the other.

Schreiber, incensed by the delay in the performance, raced down the mound. Hurling abuse at the two men, he picked up a shovel and hoisted it high before bringing it down with all his might on the head of the kneeling man. There was a sickening crunch, blood and brain spurting in all directions. Schreiber himself was hit by the human debris and this incensed him even further.

"You've ruined my uniform, you swine," he screamed at the corpse. "How dare you."

The Nazi brushed off the human offal with manic fervour, failing to notice the pitchfork being raised by the brother of the dead man. Soferman watched in morbid fascination as the two prongs came level with Schreiber's shoulders. Even though it meant his own death, Soferman willed the prisoner to strike home hard and true.

But the man, unused to the mechanics of murder, wavered for the split second that separated good from evil. A shot rang out and the prisoner crumpled, driving the pitchfork into the ground and sliding slowly down its handle.

Schreiber, visibly shaken, wheeled around to face his would-be assassin. The prisoner groaned, the red stain on his prison garb broadening. He lay on the ground face up, his left arm attempting to shield his eyes from the sun. The Nazi kicked the arm away and rolled the wounded man over with his jackboot. He then withdrew his service pistol, a 9mm Luger Parabellum, and placed the barrel against the nape of the prisoner's neck, angling it slightly upwards. Without hesitation, he fired.

Soferman flinched. In the splitting of a second one life had been saved and another taken. But the wrong ones. He watched with heavy heart as Schreiber knelt by the remains of the dead man's face and withdrew a dagger from a black scabbard at his side. The Jew could make out the SS motto "Loyalty is my Honour" inscribed in large Gothic script along almost the whole length of the blade. At right-angles to the slogan and close to the hilt were the initials HS. The Nazi began carving a swastika on the prisoner's forehead. Satisfied with its artistic merit, he passed to the other brother and repeated the procedure. Replacing his pistol, Schreiber acknowledged the guard on the bridge who had saved his life and then turned once again to the prisoners in the ditch.

"Woe betide any of you who try this sort of thing again," he cautioned breathlessly. "Otherwise there will be another couple of losers." With this, he climbed further up the mound and turned to face the prisoners from a safe distance. "Now, SOFER-man. You and that pig at the end of the line take up your weapons. I'm counting on you, SOFER-man."

Soferman felt his heart plummet. The man he was expected to fight was smaller than himself but looked about ten kilos heavier. The pug-face and squashed nose suggested experience as a prize-fighter. The man wore the yellow star but did not look Jewish. Nevertheless, he thought, it was indeed two Jews who were being ordered to fight the ultimate fight, one man having to die in order for the other to live for perhaps one more minute, one more hour, one more day.

As Soferman picked up the sharpened cudgel in his right hand and the rusting pitchfork in the other, he was reminded of the arenas of ancient Rome. The gallery was baying for blood and the supreme arbitrator, the black patrician of the Small Fortress, sat on his haunches, arms crossed and resting on his knees, watching impassively. Schreiber was not satisfied with simply killing Jews. He demanded the ultimate indignity: that

Jew should kill Jew for sport.

The Berliner turned to face his opponent. He felt Schreiber's beady eyes boring into his neck. He was the patrician's favourite. He was expected to uphold the honour of the dark empire. He was expected to satisfy his master's whim with the blood of an innocent.

"Wait!" ordered Schreiber. "Oberscharführer, where's my camera?" It was his favourite pastime. He focused the Leica and then smiled the most evil of smiles. "Okay, fight!"

"I shall live to testify, Schreiber, you bastard," Soferman muttered under his breath, at the same time raising the cudgel. "I shall never rest until you are brought to justice."

London, 16 June 1989

To: The Rt Hon Douglas Hurd, CBE, MP, Secretary of State for the Home Office

On 15 February 1988 you appointed us to undertake an inquiry into war crimes with the following terms of reference:

"(1) To obtain and examine relevant material, including material held by Government departments and documents which have been or may be submitted by the Simon Wiesenthal Centre and others, relating to allegations that persons who are now British citizens or resident in the United Kingdom committed war crimes* during the Second World War;

(2) To interview persons who appear to possess relevant information relating to such allegations;

(3) To consider, in the light of the likely probative value in court proceedings in the UK of the relevant documentary material and

of evidence of potential witnesses, whether the law of the United Kingdom should be amended in order to make it possible to prosecute for war crimes persons who are now British citizens or resident in the United Kingdom;

(4) And to advise Her Majesty's Government accordingly.

(*For the purposes of this inquiry, the term "war crimes" extends only to crimes of murder, manslaughter or genocide committed in Germany and in territories occupied by German forces during the Second World War.)"

We have now completed our inquiry and have the honour to submit our report.

Sir Thomas Hetherington
William Chalmers

Jewish Chronicle, London, 3 May 1991

There was barely enough room to nod off in the Lords on Tuesday as peers, including a feisty nonagenarian, fought to prevent the War Crimes Bill from becoming law.

It was a doomed battle against the Government, and many succeeded only in humiliating themselves and insulting the victims and survivors of the Holocaust.

The enemies of the War Crimes Bill did not suffer from self-doubt. Never, in the estimation of Lord Jenkins of Hillhead, the former Labour Home Secretary, had there been assembled against a Bill such "a combination of intellectual weight, legal distinction, and practical experience of Government ... in the highest offices of the land."

But even the best brains in the land were not going to bring victory closer, pledged former Home Secretary Lord Waddington, a mere stripling at 61. In a strong, clear voice, he said acts of appalling brutality had been committed not in the heat of the moment but as the "cold-blooded mass murder of defenceless victims ... The evidence is there and we can't close our eyes to it."

Ninety-two-year-old Lord Houghton of Sowerby thought otherwise. Opposing the Bill, he suggested to peers, meant retaining their honour. The alternative was to yield to the Commons.

He remembered as if it were yesterday how, aged 13, he had observed the progress of the Parliament Act of 1911. His memory had served him well, casting doubt over one of the main arguments against war crimes trials, that the memory of elderly witnesses would be uncertain.

Lord Hailsham, the former Lord Chancellor, urged peers to do what was right, rather than what was popular. "Populism is the enemy of justice, freedom and democracy," he said.

"This is not a house of wimps," remarked Lord Shawcross, chief prosecutor at the Nuremberg trials. "Do what your consciences tell you," he urged.

Then Lord Jacobovits, the Chief Rabbi, made his contribution. It was the peers' task to ensure the law would not exonerate those involved in horrendous crimes.

Thousands of voices were crying out from the earth, he said. The echoes were hardly heard in the chamber of the Lords.

Fifty-three speakers took nine hours to defy the Government. Full of sound and fury, they signified absolutely nothing. The Bill would still become law.

CHAPTER TWO

London

Danielle Green strode out of the glass menagerie off High Street Kensington with the sort of purpose that only beautiful career women seem to manage. Someone, somewhere, once said that looking good was three-quarters of the battle in getting any job. True, maybe, but you had to have a certain amount of talent in order to keep the job. And talent was the hallmark of her people.

Jews, however, were not especially noted for being tall or blonde, so the fact that Danielle had short satin hair and legs "all the way up to your armpits", as one of her former boyfriends once declared, proved a surprising bonus. So, too, did the emerald eyes, almond-shaped as a throw-back to some distant Sephardi scion, the high Ashkenazi cheekbones from somewhere in central Europe, and firm, well-rounded breasts. The upper of her fulsome lips, which owed nothing to collagen, supported an alluring beauty spot. The nose, small and straight, completed the perfect features. These attributes, however, were not necessarily in themselves enough to guarantee further promotion in one of the world's toughest professions.

Danielle Green, of the green eyes, firm breasts and long legs, had something else which proved highly combustible. An added ingredient in the magic potion, an ingredient that appealed only to the strongest-willed of men: intelligence.

She had entered the Associated Newspapers glasshouse six months earlier, a raw graduate trainee keen to learn what made newspapers and newspaper people tick. The *Mail on Sunday* was popular mainly by virtue of its colour supplement, the features of which balanced delicately on the tightrope separating the middle-brow from the crass inanities of the gutter press. She was now chief feature writer – a meteoric rise indeed.

Danielle Rachel Green was the second daughter of Stanley Green (whose father changed the family name from Greenbaum), a six-foot-three taxi driver from Redbridge, a borough with more black cabs per square mile than any other in the United Kingdom, and Esther (née Hyams), a petite and dutiful housewife and mother. The looks came from her, the height from him.

It was already seven in the evening by the time Danielle arrived at her rented one-bedroom apartment in the Docklands. She was running late for her appointment with a man she had been eager to interview ever since she'd been told about him by Howard Plant. While Plant was the typical middle-aged Jewish business entrepreneur who loved to court and direct publicity about himself, Henry Sonntag had been the background boy who played the money markets with such genius that he had made his clients, and himself, very rich indeed.

As she showered and dressed, choosing a smart black suit by Frank Usher, Danielle mulled over what little she knew about Sonntag. He was said to be in his early seventies and a survivor of the Holocaust. He'd come to England as a penniless refugee just after the war and got a job in the City. According to Plant, Sonntag only started to amass fortunes for himself and his clients about three years prior to the Big Bang in the eighties. The man lived alone and had been a confirmed bachelor all his life, so where would all the money go? Danielle knew there were a million questions that it was always possible to ask interviewees. There were also a million answers. Some people were more forthcoming than others, and the mark of a good interviewer was wheedling information from those who weren't. Whether or not what she was told was the whole truth was a moot point.

She gave herself the once-over in the mirror, shuddering slightly as she felt the familiar tingling sensation she always experienced before going out on a story. It would probably take about an hour to drive to Chigwell. She hoped Henry Sonntag would reveal enough to make her visit worthwhile.

The detached house was big. Too big for an old man living alone. It loomed out of the darkness like a sentinel on Salisbury Plain. It had the air of a manse about it, and she almost expected the heavy oak door to be opened by a resident clergyman.

Henry Sonntag, however, was definitely no cleric. The man who now faced her was tall, perhaps a little over six feet, and had the bearing of an aristocrat.

"Do come in, my dear," he said, his beady brown eyes glinting in the porch light. "My abode may not be humble, but at my time of life one expects a few home comforts. Please, let me take your coat."

As Danielle slipped out of the fake fox – she hadn't had the heart to buy an original and, anyway, it was almost as good as the real thing – she could feel Sonntag's breath on her neck. It reeked of lavender. The perfume permeated the house. She looked around. A first glance at the house's interior belied the impression given by the dour exterior. It was sumptuously furnished with what she could only believe were original antiques, ranging from forbidding Victorian chests to exquisitely decorated Ming vases, a few of which had sprigs of lavender protruding from them. He must have had them imported, she thought, for it was definitely out of season.

"Hmm, I see you like lavender," she said, sniffing the air. "So do I."

"Yes," smiled Sonntag. "I make sure I have a supply

year-round. Childhood nostalgia, you know."

"Quite a place you've got here, as they say."

"Never judge a book by its cover, they say also," said her host knowingly. "I know the outside's a bit drab, but ostentation attracts thieves." His accent was German, but not overbearingly so. "Please come into the drawing room and I'll fix you a drink."

The deep-pile beige carpet beckoned her into the drawing room. It too was decorated tastefully along graceful Georgian lines. A large old painting hung over a dormant fireplace.

"A Titian," said her host with pride. "Cost me a few million. It's the only classical painting I wanted to possess so I lashed out a bit ... gin and tonic?"

"That'll do nicely, thanks."

Danielle took the glass and, as she sipped, studied her host more closely. Sonntag had lost hardly any hair. It was brushed back and was the sort of yellowy white that told you its owner must have been a handsome blond in his youth. The skin, however, had the waxen texture of one who did not see much sunlight. The nose was firm and straight, the jaw strong and angular. The beady brown eyes were mobile and friendly yet curiously unreadable. The only sure impediment on the visage before her was the array of small scars around the mouth. The overall impression was of an elegant yet brittle carapace. "You know, you certainly don't look Jewish," she said, regretting the impertinence immediately.

Sonntag's laugh put her at ease. "Neither do you."

"Touché. But how did you know?"

"I told your features editor I would only consent to be interviewed by a Jew."

"Why?"

"Why not?"

"Ah ..." It was Danielle's turn to laugh. "Typically Jewish."

"What is?"

"Answering a question with a question."

"Of course. We Jews are strange and wonderful creatures. Come, my dear, now that we're family, let me show you around the hub of my fortune."

As Danielle followed her host into a room to their right, she could not help feeling slightly in awe of the big man. There was an extraordinary presence about him. In many ways he was a Jewish Tiny Rowland.

"Wow!" she exclaimed. "There are more screens here than in the whole of Northcliffe House."

"Information, my dear," said Sonntag, tapping his nose with his right forefinger, "is the key to my fortune."

"And your clients'."

"Precisely. I am successful because I always stay one step ahead of everyone else. I have built up a network of contacts in the various markets, from bonds and commodities and back again, which supplements all the stuff that anyone can get from the usual market sources."

"Why so many telephones?" Danielle asked, surveying the bank of at least twenty spreadeagled on a massive oak desk in front of what seemed like an equal number of screens.

"Quite simply, I can never afford to be engaged. Everyone who is important to my business must be able to contact me during trading hours."

"And how long are they?"

Sonntag chuckled. "Twenty-five hours a day."

"You're a workaholic, Mr Sonntag," Danielle smiled. She now understood why his skin was waxen.

"I suppose you're right, Miss Green, but I do get some time off at weekends. Come, let's return to the drawing room. I'll fix you another drink."

Danielle knew she was in for a long evening. She felt instinctively that Sonntag had a fascinating story to tell and she hoped it would not be too hard to open him up. She took out her notepad and pen as he mixed her another gin and tonic. She knew it would have to be her last. Some journalists worked better half cut, but not Danielle Green.

"Ah, I see you are ready to take notes," he said, handing her the glass. "I'm a stickler for accuracy, so make sure you get it down right."

"Then may I also use this?" she asked, withdrawing a small tape recorder from her handbag. She had a feeling she'd need more than a single long-play tape.

"By all means, as long as I can make a copy before you go."

"Of course." Danielle hesitated before adding, "Can I be blunt, Mr Sonntag?" She could feel the trepidation in her own voice.

"Of course you can." Sonntag's warm smile once again put her at ease.

"How much are you worth?"

"Many millions," Sonntag answered without hesitation, then added quickly, "but don't ask me to say how many."

Danielle smiled. "So you're never likely to go *mechulah*," she said, using one of the few Yiddish words every young English Jew used at one time or another.

"No, I'll never go bust, Miss Green. And you know why?" The journalist's raised eyebrows suggested she didn't. "Because, my dear, I now use only other people's money. I am happy just to play the markets and earn my commission."

"So you don't hope to emulate George Soros?"

"Ah, the man who broke the pound. For us he is a legend. George made more than two billion dollars on Black Wednesday, you know. Good luck to him. I'm satisfied with what I earned that day."

"How much?" she asked boldly.

"A very small percentage of what George made. But it was enough." Danielle judged by Sonntag's manner that he would not be pressed further on this matter. Still, it gave her a nice entrée into his rags to riches story. The old man duly obliged with tales of financial derring-do which occupied the next twenty minutes or so.

"Tell me, Mr Sonntag ..."

"Please, call me Henry."

"Tell me, Henry, why did you agree to this interview? You financial wizards usually like to keep a low profile."

"Strange as it may seem, my dear, nobody ever asked me before." He chuckled. "I must have kept a really low profile."

Sonntag's face then became serious. The hazel eyes narrowed as he added morosely, "Anyway, it's time."

"What do you mean?"

"I am seventy-two years old, *mein Kind*. As you know, I have never married and have lived alone all my life. I have no living relatives. No points of reference. My memories weigh on me like a ton weight. I need to unburden myself."

"You mean about what happened in the war?"

"Yes."

"Publicly?"

"Why not? I no longer believe that great distress should remain discreet. I don't think people care any more, anyway. It's far too late for the victims to see justice done and, whatever they say, I doubt whether another old Nazi will ever be brought to trial. The Demjanjuk case has seen to that."

"Do you believe he was Ivan the Terrible?"

Sonntag sighed. "Ivan the Terrible or Ivan the Less Terrible. Will we ever really know? Will it bring any of the victims back?"

"So you believe we should let all the old Nazis just fade away?"

"*Ich bin ein alter Mann*," he said resignedly. "I am too old and have hated for too long."

Danielle could feel Sonntag's hitherto suave and relaxed manner beginning to peel away. Underneath was a man obviously cut to the quick by his experiences. "Can we start from the beginning, Henry?" she said quietly, hoping against hope that her host would not dry up.

"Yes, of course." He sat back in his armchair and clasped his hands until his knuckles blanched. "I am going to tell you something now. If somebody told me this story, I would be tempted to say 'He's lying, because this simply can't be true.' Maybe you'll feel the same way, that these things could not happen. Because to really understand us, somebody has to go through it. Nobody fully understands the survivors. You can't. No matter how much sympathy you give us. To understand, you have to have been through it." He paused. "I hope this does not sound too convoluted."

"I'm trying," said Danielle half-heartedly. It was all she could think of to say.

"Good." Sonntag breathed heavily, as if he knew the knowledge he was about to impart was of necessity too much for any human being to fully comprehend.

"I was born in the Charlottenburg district of Berlin, north of the Kurfürstendamm ..."

For the next forty minutes Danielle listened spellbound to the most horrifying, and yet most inspiring, story she had ever heard. She neither interrupted nor added to her notes. By the time her first tape was exhausted, Henry Sonntag had revealed the history of his life to her. The history of a man who had lost everything dear to him, who had later gained riches most men could only dream of, but who was still essentially a husk.

She fought to control her emotions. At times she had felt close to tears, yet now that she had heard the details, she wanted Sonntag truly to bear his soul. At the same time she felt like an inquisitor, and this did not sit well with her Jewishness. As she turned over the cassette, she looked up at Sonntag apologetically. His face was ashen. Her host took out a handkerchief and blew his nose loudly. "Henry, how do you live with it?" she asked, her voice full of compassion.

"Excuse me, I don't usually show such emotion ... I don't live with it. It lives with me. It's like constant pain. You never forget, you never get rid of it. It sets you apart from other people. That's not to say I'm never happy. But I know the difference. That difference is like muzak in the background. Yet there's also another side ..."

"Yes?"

"I recognized that in order to become part of society I had a choice to make: either to stay a survivor and be in a mental prison all my life, or try to preserve my sanity by putting this away and integrating into society as if nothing had ever happened. I chose the latter." He paused, then said, "Maybe I'm fooling myself."

"What do you mean?"

Britain's richest refugee clasped and unclasped his hands. "I envy people who can really get out of themselves for one minute. They can laugh, enjoy. Deep inside I can never do those things. Only superficially, you understand. Always in the back of your mind is everything that happened. How can you ... how can you enjoy yourself? It's almost a crime against the people who died."

Danielle felt an almost overwhelming surge of compassion. The man before her was obviously coping with a thousand devils. "Would you like to break off for a short while?"

Sonntag cleared his throat. "No, it's quite all right." He smiled weakly. "This is doing me a power of good. And anyway, you haven't really started asking me questions yet. The third degree, as they say."

Danielle smiled. There were so many questions in her mind. She stared at her blank notepad. "Tell me, Henry," she said at length, "these Nazis ... what, if they were going to kill you all anyway, was the point of all the humiliation and cruelty."

"Pavlov's dog," replied Sonntag sharply, eagerly. "To

condition the reflexes of those who had to actually carry out the policies. After you've butchered one man, it becomes easier. Also, to achieve the extermination of those millions of men, women and children, the Nazis committed not only physical but spiritual murder ... on those they killed, on those that did the killing, on those that knew the killing was being done and did nothing and also, to some extent, on future generations. It was dreadful."

Every word struck home for Danielle. Both sets of her grandparents had lost relatives in the Holocaust. In the final analysis, it all boiled down to an accident of birth; being in the wrong place at the wrong time. Whenever she read books or saw films about the Holocaust, she had tried to envisage herself and her loved ones in the same circumstances, yet the vision was always incomplete. Sonntag was right. No one could put himself in the place of a victim.

"You spoke earlier of Demjanjuk," she said. "Was there anyone in Theresienstadt who was particularly brutal?"

Sonntag's eyes glazed. His lips quivered, prompting the collection of small scars into a macabre dance. He breathed deeply as if some memory was too terrible to reveal. "There were individuals with their own peculiarities," he said quietly. "Some worse, some better. There was incredible rivalry amongst the SS. Almost everyone had his protegé among the prisoners. The SS played one off against the other."

Apparently warming to his task, he became increasingly animated. "You see, Danielle – may I call you Danielle? – everything was reduced to a primeval level: life and death. Some SS men developed a kind of loyalty to one prisoner or another, though one hesitates to call it that for there was always a nefarious reason for any sort of kindness or charity. Never forget the incredible power they had. Yet most of the Nazi officers hated and despised one another. They would do almost anything to get at each other. This created an indescribable climate of fear for the prisoners. Spared one moment, damned the next."

Danielle sat transfixed by the intelligence of the man before her. She began to feel it an honour to be in his presence. Even before he had paused for breath, she asked the question that had been bothering her for some time.

"Tell me, Henry, what is the secret of survival in these circumstances?"

"People just do not understand, my dear, that it wasn't ruthlessness which enabled us to survive, but an intangible quality, not peculiar to educated or sophisticated individuals. Anyone might have it. It is best described as an overriding thirst, perhaps a talent for life and faith in life."

"A tremendous will to live."

"Yes, but I don't mean to say that these were deliberate acts or even feelings. They were largely unconscious qualities. Another talent needed was a gift for relationships. There were people who survived who were loners. Maybe they say they survived because they relied solely on themselves. But even if they don't admit it to themselves, they survived because at some stage or other they were carried by someone, someone who cared for them as much as for themselves. They are now the ones who feel the guiltiest ... not for anything they did, but for what they didn't do."

"Did anyone help you, Henry?"

"Yes," he sighed, "but they were all murdered for their pains. You see, Danielle, to be chosen to live an extra day was nothing but luck, one chance in a thousand. Luck combined with the qualities I have mentioned gave us a chance to survive longer. In the Small Fortress you could never pretend. You could never take refuge in the imaginary."

"What do you think of Germans today?" Danielle asked. She herself had found it hard to blame the sons for the sins of the fathers.

Sonntag raised his hands in a gesture of resignation. "Listen, Jews have lived in Germany for sixteen hundred years. Anti-Semitism was nothing new when Hitler came to power. You know what they say: anti-Semitism is hating Jews more than is necessary."

Danielle smiled. "Yes, I've heard that one before."

"I would never personally step on that tainted soil again," the old man continued. "It's the fatherland of barbarism. It's not that I hate the young Germans of today – except the neo-Nazi thugs, that is – but they must accept that they were responsible for the Holocaust as much as for producing the likes of Goethe, Bach and Beethoven. We Jews will never forget, but neither must we allow the world to forget, otherwise it will happen again."

Danielle pushed her point. "But do you believe in collective guilt?"

Sonntag hesitated. The beady eyes misted. She knew he was undergoing a moral crisis.

"Listen, Danielle," he said at length, "it was Simon Wiesenthal who said that any Jew who believed in God and in his people could not believe in the principle of collective guilt. We Jews suffered for thousands of years because we were said to be collectively guilty – all of us, including the unborn children – guilty of the Crucifixion, the epidemics of the Middle Ages, communism, capitalism, bad wars, bad peace treaties. All the ills of mankind, from pestilence to the atomic bomb, are supposed to have been the fault of the Jews. We are the eternal scapegoats. We know that we are not collectively guilty, so how can we accuse the other nations, no matter what some of its people have done, of being collectively guilty?"

"I think you're right, Henry, and there are many who say we brought this catastrophe upon ourselves."

"What do you mean?"

"I mean that a lot of young people, that is young Jews of

today, especially in Israel, think that the older generation didn't put up enough of a fight."

"There was the Warsaw Ghetto, Treblinka, Sobibor ..."

"Yes, but the incidences were few and far between."

The old man pondered for a few moments. He then stared at Danielle with a steely gaze that made her feel slightly uncomfortable for the first time.

"My dear," he said, the eyes narrowing, "do you know what happens to an animal, say a wildebeest, when it is attacked by a pride of lions? As soon as it is caught, it goes into mind-numbing shock. When the lion applies the coup de grâce, the poor wildebeest doesn't feel a thing. From the moment the Nazis dehumanized us, we were in that state of shock."

For a moment the whirr of the cassette recorder seemed to take over the room. Danielle felt that she, too, was in a state of shock. Everything the man had said made complete sense. She glanced at her tape. It was nearing the end. She still had a couple of questions left.

"Henry, in a way I asked this earlier, but do you believe it's right to continue to prosecute war criminals?"

"Yes. There are still Nazi criminals around, and the only thing they regret is not winning. They are my generation and their presence among us casts a shadow, even now."

"What about revisionist historians like David Irving?"

"Those who try to rewrite history by saying the Holocaust never happened are the worst type of evil. I hate them."

She skipped back through her notes. "But before you said you had hated too long."

"Correct. Hate clouds the mind. But you see, and this is off the record, I cannot stop hating. I hate myself for being German. To be sure, I never deny being Jewish, but I have never come to terms with the fact that I am a German myself, that part of me is German, part of me is Jewish. You see, my dear, I hate to some extent both the Germans and the Jews. And I am both. I find the mixture unbearable and I am part of that mixture. You have the cringing, arrogant Jew and you have the superior, arrogant and insensitive German and all that is part of me as well. And in any case, if I had not been a Jew I might have made a very good Nazi. I am an absolute perfectionist, you know."

For a few moments Danielle was dumbstruck. Henry Sonntag's words were extraordinarily candid. This was a man who was hurting badly, a man whose patent honesty allowed him to admit that, had he not been a Jew, he might have been one of the very monsters who had tormented him. He would no doubt suffer this torment until his dying day.

She cleared her throat, but the words still came out hoarsely. "Henry, can you ever bring yourself to forgive?"

"Forgive?" The old man laughed, relieving the gloom once again. "Ah, now that is an interesting question." He raised his thin yellowy-white eyebrows. "If I may, I'd like to tell you a story. It's long, so bear with me. Many years ago there was a rabbi from Brisk, a scholar of extraordinary renown, revered also for his gentleness of character. One day he boarded a train in Warsaw to return to his home town. The rabbi, a man of slight stature and not particularly distinguished, found a seat in the compartment. There he was surrounded by travelling salesmen. As soon as the train began to move, they started to play cards. Now, as the game progressed, the excitement increased. The rabbi remained aloof and was absorbed in meditation. Such aloofness was annoying to the rest of the people and one of them suggested to the rabbi that he join in the game. The rabbi answered that he never played cards. As time passed, the rabbi's aloofness became even more annoying and one of those present said to him, 'Either you join us, or you leave the compartment.' Shortly afterwards, he took the rabbi by his collar and pushed him out of the compartment.

For several hours the rabbi had to stand until he reached his destination, the city of Brisk."

"Where's that?" Danielle cut in, fascinated.

"Poland somewhere. It doesn't matter. Anyway, Brisk was also the destination of the salesmen. The rabbi left the train and he was immediately surrounded by admirers welcoming him and shaking his hand.

"'Who is this man?' asked the salesmen who had spoken to him. 'You don't know him? You don't know the famous rabbi of Brisk?' The salesman's heart sank. He had not realized whom he had offended. He quickly went over to the rabbi to ask forgiveness. The rabbi declined. In his hotel room, the salesman could find no peace. He went to the rabbi's house and was admitted to his study. 'Rabbi,' he said, 'I am not a rich man. I have, however, savings of three hundred rubles. I will give them to you for charity if you will forgive me.' The rabbi's answer was brief: 'No.'

"The salesman's anxiety was unbearable. He went to the synagogue to seek solace. When he shared his anxiety with some people in the synagogue, they were deeply surprised. How could their rabbi, so gentle a person, be so unforgiving? Their advice was for him to speak to the rabbi's eldest son and to tell him of the surprising attitude taken by his father.

"When the rabbi's son heard the story, he could not understand his father's obstinacy. Seeing the anxiety of the man, he promised to discuss the matter with his father. As you know, it is not proper, according to Jewish law, for a son to criticize his father directly. So the son entered his father's study and began a general discussion about Jewish law and in time turned the conversation to the laws of forgiveness. The son mentioned the name of the man who was so anxious. The rabbi of Brisk said, 'I cannot forgive him. He did not know who I was. He offended what he thought was a common man. Let the salesman go to him and beseech forgiveness.'"

Sonntag paused for a moment, as if waiting for a sign that his guest fully understood the implications of the story.

"The moral is," he continued, "that no one can forgive crimes committed against other people. It's therefore preposterous to assume that anybody alive can extend forgiveness for the suffering of any one of the six million people who perished. According to Jewish tradition, even God himself can only forgive sins committed against Himself, not against Man."

Danielle, in the pregnant pause that followed the apocryphal tale, was once again astounded by her host's conviction and learning. "That's some story," she said at last. "Certainly a provocative after-dinner turn."

"What do you mean?"

"Nothing," she shrugged, adding quickly, "It's just that I imagine you must have told this story to friends before. It's the sort of thing that exercises the grey matter. Tell me, Henry," she continued, altering course, "are you religious? I believe you belong to the local *shul*."

"I'm like most of my Jewish clients. I go three times a year on the High Holy days. You're the same, aren't you?"

Danielle suddenly wished she had been a more observant Jew. "I'm afraid I don't even bother to go on Rosh Hashanah and Yom Kippur, although I do take the days off work. I spend most of the time in bed."

"Do you fast?"

"Sometimes, if the mood takes me. Do you?"

Sonntag smiled conspiratorially. "Off the record, no. I'm a bit of a chameleon, in point of fact. I act religious if I need to."

"What do you mean?" asked Danielle, genuinely surprised.

"With my ultra-orthodox clients I wear a *kippa*. It makes them feel more comfortable."

"It's funny," Danielle laughed, "but I can't imagine you wearing a skull-cap."

"No, I suppose not." He winked.

Danielle returned to her point. "By religious, I really meant in a spiritual way. In effect, do you believe in God?"

Sonntag's eyes glazed momentarily. "It depends on how you define God," he said wistfully. "The God of the Jews?"

"If you must."

"The God of the Jews died in the concentration camps," he said dully. "This is off the record, you understand. Officially, to paraphrase Ivan Karamazov, it's not that I don't accept God, it's the world created by Him that I don't and cannot accept." The pain in Sonntag's voice was tangible.

Danielle breathed deeply. "I'm sorry, Henry, maybe I'm being too personal. It's not really germane to the article I want to write."

The old man smiled kindly. "It's the prerogative of a beautiful woman to make mistakes ... and to be forgiven instantly."

She nodded in relief. "Just one final question, Henry, and then I'll leave you in peace."

"So soon?" He smiled again.

She looked at her watch. "My goodness, it's been nearly two hours. Where do you get the strength to go through all this? What keeps you going?"

Sonntag stroked his chin, "I often think about that. I suppose it's a bit like schizophrenia. One cannot allow the past to become so overwhelming that it will make one unable to function in so-called normal life. Yet it's always there, giving me a total world view. You might call it extreme pessimism – really knowing the truth about people, about human nature, about death, really knowing the truth in a way that other people don't know it. And all of this truth is harsh, and impossible to really accept, and yet you have to go on and function. I suppose I have a complete lack of faith in human beings, whether it's politics or anything else. You hear one thing and you believe another."

Once again Danielle felt an overwhelming sense of humility before her elderly host. It was as if he encompassed all the terrible trials of a lost generation.

"I think we'll leave it there," she said, switching off the tape recorder. "All I can say is that it's been a privilege meeting and talking with you. I only hope my feature will do you justice."

"I'm sure it will," beamed Sonntag. "I feel better for getting all this off my chest. Thank you."

Glancing at her watch, Danielle smiled sweetly. "By the way, our photographer, John Chivers, will be here shortly as arranged. He knows what shots to take. Usual stuff. A head and shoulders and some in the dealing room."

"I don't photograph very well."

"Don't worry," she laughed, "with modern technology we can make the Elephant Man look like George Michael."

"Who's George Michael?"

"A pop star."

For a fleeting moment Sonntag looked sad. He sighed. "Having no wife and children means I've missed out on all those sorts of things. I'm what you English call an old fuddy-duddy."

"It's never too late for romance, you know."

"Maybe. One day. In the meantime, *zeime gezint*.

"And you should be healthy too, Henry. Until one hundred and twenty, as they say." She held up the tapes. "I'll make copies of these tomorrow and send them to you right away. Don't worry, I won't misquote you."

"I have complete faith in your journalistic principles, my dear," Sonntag responded. "Just make sure whoever edits the feature doesn't distort the truth. It's so easily done."

"I'll make sure I have the last word on this one," she said reassuringly. She allowed Sonntag to help her with her coat.

"Take care, it's a horrible night for driving."

"Thank you once again, Henry," she said, shaking his hand warmly.

As she took her leave of her host she could not help feeling that the *Mail on Sunday* magazine was the wrong forum for the story of this remarkable man. Only a book could do Henry Sonntag real justice.

CHAPTER THREE

Joe Hyams was dog tired. He was tired because he was working all God's hours in order to pay the household bills. He was tired because his wife and children demanded more than he could give them. Anyway, that's what he tried to convince himself. If the truth be known, of course, it was them he was trying to keep away from. There was only one thing worse than the Jewish mother syndrome. The Jewish wife and kids syndrome.

Joe picked thoughtfully at his fleshy nose and prayed that the next fare would be going his way. True, there was less traffic on nights, but six years of working through the early hours was getting him down. It had ruined his metabolism and had probably ruined his marriage.

Still, the Heathrow run wasn't too bad. At least he usually got a decent class of fare. No drunks, no anti-Semites. He knew he looked very Jewish and it didn't happen very often, but there was always the odd occasion when he might pick up a fascist, drunk or otherwise.

Joe spotted Sam Spiegel two cabs ahead in the rank. Bastard had nicked a good fare off him more than once. Now lived with the *hoiche Fensters* in Edgware. Ilford was no longer good enough for him. "I hope you get a last fare to Croydon, *mumser*," Joe mouthed as Spiegel leant out of his cab and smiled.

"How's things, Joe?" the man with flat cap asked.

Hyams gave Spiegel a middle-finger salute. Why waste breath on the man, he asked himself as he edged the cab closer to the front of the rank. Please let him get Croydon and me Ilford. Please.

There they were. A couple of Yank tourists by the look of them. Lucky bastard'll probably get Edgware. One straight road. All the way home.

Joe watched Spiegel pull away and then jumped out of his cab.

"Hey, you," he called to the cabbie in front, "did you hear where his fare was?"

"Yeah, Croydon, I think."

"Bingo!" Now all he needed was for the second half of his win-double to come true.

The driver in front was soon loaded up with a couple of Pakis and now it was his turn.

"Over here, sir," he called out to a man leaving the exit to the terminal carrying a briefcase. It was obvious he was looking for a cab.

"Where to, guv?" Joe Hyams called out with false nonchalance.

"Do you know Ilford?"

Bingo! This time Joe Hyams exulted inwardly.

"Of course, guv," he enthused. "Know it well."

"Drive to Fairlop station. I left my car there."

Strange accent, thought Hyams as his fare climbed in. Like someone trying to pretend to be a Kraut in a bad war movie.

"Where have you just come from, guv?" the cabbie called out as he drove away. "Anywhere nice?"

"Berlin," said the fare. "But you'll have to excuse me. I'm not feeling so well and I'd like to get some sleep, if you don't mind."

"No trouble at all, guv," said the cabbie kindly, and he closed the glass partition. What did he care? The man was going his way and Joe Hyams Esquire wasn't bothered if he kept *shtum* all the way home.

Joe switched on the radio. The dark early-November night was damp but not cold. Just the way he liked it. Although he preferred to do the North Circular, the shortest route was through the West End and City. Best not to bother the fare again, he thought. The man seemed all in. Must have had too much schnapps.

Joe Hyams knew the way blindfolded. At Stratford Broadway he tired of listening to James Last and the other muzak of the night. As he leaned forward to switch off the radio, his horn-rims did their usual skiing act. He was always meaning to get his nephew Stephen the optician to tighten them up but never seemed to get around to it. "Maybe I should try out some contact lenses," he muttered, suddenly startled by the sound of his own voice. Becky might fancy him more without glasses. She certainly couldn't fancy him any less. That's why she made him do nights. It was Becky's way of saying she had a headache. On the other hand, maybe it was his own way of saying *he* had a headache. The plain fact is, Joe Hyams, old boy, he mused, your whole bloody life is a headache. Your wife doesn't understand you, and your two sons, glorified barrow-boys each, are consumed by dreams of bright-red Porsches. Love and respect for the father didn't matter any more. Not like the old days, when children catered to their father's every whim and the mother was a *balabusta* who was for ever tidying the house and could cook the hind legs off a donkey. His wife must have been one of the first Jewish princesses. To boil an egg she had to consult a cookery book.

Consumed by his cheerless existence as a balding, bespectacled and powerless Jewish patriarch, Joe Hyams was startled to find himself already driving along Forest Road and nearing his destination. He stopped by the entrance to Fairlop station.

"We're here, guv."

"Just drive on a little further, please. Closer to the car park entrance. It has started to rain and I don't want to get wet."

Joe Hyams, accustomed as he was to taking orders from fares, duly pulled to a halt a few yards further on. The wind was starting to get up and the rain whipped cruelly against his windscreen. It was turning into a filthy night. "That'll be forty-five pounds please, sir," he said, stretching to open the partition window without turning round.

There was precious little time for Joe to appreciate the tickle of cold steel against the nape of his neck. No time at all to make peace with his Maker. The worries of Joseph Stanley Hyams were truly over. He was also spared the indignity of knowing that his killer had left as a calling card the symbol most despised by his race.

Discounting dreams, it was only when he was asleep that Mark Edwards did not breathe, eat and drink newspaper reporting. Many had forecast that he would burn himself out by the age of forty. Well, that was ten years away and too much of a distant threat to worry him.

His list of police and criminal contacts was second to none, and even the old hacks among the nation's crime reporters were forced to give him his due. Respect from those who could still remember when Fleet Street was more than just a generic term was respect indeed.

Edwards switched on the table-lamp by his bed. After a couple of seconds his eyes managed to focus on his watch. It was five-thirty in the morning. Not the time he usually awoke. But now he was up he knew he was unlikely to doze off again. He was a morning person. The bio-rhythms dictated that. He really believed that some people were night owls; the sort that loved to go to bed in the early hours but could never get up in the morning. Their minds just could not function as well in daylight. He was different. He could function on six hours' sleep, as long as it was early to bed and early to rise.

He thought back to the dream that had woken him. There he

was, on yet another story about police corruption. Some of his best friends were coppers, and the bad press worried him as much as it did them. He knew his reports were bound to tarnish the innocent, for Joe Public was beginning to believe that all coppers were bent. He, Mark Edwards, might work for one of the popular newspapers, but he prided himself on searching for and writing the truth. The headlines, however, were not his responsibility, although he sometimes wished they were. Some of the sub-editors in the glass menagerie got carried away. He often wondered whether they ever read the stories they subbed.

Light worrying plagued Edwards most mornings until he actually got out of bed, or until it was interrupted by something more stimulating. A sigh to his right proved the catalyst. She was a mood-changer. She had a sensuality that could make a shoal of barracuda turn on each other. Propped on a pillow, Edwards gazed down at the sweeping lines of the form beside him. His restlessness had caused him to pull the duvet almost completely off her. Her skin was like satin, her long and shapely legs, drawn up slightly, rose inexorably towards the most perfect bottom he had ever seen, then up, past the small of the back, and along the delicate delineation of her spine towards the nape of a neck that was half lapped by gold leaf. God, she was beautiful.

His lover's right leg straightened languidly and the combination of the ripple of her buttocks and the lingering fragrance of Ysatis caused his mood to alter. He placed the duvet delicately around her and pressed his naked form against hers. She did not respond for a full two minutes. It just so happened that she was in the middle of an erotic dream. In the delicious and relaxing glow of half-sleep and sexual arousal, she luxuriated in the dream as if it were reality.

"Oh, God," she groaned. She was already wet when she turned to face him. He was beautiful – the bright blue eyes and thick wavy blond hair, the snub nose and square jaw. She smiled, feeling her own lips and face beginning to flush.

"You don't have to warm me up," she moaned. "I'm almost coming already." It would be her third orgasm of the night.

Edwards needed no further invitation. He allowed her to guide him into her and began to stimulate her and himself, gently at first and then with increasing vigour.

They came – she slightly ahead of him, the way she liked it – and lay spent in one another's arms. Only the intrusive resonance of the telephone spoiled the idyll.

"Damn!" muttered Edwards. He knew the interruption had to be work-related. It had happened a few times before. But this time was the cruellest. He had been wining and dining the girl for two months and this was their first night together. The way she made love had matched her looks. She was simply stunning, and he knew he must be the envy of his colleagues. Maybe this was one of them on a spoiling mission. The receiver was by his bed, so he could still cradle her as he spoke.

"Oh, hello, Bob. What's up? ... Where? ... I'll be there in ten minutes."

Edwards grappled with the phone. He'd have to ring Fred Diamond, the local freelance photographer. He wanted someone at the scene as soon as possible.

"What's happened?" she moaned.

"A murder. Ten minutes up the road. My contact says it's a biggie. I'll contact you at the office later."

Danielle Green hugged her new lover. He was only her second, but she felt instinctively that the relationship could flourish. Mummy and Daddy might not be too pleased, but the fact that he was a gentile caused her only slight disquiet.

Detective Inspector Robert William Webb knew local commuters would not be appreciative, but there was no question of Fairlop station being re-opened until the evening rush hour. In fact, he doubted whether he could allow the hordes near the place for at least a couple of days.

"Smith, Carter," he called out to two uniformed bobbies near by, "rope off an area fifty yards either side of the station entrance. The early morning mob'll be here any moment. They'll just have to walk to Barkingside."

Webb noted their acknowledgement and then turned his gaze on the station foreman. Poor sod. No fun in opening up in the morning and finding a stiff on your doorstep. And this was no ordinary stiff. This was a humdinger of a stiff. A shock-horror-drama headline-grabbing humdinger of a stiff.

"Are you all right, mate?" he called over to the man, who was ten yards away, slumped against a wall by the station entrance, the dawn's early light causing a halo to play around his head.

"I'll be all right, mon," the man called out in thick West Indian brogue. "I just got to compose myself."

Looked as white as a sheet, thought Webb, and then he quickly turned his ensuing chuckle into a smile of reassurance. "Take as long as you like. We're arranging for you to get the day off."

The policeman knew the foreman would have a whole day of exhaustive questioning to go through. It was odds-on the man was an innocent party, but nothing would be left to chance. Not on this one. Not with the Super breathing down his neck, the Commissioner breathing down the Super's neck and the politicians huffing and puffing down everyone's neck. He had premonitions of a disaster if no arrest was quickly forthcoming.

"Hi, Bob. What's up?"

Webb's gangling six-foot-two frame started at the voice by

his side. It belonged to a young man with whom Webb had many shared interests besides police work, such as soccer, tennis and more than the occasional round of golf. Although Mark Edwards was six years his junior, Webb could still match him at most sports.

"What took you so long?" the policeman smiled. "The body's already cold."

The mere mention of the word made Edwards shiver. The body was not all that was cold that morning. His side of the bed would soon be stone cold. Criminal, he thought, absolutely criminal. He was having a hard time keeping his bearings. He'd certainly never felt this way about anyone before. Danielle Green was simply mind-blowing.

"Are you with us?"

"It's okay, Bob, I'm still half asleep."

"She must be some lady." Webb winked knowingly.

"Is that an educated guess or do you have inside information?"

"Nothing. Nothing, Mark, mate, it's just that that girl journalist you introduced me to last week was an absolute knockout."

"Talking about bodies, Bob," said Edwards, "what gives on this one?"

"Cabbie murdered. A molto bad one. Before you ask, I can't let you or your photographer near the scene. Forensic already have their dabs on it. He can take a shot of the cab and I can let him shoot these."

Edwards examined the police photographer's preliminary Polaroids. "Jesus Christ!" he whistled.

"No, he was crucified," said Webb humourlessly.

Edwards looked again at the pictures. The first one showed clearly a swastika carved into the victim's forehead, the others the points of entry and exit of a bullet.

Webb pointed a finger. "Shot through the nape of the neck

first and then the killer left his calling card. This was an execution, mate, pure and simple."

"I don't think we can use these, Bob, they're too horrific. We'll shoot 'em to keep 'em on file, but I know the editor'll have his reservations. The Jewish community is going to be up in arms and the *Standard* is very pro-Jewish and very pro-Israel. Is this the work of fascists or Arabs? Any clues?"

"Nothing much to go on at the moment," Webb lied. As much as he cherished their friendship, there were some things a policeman had to keep secret. Information was a two-edged sword and there were always some clues which it would be injudicious to reveal. Timing was everything in a murder inquiry. "We'll check out the Claybury nuthouse first, but somehow I don't think we'll find an inmate missing. Local nutters tend to belong to the dirty raincoat brigade."

Edwards watched in fascination as the forensic boys milled around the black cab. The body of the cabbie was slumped over the steering wheel. He was thankful he could not make out the man's altered features. The Polaroids were horrific enough.

"Okay, Bob, shoot. What's known?"

Webb yawned and stretched his large frame. The breath exuded from his generous mouth in a fine mist. Reflectively, he ran his thumb and forefinger along a pencil-thin moustache, slowly bringing them together at the foot of his lantern jaw. "Hyams. Joseph Stanley Hyams. Aged fifty. Married to Rebecca. Two sons, twenty-three and twenty-one. All living in Beatyville Gardens. Typical middle-class Jewish family, if you ask me. Hope she's not the hysterical type. A couple of my boys are with her now."

"Do you think a passenger did it?"

"More than likely. The meter had forty-five pounds on the clock. At first glance it looks like a Heathrow job. The cost per distance is about right. Funny, though ..."

"What?"

"The killer was obviously a pretty cool customer. He switched the motor off but didn't try to destroy the evidence on the meter. Somehow, I don't think it's going to yield much. We'll go through the flight lists, but I think we'll probably be wasting our time."

"What about known fascists?"

"The usual suspects will be questioned. Special Branch have a list of known activists in this area. The Yard's method index may help, although I doubt whether there's any previous form on this particular modus operandi."

"You sound pretty depressed, Bob."

"I've got bad vibes on this one, Mark." Webb stared straight ahead. "It's got all the hallmarks of the beginnings of a serial killing. Nobody bothers to carve a swastika on someone's forehead unless he's leaving some kind of message."

"What do you mean?"

"I can't tell you just yet," said Webb, regretting his observation. "But I promise you you'll be the first to know if we come up with anything."

"Don't bugger me about, Bob," said Edwards, sensing his friend was being a little too circumspect.

"Look, mate," the policeman rejoined tetchily, "don't press me too far. You know all the big nobs will be breathing down my neck on this one. It's got political overtones."

Edwards realized he might indeed be pushing too hard. He respected Webb's abilities as a copper and he knew the man was going to be under intense pressure to come up with something. The middle echelon in the police pecking order was always the hardest pressed. Those at the bottom of the heap had the least responsibility and those at the top could dump their frustration on the likes of Webb.

"Okay, Bob," said Edwards, changing the subject, "let's talk about the murder weapon."

"Dunno yet. Forensic says the wound is typical of close quarters with a silencer. But as to the make of weapon, we'll have to wait for the lab report on the bullet we found."

"Where was it?"

"Lodged in the dashboard."

"What was used to carve the swastika?"

"A knife, probably. We've only just started combing the area."

Edwards closed his notebook. "Bob, can I interview the guy who found him, and then I'll be off?"

"Sure," said Webb. "He's the station foreman. Sitting over there by the wall. He's pretty shook up. I'll give you five minutes."

"Thanks. I'll see you a bit later. There'll probably be a news conference, right?"

"Probably," Webb grimaced. "But I think we'll hold you lot off until tomorrow."

"Unless you have a little exclusive something just for little old me, eh?"

"Go on, bugger off. I'll see you later, no doubt. I'll get you on your mobile if anything comes up."

Webb watched the reporter approach the West Indian. Edwards was a good journalist, a man who could be relied on to write the facts without too much embellishment. But he himself was a good policeman. And good policemen had to play some of their cards close to their chests. He withdrew the note from his breast pocket and re-read its contents. "All in good time," he muttered. "All in good time."

Mark Edwards, having filed his story on the hoof, knew he was in for a long and exhausting day. Nick Logan, his news editor, was a demanding tyrant. The man had decided to dispatch a relief reporter to the scene, while Edwards was to interview the widow and get hold of some family photos. It was always the shittiest part of being a crime reporter. He had to be pretty thick-skinned to do the job anyway, but bereaved relatives always got to him.

Driving back to his flat to wash and shave, he couldn't help feeling that he'd be a fish out of water with the Hyams family. People always responded better to their own. He thought of Danielle. He'd ask her to accompany him. She wasn't due in her office until lunchtime, anyway.

Edwards parked his car in the lay-by outside Redbridge Court. Although traffic was light, some commuters were already making their way towards Redbridge station nearby to begin their regular boring journeys to the City. But at least they were alive. Not like poor old Joe Hyams.

He took the lift to the third floor and let himself in quietly. The flat was silent, save for the familiar hum of the refrigerator. Permeating the apartment was her favourite perfume, a strong yet delicate reminder of the carnal pleasures of the previous night. For one moment he felt like telling Nick Logan where to stick his orders. Professionalism, however, restored itself quickly. Edwards entered his bedroom. He could feel his desire welling up once again as he gazed at her form. Sitting gently on the bed, he stared at her bare white shoulders. Her gold Star of David had somehow worked its way around to the back of the chain. He fingered it delicately and then returned it to its rightful place just at the top of her cleavage. Danielle moaned as she attempted to pull the blankets higher.

"Dani," he whispered. "Dani, please wake up."

She sighed and lingered a few more seconds before turning slowly towards him. "Mark, is that you? What time is it?"

"It's seven-thirty, darling. I wish I could get back into bed with you, but I need your help."

"What's happened?" she asked, propping herself on her

right elbow, the sheet and blankets slipping below the line of her ample breasts.

Edwards ran his fingers through his hair. He sighed, not really knowing where to begin. The news he had to impart was horrible enough. The fact that the victim was one of her own people meant he had to be especially sensitive. He breathed deeply before saying simply, "The murder."

"Yes?" she asked with obvious concern.

Edwards related the gruesome details, being careful not to over-dramatize.

"What was his name?" she asked. She'd left the question to last, fearing that perhaps he had been an acquaintance of her father's.

"Joe Hyams."

"Oh no," she gasped. The emerald eyes opened wide in surprise, closing only when the emptiness reached the pit of her stomach.

"Do you know him?" Edwards' voice carried genuine concern.

She pulled the sheet up and bit hard on the edge. "He's my uncle. My mother's brother."

Edwards leaned over and began caressing her hair. "I'm so sorry, Dani. It's just unbelievable." He wiped away her tears with his forefinger.

"Uncle Joe was always a loser," she sighed. "He's what we call a *nebach*, always complaining about how life was treating him. But he was a lovable *nebach*. Auntie Becky'll be devastated."

Edwards felt he was intruding on her personal grief, yet he knew Nick Logan was unlikely to take him off the job.

"Dani," he said with trepidation, "I don't know how to say this, but I've been told by my office to get some pictures and interview the bereaved wife."

If Danielle Green was upset, she did not show it. She leaned

over to her side of the bed and withdrew a tissue from a pink
box on top of the bedside cabinet. Blowing her nose forcefully,
she muttered, "I can supply you with the photographs. We'll
pop into my parents' home on the way. My mum probably
doesn't know yet. It's not the best circumstances for you to
meet them in, but that's all I can do for you."

"Thanks," said Edwards simply.

As Danielle left the bed to wash and dress, it was not her
uncle and his family who were uppermost in her mind.
Another man, in a way a distant relative, dominated her
thoughts. What would Henry Sonntag make of this incredible
horror?

CHAPTER FOUR

House of Commons, London

"Mr Speaker," intoned the Right Honourable Member for Ilford North, "I'm sure the House would like to register its shock and disgust at the appalling nature of the murder which has taken place in my constituency and to voice its condolences to the victim's family."

"Hear, hear," bayed members on both sides.

"I'm sure my Right Honourable colleague the Home Secretary can assure the House that the police are doing all within their power to bring the perpetrator to justice speedily."

The Home Secretary rose slowly. Removing his gold-rimmed spectacles, he cleared his throat before replying. He knew the Opposition was waiting to pounce on the question of law and order. "I can assure the House", he stated, "that the police will leave no stone unturned. This is ..."

"Shame, shame," cried a group of Opposition backbenchers. "The Government's record on law and order is shameful. Shameful."

"Order, order," cried the Speaker.

"This is a crime", the Home Secretary continued, "the specific nature of which recalls the worst barbarism of the Nazis. As I said, the police will leave no stone unturned."

This was the cue for the portly Shadow Home Secretary to jump to his feet. In booming Yorkshire brogue he launched his attack. "I'm sure that my Right Honourable friend the Home Secretary is aware that this crime is the latest in an ever-growing catalogue of racist attacks which are shocking the people of Great Britain. The Asian community has been hardest hit until now. However, as he rightly says, the nature of the crime in the early hours of this morning defies belief.

The racist and criminal elements in our society are having a field day."

"Hear, hear," bellowed the Opposition. The back benches were afire with indignation.

"Order, order," cried the Speaker. "Order, order."

Twelve miles to the east of Parliament, another man was burning with indignation. "Bring him in," barked Detective Inspector Robert Webb with undisguised contempt. "Sit him in that chair."

"Fuckin' leave off, will yer. I ain't done nothin'."

The detective glared at the man before him. Colin Smith was the dregs of the earth. Obese, obnoxious, his body covered with tattoos ranging from the slightly amusing to the outright racist. Swastikas and other symbols of hate abounded within the undulating folds of blubber. "You're scum, Smith."

"I ain't done nothin', I tell yer," Smith pleaded in an accent that was pure Canning Town.

"Where were you in the early hours of this morning, scum?"

"'Ere, don't call me that. I've got my rights."

Webb's steel-grey eyes narrowed. "The only rights you will ever be entitled to, Smith, are the last ones. Now annoy me too much and you'll be begging me to call in a priest."

"What's all this about, guv?"

"You mean you haven't heard?"

"No, honest."

Webb moved behind the thirty-year-old fascist and stooped to whisper menacingly in his ear, "You couldn't be honest if your life depended on it, Smith."

"Look, I tell yer I don't know what yer talkin' abou'."

The detective circled the fat man. "I'm talking about the brutal murder of a Jewish taxi driver. Where were you in the early hours of this morning?"

"In bed wi' me wife."

"Fuck me how anybody could sleep with you, Smith."

"Now there's no need to get personal, guv. I tell yer I don't know anythin' about this taxi driver."

Webb looked squarely into the fat man's baby-blue eyes. The picture of innocence before him was a leading heavy for the ultra-right-wing British National Party. He was also a part-time thug for Combat-18, a virulent fascist group that had close ties with German neo-Nazis, and had been responsible for attacks on Asians and Jews.

"Convince me, Smith," the detective snarled, switching on the tape recorder. "Convince me."

Mark Edwards sat at his desk on the third floor of Northcliffe House and stared blankly at the VDU screen. The previous day had proved cathartic. Not so much because of the actual murder, but because of the hysterical wailings of Becky Hyams. He was used to English stoicism, the sort of reserve that could sometimes mask feelings just as strong as those of Mrs Hyams but would not impinge on the neutral observer's emotions. Safe. Clean.

Becky Hyams, however, made sure the whole world knew about her tragedy. Danielle had tried to calm the woman, but emotions ran so strongly that soon all the family were wailing. Dani had explained to him that under Jewish law the body had to be buried as soon as possible and that seven days of mourning, a *shiva*, would follow. She had described this period as vital in the family's attempts to come to terms with bereavement.

Edwards had found Dani's parents courteous and polite. Given the circumstances, they had not asked him too many questions, although he had detected one or two knowing glances directed his way. If they were concerned that their favourite daughter was dating a *goy*, they did not show it. He smiled to himself at the thought of being Dani's "goy boy".

"Penny for your thoughts, old chap."

The West Country drawl and the intrusive odour of an early morning dram told him the speaker was Jim Pottage. Gentleman Jim, the police's favourite reporter, was a man who could hold his drink with the best of them, from the Commissioner down to the bobby on the beat.

"Good morning, Jim lad," said Edwards. "Starting a bit early today, aren't we?" The comment was entirely without rancour, for Edwards respected Jim Pottage both as a man and as a damned good crime reporter.

"Abso-bloody-lutely, old bean," replied Pottage jovially, fingering the spotted bow-tie that was his trademark. Navy blue spots on crimson this time, matching his pickle-nose. Side-whiskers, a ruddy complexion and the obligatory beer-gut completed a character straight out of Dickens.

Edwards turned to face his colleague. Gentleman Jim was an apt name for him. The older man had had every right to give him a rough time. Going on fifty and with a reputation as a hard drinker, Pottage had been passed over for chief crime reporter at least three times in the last decade. Nine months ago it had been his turn to upstage the old man. But if Pottage felt any bitterness, he never showed it.

"What's up, Jim? Anything from the Yard?"

"Chasing blue-bloody-bottles, old man. They haven't a clue on this taxi-driver murder and the Chief Rabbi's giving them hell. They're sure it's the work of a fascist and not an Arab, but the world's more full of fascists than it is of Arabs. Like looking for a needle in a hay-bloody-stack."

"What do they call that, Jim?"

"What?"

"The way you speak."

"Oh, you mean bloody this and bloody that. It's a figure of speech, a tmesis – you try saying that when you're pissed – a separation of the parts of a word by the insertion of another word." Pottage laughed. "Bloody seems to fit every bloody time. Like I'm the Cinder-bloody-rella of this organization."

"Come on, Jim, you get all the fun and none of the responsibility."

"True, dear boy, true."

"Logan's breathing down my neck for a new angle," said Edwards, rubbing his square jaw roughly in thought.

"Leave him to me, Mark. If I breathe on him, he'll be in a stupor for a week."

"No, seriously, Jim. Have you got any ideas?"

"Aar, I think the police be holding something back," said the older man, slowly taking his seat at the screen opposite.

"Funny. I've got the same feeling. Bob Webb intimated something at the scene. Damned if I can guess what, though."

The conversation was suddenly interrupted by the telephone on Pottage's desk. Picking up the receiver, he greeted the caller and then quickly placed his hand over the mouthpiece. Mouthing the words "talk of the devil", he handed the phone to Edwards.

"Hello, Edwards here. Oh, hi, Bob, what's news?"

"When's your next edition due out?" the policeman asked, his voice scratchy with urgency.

Edwards glanced at his watch. "About an hour."

"Good," said Webb. "Listen, we found a note by the body."

"Jesus, Bob, how long have you been holding out on this one?"

"Don't blame me. It was a board decision."

"Well?" asked Edwards eagerly. He could already see Pottage champing at the bit.

"'Just for you – HS'. That is, there's a dash between 'you'

and the initials. We don't know what they stand for. It's typewritten and we're checking out the make."

"What do you think it means, Bob?" Edwards asked, scribbling the contents of the note on a piece of paper. He could smell the presence of Pottage behind him.

"Look, I can't talk for long, Mark. We think that whoever did this thing may be HS, although why he should leave his initials, I don't know. It may be a decoy. The Hyams family don't know any HS. We'll be putting out an official statement soon."

"Thanks, Bob. I appreciate it. By the way, any news on the weapons used in the murder?"

"Oh, yeah, forgot all about it," came the sheepish reply. "Point thirty-eight Smith and Wesson with a silencer. We haven't found the gun or the knife. Looks like he took them with him."

"Thanks, Bob. Keep in touch."

Edwards leaned over to replace the receiver and then swivelled to face Pottage.

"So Logan'll get his new angle," smiled the older man. "A note on the body, I presume. Just love those notes. Adds so much spice."

"Right, Jim, but it doesn't really amount to a lot, does it?"

Pottage leaned over to look once more at the note on the desk. "Hmm. The way it's written you would have to believe that HS is taking the mickey out of his victim. On the other hand ..."

"Yes?"

"Well, it could be the other way round. That is, the killer's leaving a message for someone with the initials HS."

Edwards stared once more at the words. Pottage was right. It was ambiguous. Still, he had his new lead, however skimpy. With all the furore going on, it would probably be worthwhile bringing forward the second edition. Another Edwards exclusive. He looked up at Pottage. "Try to get me some more quotes from the Hyams family about this, will you, Jim, and anybody else you think would have an interesting comment. Also, go and let Logan know what's happened."

"Aye, aye, sir," said the corpulent Pottage, wheeling away. There was nothing he enjoyed better than a juicy murder mystery.

Edwards turned to face his VDU. He had the bare bones of a new lead. He'd flesh it out later with Pottage's gleanings and background material. Just as he placed his fingers over the keyboard, he could not help but think once more of Danielle and their first night together. They had arranged to meet in the Czar Ricardo wine bar, the *Mail*'s watering hole, that evening. He knew he was getting in deep, and for the first time in his life he felt unafraid of commitment. Little did he realize that the story he was about to write would change both their lives irrevocably.

An hour later and two floors up, Danielle Green sat at her desk reading the front page of the second edition of the *Standard*. Mark's byline was larger than usual and a small and rather unflattering photograph sat above it. Picture bylines were rare accolades indeed. However, apart from details of the note and the gun, the story was mainly a rehash. Try as she might, she could not think of any connection between the initials HS and her uncle, her family. Joe Hyams would be buried tomorrow. His two sons would say *kaddish* and only God would know the connection between the note and their father.

Danielle read Mark's story once more. She was finding it hard to concentrate on anything much since the murder. Two men dominated her thoughts, one who had loved her with tenderness and passion and another who had probably been too brutalized to be able ever to truly love anyone.

She had begun to write the feature on Sonntag, although it had taken her more than an hour to get past the first sentence. Somehow the enormity of the man's wartime experiences had dwarfed the fiscal achievements that had been the main purpose of the interview. She believed he would have exchanged all his millions just to have had a normal childhood, to have had at least some remnants of his family left alive. The old man was so totally alone, probably the loneliest person she had ever met.

Danielle sighed deeply and steeled herself to complete the article. She was under little pressure, for most features were the product of forward planning. Most were sat on for a few weeks unless they were topical. Some never made it into print at all. The only connection between Sonntag and recent events was the fact that both he and her deceased uncle were Jews who had apparently suffered at the hands of fascists. She herself was convinced that Uncle Joe had been the victim of some right-wing nut. No explanation, however, could alleviate the plight of Auntie Becky, who had been so dependent on Joe that finding herself having suddenly to fend for herself in a cruel world was trauma enough. Having sons like Jason and Bradley only made matters worse. Danielle believed her cousins were the most selfish children she'd ever known. She flinched at the memory of the times she had been forced to babysit for them. There was only a four-year age gap but the boys had been especially immature in their pre-teens and had made her life hell.

Forcing herself to forget the Hyams family for a while, Danielle's mind drifted back to her night with Edwards. It had been so exquisite, spoiled only by the telephone call. She would have loved to have awoken in his arms, to have explored his body and her own feelings in that time of special tenderness. Still, she believed there would be opportunity enough for that. She would not agree to sleep with him again just yet, for she felt she needed a few days to herself. Recent events and the thought of the forthcoming *shiva* conspired to put a dampener on her ardour. She sighed and turned once again to face the VDU. The cursor blinked threateningly. It seemed to dare her to finish her article. She had barely concluded a sentence before her telephone rang.

"Hello, this is Danielle Green."

"Danielle!" It was Henry Sonntag. She thought maybe he was phoning to remind her to send a copy of the interview tape.

"Yes, hello, Henry. How are you? I'm just working on the article now."

"Danielle, please listen to me. Please do not publish the article."

For a moment she was stunned. His voice was pleading, desperate, so unlike the strong character she had interviewed. "I don't know, Henry. Why? What's happened?"

"I cannot elaborate, Danielle. Please do as I say. You will never understand."

"But, Henry, it may not be so simple. How will I explain to my editor?" Danielle's mind was racing with a hotch-potch of excuses.

"Then hold fire for a while," came the urgent reply. "There is so much you do not know. Maybe I can give you an even better story later."

Danielle felt she had been let off the hook, for Sonntag obviously did not know that the interview might be on hold for weeks. She was intrigued.

"Okay, Henry," she agreed. "But be in touch soon, okay."

"Bless you, my dear," he said, clearly relieved. "I will, I will. Goodbye."

"Goodbye, Henry."

Danielle spent the next few seconds staring at the receiver. How extraordinary. She tried to analyse the resonance in Sonntag's voice. It had been a mixture of excitement, entreaty, and stratagem. But most of all, Henry Sonntag's voice had contained an element far more disturbing: fear.

CHAPTER FIVE

Theresienstadt

Herschel Soferman felt cold. Very cold. Although only a dusting of snow lay on the ground, the external temperature was at least ten below. A biting wind increased the chill factor to an unbearable degree. It would have been bad enough for a well-fed and well-clothed citizen in normal times. For an inmate of the Small Fortress in a cruel and unceasing war, however, each gust carried with it the torture of a thousand needles.

He was still alive, though how he had survived the past month was nothing short of a miracle. He was now a veteran of the place, for all the Jews who had entered this hell around the same time as himself were no longer alive. And to what did he owe his survival? To the whim of one Hans Schreiber, benefactor and torturer. And how had Schreiber managed to keep his protégé alive? By giving him extra rations and selecting only the weakest opponents for him to fight in the gladiatorial contests.

Hate had been Herschel Soferman's best friend. His hatred for Schreiber had given him the strength to kill his first opponent, much heavier but so much less fleet of foot. Yet he had still been human enough to have felt utter self-disgust at what he had done. He had still been human enough to have felt revolted by the sticky warmth that splattered him as he destroyed another man's life.

That was then, however. Almost six months ago. And between then and now the humanity of Herschel Soferman had been whittled away until only a splinter remained. Hans Schreiber had stripped Herschel Soferman of his past and robbed him of his future. Maybe there could be no escape from death. On the contrary, maybe it would come as a welcome relief. Maybe he would shortly join Springer and all the others in eternal release, for it was obvious that Schreiber was becoming tired of his plaything. In the last contest, Soferman could have sworn that Schreiber was giving vocal support to his opponent. The Jew thought he had detected a flicker of disappointment in the Nazi's evil eyes as victim number four had been dispatched. It may simply have been paranoia, but then paranoia was a constant companion in the Small Fortress.

Herschel Soferman sat on his haunches and consumed the last morsel of bread and wurst which had constituted his noon meal. The room was full of shivering prisoners, yet he was alone. Their eyes avoided his, for he knew he was damned, both by his reputation as Schreiber's favourite and by the purpose he had shown in competition. Each one of the prisoners was right to believe that he might be Herschel Soferman's next victim. In an even contest, some of them might have believed that they would have a chance. Yet the main great divider was nothing more mundane than food. Compared to normal times it was all pig-swill, yet pitting a man who ate three such meals a day regularly against a man who had survived for months on a single daily helping of gruel and mouldy bread was a no-contest. Will without strength spawned an empty threat.

Soferman, morose and old beyond his years, was little more than an automaton. When Hans Schreiber told him to eat, he ate. When Hans Schreiber told him to kill, he killed. Yet, paradoxically, while the Jew thought he would die, he also believed he would live. Hans Schreiber was the very reason he clung to his instinct for survival. Revenge was his motive and hate his strength.

"Soferman!"

The voice and all it represented still succeeded in striking a chill through the hearts of men already numbed by cold and hunger. The forty-three men in the room struggled to attention.

"Soferman, choose twenty men and come with me."

"*Jawohl*, Herr Obersturmführer."

Herschel Soferman threaded through the ranks of the prisoners like the angel of death. All stood with heads bowed, as if knowing they were in the presence of their executioner. "*Eins, zwei, drei ...*" Under the watchful eye of Schreiber and two SS guards, he tapped twenty men on the shoulder.

With Soferman at their head, the prisoners filed out into the courtyard. The wintry sun provided scant warmth as they stood and waited for further orders. The chattering of teeth provided macabre audible testimony to their plight.

"This is a special detail," Schreiber called out. "You will follow the guard in single file. Anyone stepping out of line will be shot."

The first guard stepped forward and stood with his back to Soferman. The men shuffled into line and the second guard took up the rear.

"*Links, rechts,*" Hans Schreiber called out in a bored monotone as the group started to trudge forward.

The first guard led them out of the compound of the Small Fortress and towards a copse about half a kilometre distant. Across the river Ohre they could see the large fortress, their previous home and a haven compared to where they were currently incarcerated.

However, the smell of nature, sweet even in the dull depths of winter, was soon replaced by an odour as pervasive as it was pungent. The familiar smell of death hung heavily in the air.

Some of the men began gagging as they neared the copse. Even the forward guard was forced to cover his face with his handkerchief.

"Halt!" shouted Schreiber.

As the prisoners turned to face him, a brave man might have been tempted to laugh. Hans Schreiber, the devil incarnate, indeed looked comical as he spoke from behind the sprig of lavender held in his right hand.

"Ahead of you you will see a collection of shovels protruding from the mound of a ditch," he said. "Each one of you take a shovel and stand in line facing the ditch. Wait for me to give you the order to begin filling it."

Herschel Soferman and his companions shuffled towards the ditch. There was no doubt as to what it contained. Each stood by his shovel. No one dared look down. No one, that is, except Herschel Soferman. Oblivious to the stench, the Berliner gazed at the putrefying flesh below. Like abandoned marionettes, the bodies were twisted in affirmation of the obscenity of their demise. Called upon to do the work of the Devil, Soferman felt no sense of pity for those in the pit. They had gone to their deaths meekly, while his heart still throbbed with the vitals of life, for he was a man with a mission to live, a mission to bear testimony, a mission to avenge.

"When I whistle, start to dig," came the dreaded voice. In the short hiatus that followed, Herschel Soferman's mind drifted back to his childhood and the magical city that was Berlin before Hitler. Incongruously, he thought of the adventures of Emil and the Detectives. What would Emil have made of all this? Had the book been written a few years later, the little boy who represented good against evil might have been a model member of the Hitler Jugend. The world was indeed doomed because even little children were no longer innocent. He closed his eyes and felt his body sway towards the pit. Maybe it was just a distant memory, but he thought he could hear a pigeon cooing.

It was then that Herschel Soferman heard another sound, as familiar as it was threatening. The sound of machine-guns being cocked echoed through the trees.

"No!" roared the raging tiger in his mind. "Not this way. Not like them."

Behind them all Hans Schreiber held his left arm aloft.

"Goodbye, SOFER-man," he shouted. "FIRE!"

London

It was already late afternoon and Mark Edwards would have been justified in leaving the office for home, satisfied that a good day's work had been accomplished. He sank deeper into his chair and stared at his shoeless feet resting on the desk. There was no one around to take umbrage. A somnolent Pottage had dozed off opposite him after imbibing one too many during a late lunch at the Elephant, an apt name for a pub frequented regularly by such a larger-than-life character.

With sonorous accompaniment, Edwards' daydreaming turned to thoughts of Danielle. They had agreed that he would not accompany her to tomorrow's funeral, but that he would take her to the first night of the *shiva* that evening. In a curious way, he was looking forward to it. He had known little or nothing about Jews until he had first dated her two months ago. Northcliffe House was not short of Jewish journalists, but they tended to keep their own company. The pub, that greatest of all English institutions, was the best place for encouraging guards to be lowered sufficiently to inspire social intercourse. Jews, however, generally treated them as no-go areas. He believed it was more of a cultural than a religious thing. Danielle had said that the tradition of taking sacramental wine on Friday nights, their sabbath eve, was as close as her family ever got to alcohol.

Ironically, it had been in one of the *Mail*'s watering holes, the Greyhound, that he had first got up the courage to ask her out. They had been there celebrating a mutual friend's birthday, and he had made his move at a moment when conviviality had not yet been overcome by boorishness, a constant threat at newspaper drink-ups. He knew he was not entirely on unsafe ground because initial eye contact in the lift at Northcliffe House had suggested that she too might be interested. Edwards smiled to himself as he recalled how Danielle's emerald-green eyes had caused him to quake inside. Had she spoken to him then, he knew he would have remained mute or stuttered some inanity. It would probably have spoiled his chances comprehensively, for although he did not lack experience with women, ice-breaking was not exactly his speciality. He was thankful that she had taken the initiative that evening in the Greyhound, quizzing him about a fraud story he had written. A rum and coke had been enough to prevent him from getting tongue-tied and from there on in it had been plain sailing. By way of conversation, Danielle had told him that she always used the Underground to get to work and they bitched mutually about the difficulties of crossing London from east to west and back again, whether by public or private transport.

"I can give you a lift home, if you like," Edwards recalled himself saying. "I live in Redbridge and often use the A13."

Danielle had acquiesced and within the hour he found himself sipping piping-hot black coffee in her pied-à-terre in Docklands. They had talked a little about likes and dislikes before she had packed him off with a thank-you kiss. At the door, he had asked her if she'd like to accompany him to the theatre that week. His heart had skipped a beat as she first pursed her fulsome lips and then smiled knowingly. Between then and the night they made love, they had seen one another at least four times a week. Her one stipulation had been that they agree never to talk shop. She had wanted to know so much more about him than could be garnered from newspaper talk. For him, too, it had been as much a gradual meeting of minds as of bodies.

"Penny for your thoughts, old chap."

The avuncular leviathan had stirred. Jim Pottage emerged from alcohol-induced slumber with no visible signs of a hangover apart from rheumy eyes and a purplish nose. He stared at his number one benignly. Handsome bugger was Edwards. Probably a wow with the ladies.

"Nothing, Jim," replied Edwards, looking at his watch. "It's time we were both making tracks."

Pottage stretched his stout frame and was in the middle of a vulgarly loud yawn as the telephone rang. "Oh no, not this time of night," he complained. "Hello ... who is this?"

Edwards watched as a look of puzzlement spread across Pottage's features.

"It's for you. Again," said the older man, pressing the mute button. "Foreign-sounding chappie. Sounds a bit agitated."

The chief crime reporter took the phone. He did not fancy getting involved in any more work that evening. "Hello, Edwards here," he said resignedly.

"Are you the Mr Edwards who wrote the stories?" the voice asked.

"If you mean on the murder of the cab driver, yes." Edwards could tell by the caller's accent that he was of German or Austrian origin. He himself had studied German at university and was fluent in the language.

"Please, listen to me carefully, Mr Edwards. It is about the murder. I know who did it."

Edwards took his feet off the table and sat up straight. "Who are you? Where are you calling from?" The urgency in his voice had Pottage agog.

"This is immaterial at the moment," came the reply. "Please do not press me too closely. I am afraid. The man is pure evil and I believe he is trying to find me and kill me."

85

"Who is this man?"

"The man who wrote the note ... HS."

Edwards felt the familiar tingling sensation along his spine which usually signalled a good story. Yet the world was full of cranks and he was not going to jump to conclusions on this one. "Who is this HS?" he said, a note of scepticism creeping into his voice.

"Hans Schreiber, the Beast of the Small Fortress," replied the caller, spitting out the word "Beast".

"The what?"

"Please, Mr Edwards, do not believe that I am crazy. I am deadly serious. The murder of the taxi driver was the modus operandi of Hans Schreiber. He was an Obersturmführer, an SS lieutenant, at the Small Fortress in Theresienstadt. He used to kill people with a bullet through the nape of the neck and then carve a swastika in the forehead. He is a monster."

Edwards' mind raced. "How do you know all this?"

"I was there, Mr Edwards. I suffered. I survived."

"But he must be an old man by now."

"He is the same age as me, Mr Edwards. Is seventy-one too old to kill?"

"Tell me, how can I contact you?"

There was a pause as the caller took stock. "I am afraid, Mr Edwards. Very afraid. I will call you with further information as long as you do me one favour."

"Yes?" Edwards said hesitantly.

"Please keep me informed of latest developments as far as the police are concerned. I need to stay one step ahead of him. Please tell me you will do this and I promise I will help you."

A thousand thoughts flashed through Edwards' mind. The whole thing was bizarre, yet he knew he must check it out as best as he could. "Listen, I will give you my direct line here at the office and my mobile phone number. If you can't get me at my office, dial this number. Are you calling from a call-box?"

"Why do you ask?" came the suspicious reply.

"Because you'll need to have plenty of money on hand. The calls cost about thirty-five pence a minute."

"Thank you, I'll manage."

"By the way," said Edwards, "*ich spreche deutsch. Ich studierte es in der Universität. Sie können deutsch sprechen, wenn Sie wollen.*"

Again there was a long pause before the bitter reply came. "I vowed never to speak that accursed language again. Speak to me only in English."

Edwards coughed awkwardly before giving the caller both phone numbers. "Please be in touch," he said firmly. "I will do all I can."

"Who the hell was that?" asked Pottage as Edwards replaced the receiver.

"Probably a crank," sighed Edwards, "but you never know."

"Well, give to Uncle Jim," said the older man, beckoning with both hands.

"I'll explain later, Jim. Tell me, what's the name of that place where you check out books and info on the Holocaust? In the West End somewhere."

"The Wiener Library, Devonshire Street."

"Yeah, that's it," said Edwards, rising. "I'll see you tomorrow, Jim."

James Harold Pottage sat back in his chair nonplussed. Suddenly finding his tongue, he called out to the receding figure of the chief crime reporter. "Bugger you, Edwards," he shouted, only half jokingly.

The following morning, as Edwards rode the Circle Line to Great Portland Street, his thoughts were mainly of Danielle. She had rung him at the office about an hour earlier and had described the previous day's funeral. It had been a rather desperate affair, with Auntie Becky beside herself with grief. Danielle had told him she would be taking a second day off and would pick him up at seven-thirty in the evening in time for the eight o'clock start of the *shiva.* "I'll bring a *kippa*, a skull-cap, for you," she had said. "Don't worry, you'll be okay. It'll be an experience."

During the train journey, he had dwelt little on his destination and the purpose of his visit to the Wiener Library. He needed to know about Theresienstadt, about the Small Fortress and about Hans Schreiber. The strange caller had not given much detail. Edwards knew that if he could gen up he might win the caller's confidence. He also knew that should he decide to write the story, all hell would break loose. An incensed Webb would demand that he divulge his source. The police would probably suspect that the caller knew the killer or, for that matter, was the killer himself. He had the distinct feeling that the case was going to run and run. Meanwhile, in order to concentrate on the job in hand, Edwards was forced to place the moral issue on the back burner.

Considering it was in the heart of the West End, the terraced building housing the Wiener Library at number 4 Devonshire Street, W1 was unprepossessing. The grey slabs that made up the façade were covered in a patina of sooty deposits left by the incessant flow of traffic. Edwards stared up at the entrance, a large black door which stood at the top of a small flight of stone steps. To the right of the door was a small brass name-plate declaring that it was the home of the Institute of Contemporary History and Wiener Library. Pottage had told him that inside its portals were almost thirty-five thousand books on the Third Reich, the survival and revival of Nazi and fascist movements, anti-Semitism, racism and post-war Germany. As he pressed the buzzer and was granted entrance, the reporter hoped he would not have to read through all of them to find what he was looking for.

He was directed to a first-floor room that was as unexceptional as the exterior. Compared to his local borough library it appeared minuscule. The room was empty apart from a junior librarian and an older grey-haired man who was studying intently at the long table that ran down the centre.

"We have more documentation downstairs," said the librarian. The bespectacled young man was also a part-time clairvoyant, thought Edwards.

"Oh, er, thanks," the reporter stammered. "I'd just like to see some documentation on the SS, please. And also if you have any information on the Small Fortress at Theresienstadt."

A few minutes later, Edwards was poring over a heavy leather-bound tome. He knew that much of the early Nazi documentation was written in Gothic script. As a student, Edwards had always found the script burdensome. The Nazis had worshipped it as a symbol of Germany's glorious and heroic past, using it at every opportunity until one bright bureaucrat decided it was not the easiest way to make the ordinary German citizen literate.

Delving into the tome, the reporter was unaware of the stranger at his side.

"You look puzzled, my friend. Can I be of some assistance?"

Startled, Edwards looked up to see the grey-haired man standing over him. He was early-middle-aged and about six feet tall with thin, almost gaunt features. Horn-rims and a wispy goatee lent him a rather bookish appearance. An empty pipe protruded from thin, colourless lips. From his accent, Edwards knew the man was German.

"I'm afraid I'm having a bit of trouble with this Gothic script," he said apologetically. "My German's not bad, just a bit rusty. *Ich studierte es in der Universität.*"

The stranger shook his head and removed his pipe. "*Es*

macht mir nichts aus. Sprechen Sie was Sie wollen. I'm easy."

Edwards smiled. The man's casual manner put him at ease immediately. Besides, the reporter knew he could do with some help. "What does this sentence mean?" he asked.

The man leaned closer and proceeded to give an explanation in flawless English which made complete sense.

"*Danke,*" said Edwards, rising and stretching out a hand. They were around the same height. "I'm Mark Edwards."

"*Sehr erfreut.* Dieter Müller, at your service."

Typically Germanic, thought Edwards, as the man shook his hand firmly. He could have sworn there was a slight clicking of the heels. The reporter leaned on the table and folded his arms. "How do you like our wonderful city?"

"Ah, my friend, there is one thing that makes London so much more attractive than Berlin."

"And what's that?"

"It's dirtier."

Edwards laughed loudly and then covered his mouth as he caught sight of the librarian's unappreciative gaze.

"What are you doing over here?" he asked in a more hushed tone.

"I'm a history professor at Heidelberg on a sabbatical," said Müller, scratching his angular chin. There was the light of pride in his steel-blue eyes. "*Ich hab mein Herz in Heidelberg verloren.*"

"My heart's closer to home, Dieter. But I know what you mean about Heidelberg. I've been there myself. It's a truly beautiful town. The university is magic. Do you specialize in anything in particular?"

"I'm an expert in the rise and fall of Nazism and Holocaust studies. I also have a Master's in psychology."

"Phew, pretty impressive. I thought most Germans were only interested in sweeping the past under the carpet."

"They are," smiled Müller, showing rows of teeth stained by

pipe tobacco. "I am their nemesis. Mind you, the number of politically active neo-Nazis and right-wing nationalists in Germany is relatively small, about forty thousand in all, but the shadows they cast are long because of my country's past. But as it says on the gates of Dachau, *Nie wieder*. Never again."

"Good for you, Dieter, although it seems that those old Nazis never seem to die or even fade away."

"What do you mean?"

"You must have heard about the Jewish taxi driver who was murdered the other day."

"Yes, terrible thing. The papers seem to think the killer is this HS and that he is probably a neo-Nazi."

"Maybe," said Edwards, wiping the corners of his mouth. "That's why I'm here, actually. I'm a reporter for the *Evening Standard*."

"Yes, now I remember why I thought I had seen you before. Your photograph was in yesterday's newspaper."

"I'm surprised you recognized me from that," Edwards laughed.

"True, it doesn't really do you justice."

Edwards, beginning to warm to the professor, was coming to believe that the man might indeed be able to help in the search for background on Schreiber. "Can you keep a secret?" He winked conspiratorially.

"Try me, my friend," said Müller, switching comfortably back to English.

Edwards paused, thinking the whole thing might sound a bit far-fetched. He looked past the German and at the librarian. Taking the hint, Müller suggested they go into a side study to continue their conversation.

"I suppose I'm here because of a phone call," said the reporter, leaning against a table. Müller's raised eyebrows betrayed an eagerness to know more. "I received a rather strange call from a man with a German accent. He said that he knew who the killer was, that this HS was a guy by the name of Hans Schreiber, a junior SS officer at the Small Fortress in Theresienstadt. He was very agitated and might just be a crank, but I don't think so."

If Müller was surprised, he did not show it. He stroked his goatee for a few seconds. "I think it is fortuitous that we met here today, my friend."

"What do you mean?"

"It just so happens that I'm currently researching Theresienstadt. I can save you a lot of leg-work, although I don't think you'll find much on Schreiber."

"Why's that?"

"Simply because the files on junior SS officers are not as thick as the files on the big fish. I mean, there's plenty about Joeckl, who was also called Pinda and was commandant of the Small Fort. He was executed in Prague in the autumn of 1946. A fitting end for an arch-criminal. But Schreiber ..." Müller shrugged.

Undeterred, Edwards pressed on. "But this Schreiber must have been a pretty mean character. I mean, to shoot prisoners through the nape of the neck and then carve a swastika in their foreheads must have made him a number-one target for the investigating authorities after the war."

"Is that what the caller told you?"

"Well, he told me about Schreiber's modus operandi."

"What did he sound like, may I ask?"

Edwards scratched his chin. "Elderly, I suppose. Must be, as he said he was a victim of Schreiber."

"A victim?" Müller's voice held a trace of scepticism.

"Yes, he said Schreiber made him suffer but he lived to tell the tale."

"Was he Jewish?"

"Maybe. He had a heavy German accent. He might be

Jewish, but he didn't say."

Müller's voice softened. "I'm afraid, Mark, that as far as my knowledge goes, there were no Jewish survivors of the Small Fortress."

"What do you mean?" Edwards asked, genuinely shocked.

"I mean that it was a place where those who had been particularly irksome to the Nazis were sent for rehabilitation. There were plenty of survivors among the criminal and political fraternity of Theresienstadt. But Jews were singled out for special treatment. The Americans have a wonderful phrase for it ... extreme prejudice."

"You mean they were all killed?"

"Yes, I believe so."

"But surely you cannot be one hundred per cent sure."

"No one can," said the professor, shaking his head. "However, it would have been extremely unlikely that any survived."

"I need to know about this Schreiber," said Edwards. His need was urgent, and he did not fancy ploughing through reams of documents in German. It would take him hours, probably days. Realizing that Dieter Müller might be an extremely useful asset, he decided to take the plunge. "Dieter, I know we've only just met and I hope you don't think me rude, but as you're studying here anyway, would you be prepared to help? *Mit meinem Deutsch ist es nicht weit her.*"

Dieter Müller smiled broadly. "*Das ist nicht weiter schlimm.* Really, your German is not too bad." He thrust out his hand and shook the reporter's warmly. "*Jawohl!* It will make my research very exciting."

"Good," said Edwards. "Here's my card. It's got my work number and my mobile phone number. If you come up with anything, please let me know immediately. By the way, where can I get hold of you?"

"I'll be here most days working on my new book on the

Holocaust," replied the German, taking the card. "You can leave a message if I'm not. Also, I'll give you the phone number of my rented apartment. You might catch me there in the evenings."

"Thanks, Dieter. I really do appreciate this. We'll have to get together for a drink. It's nice to know there are people like you making sure the youth of Germany know the truth."

"Thank you, Mark. That is very kind of you. I try to do my best."

Müller wrote out a couple of telephone numbers on a slip of paper. The two then shook hands again. Edwards, thankful that he had found an ally to plough through the records, turned to leave.

"Oh, Mark," his new friend called out. "Keep me up to date with developments, eh? ... Especially on this anonymous caller. He seems a strange one. And one more thing ..."

"Yes?"

"This stranger might conceivably even be the killer."

Mark Edwards nodded in agreement. The thought had crossed his mind more than once.

Seven hours later, Edwards sat alone in his flat waiting nervously for the doorbell to ring. Danielle would be arriving any moment to pick him up and take him through a new religious experience. He saw himself as an agnostic rather than a godless atheist. Yet the trappings of religion, the ceremony and the cant, bothered him. It did not matter whether it was a church, a mosque or a synagogue, he knew he would not feel comfortable in any of them. His parents had been nominal Anglicans and he and his brother had enjoyed all the trappings of Christmas as did most other families in Britain. Yet he only remembered going to church once, around the age of five, and that it was a frightening experience. He recalled being surrounded by straight-faced strangers and being scared by the booming echo of the vicar's voice. No, organized religion was definitely not his cup of tea.

The front-door chimes stirred Edwards from his musings. He knew it could only be Danielle.

"Hi, darling." She smiled warmly as he opened the door. Standing before him in an exquisitely cut charcoal two-piece, Danielle displayed two rows of the most perfect teeth he had ever seen. Everything about her seemed to be in perfect proportion. He was as excited as a schoolboy to see her. He knew these feelings were transparent and he did not care. For a moment the two stood staring at each other, their eyes bright not only with obvious approval, but with the memory of their first night of lovemaking.

"Well," she said at last, "are you ready to go?"

"If I can kiss you first."

"You may," said Danielle, leaning forward.

Edwards pulled her towards him and, holding her tight, gave her a kiss that lingered long enough for him to feel the familiar stirring.

"Whoa," she laughed, "down, boy."

"Sorry. I just get carried away when I'm with you."

"Mark," she sighed, "believe me, I feel the same. But let's cool it over the next few days. It's a pretty rough time."

"I'm sorry," he said. "I understand. Where's the synagogue?"

"Oh, Mark," she laughed, "I see I'm going to have to give you a crash-course in Judaism. The *shiva*'s held in the home and not in the synagogue."

"Sorry," he said, hoping his relief was not too obvious. "It just shows how ignorant I am."

"Come on, let's go," she said, grabbing his hand. "We'll take my car."

Neither talked much during the short journey, both reflecting on the solemnity of the occasion.

Danielle brought her red Vauxhall Cavalier to a halt about fifty yards from her aunt's home. She could see by the number of mourners' cars that it would be pointless trying to park nearer. She took her handbag which Edwards had been holding and opened it. Withdrawing a dark blue *yarmulka*, she placed it gingerly on his head.

"Okay, Mark," she said firmly, "this is where you get your first lesson in Judaism. You have to wear this whenever we're in a house of worship, at a wedding, a *barmitzvah* or, God forbid, a funeral or *shiva* like tonight. As I told you before, *shiva* simply means 'seven' and we traditionally have seven days of mourning after someone dies. Got it so far?"

"Yes, teacher."

"Good. Now, so's you shouldn't be too surprised, you'll see Auntie Becky, her two sons and Joe's two brothers sitting on low chairs. They'll all be wearing an item of clothing torn over the heart. There'll be about half an hour of prayers in Hebrew, but don't worry ..."

"What?"

"Neither you nor I nor most of the people in the room will understand it."

"What do you mean?" Edwards asked, genuinely intrigued.

Danielle smiled. "It's quite simple, really. As far as the Jews in this country are concerned, Hebrew is purely liturgical. Like High Church Latin. It's as if you pray in it not for its meaning to you, but maybe for its meaning to God. After all, when we envisage our God it's as a Hebrew-speaker, not someone versed in Swahili or Outer Mongolian."

Edwards could not contain himself. He burst out laughing. *Shiva* or not, he found all the paraphernalia surrounding religious ritual highly amusing.

"Don't be so blasphemous," Danielle scolded, and then

burst into a fit of giggling.

"Okay, let's go, mademoiselle. We can't go in there with smiles on our faces."

"That's true," said Danielle. "And we can't leave with smiles either. But after you arrive and before you leave you might be permitted the occasional smile."

"What do you mean?"

"I mean that at Jewish functions, even funerals, you meet old friends and acquaintances and it's impolite not to smile. Amongst our own we're as gregarious as a bunch of rabbits. C'mon."

Danielle led him up the path of a typical bay-windowed three-bedroom semi. People wearing skull-caps were standing around outside.

"It's far too crowded in there, Danielle," said a small bald-headed man. "It's bloody murder."

Danielle smiled and then said out of the corner of her mouth, "What a wonderful way Uncle Monty has with words."

Edwards, trying hard to look grim, gripped her hand even harder. He felt so much the outsider. As Danielle led him through the throng and into a packed through-lounge, he felt a rising sense of panic. A heady brew of perfume and sweat engulfed him. A tall, bearded man thrust a prayer book into his hand.

"But ..." Edwards stammered.

"Sshh, Mark," said Danielle soothingly. "Don't worry. It's in Hebrew and English. The rabbi will tell you in English which page to turn to."

"Who's he?"

"The one over there with the hat," she whispered.

Edwards craned his neck. "Doesn't look like a rabbi."

"Just because he doesn't have a beard?" she said with raised eyebrows. "Not many of them do nowadays."

Edwards suddenly felt ashamed. His reaction had been

typical of someone who had been brought up on stereotypes, encouraged not so much by his parents as by his peers.

Danielle, sensing his discomfort, gave his hand a gentle squeeze. She knew how strange and difficult it must be for him. "I've got to go out of the room while the men pray, Mark. Just stand looking down at the book. Nobody will take any notice. See you in a few minutes."

For the next half an hour Edwards remained a mute sentinel amid a sea of swaying incantation. He spent the time reading the English translation of the prayers, but was more fascinated by the Hebrew characters. They were unfathomable, yet their very shapes seemed to jump out at him. They seemed to have an extraordinary power compared to the smaller and blander Latin-based characters on the opposite page.

A proferred hand at last told him the service was over. He almost felt reluctant to hand back the prayer book. He looked up to see Danielle eyeing him from the hallway. His heart skipped a beat. This was stupid, he told himself. He had known her only a couple of months. She weaved her way towards him.

"We'll stay around for a few minutes," she whispered in his ear. "I told everybody I had to interview somebody tonight, but you can take me for a drink round the corner. There's no chance anyone here will be there."

"Do I say anything to them?" said Edwards, eyeing the row of bereaved seated on the odd chairs that had had their legs cut off halfway down.

"Yes, just shake their hands and wish them a long life."

"A what?"

"Just say, I wish you a long life."

A few minutes later they both joined the procession of people paying their respects. There were a few cousins there Danielle had not seen in years. Cousin Stephen the optician, cousin Melvyn the chemist, cousin Roy, big in ladies' skirts.

She kissed them all warmly except for Joe Hyams' two sons. They got more of a peck. Edwards grimaced as he passed down the line. He felt acutely embarrassed.

The reporter only wound down after the first swallow of a whisky mac in a local pub burnt its way down his throat and gave him a warm glow in the pit of the stomach. "Phew, I needed that," he said in relief.

"Come on," said Danielle, "it wasn't that bad, was it?"

"I suppose not. But I'd much rather be at a wedding than a funeral."

"Here's to *simchas*, then," she said, raising her glass of gin and tonic.

"What's *simchas*?"

"Happy events," smiled Danielle, the perfect teeth framed by lips that glistened.

"Not many of those around at the moment, are there?" he sighed. "Dani ..."

"Yes."

"I know we agreed not to talk shop, but something's been bothering me and I just feel I want to get it off my chest."

"Shoot," she said, placing her hand on his.

Edwards, looking squarely into his lover's emerald-green eyes, spent the next twenty minutes telling her about everything that had happened to him during the past few days.

Danielle, listening intently, did not interrupt him until he had signalled that he had finished. He had not noticed her eyes widen at the mention of the strange caller and was unaware of the turmoil in her mind.

"Mark," she said, gripping her glass, "you are saying that this caller claimed the killer is a man called Hans Schreiber who was an SS officer at the Small Fortress in Theresienstadt?"

"Yes."

"How odd."

"What do you mean?"

"I don't know whether there is anything in this, but it seems an amazing coincidence." She paused to take a long swig of the gin and tonic.

"Well?" said Edwards, intrigued.

"Henry Sonntag," she said bluntly.

"Who's he?"

"He's a Jewish multi-millionaire bonds dealer I've just interviewed, a sort of British George Soros. He made his fortune after arriving here as a penniless refugee after the war. He made no mention of this Schreiber, but he did say he was a survivor of the Small Fortress. The things he described that went on there defy belief. Mark ..."

"Yes," he said, eager to hear more.

"I got a strange phone call at the office from Sonntag the day before yesterday. He pleaded with me not to publish my interview. He said he couldn't explain and sounded really scared."

"Jesus!" Edwards exclaimed. "What the hell's going on?"

"I think you'd better chase up that German professor friend of yours. I'll try to make contact with Sonntag again, but he sounded pretty agitated."

"Maybe I should give him a ring," said Edwards, the crime reporter's inquisitiveness rising to the fore.

"No, Mark," she said firmly. "I promised him. I like the man. I don't want you barging in like a bull in a china shop. He's suffered enough."

"I can be diplomatic, you know," he said in a hurt tone.

"I'm sure you can, darling, but let's just try to get some more information before we jump to any conclusions."

Edwards nodded in agreement. Only two things were uppermost in his mind. He was hoping that Dieter Müller would find something on Schreiber. More importantly, he was praying that his anonymous caller would continue to ring him.

CHAPTER SIX

Howard Plant was the sort of man whose favourite perfume epitomized his psychological make-up. He doused himself in Calvin Klein's Obsession, hardly the subtlest of fragrances, with the passion of one who believed that natural body odours were an affront to olfaction. Plant's other obsessions were myriad: fast cars, large houses, small boys, money. But not necessarily in that order. Howard Plant was not a very nice man. Unsurprisingly, therefore, Howard Plant tended to have more enemies than the Leader of All the Russias.

"Bates!" he bellowed. "Bates, where are you?"

"Coming right away, Mr Plant," came the effeminate reply. The squeaky voice emanating from the kitchen carried nuances both of obeisance and sarcasm. For Richard Bates, a gangling and prematurely bald leech, was nothing if not used to his master's idiosyncrasies. Ten years of catering to Plant's every whim, from the procuring of various new "toy boys" to allowing even the occasional sexual violation of his own body, meant that Richard Matthew Bates had earned the right to share in some of the multi-millionaire's extravagances. If ostentation was the mark of the insecure, then Howard Plant was a brightly hued dragonfly, darting to and fro in a desperate attempt to impress the world. The biggest house in Chigwell, two Rolls-Royces, three Lamborghinis, two Maseratis and the odd Ferrari made it clear that Plant enjoyed being the oldest "Essex boy" in the county. Despite his proclivities, he had become the darling of the press thanks to a burgeoning software company that was the Great English Hope, expected to counter the Microsoft explosion. Plantware was gobbling up the market like a deranged Pacman.

"Here it is, here it is," the manservant said soothingly as he entered the TV room where his master lay naked and spreadeagled on the floor, his large genitalia grotesque appendages to what was in effect a slight and somewhat emaciated frame. The man was a middle-aged weasel, and although Bates was used to seeing his boss naked he believed fifty-year-olds were better satiated under the sheets and with the lights out.

Plant continued with his gentle callisthenics as Bates placed the tray gently on a side table. The tray held the usual selection of vegan supper dishes and vitamin supplements.

"Did you blend the carrots with the tomato juice, Master Bates?" asked Plant in time-honoured fashion. Plant's continual use of the honorific as a synonym for "mastur-bates" had become a repetitive form of verbal torture for Bates, assuaged only by the luxury of a lifestyle that most other servants would envy.

"Yes, sir," sighed the hireling.

"Did you make sure you extracted all the pips from the fresh orange juice. I found one in there the other day."

"Yes, Mr Plant."

"Good, Bates. Now run along and get my clothes ready. My visitor will be here shortly. It's Henry Sonntag. He's been here before. Lives up the road, on the border with Abridge. You remember him, don't you?"

"Yes, sir. Nice chap."

"Well, he's going to be in a for a bit of a shock tonight."

"What do you mean?"

"I mean I haven't been too satisfied with his performance lately."

"Funny, I thought you always swore by him," said the servant, who knew full well that Sonntag had helped make Plant very rich.

"No, not any more. I think I'll dump him."

Richard Bates paused. He had always believed that Jews did not do this kind of thing to their own. Still, if there were going to be any fireworks, he did not want to be around. He had other plans for the evening.

"Er, Mr Plant ..."

"Yes," said Plant, tucking into his health-food supper.

"May I, er, take an hour off after Mr Sonntag arrives?"

"Perhaps. Where are you going?"

"The King's Head. I'm meeting someone there."

"Does he have a friend?" asked Plant lasciviously.

"Maybe. I'll ask him for you." Bates knew how to hook his master. If the truth be known, Plant was like putty in his hands.

"Okay," said Plant, wiping along his pencil-thin moustache and the corners of his rubbery mouth with a red serviette, "but don't be gone too long. It's not your usual night off."

"Thank you, sir. I'll go and prepare your clothes."

Plant continued his naked callisthenics for the next ten minutes while his trusty manservant prepared a charcoal-grey Armani suit and a handmade white shirt from the Burlington Arcade. Bates could never understand why his master insisted on dressing formally to receive his business cronies in his own home. The man frolicked naked one minute and dressed to the hilt the next. Still, he thought, rich men usually exercised their right to do whatever they damn well pleased.

"Here are your clothes, sir," he said. "Shall I dress you?"

Howard Plant growled an affirmative and then stood transfixed with arms outstretched as his manservant dressed him speedily and skilfully. Within a few minutes, the man who had gone from rags to riches in less than a decade was preening himself before his hall mirror. "Dapper" was how the newspapers labelled him, and dapper he was. He accepted the various labels with equanimity, for image was no strange bedfellow to vanity.

"Ah, it must be Sonntag," he called out as the doorbell sounded. "Bates, be ready to fix our guest a stiff drink. I think he'll be needing it."

Plant opened the front door himself. "Ah, Henry, my good friend," he enthused. "I hope you didn't get lost on your way from the front gate."

"Still the same old jokes, eh, Howard?" smiled Sonntag.

"Come in, come in." Plant took his guest by the arm with all the bonhomie of a Black Widow and led him into a drawing room festooned with Old Masters. "There's lots to talk about. Bates, fix Henry's usual. Never forgets a face and never forgets a drink to go with it, does our Bates."

"Yes, sir. Whisky and dry on the rocks, wasn't it, Mr Sonntag?"

"Well remembered, Bates," said Sonntag, handing the manservant his coat.

Plant ushered his guest towards a Regency chaise-longue. "Terrible goings-on, eh?" he muttered.

"You mean the murder?"

"Yeah. Must bring back memories of the war for you. Must have been a fascist bastard."

"They never really go away, Howard."

"Yeah, I know. But who would have thought that this kind of thing could happen in our own back yard. It's a fucking disgrace."

"I'm sure the police will catch the man responsible," said Sonntag, trying to calm the fear that had crept into the younger man's voice.

"I tell you, I'm dead scared, Henry. No Jew is safe while this nutcase is on the loose. A cab driver, *noch*. Maybe next time he'll go up-market."

"Calm down, Howard. You know my philosophy ..."

"That the only time someone should worry is when a gun is held to his head. Yeah, sure, Henry. Go tell that to Joe Hyams. Talking about dangerous weapons, Henry, how go the markets?"

"Up and down," said the older man. "You know how it is."

Howard Plant certainly did know. Of late it had all been down. He was convinced that his guest was getting too old for the job. "Sit down, my friend. Sit down."

Bates, having hung Sonntag's coat on an ornate baroque stand in the entrance hall, sidled into the room towards the drinks cabinet. He kept his gaze averted but his ears open. Having been forewarned, he was eager to hear Sonntag's reaction.

"Ah, thank you, Bates," said Plant, taking his usual whisky and dry on the rocks. "Bring us some peanuts, will you."

"Right away, sir."

"Now, Henry," said Plant, turning towards his guest. "You know me. I'm not one to bandy words."

Henry Sonntag smiled. He knew what was coming next. It was the Italian job. The Italian government had collapsed once again, only this time he had missed out by a whisker on making a killing.

"My dear Henry," the weasel continued, "you've lost me a lot of money this week."

There was a pregnant pause while Sonntag considered his reply. The little man was irritatingly avaricious and had been spoilt by too many years of unbridled prosperity. "You know the old adage, Howard: what goes up can also come down. Not every day is Christmas. You are still way ahead in the game."

"True, true. But when I lose a couple of million, it really hurts."

"How much have I made for you over the years, Howard?"

Plant squirmed. He hated being in debt to anyone. He hated paying anyone. He especially hated the ten per cent merchants. Sure, they made him a lot of money. Millions. But while to lose a million might be considered an accident, to lose two million was carelessness. "I don't know, Henry. I don't keep count."

The beady hazel eyes narrowed in contempt. Sonntag knew that if anyone kept a constant vigil on his finances, it was Howard Plant. "By my reckoning, my trading for you over the years has earned you at least thirty million."

Whereas Howard Plant's lupine features betrayed little emotion at the enormity of the figure, the bald-headed eavesdropper in the next room whistled sharply under his breath. Bates glanced at his watch. He was torn between the prospect of a good old-fashioned altercation and the possibility of setting up a seduction.

"Maybe, maybe not," said Plant. "But time moves on, Henry. No one can afford to live on past glories." Then, after a short pause, he continued, "We all have to retire sometime."

So that's it, thought Sonntag. The big shove. The little weasel couldn't take a downturn. So be it. There were plenty of other fish, albeit not quite so fat. As long as the little bastard settled his account. "So, Howard, you want to dispense with my services."

Plant cleared his throat nervously. "Well, maybe it'll do both of us some good. You know, pastures new, so to speak."

"Okay, Howard," said Sonntag, the contempt in his voice now clearly discernible, "we'll settle up here and now. You owe me a million in unpaid commission."

"Ahem. I, er, don't think so."

"What do you mean?"

"I mean there's nothing in writing."

"There's never been anything in writing, Howard." Sonntag's words, delivered slowly, were heavy with sarcasm.

"Yeah, I know," the little man squirmed. "Come on, it's not as if it's costing you personally. What you've never had, you never miss. You've earned a fortune from playing with my money."

Henry Sonntag felt a sense of hatred the like of which he

had not experienced since Theresienstadt. "You English Jews are all the same. Always complaining. No patience to wait for an upturn ... I could kill you for this."

Howard Plant sank further into his armchair and spread his palms. "Now, now, Henry," he cajoled. "Take things easy. We can talk this through."

Neither protagonist heard the front door close. Richard Matthew Bates had a more pressing need than to listen to the bickerings of rich men.

About five miles away, Mark Edwards was propped up in bed perusing his weekly issue of *Time* magazine. He had decided to have an early night and thought a little light reading might help him doze off. However, apart from a few lines on the murder in the review-of-the-week section, he could not concentrate on anything. His mind was juggling with three images, only two of them morphologically definable. The third was a phantasm, a collage of the haunted features of concentration camp victims. The anonymous caller kept invading his thoughts of Danielle and Dieter Müller. Was he sinner or sinned against? Would he call again? Would Müller find anything on this mysterious Hans Schreiber?

Turning his head, he stared at his mobile telephone and the regular apparatus lying next to it, the number of which he divulged only to close friends. Edwards found himself willing the mobile to ring with the intense concentration of a practitioner in telekinesis.

It did.

The reporter's heart leapt into his mouth. For a few seconds he sat ossified. "Hello, hello ..." he said at last, fiddling with the talk button.

"Hello, Mark, this is Dieter. You sound out of breath."

"Oh, hi, Dieter. I – I just got in."

"I've got some important news for you. Have you got a pen?"

"Hold on a minute," said Edwards, grabbing the pen and notepad he always kept by the bedside phone. "Fire away."

"In the *Dienst Heerliste der Waffen-SS* there is a listing for an Obersturmführer Hans Schreiber. His SS number was 675951. His date of birth was 10 June 1922. He was accepted into the SS on 15 July 1940. There were about twenty Schreibers in the listings, but only three named Hans."

"Fantastic, Dieter," Edwards replied excitedly. "How did you do it?"

"Elementary, my dear Edwards."

"Listen," said the reporter, "did you find out if this particular Schreiber had any connection with Theresienstadt?"

"I'm trying, Mark, I'm trying. Unfortunately, there is so little written about the Small Fortress. There used to be a Small Fortress Association in a place called Littlehampton ..."

"Sussex."

"Yes. But it doesn't exist any more. They must have all passed on."

"Keep looking."

"I will, Mark, I will. What about your end? Anything new from the police or that mysterious caller?"

"Nothing, Dieter, sorry."

"Let's compare notes soon, Mark, okay?"

"Sure. I'll give you a ring as soon as there are any new developments. Thanks once again, Dieter. 'Bye."

Edwards, his heart pounding, pressed the talk button again. He was already formulating the next day's lead in his mind. He'd have to run the gauntlet from Webb, but the DI could not expect him to pass on this opportunity. Rejuvenated by Müller's call, he sprang out of bed, paced around the room for a few minutes, and then made for the bathroom. He splashed his face with cold water and ran his wet fingers through his hair. He desperately wanted to speak to Danielle, but he knew she would be spending the night with her inconsolable aunt.

The phone rang again.

"Damn it," he muttered, "who can that be?"

He strode back into the bedroom and picked up the mobile. "Hello, Edwards."

"M-Mr Edwards."

The reporter sat on the side of his bed. It was the anonymous caller and he was obviously distressed. "Yes, yes. What's the matter?"

"I am frightened, Mr Edwards. I am so frightened."

The man was sobbing, and Edwards felt at a loss as to how to react. "Look, whoever you are, try, er, try to compose yourself. What's happened?"

"He is going to kill again. I know it. He will kill again and again until he finds me. He is evil. Please protect me, Mr Edwards. Please protect me."

"How can I protect you when I don't even know your name or where you live?"

"I can't, Mr Edwards. I am too afraid. I lost my faith in humanity fifty years ago."

"I can arrange it so you'll get round-the-clock police protection. You see, I believe you. I know that Hans Schreiber existed." There was a long pause. "Hello, hello ... are you still there?"

"Thank God," came the whispered reply. "The whole world must know his name and what he did."

"Can you give me any more details?" the reporter asked, flicking over to a fresh page in his notepad. Again there was a long silence.

"He was an animal, Mr Edwards." The voice was low and bitter. "He would take a special delight in making a spectacle of killing."

"What do you mean?"

"Did you ever see the film *Spartacus*, Mr Edwards?"

"Yes, of course. With Kirk Douglas."

"For Hans Schreiber the Small Fortress was a Roman arena. He would arrange gladiatorial contests ..."

"Go ahead, sir, I'm listening." Edwards gripped the mobile hard.

"Schreiber would pit one Jew against another and make them fight to the death."

"What?" the reporter gulped.

"I know this," the caller continued. "I saw it with my own eyes."

Edwards sat on the bed transfixed. His hand refused to write. His head was full of a thousand terrifying images of the worst excesses of ancient Rome.

"I-I don't know what to say," he stuttered.

The stranger's voice suddenly became calmer. "He enjoyed it. He actually enjoyed watching men kill one another. I think he enjoyed it more than killing them himself."

"Now listen, please. Please do as I ..."

"I cannot, Mr Edwards. I will call you again."

"No, don't go ..."

Click.

"All right, calm down," snapped Bob Webb. "For God's sake, calm down!"

The manservant stood trembling by the twisted body of his late employer and whimpered, not because of the grotesque manner in which his benefactor had met his end, but because he was about to be put out into the street. Knowing Plant as he did, he was sure that a will, if there indeed was one, would contain no provision for him. It had always been a case of enjoying the good life while it lasted. Richard Matthew Bates was crying because he was feeling sorry for Richard Matthew Bates.

"Now let me get this straight," boomed Webb gruffly. "You left the King's Head to walk home about fifteen minutes ago. It took you five minutes to reach the front gates and you found Mr Plant where he's now lying, about fifteen yards down the path from the gates."

"Yes," Bates squeaked.

"Is there anyone at the pub who can vouch for you being there?"

"Yes, of course. Ask any of the barmen. They all know me." Bates knew he was squirming, but he was damned if he was going to divulge the name and address of his new-found friend. He did not want the fresh meat spoiled.

"Now you garbled something before about leaving Mr Plant with a guest."

"Guv!"

Webb looked over his shoulder as Detective Constable Jim Simmonds, his ruddy face streaked by the rain, entered the hall. "Wipe your shoes, Jim, there's a good lad. You look like you've been working on a farm."

"Yes, guv," said Simmonds apologetically. "It's starting to rain heavily. Everything's muddying up. But look what we've found already."

Webb took the transparent plastic bag and smoothed it against the object inside. It was clearly a dagger, displaying the runes of the SS on the hilt and some kind of German motto along the blade. The tip was tinted with blood. But what concerned Webb most were the initials HS carved on the hilt between the Nazi winged eagle and swastika emblem and the runes.

"And there's also another note," said Simmonds, handing his boss a second plastic bag.

Webb stared intently at the printed message. It was the same as the first, but with a rider: "Publish this note and maybe I will stop enjoying myself killing Jews".

The gangling DI took a deep breath and turned round to face the ashen-faced manservant. "Does this mean anything to you?" he said, showing him the knife.

"N-No," stammered Bates. "Oh, look at the blood. I feel faint."

"Before you pass out, Mr Bates, you were saying that you left your boss in the company of a stranger."

"Well, not exactly a stranger. It was Henry Sonntag, Mr Plant's financial adviser. They were discussing business."

"Where is this Sonntag now?"

"He must have left before I got back," came Bates's tremulous reply. "Oh dear."

"What, Mr Bates?"

"They were having a bit of an argument ... over money. I – I – oh dear ..."

"Yes, Mr Bates?" said Webb, becoming increasingly irritated.

"I thought he was joking ..."

Webb's imposing eyebrows lifted and his steely eyes bored into the manservant's.

"Just before I went out, I thought I heard Sonntag say he could kill Mr Plant. They were arguing about some commissions that Sonntag said Mr Plant owed him. I thought it would all blow over. Oh dear."

Webb pursed his lips. He felt like throttling the queer. "Right, Mr Bates. What does this Sonntag look like?"

"He's about six feet tall with thinning yellowy-white hair. Must be in his seventies. He's a German Jew, I think."

Webb's ears pricked. The word "German" had set the alarm bells ringing. "Where does he live, this Sonntag?"

"He lives about three miles away, off the main Abridge

112

road," said Bates, moving shakily towards the telephone table to his right. "I think his address and telephone number are in Mr Plant's telephone book here." The manservant picked up the leather directory. "Yes, here it is."

Webb ripped out the page. He knew the country lane in question and the few detached house along it. "Jim, you come with me. Get Fairbrother in here to look after Mr Bates. Give these to Swanson for safe keeping."

"Right away, guv," said Simmonds, taking the two plastic bags. Webb loped out towards his car, its blue light playing intermittently over the dark rain-soaked bushes. He strode towards his colleagues, who had set up arc lights by the body further down the path. He felt elated, certain he was on the verge of some kind of breakthrough. The poof was a suspect and so was the character named Sonntag. Something was telling him he should put his money on the latter.

The detective inspector climbed into the passenger seat of his new Ford Mondeo. Within seconds his subordinate was at the wheel. "How long will it take you to get there, Jim?" he asked.

"Seven minutes for an ordinary driver, three for me."

"Step on it then, Jim lad."

Simmonds swung the Mondeo out of the late Howard Plant's driveway with a vengeance. Neither man spoke as they sped along the A113. Sonntag's home was just inside the border that separated the Met from the Essex constabulary. Webb was glad. He did not want any country yokels in on this one. The detective felt the familiar surge of adrenalin through his veins. The prospect of an arrest was what kept every good copper on his mettle. He just hoped this Sonntag character was still at home.

Simmonds switched off the blue light and the headlights as he swung the car into the short driveway of Henry Sonntag's home. Both men were relieved to see that the house was ablaze with light. They had every reason to believe that their suspect was present.

Three times Webb pressed the white ceramic button that was set into an oval brass plate to the left of the oak door. Three times he could hear the bell ring from within, yet there was no sign of any life.

"Okay, Jim," he said, exasperated, "force it."

Simmonds tested the door. He prided himself on being able to make a forced entry using the minimum of force. The owner had thankfully not engaged the mortise lock and ordinary Yales were a piece of cake. Within seconds both men were inside.

"Phew, pretty lavish, eh, guv?" Simmonds whispered.

"Par for the course round here, Jim ... Ssh." Webb suddenly put his forefinger to his lips. Both men listened intently. They could hear the sound of running water. Someone was having a shower. Suddenly they heard a voice singing. In German. "Bloody awful language," the big man muttered.

"Shall we go up, guv?"

Webb nodded and placed his foot firmly on the first step of a large spiral staircase leading to the upper floor. For two big men they made surprisingly little noise as they ascended.

"We'll have a look around before we confront him," Webb whispered.

The singing, a croaky baritone, continued to emanate from a room to their right as they reached the top of the stairs. The detective inspector motioned to Simmonds to stay by the bathroom door while he went to investigate the three rooms to the left of the central balustrade. He quietly opened the first door, his sweaty palm luxuriating in the coolness of the round gold-plated doorknob. It was a broom cupboard. Moving along to the second door he sent a furtive glance towards Simmonds before opening it. He could see right away that it was the main bedroom.

Bob Webb entered Henry Sonntag's bedroom and came face to face with further proof that he had indeed found his man. On the bed was a large brown suitcase which its owner was clearly in the process of packing. Some shirts and a pile of underwear lay next to it. To the left of the suitcase was a European Community passport and a British Airways airline ticket. The detective inspector opened the passport and stared at the photograph of Henry Sonntag. Pretty distinguished-looking guy, he thought. He noted with interest that Sonntag's place of birth was given as Berlin.

Webb placed the passport back on the bed and picked up the flight ticket. The fact that the destination read "Rio de Janeiro" hardly surprised him. Forget Colin Smith and his bunch of yobbos. This was their man, all right. He replaced the ticket and left the room. Motioning to Simmonds to stay where he was, he then walked into the third room which was facing him at the end of the landing. The room was cold and musty. He groped for the light-switch.

"Jesus H. Christ," gasped the policeman as the room flooded with light. Nothing in his previous experience had prepared Detective Inspector Robert William Webb for what now confronted him.

Theresienstadt

In the split second between Schreiber wishing him farewell and the staccato chatter of the machine-guns, Herschel Soferman made and acted on a decision intended to give him the only possible chance of survival. Throwing himself headlong into the ditch of putrefying flesh, he barely had time to gag on the oild stench before another body hit him full force in the back. Slipping into welcome oblivion, Soferman thought he heard Schreiber berating his men for forgetting to bring the quicklime.

When the Jew regained consciousness it was not his olfactory sense which was first assaulted, but that part of the brain that triggers panic. Oxygen, the very stuff of life, was being denied him. Squirming with all his might, he tried desperately to shift the heavy weight that was crushing him.

It was only when he had manoeuvred free of the corpses and taken a deep lungful of fetid air that the subsequent rush of adrenalin enabled him to clamber from the ditch. He hardly had time, however, to savour the most intoxicating elixir that life has to offer: freedom coupled with the knowledge that one has cheated death.

"*Schnell! Schnell!* Guards, hurry them up." The stentorian voice of Hans Schreiber echoed through the trees, their branches almost seeming to wilt in servile deference to the black-garbed arbiter.

Soferman summoned what little energy he still possessed and flung himself into a small clump of bushes at one end of the ditch. This time, instead of gasping for air, he reduced his breathing to the barest minimum. He knew that the slightest movement would bring a most terrible retribution.

"Stand by your shovels," came the familiar refrain.

Soferman peered through the leaves with morbid fascination as another group of men shuffled to their positions, as gullibly as he had. For the mind refused to believe the worst. Instead, it embraced every opportunity to indulge in wishful thinking, to believe in the sanctity of life even when death was inevitable.

"When I give the order, you will begin to cover the bodies," Schreiber told nineteen more doomed inmates of the Small Fortress.

As the Nazi boomed out the order to fire, Herschel Soferman screwed up his eyes and prayed that no loose bullets would find his refuge. He trembled as the withering hail cut the prisoners to the quick, allowing them no time to protest at the duplicity of their tormentors.

"Cover them with lime," declared Schreiber, "and we'll come back tomorrow to finish the job."

The smell of cordite hung heavily in the air as Soferman opened his eyes. His heart leapt into his mouth as he saw Schreiber approaching the ditch. If he inspected it too closely he might notice that one Jew was missing. A very special Jew. His erstwhile favourite Jew.

Hans Schreiber neared the ditch of death and then veered suddenly to his right until he was standing only a yard from the bushes that protected the man whom he supposed to be dead. The Obersturmführer took out a small pink handkerchief and put it to his nose. Soferman could smell the heady scent of lavender as it wafted through the air to season the stench of death. The drumming in his ears seemed to pound even harder. He willed Schreiber to move away.

"So," said Schreiber at last, "let's go. Tomorrow we shall have more fun." The six guards laughed heartily along with their mentor.

Soferman watched the monster and his henchmen march away from the copse, daring to move only once the canorous chirping of the birds had begun to replace the evil prattle of murderers.

CHAPTER SEVEN

Mark Edwards snubbed the lift to the fifth floor. Instead, he bounded up the two flights of stairs to the *Mail*'s offices. Breathless, he raced into the features section. Grabbing a startled Danielle by the arm, he implored her to find a side room where they could talk. Danielle, shrugging her shoulders at her colleagues, led him into an empty office.

"For God's sake, what's happening, Mark? You look like you're about to have a fit."

"Dani," he gasped, trying to regain his breath, "all hell's broken loose."

"Now calm down and tell me what's going on." She could hardly restrain her own eagerness.

"Howard Plant."

"The software man?"

"Yes. The old poof's been murdered. At his home in Chigwell."

"What!" Danielle exclaimed. "We only ran a feature on him a few weeks ago."

"That's not all," Edwards went on excitedly. "Bob Webb says it's the same modus operandi as your uncle's. What's more, they found an SS dagger near the body. The bloody Yard's been sitting on this all night, and you know why?"

Danielle shook her head.

"Because, as they say, a man is helping them with their enquiries."

"You mean they think they've got the killer?"

"They're not saying that officially yet. But Webby thinks it's an open and shut case. But until they charge anyone, I've got a free hand."

"What do you mean?" asked Danielle, feeling a sudden urge to support herself on the room's large grey desk.

"I mean, darling, that besides writing about the murder, I'm going to write about my anonymous caller and about this Schreiber character. It may be the only chance I get. Once it all goes *sub judice* I've had it."

Feeling a sense of elation and with the adrenalin pumping wildly, Edwards clasped her to him and gave her a long hard kiss on the lips. "Dani," he blurted, "I love you."

Danielle watched in shock as her lover then wheeled away and raced from the room. It was the first time he had uttered the three words that were the most potent in the English language. In any language, for that matter. She was not sure whether he meant them or whether they were a consequence of the excitement he was feeling over the story. Nevertheless, her own heart had begun pounding in response to his outburst. She at once felt the heady brew of elation and apprehension.

Two hours later, Mark Edwards was sitting back in his chair and admiring his front-page lead.

SS dagger and second 'HS' note found near body
MAN ARRESTED AFTER HOWARD PLANT
DIES IN COPYCAT SWASTIKA MURDER

by Mark Edwards

A man is expected to be charged later today with last night's brutal murder of Jewish software billionaire Howard Plant.

In a carbon copy of last week's murder of Barkingside taxi driver Joe Hyams, Mr Plant was found dead in the grounds of his palatial Chigwell mansion. Police said he had been shot through the nape of the neck and a swastika had been carved into his forehead. A bloodstained SS dagger was found near the body. The letters "HS" were inscribed near the hilt. Also found was a typewritten note with the same message as that found on the body of Joe Hyams: "Just for you – HS".

Detective Inspector Bob Webb, leading the police murder team, said Mr Plant was found by his butler and long-time companion, Mr Richard Bates. He said Mr Bates had helped police with their enquiries and had been ruled out as a suspect in the case.

Police said a man is expected to be charged later today.

Besides being fabulously wealthy, Howard Plant was also a leading Gay activist and donated large sums towards promoting Gay rights. He also ...

Edwards switched his gaze to the box that had been placed alongside the main story:

ANONYMOUS CALLER TELLS ME MYSTERIOUS 'HS' IS SS BEAST HANS SCHREIBER

by Mark Edwards

Following news of the brutal killing of Howard Plant, I can now reveal that an anonymous phone caller has informed me that the HS referred to in the death notes is an SS officer named Hans Schreiber. The caller rang me shortly after the murder of Joe Hyams. He said Schreiber was known as the "Beast of the Small Fortress" in Theresienstadt, a town near Prague used for the transit of Jews on their way to the Nazi death camps. He said he was convinced that Schreiber was in England and had murdered Hyams.

The caller, who had a German accent and sounded very afraid, claimed he was a survivor of the Small Fortress and that Schreiber's favourite method of killing a victim was with a bullet through the nape of the neck. He would then carve a swastika in the prisoner's forehead. The caller said Schreiber also used this method to finish off prisoners who had lost gladiatorial contests that he had arranged.

The caller demanded that I respect his anonymity and I decided not to report this matter until I had undertaken some research of my own. I can now reveal that there was indeed an Obersturmfüher Hans Schreiber who served in a Totenkopf, or Death's Head, division of the SS. His number was ...

Edwards put the newspaper down and leaned back in his chair.

"If you were a Yank you'd get a Pulitzer for this," said Jim Pottage, waddling towards him with a sheaf of news copy. "Abso-bloody-lutely brilliant, old man."

"Thanks, Jim. You've also been great on back-up. I mean it."

"Mind you," said Pottage, his West Country drawl exacerbated by a lunchtime tipple, "I be thinking that the shit's going to hit the fan soon."

"What do you mean?"

"I mean old Webby ain't going to be too pleased you didn't give him the low-down on this 'ere caller."

"Oh, don't worry about that, Jim. He's probably going to wrap it all up later tonight. It's not as if they're still searching for someone. I mean, I had to get the story in before it goes *sub judice*."

Pottage pulled at his purplish bulb of a nose. "Be a real hoot if this bloke they arrested is this Schreiber character. Odds on he's using an alias. Have you any idea who he might be?"

"No, the police are being cagey. My money would have been on his poof companion. You know, the butler did it, and all that."

"But his bum-boy's been ruled out," said Pottage. "My money's still on the queer connection, though. It's ..." His observations were cut short emphatically by the telephone. "Here we go," he laughed, "probably the Nobel people wanting to confirm your nomination for the literature prize.

Hello, Pottage here ... just a minute." The older man passed the phone to Edwards. "It's the scarlet woman," he winked.

Edwards took the phone. "Hi, Dani, how's it going?"

"Thanks, Mark," she said simply.

Edwards, thinking she was referring to his words of endearment, sought to reassure her. "I meant what I said, darling."

There was a pregnant pause before Danielle answered. "Oh, no. I-I didn't mean that. I meant thanks for not mentioning Henry Sonntag in your sidebar."

For a moment Edwards was nonplussed. Then he whistled. "Shit. I forgot all about him. Of course, you mentioned he'd been in that Small Fortress place. Jesus, what a balls-up. Listen, give me his number. It's too late for today's edition but if the police don't charge anyone tonight I might be able to write something about him tomorrow. I ..."

"Mark ..." Danielle cut him short.

"Yes, darling."

"Don't."

"Don't what?"

"Don't contact him. Please. He's been through enough already. The police have got their man, so there's no point."

Edwards hesitated. What she was asking went against all his reporting instincts. "You've really got something going for this man, haven't you?" he said, regretting the words instantly.

"You know how we Jews close ranks," said Danielle indignantly.

He heard a click. "Shit!" he exclaimed, and slammed down the phone. His gaze was met by Pottage's raised eyebrows. "Lovers' tiff?" smiled the older man. "Don't worry, she'll get over it."

"Damn it," Edwards muttered, as the phone rang again. "Hello, Dani ..."

"Mr Edwards," came the familiar fearful voice, "who have

122

the police arrested? Is it him? Is it Schreiber? You must tell me."

The reporter's mind was racing. He pushed all thoughts of Danielle aside. This meant that his anonymous caller was definitely not the police suspect. "I don't know," he answered. "The police will probably name him tonight."

"Please, Mr Edwards. I must know if this is Schreiber."

"Look, whoever he is, he probably won't be using that name. Anyway, you could be a vital witness. Please let me know how I can get hold of you."

"I can't, Mr Edwards," the harsh Germanic voice said. "I can't until I know that it really is Schreiber behind bars. You must understand me."

Edwards sighed heavily. The man sounded petrified. It was useless trying to persuade him to co-operate, and the reporter did not know what else to say.

"There is a way I can help you," said the caller, breaking the silence.

"How?"

"Only after you publish the accused man's photograph."

"We can't."

"What do you mean?" asked the caller, a note of panic entering his voice.

"I mean no one can. The case is *sub judice*. No photographs or information likely to be detrimental to a defendant can be published. Just his name, age and the town he's originally from."

"But you can pull strings, Mr Edwards."

"Maybe," said the reporter, thinking on his feet. He did not want to lose contact with this strange man.

"I will promise you every co-operation, Mr Edwards, if you let me know this man's name and send me a photograph."

"Firstly, the man's name will be on TV, radio, and plastered all over the papers as soon as the police charge him. Secondly, how can I send you the photograph if I don't know where you live?"

"I will think of a way, Mr Edwards."

"Okay, we'll play it your way. Give me a call this time tomorrow. Either on this line or my mobile."

"Mr Edwards ..."

"Yes."

"No police, Mr Edwards. You must promise me that you will not involve the police."

The reporter took a deep breath. He knew he was already in enough trouble with the police. What might previously have been a case of a hoax caller was now a case of withholding evidence. With the arrest, the stakes had moved up a gear. Yet he had always respected anonymity in the past and his sources knew they could rely on him. "Okay," he sighed, trying to sound convincing, "as long as it's clear that you will come forward if the man in the photograph is who you claim it is."

"I promise, Mr Edwards. Once I know he cannot reach me, I will co-operate fully."

Click.

Edwards replaced the receiver slowly.

"Was that the invisible man?" asked Pottage, already knowing the answer.

"Yes, Jim," said Edwards, rubbing his eyes hard with his palms. "I don't know what to do about him."

"There's only one thing you can do, my boy. You've got to tell Webb."

"I know. But I don't want to lose him. If the police cock everything up ..."

The phone rang again.

"Bloody hell," cursed Edwards, "I don't believe this."

"What did you expect," said Pottage, picking up the phone and handing it to the younger man, "anonymity?"

Edwards smiled. He could always count on the old man to

bring a little perspective to things. "Hello, Edwards ..."

"Hello, Mark, it's Dieter. Congratulations on the article."

"Thanks, Dieter. Most of it was thanks to you."

"I'm glad I could be of help, old man. Tell me, though, do you know who this man the police have arrested is?"

"Got no idea, Dieter. They're being a bit cagey. But I think we'll have a result by tomorrow morning."

"I'm intrigued, Mark, although it would be too far-fetched to believe it was this Schreiber fellow."

"I tend to agree with you, although there's one thing I can tell you for definite."

"What's that?" Müller asked eagerly.

"It's not our anonymous caller."

"How do you know?"

"He just rang me. I'd hardly think he'd be allowed to do so whilst in police custody."

Müller laughed. "Maybe they allowed him one phone call and he chose you instead of his lawyer."

"Dieter, I thought you Germans didn't have a sense of humour."

"True, we don't laugh at ourselves much. But we sure as hell laugh at others."

Edwards' loud guffaw had Pottage off his seat. "Who is this guy, some kind of comedian?" the West Countryman asked.

Edwards placed his hand over the mouthpiece. "He's that German professor chappie I told you about," he whispered, then, removing his hand, "Hello, Dieter ... listen, the caller said he wanted to see a photo of the man the police are going to charge and only then would he reveal himself."

"What are you going to do, Mark?"

"I don't know yet. Look, Dieter, I'll be in touch. Once the charge is formalized, I won't be able to write anything appertaining to the trial. But this whole affair is bugging me. I think we should get together again. I'll buzz you once things become more clear, okay?"

"Gut, mein Freund. Ich muss weg. Auf Wiedersehen."

Edwards had barely replaced the receiver before the telephone rang again. "I don't believe it," he groaned.

It was Bob Webb, and the man was angry.

"Edwards, you bugger!" the policeman bellowed. "You're gonna get your arse down here to the incident room at Barkingside nick right now. A squad car'll be with you in five minutes."

"Look, Bob, I ..."

"Just meet my man at the information desk in the lobby, okay?"

"Okay, Bob, I'll do all I can to help," the reporter said meekly.

"You'd better," said Webb fiercely, and terminated the call.

Jim Pottage gave his colleague a knowing wink. "Aar, I told you he'd be livid."

Edwards tried ringing Danielle's extension but it was engaged. He knew there was no time to speak face to face. "Look, Jim," he said, scribbling a note, "this is Danielle's extension number. Give her a call. Tell her everything and tell her where I've gone. Tell her I'll be round at her place later this evening. Tell her I'm sorry and I'll explain everything then."

"Sorry?"

"Lovers' tiff, remember?"

"Abso-bloody-lutely, old boy."

Within the hour, Mark Edwards was seated in the waiting room of the newly built police station at Barkingside. A thousand thoughts flashed through his mind as he prepared to face the ire of his friend. Who was the man the police were about to charge? Who was the anonymous caller? Would there be any connection with this man Schreiber? It seemed preposterous that an old Nazi would come out of the woodwork and start bumping off Jews as he had done in the old days. These things just did not happen.

"Please come with me, Mr Edwards." The order, emanating sweetly from the mouth of an attractive woman police constable, stirred the reporter from his musings. He thought she must be new because he could not recall seeing her there before. He followed her down a long corridor into a small side room, the sort used to interrogate prisoners. He felt almost overpowered by the smell of fresh paint and the heady aromatics of virgin furniture.

"Please wait here," said the crisp white shirt and stiff navy skirt. "Detective Inspector Webb will be with you shortly."

Oh, thought Edwards, not "Bob", not even "DI Webb". It was all getting too formal for the reporter's liking, and he was beginning to feel more like a prisoner than a witness. He half sat on the new table and folded his arms. It was a full five minutes before his golf buddy entered the room.

Bob Webb's steely grey eyes bore into the reporter. "You'd better sit down, Mr Edwards," he ordered in a low growl. The policeman scratched his thin moustache, an act that the reporter recognized as a prelude to an angry outburst.

Edwards sank into the chair to his left and faced the slowly narrowing eyes of a man about to lose his temper. Webb's features began to contort into the sort of grimace normally reserved for a sliced tee-shot.

"You fucking bugger, Edwards," the policeman seethed. "What the fuck do you think you've been playing at?"

"I ..."

"You've been playing silly buggers on the most important fucking case I'm ever likely to handle. I mean, even the Prime Minister's got involved in this one. The Queen's probably having kittens. I mean, her mob are all Germans, aren't they? And you, the fledgling press baron, decide to withhold a vital piece of evidence."

"But I ..."

"Let me finish, Mr Sleuth-Hound," Webb said menacingly. "What's more, you publish the story before consulting the man who's given you more leads than hot dinners. I've given you more exclusives than other reporters get fillers. Now what's it all about?" Having vented his spleen, the detective leant back in his chair and folded his arms.

Edwards' raised eyebrows sought permission to speak. He swallowed a lungful of paint fumes before launching into what he knew was a pretty lame explanation. "Look, Bob," he cajoled, "I didn't know whether or not this caller was just an old hoaxer. You know, he still might be."

"Hoaxer or not, my boy, we've had some murders on my patch. Or hadn't you noticed? My God, one of them's your girlfriend's uncle. I need every bit of information I can get, so let me decide whether it's important or not."

"But you've got your man, haven't you?"

"Maybe," said Webb cagily. "He might have been your anonymous caller."

"But he's not."

"How do you know?"

"Because the guy rang me again today. You'd hardly allow your man to do that, would you?"

Webb stroked his moustache thoughtfully. "I want him, Mark. He could be a vital witness for us."

"When are you going to release your man's name?"

"Oh," said Webb, looking at his watch, "the Yard'll issue a statement in the near future."

"So you can tell me who it is now. It's not going to make much difference, is it?"

"Eager beaver, aren't you, mate. First of all, I want you to promise me you'll co-operate."

Edwards smiled. "I promised my man I wouldn't betray him to you lot."

"Bullshit," said Webb, shaking his head slowly.

"Yeah, I know," sighed Edwards, running his fingers through his hair. "What do you want me to do?"

"Is he planning to contact you again?"

"Yeah, I told him to ring me at my office at around five tomorrow afternoon. He wanted me to confirm whether your prisoner is this Schreiber character. He still sounds pretty scared."

"Can you stall him long enough for us to trace the call?"

"How long does that take?"

"New technology's enabled us to cut it from four minutes to just over a minute."

"Phew," said Edwards, impressed, "that shouldn't be too much trouble, then."

"As long as you don't blow it, mate."

"What do you mean?"

"You mustn't give him any idea you're stalling for time, or that you've spoken to us."

"Come on, give me some credit, Bob," said Edwards. Then it suddenly hit him. "Wait a minute. If you're so interested in my caller, then there must be something in this Schreiber thing." The reporter cocked his head to one side. "Give."

"Maybe, maybe not," Webb replied with a broad grin. "This is a real beauty, though."

"Look, Bob," said Edwards animatedly, "I know I fucked you about and now you're fucking me about, but if it's going to be announced soon then what's the big deal?"

"Just wanted to make you sweat a bit. Anyway, it'll only be announced when I give the go-ahead. And I don't really want to do that until I've at least made an attempt to wrap up the invisible man. Anyway, I don't know why you're getting so excited. Once we arrest someone, it's *sub judice* for all you lot."

"I'LL CO-OPERATE, OKAY!"

"Good." The policeman beamed. "Now you know how I felt when I read your story." He carried on, without hesitation, "You know, after what we found in this guy's home, it's an open and shut case." He paused to savour his friend's perplexity.

"Look, stop talking in riddles, Bob, and get to the point."

"Okay, okay. Easy." Webb gestured with open palms. "The fact is our man was Plant's financial adviser and was visiting the poofter on a business matter. The other poof, the manservant, overheard them arguing over money before he scarpered off for some dangerous liaison at his local. Plant's guest even threatened to kill him. Lo and behold, when we get round to the guest's home, it's a real classic. He's singing in the shower, and on his bed is an open suitcase with your usual holiday gear and, wait for it ... a first-class ticket to Rio. Boom-boom!"

"No shit," whistled Edwards. He could just imagine Webb's glee on finding the incriminating evidence. Then it struck him that he still did not know the killer's name. "Haven't you forgotten something, Bob?"

"Oh, yeah, sure. There's more."

"No, I mean, what's the guy's name?"

"Oh, he's another big-time moneybags. Henry Sonntag."

Edwards stared at Webb as if the detective had lost his marbles. Dumbstruck, all he could envisage was Danielle's disbelieving face.

"What's the big surprise?" asked Webb. "Do you know this guy?"

"But he's a Jew," said Edwards, breathing deeply. "He couldn't have done those things."

"Sure, he protests his innocence. But I don't think he's a

Jew, my friend. I think he's a fucking Nazi pretending to be a Jew. After what we found in his home there can be no doubt. Sonntag is your man Schreiber. One and the same."

"What do you mean?" Edwards asked incredulously.

"I mean these," said Webb, withdrawing five large black and white photographs from the desk drawer.

"It looks like some kind of museum," said Edwards, his brain almost refusing to accept what his eyes were seeing.

"Too true, mate. That bastard had a whole room full of SS memorabilia. Guns, uniforms, the lot. Photos of Theresienstadt were hanging on the walls and he had his own personal library of books on the SS and the Holocaust."

"It's unbelievable," Edwards muttered.

"And we even found one of these," said Webb, withdrawing a sixth photograph.

Edwards stared at the close-up shot of the SS dagger.

"We found one in his home," Webb continued excitedly. "It was exactly the same service dagger as found near Plant's body. Now you know why we need to interview your anonymous caller. You know, it's strange ..."

"Yes?"

"We searched all over but couldn't find any personal photos. You'd think the guy would have had an album or something."

"What did Sonntag himself have to say about all this?"

"He refused to say anything much other than declare his innocence. He just sat there and looked at us with contempt. He said that whatever he might say we were going to charge him anyway and so it was best to get it over and done with. We're going to let him sweat a little more before we charge him. I want you to help me get this caller bod. It'll round things off nicely for the Crown Prosecution Service. One thing's for sure. Sonntag can afford to have the best defence money can buy. His personal friend is no less a personage than Sir John Tilson, QC."

Edwards whistled, conjuring up a vision of one of Britain's foremost Queen's Counsels. "I've seen him in action a few times. He defended Sims, the alleged Warwickshire serial killer, didn't he?"

"Alleged is right, my friend. Got the bastard off."

"But, if I remember right, there was a shadow of a doubt, Bob."

"Doubt, my arse. Sims was as guilty as hell. Did a Hannibal Lecter and pissed off abroad. He's probably knocked off more than a few natives by now. Only difference between him and Lecter is that he didn't eat 'em."

"What about the Hyams murder?" asked Edwards, aware that this was of paramount interest to Danielle. "Are you going to charge Sonntag with that?"

"We don't really need to, mate. It was in the early hours of the morning. Although Sonntag has no alibi apart from being tucked up in bed, we don't have any witnesses. But the modus operandi was the same as the Plant murder and that should be enough for the Crown Prosecution Service to get him on both counts."

"You have no doubts as to Sonntag's guilt, Bob?"

The steel shavings that were Webb's eyes narrowed to slits as he spoke through gritted teeth. "No doubts at all, mate. Open and shut. Open and shut."

CHAPTER EIGHT

Edwards drew up behind Danielle's red Vauxhall outside her Docklands flat. It was already eight o'clock on a dark and wet night, and he had just spent an exhaustive two-hour session with Webb going over old ground and being briefed on how to help trap the caller. He had decided not to ring her from the cop-shop. They both needed to talk face to face. So much had happened that he was at a loss as to how to begin. He took a deep breath and pressed the buzzer, his stomach tightening with apprehension.

"Hello," came the familiar voice through the intercom.

"Hello, Dani. It's me."

There was a short pause before the door lock clicked open, as if she were weighing up the pros and cons of granting him entrance. By the time he reached her front door it was ajar. He did not know why he knocked. Considering they were lovers it seemed faintly ridiculous.

"Come in, Mark," came a voice that was on the warmer side of formal.

She was seated on the red leather settee, wearing black slacks and a pink roll-neck sweater. Her satin hair was still dank from showering. Somehow it made her look even more stunning. Prolonged abstinence prompted an urge in him to sweep her into his arms, but her half-smile signalled caution rather than invitation.

Edwards sank into the armchair opposite. "I'm sorry for what I said on the phone. It was a stupid thing to say."

Danielle gave a cursory nod. Her emerald eyes seemed to bore through him, destroying his concentration. He had rehearsed over and over what he must divulge and yet his mind was now confused.

"I, er ..." He scratched his head and took a deep breath. "I have to tell you something."

Danielle, sensing the tension in his voice, frowned slightly. "I'm listening," she said simply.

Edwards took another deep breath. "The man the police have arrested is going to be charged with the murder of Howard Plant very soon. They say it's an open and shut case. They say he probably killed your uncle as well, but the evidence around the second murder makes it cast-iron that he killed Plant."

Danielle wiped away a water droplet that had trickled from her hair into her right eye. "Who is he?" she enquired quietly.

"I don't know how to say this, Dani," he said, scratching his head defensively once again. "I, er ..."

"Who is he, Mark?" Danielle asked again, her voice now laced with apprehension.

Edwards pursed his lips. "It's unbelievable," he shrugged, "but I'm afraid it's Henry Sonntag."

For a few moments Danielle stared at him in silence, her brow furrowed. Then, quietly, she said, "I can't believe it."

"I couldn't either. I told Webb that Jews didn't do this type of thing."

"What kind of things do Jews do?" she enquired with wide eyes, her composure regained. Edwards could sense that she was on the defensive. He also knew that the only fact at her disposal was bald: Henry Sonntag had been charged with the murder of Howard Plant. He pushed to the back of his mind the caller's words about Jews being forced to kill fellow Jews. The time was inappropriate, and maybe the man was lying anyway. "What they don't do is murder anyone, let alone one of their own," he said, fingering the cleft in his chin nervously.

"Precisely. And that is why Henry Sonntag is innocent."

Edwards sighed deeply. He hated to disavow her, to irritate the hypersensitivity that seemed to be part and parcel of the Jewish character whenever it felt threatened by outsiders. He knew he was still an outsider and that therefore it was incumbent upon him to choose his words carefully. She had already told him that Jewish jokes could only be told by Jews; that however innocently a gentile told one, he stood the risk of being regarded as anti-Semitic. She had said that thousands of years of persecution had given her people a thin skin; that it was words, rather then knives, which hurt them most.

"Dani," he said quietly, "there is something I have to tell you. Something that because of the law of *sub judice* will now only come out in the trial." The reporter swallowed hard before relating to her all that Webb had told him.

Danielle Green did not bat an eyelid as her lover described the deeds of a man who was beyond evil. A man who inhabited the nether world of the damned. A man who at such an advanced age still enjoyed bloodlust. She listened carefully to each and every word, weighing up the incredible implications of a story that defied belief. And this was precisely the conclusion to which she came.

"I still don't believe it," she said simply.

"But, Dani," he said incredulously, "Webb's as straight as a die. He'd never concoct evidence."

"I'm not calling Webb a liar, Mark. What I'm saying is that Henry Sonntag is a Jew. Therefore, per se, Henry Sonntag cannot be a Nazi. He cannot be Schreiber. And if he is not Schreiber, then he did not kill Howard Plant, or my uncle for that matter. Are they going to charge him with that, too?"

"Probably."

"Henry Sonntag is innocent."

"But how can you be so sure?" stammered Edwards, scratching his temple. The evidence in the Plant murder was so incriminating that her obduracy puzzled him.

"Wait here a moment," she said, rising and making towards the dining table. On it was a black leather briefcase. She opened it and withdrew a sheaf of papers. "Read this. It's my article which will now probably never see the light of day."

Edwards took the papers from her outstretched hand. He spent the next ten minutes in rapt silence. The article was beautifully written and told an enthralling story. "It's an amazing tale," he said at last. "But maybe that's all it is. He could be making it all up, you know."

Danielle frowned, although deep down she knew he had every right to play the devil's advocate. "Remember I once told you that only a Jew could truly recognize another Jew?"

"Yes."

"Remember I told you about that Israeli friend of mine who said he could stroll down Oxford Street and identify Israeli tourists just by their gait?"

"Yes, but ..."

"That is why I know Henry Sonntag is innocent. He's a Jew, Mark. Jews are sharp in business. They can conspire and intrigue with the best of them. But Jews are not murderers."

"But what about all that Nazi stuff found in his home?"

"You know, I once wrote a feature about a survivor of the Holocaust. Bernstein was his name. His whole raison d'être was collecting memorabilia of his persecutors. He even slept with a bottle of Zyklon B in his bed."

"He was mad."

"Possibly. But he wasn't a killer."

Edwards was mesmerized by the defiance in her eyes and the beauty spot that bobbed as her lips pursed and pouted. God, he was crazy about her.

"Dani," he said, running his fingers nervously through his thick, wavy hair, "you know I don't really understand about these things. Webb believes Sonntag is pretending to be a Jew. Maybe these traits can be learned. Can one learn to be a Jew?"

Danielle hesitated. He had expressed his love for her and she, too, felt a yearning to reciprocate, to lose herself in these new emotions. He had been so gentle, leading her tenderly through the maze of sexual awareness until both had felt the time was right to consummate their relationship. The last thing she wanted to do was hurt him. But there were some truths that had to be told.

"Sure," she said at last, "there are gentiles who convert to Judaism. If they do it the orthodox way, then they often end up having a far greater knowledge of the religion than someone born a Jew." She hesitated again. She always felt strange discussing her faith with outsiders. Maybe it was a ghetto thing. "But," she sighed, "however he or she acts the Jew, another Jew will be able to tell. You see, we have an umbilical cord linking us through thousands of years of history. You know, in Israel, there are more than a million Jews from Arab lands. They are dark, Mediterranean types. Yet that Israeli friend I was talking about said he could tell Jew and Arab apart just from their features and their mannerisms. But to outsiders they would all look like one people."

"Could you tell the difference?"

"I don't know. I haven't visited Israel yet. But I can tell whether a person is an Ashkenazi Jew or not."

Edwards was puzzled. In the few months they had known one another they had not delved deeply into the mysteries of her faith. The *shiva* had been his first brush with orthodox tradition and a culture about which he was almost totally ignorant.

"An Ashkenazi", she smiled, "is a Jew of European stock. Other Jews are called Sephardim. It literally means 'Spanish' but nowadays encompasses all Jews from Arab lands. I'm mainly Ashkenazi with a little Sephardi thrown in for good measure. Maybe one of my ancestors fled eastwards from the Inquisition."

Edwards scratched his head. "I'm afraid I don't have that much pride in my ancestry," he said. "I know my great-grandfather was Welsh, but I regard myself as English, a

Londoner through and through. I only remember going to church once, so I suppose I'm as ignorant about religion as anyone can get."

"It doesn't matter, Mark. You were brought up in a nominally Christian society. You are Christian by osmosis. Because we're born and raised here, we Jews probably know more about Christianity than Christians know about Judaism."

"What about you, would you call yourself orthodox?"

She ran her fingers through her wet hair and smiled. "No, I'm probably what you would call secular, but ..." She hesitated.

"Yes?"

"I feel just as proud of my heritage and as much a Jew as any of those in Stamford Hill."

"Stamford Hill?"

Danielle laughed out loud, two rows of perfect white teeth breaking free of their luscious frame. "You know, the Hassidim. The guys with the funny hats and the side-curls. In their minds they inhabit nineteenth-century Poland and consider themselves the real Jews. It is preposterous. They are faintly amusing." Her eyes suddenly narrowed. "Frankly, I just don't relate to them."

Edwards was surprised by her attitude. "I don't understand. They're fellow Jews, aren't they?"

"They are and yet they're not. Their lifestyle is so dictated by religious dogma that we are worlds apart. I know they don't even consider me a true Jew, and I resent that."

Edwards, trying hard to keep pace with what was turning into a complex cultural lesson, stroked his chin. "I suppose that doesn't make them much different from the ayatollahs and other crazy fundamentalists, does it?" he said.

"Maybe," she smiled, "but there's one thing our ultra-orthodox mob definitely don't do. They don't proselytize. They don't go out trying to convert the world. In fact, the opposite. You know something, Mark ..."

His raised eyebrows urged her to continue.

"... if I was a Martian who arrived suddenly on Earth and was given the choice of adopting one of the three great monotheistic religions, I'd choose Judaism. And do you know why? Because it's the only one that would allow me to choose."

"I think I see what you mean," he said pensively. "Perhaps that's why Jews have died by the sword rather than lived by it."

For a few moments there was complete silence, and Edwards thought he might have said something wrong.

"Darling," she said softly, "that is one of the most profound statements I have ever heard. I think you're right. And, if you'll pardon the pun, I think that's a cross we have to bear."

Edwards gazed at her hard and long, the desire in him welling up once more. He knew she was intellectually his superior and yet he felt able to discuss any matter with her on equal terms. Her manner had never been condescending.

"Aren't you going to kiss me, then?" she said, her lips beginning to swell and glisten like red peppers. "I forgave you as soon as you walked through the door."

He smiled and crossed the room to join her on the settee. Putting his arm around her, he nuzzled the nape of her neck, luxuriating in the dampness of her hair and the appley fragrance of aloe vera. "I love you, Danielle. I've never felt this way about anyone before."

"Ssh, my darling. Let's take our time. Let's grow into this thing. It's new for me, too."

Edwards turned her face towards him and kissed the swollen lips with a passion that almost frightened him. His lips lingered on hers before sliding to nestle in an area just below the chin-line.

"Oh, darling," she gasped. "I want you."

Taking her hand, he began leading her towards the bedroom, his excitement heightened by the knowledge of what was to follow. A trail of discarded clothing pointed the way. Once on the bed, she wallowed in the affectionate kisses with which he covered her naked body. Then she took the initiative, teasing him a little before satisfying what she knew he was craving. "Oh, God," he murmured as she slid down, "oh, God."

Danielle gazed into her lover's widening ice-blue eyes and delighted in his ecstasy. They did not share a common heritage and yet she felt she had known him all her life. She knew she would have to concede that she loved him too, and that she could envisage sharing the rest of her life with him.

Totally oblivious to the passage of time, the lovers coupled and uncoupled in a frenzy of pleasure. The climax, when it finally arrived, was a paroxysm that was at once both satiating and debilitating.

Mark sighed deeply as he lay exhausted beside her. "Jesus," he said, "I don't think it can get any better."

Danielle snuggled into his hairy chest for a few moments and then burst into a fit of giggling.

"Hey, what's so funny?" he moaned quietly, his post-coital strength still on the wane.

"You know, I'm glad you're circumcized, Mark," she laughed. "I've never seen an uncircumcized man. Not in real life, anyway. I must say I worried about it a bit before I went to bed with you."

"You have my parents to thank for that, my darling," he said, gently stroking her hair. "They read somewhere that it was more hygienic, so I had it lopped off as a baby. Didn't feel a thing ... Hey, I've just thought of something. I wonder whether Henry Sonntag is circumcized? If he is isn't, then he sure as hell ain't Jewish."

Danielle remained silent. The question had never entered her mind because she was so convinced of the man's innocence. If Henry Sonntag was indeed uncircumcized, then she knew she would be forced to rethink.

"Mark," she said, "what will happen to Sonntag now?"

"Oh, he'll go for committal proceedings at a magistrate's court. There's obviously a prima facie case to answer, so it'll be referred to the Central Criminal Court, the Old Bailey."

"How long before he comes to trial?"

"Could be anywhere from four to eight months, even longer."

"You mean he could spend all that time in jail, even if he's eventually declared innocent?"

"'Fraid so."

"Mark."

"Yes, darling?"

"Can you arrange something with Webb for me?"

"Like what?"

"I'd like to visit Henry Sonntag in jail. If he'll agree to see me, that is."

"You must be joking."

"No, I'm serious," she said, propping herself on one ivory arm. "I want to look into his eyes again. I want to know if he's lied to me."

"I'll see what I can do." He shrugged. "Webby wants me to trap this anonymous caller. If he identifies Sonntag as being Schreiber, then that's another nail in your man's coffin."

"You're my man, darling," she said, stretching to plant a kiss on his forehead. "Don't you ever forget it." She smiled demurely. "Now, does little Willy want to pay another visit."

"Little Willy does," he laughed, "but big Willy will."

Straelen, North Rhein-Westphalia, 1931

The little boy sobbed bitterly in his nakedness. Why were they making fun of him so? Why were they so cruel to him? Why was he different from them? "Leave me alone," he pleaded. "Please leave me alone."

"Quick, you guys, come and look at the new boy's willy," cried fat Friedrich, the local bully. He was one year older than the others in the Grundschule, one year bigger. A year in which his mental development had allowed evil thoughts to puncture the innocence of early childhood. Simply put, fat Freddy was old enough to understand what he now enjoyed. Power.

"Please, please," the little boy implored, clutching his vitals and shrinking back against the cool ceramic wall of the shower-room. How he wished he were like fat Freddy. How he wished he could order the others to hurt fat Freddy.

He struggled vainly to stay against the wall, as if the impassive surface could protect him from his humiliation. The shouts of the boys echoed through the dank atmosphere as they dragged him into the centre of the room.

"Look," giggled one of his tormentors, "he's only got half a willy. The Berliner's only got half a willy."

"Half-willy Hans," cried fat Freddy. "That's what we'll call him."

The boys linked arms and began circling their prey. "Half-willy Hans, half-willy Hans," they chanted in unison.

The new boy sank to his knees and covered his ears. "Leave me alone," he sobbed ever more bitterly. Curling into a foetal position, he remained motionless until his persecutors grew tired of their sport. He did not leave the shower until after they had dressed and left the adjoining dressing room. Only then did he stir. Hans Schreiber dressed with the torpor of the weak and humiliated. He did not know why he was different from the other boys, only that they had an extra piece of skin on their willies. He so desperately wanted to be like them.

Thankful that games had been the last lesson of the day, the small boy ran through the sun-drenched streets of the little town. Everything was so quiet compared to where they had moved from a few weeks earlier. No big buildings. No noisy automobiles. Only the lazy rustle of leaves gave him some succour as a light breeze relieved the heat of the afternoon.

Turning the corner, he saw his father hoeing the front garden. Sight of the familiar figure induced in him another burst of sobbing. He ran into his father's arms.

"There, there, Hans," soothed Dr Wolfgang Schreiber. "What's the matter?"

"They made fun of my willy, Father," he cried, the tears cascading down his pale cheeks.

Dr Wolfgang Schreiber stiffened, as if some unpleasant memory had had the audacity to spoil such a pleasant afternoon. He held the boy at arm's length and looked squarely into the reddened eyes. "You must be strong, Hans. Never show them you are weak."

"But why am I so different, Father?"

"You had an infection in your pee-pee, Hans. When you were a baby, it was necessary to remove what we call the foreskin."

"Can I have it put back, Father?"

Wolfgang Schreiber smiled and patted the boy's dank blond head. "I'm afraid that's impossible, Hans." The good doctor tried to subdue the wrenching in the pit of his stomach, for the boy's humiliation was his own. "Here," he said, pulling a sprig of lavender from the large bush that dominated the front garden, "smell this. It's wonderful. It will make you feel much better."

Hans Schreiber clutched the sprig to his nose and breathed deeply. It had quite the most wonderful scent he had ever experienced.

CHAPTER NINE

Detective Inspector Bob Webb looked impatiently at his watch. It was already almost half past five. He peered intently at the two telephones, praying, firstly, that the anonymous caller would ring and, secondly, that he would use British Telecom rather than Vodafone. He had a team set up at Vodafone to trace the call if the caller rang Edwards' mobile, but the whole thing was a bit hit and miss. The reporter's personal extension at the *Standard* was the best bet. He was willing to wager that the caller was somewhere in the Greater London area covered by the Metropolitan Police. He had put out an all-stations alert throughout the Met. Once BT had informed him of the source of the call he would flick through the almanac that gave him details of every station in the country. If the call came from outside London he'd have to rely on whatever nick was involved not to waste time questioning him needlessly.

"Penny for your thoughts, Bob."

"My thoughts are, Mark, that if your guy doesn't call again, I'm gonna wring your neck."

Edwards laughed nervously and then glanced sheepishly at the two detectives who were sitting either side of the phones. One of them was twiddling a knob on a tape deck which was connected to a receiver planted in the main body of the phone.

"Come on, you bastard," said Webb. "I don't want to be sitting here all night."

"How long will you give it, Bob?"

"If he doesn't ring your office number by six, me and you are getting married."

"What do you mean?"

"I mean, dear friend, that I go where you go where your mobile goes. If he can't raise you on BT, he'll more than likely ring the mobile. The poor sods at Vodafone will have to be on stand-by for as long as I deem it necessary. But, old buddy, I want to be around you if and when this guy rings. Your place or mine?"

Before Edwards had time to reply, both men started as the reporter's direct line burst into life. Edwards took a deep breath. He just hoped it wasn't his mother. Webb signalled to his two cronies to switch on the tape. He then rose, swiftly for a big man, and seated himself at an adjacent desk. Upon it was the lone grey telephone which would ring as soon as BT had the necessary information.

"Hello, Edwards here."

"Mr Edwards ..."

Blue met steel-grey as the eyes of the reporter and the detective registered recognition.

"... Mr Edwards, are you there?"

"Yes, I'm here," the reporter said slowly, although not slowly enough to raise doubts in the caller's mind.

"I have heard the radio and read your newspaper, Mr Edwards. Who is this Henry Sonntag? What does he look like?"

"I honestly don't know."

"Do you think you can get me a picture of this man?"

Edwards took the lead from Webb's nod. "Yes ... I think I can get hold of a photograph of the accused man."

"How? I thought you said there was a ban on publicity."

"I'm sure I can arrange it."

"With the police?" The caller's voice was heavy with anxiety.

"Of course not," Edwards improvised, suddenly remembering that Danielle had mentioned a photocall when she had done the interview with Sonntag. "One of my newspaper colleagues is sure to have a file photo. In fact, I recall one of them saying he had recently interviewed Sonntag." He tried to stretch his answer for all it was worth. "It was very interesting, actually. He said that ..."

"Never mind, Mr Edwards. How long will it take to procure the photograph?"

"Er, not too long, actually. I'll have to phone a few people."

"As long as you do not go to the police, Mr Edwards. You promised me, remember?"

Edwards felt his face flush. Duplicity did not rest easy with him. "Of course, I ..." The reporter hesitated in response to the urgent ring of Webb's telephone. The sound lasted only as long as a semi-quaver as the policeman snatched it to his ear.

"Got it," Webb whispered sharply, motioning to Edwards to keep dragging out the conversation. As luck would have it, he did not even have to consult the almanac. The caller was using a public phone box in Leyton, east London, and he knew the local nick's number by heart. He also knew several senior officers there personally. Within seconds a car would be racing to the scene. One thing was sure: their prey was too old to run away.

"... I believe you said you would come forward if you identified this man as Schreiber," Edwards continued. "Does that offer still hold?"

"Of course, of course. My word is my bond, Mr Edwards. I must be sure that the mumser is behind bars."

"Sorry?"

"The bastard. Once I am sure he can no longer torture me, I shall be glad to testify. I told you this before."

Edwards had to think on his feet, for Webb was signalling ever more frantically for him to prolong the conversation. "Tell me," the reporter asked, "do you know of anyone else who might back up your testimony?"

"I have lived my life alone with my memories, Mr Edwards. I am not what you call a mixer. Schreiber made sure of that. I lost all my family in the Holocaust. There is no one. No one

146

that I know personally. Maybe there are other survivors of the Small Fortress in other countries, but not here. Not that I know of."

"I'm sorry about your family ..." Edwards hesitated. It was so frustrating not being able to pin a label on the voice at the other end of the line. "I shall try to help you all I can," he lied uneasily. "It would help, though, if you would tell me your name."

"I cannot, Mr Edwards. Not yet. If I tell you my name and your prisoner is not the killer, then it will be a death sentence for me."

"I give you my word that I will not publish anything."

"I'm afraid I cannot take that chance. Not because of you, but because of what others might do."

"It would be in contempt of court if we published anything. No newspaper would risk it. That is your guarantee."

"No, Mr Edwards. I shall remain anonymous until I am sure that Schreiber is behind bars. I shall ring you at the same time tomorrow. If you have the photograph, I will tell you how to get it to me. Do you understand?"

"Of course."

"I trust you, Mr Edwards."

The reporter felt the twinges of conscience knotting his stomach. There were no more words with which to satisfy Webb's imploring eyes.

"Hello ... hello. Mr Edwards. Are you there? Now I must cut short this conver ..."

The caller's voice stopped abruptly. Edwards heard a crashing sound, which he guessed was the telephone falling from the man's grasp. Then came a hotch-potch of scratchy-thin voices.

"No ... now come along quietly, please sir ... No, leave me alone. You are like the Gestapo. Why? Mr Edwards, why? ... We won't harm you sir. Please do not put up an unnecessary struggle ..." Then came the sound of uncontrollable sobbing. It quickly grew less and less distinct.

"Hello, hello," shouted Edwards, feeling like the proverbial heel. "Don't hurt him. Please don't hurt him."

Silence. Then a gruff voice from the telephone box. "Hello, is Bob Webb there?"

Edwards grimaced and handed over the receiver. "It's for you. They've got him," he said simply.

"Hello, Webb here."

"Hello, Bob. It's Jim Wetherall. We've got him ..."

Both men could hear the bleeps.

"Hang on. I'll just put another ten pence in ... Listen, Bob, what do you want us to do with him?"

"Right, Jim. Look, it's a murder inquiry, so take him in on suspicion. I'm sure he didn't do it, but I need to interview him to get his alibi. I'll meet you at Leyton nick in about forty minutes."

Webb slammed the phone down with a grin as wide as the Thames. "Edwards, you bugger," he beamed, "all is forgiven."

"What are you going to do with him?" the reporter asked in a voice that was as flat as his emotions.

"I'm going to interview him, sonny boy. And then I'm going to take him on a little trip to the nick at St Ann's Road, Tottenham, where he can be our star witness in a police line-up. They've got the best facilities in the capital." Webb rubbed his hands gleefully. "I can't wait, my little beauty."

"Bob ..."

"Yes?"

"I want you to do me a favour."

"Depends what," Webb said sharply.

"I want to come with you to see the identity parade."

"Sure. I'm PC Plod and you're my sidekick, Noddy."

"No, I mean it, Bob."

"You know, you crack me up. I think you're the one who

should be doing all the favours."

Edwards' voice grew more desperate. "I've got to see it, Bob. Just this once."

Webb sighed. "Blimey, I'll swing for you one day, you bugger."

"Thanks, mate. Er, there's just one more thing."

"Now, don't get too pushy."

"If he'll agree, I want to speak to this guy privately."

"You can speak to him for as long as you like, mate – only after we've checked him out and got our statement. Okay?"

Edwards nodded purposefully. He knew that whatever the man had to tell could not be published, yet he was fascinated nonetheless. The caller could well turn out to be the final nail in Henry Sonntag's coffin.

"Anyway," Webb continued, "once we charge Sonntag, the whole thing'll be out of my hands. The Crown Prosecution Service will take over."

"What about visiting Sonntag in prison?" asked Edwards, remembering Danielle's request.

"That's up to the prison authorities, I should think. I can't see there being much objection. The man himself may not want to see anyone except his lawyer. He doesn't appear to have any family at all."

"Thanks, Bob," said Edwards, shaking Webb's hand warmly. "Let me know on my mobile when you're ready to do the identity parade."

"Next round of golf on you, then, is it, mate?"

"I invite you to get beaten yet again," grinned the younger man.

The twelve-mile journey from Kensington to Leyton gave Bob Webb time to reflect on what was rapidly developing into an extremely satisfying case. Kudos was the name of the game, and it was coming his way in buckets. Diluted, maybe, on its way down from the Home Secretary, but there would still be enough left to look good on his record.

The detective already knew he had enough evidence on Sonntag to nail him regardless of any witness from the past. But it was nice, very nice, to have a killer damned by his previous actions. There was motive, murder and modus operandi. The motive, money, had triggered off a terrifying vengeance from a man who had for years successfully hidden his past. Call it a brainstorm, if you like. Who cared? Henry Sonntag was as guilty as hell, and that was precisely where he would rot.

"Penny for 'em." It was his driver.

"I was just wondering why the bloody hell it's taking you so long," Webb huffed.

"Don't worry, sir. The nick's just up ahead."

Webb could barely hide his eagerness as he hauled his huge frame out of the car and loped into the station.

"I'm DI Webb from Barkingside," he barked at the duty officer. "You've got a murder case witness here for me."

"Oh, yeah, that old foreign bloke." The duty officer, ruddy-faced and pimply, looked at the last name on his custody record. "Resembled a frightened rabbit. I don't think this is going to do you much good, sir." The man swung the book around.

Webb peered at the entry. It read simply, "A. N. OTHER". "What the bugger's going on?" he growled.

"Wouldn't give his name and didn't have anything on him that would reveal his identity. A real strange one, sir."

"Where is he?"

"First floor, sir. First room on the right. Jim Wetherall's with him."

"Thanks."

Webb took giant strides up the stairs. The door to the room was ajar. An old man in a dirty brown raincoat was peering through a window at the darkened street below. A shock of white hair formed a semi-circle around the back and sides of the old man's otherwise bald pate. The detective pushed the door fully open and received an acknowledging nod from Wetherall, who was sitting by a table. The man in the raincoat was still unaware of Webb's presence.

"Hi, Bob," said Wetherall, grinning with the confidence that went with a mission accomplished, "this is, er ..." His shrug spoke volumes.

The old man turned slowly, grunting and groaning as if the effort were causing him considerable pain. He faced the detective with eyes that betrayed a man tortured beyond human comprehension.

Webb's lantern jaw dropped open. "Jesus H. Christ!" he gasped.

Mark Edwards felt distinctly uneasy as he entered the police station in St Ann's Road, Tottenham. Webb had telephoned him an hour earlier and the consternation in the policeman's voice had been clear. The anonymous caller had agreed to co-operate only if the reporter were present at the identity parade.

"I know it sounds crazy," Webb had said, "but despite you shopping him, he still wants you to be there. I didn't tell him we were planning to have you present anyway."

But it was what Webb had said next that really baffled the reporter. "Mark, there's something else, but I don't want to say anything at this moment. I don't want to prejudice your reaction in any way. I want you to describe to me your feelings after the line-up. I don't want to believe that I'm the only bloke going mad around here. Get here as quickly as possible."

Edwards had spent the next few seconds staring at the mute handset, his jumbled mind trying vainly to figure out what the policeman had meant. He then rang Danielle and informed her of developments. Her voice had conveyed the sense of intrigue that now gripped them both. The reporter's daydreaming ceased as soon as he caught sight of Webb in the corridor. Without further ado, the detective beckoned him into a side room. "Look," said Webb, "before we start, I want to explain to you some of the procedure. The identity suite is in a new purpose-built centre attached to the nick. To comply with the law, you and I are not allowed to be present at the parade."

"But ..."

"Don't worry, Mark, we'll be in the adjoining control room, which has a view of the whole shebang. The suspect will be amongst seven other men of similar age, build and standing in life. They have all been vetted by Sonntag and his solicitor."

"Does his solicitor get to see our friend?"

"Yup. He'll be standing next to an inspector in charge of the witness. The three of them will be together looking through the two-way mirror."

"When do I get to see my man?"

"Straight afterwards. I told him I'd prove to him you were present."

"By the way, what were you nattering about on the phone?"

"Patience, dear boy. Patience. No more questions for now. Let's go." The detective glanced at his watch. It was already seven-thirty.

Shivering in the evening chill, Edwards followed Webb stride for stride out of the station. Turning sharply to the right, they came to the new chalet-type building at the rear. A balding middle-aged policeman in a dark blue shirt met them in the lobby.

"Hello, Paul," said Webb to the duty inspector. "All ready, then? This is Mark Edwards of the *Standard*. Mark, this is Paul Brand. He's in charge around here."

The reporter and the uniformed man shook hands.

"This is highly irregular, you guys," said Brand. "Just don't make any sound when you're in the control room. We banned arresting coppers from being present because some of them started whooping it up when their suspect was identified."

"Not very edifying, I'm sure," smiled Webb. "I don't go in for whooping much myself and neither does this young man here."

"Oh, good," said Brand, his face rapidly turning the colour of cooked beetroot. "Now follow me."

The inspector led them through the front office and into the control room. The first thing that struck Edwards was how everything appeared so antiseptic. Looking through a large plate-glass window to his right, he perused the parade room. Although about thirty feet long, and bare, it had the look of a modern office about it. On the right was the mirrored surface of large plate-glass panels which stretched the whole length of the room. It was obvious that witnesses viewed the parade from behind it. The room itself was tastefully carpeted in grey, and the lighting, though bright, was filtered. In a row along the floor and in front of a bench were white discs with numbers one to twelve in ascending order, leading away from him.

"Makes a change from the old days," said Brand, as if reading the reporter's thoughts. "Then it was a seedy old room and the witness had to come face to face with the suspect, even put his hand on the bloke's shoulder."

"I can't think of anything more intimidating for a witness," observed Edwards.

"Precisely," said the inspector. "That's why it's not done that way any more. This, my friend, is state of the art."

Edwards turned his attention to the television screens and

electronic hardware directly in front of him. One screen focused on the parade area and another was split into various views, including one of the witness's gallery.

"When the line-up people come in you'll notice their movements on-screen will be jerky," the inspector explained. "This is because there are seven cameras operating at the same time. The camera in the witness area is black and white because the lighting has to be very subdued in there, otherwise the suspect in the line-up may see the witness through the two-way mirror. It doesn't give a very good image, I'm afraid."

"Where is the witness?" asked Edwards with a hint of irritation. He wanted them to get on with it. "And did he give his name?"

"One of my colleagues is waiting with him in the TV room adjoining the corridor behind the mirror. The witness will be required to give his name to the duty inspector for the official record of the ID parade. I haven't even seen the witness yet. I've been more concerned with the suspect."

"How does the suspect seem to you?" asked Webb. "I haven't seen him since they shipped him here."

"Calm," said Brand. "Very calm."

"But then he's a professional chameleon, isn't he?" said Edwards.

"Ahem." Webb cleared his throat. "We'll soon find out. Here they come."

The three onlookers in the control room turned their attention to the parade area. Eight men and an accompanying police officer filed into the room. They were all elderly and of similar stature. Each was smartly dressed in suit and tie.

"We've got a lot of pensioners on our books," explained Brand. "They get four quid and a cup of tea for standing in line for few minutes. Not a bad rate, really."

"Which one is Sonntag?" asked Edwards eagerly, suddenly

remembering that he did not even know what the man looked like.

"Number five," said Webb. "Handsome bugger, isn't he?"

The reporter strained to get a clearer view of Sonntag. He found it more rewarding to peer at the colour screen in front of him. The man had a military bearing and was certainly more handsome than the others. Each of them had a full head of yellowy-white or white hair. Obviously this must have been a stipulation demanded by Sonntag's solicitor. His aim, after all, was to make identification as hard as possible for the witness.

The members of the parade were then requested to sit on the bench running the length of the rear wall and behind the allotted numbers placed at their feet. They were told by their escorting officer to sit with their heels together, hands on laps, and to stare directly at their reflections in the mirror. Edwards found the whole process fascinating.

"Here comes the witness," whispered Brand. "We must keep silent during the ID. You can only see him from here on the video screen."

Edwards' heart pounded as the witness was ushered into the viewing area. The image, in black and white, was disappointing. It was difficult to make out the man's features or his reactions.

The three onlookers then heard the voice of the inspector who was accompanying the witness. He was standing by a lectern at the near end of the viewing corridor. Sonntag's solicitor was also present, although out of view.

The inspector's address to the witness was formal and precise and could only be heard in the control room. "You have been asked here today to see if you can identify the person you saw in the Small Fortress of Theresienstadt transit camp during the winter of 1942 and '43. I am going to ask you in a moment to walk along the line at least twice, taking as much care and time as you wish. I want to make it clear to you that the person you saw may or may not be here. If you cannot make a positive identification you should say so. Please indicate the person by calling out his number. Do you understand?"

The witness's affirmation was muffled.

"You may go ahead, sir."

The old man shuffled slowly along the line and then appeared to press himself against the glass. The tension in the control room was almost unbearable. Edwards stole a glance at Webb. He knew his friend was counting on a positive ID to help sew up his case. This was one hell of a moment.

The witness continued staring ahead for what seemed an eternity. Then he croaked, "It is him. My God, it is really him. It is Hans Schreiber."

"What number are you referring to, sir?"

"Number five," came the faltering reply. "Number five is Hans Schreiber."

Webb gave a huge sigh of relief. "That's it, my boy," he hissed. "Open and shut."

"Please sign here," came the officer's voice from the viewing corridor.

"Okay," said Brand, "we'll wait a bit. Bert will check with the suspect and his representative on whether they have any comment to make and then you can have both of your men back."

When Edwards and Webb finally left the control room, a grey-suited, weedy fellow carrying a briefcase scurried past.

"That's your suspect's solicitor," grinned Brand. "Looks as though he's seen a ghost."

Webb smiled. He knew why the man was ashen-faced and his golfing companion was just about to find out.

"And there's your suspect."

Mark Edwards stared hard and fast at the man who now stood only five yards from him, handcuffed to a uniformed constable. Henry Sonntag was even more imposing in the flesh. No wonder Danielle had been taken with him. Edwards felt his skin creep as the small brown eyes returned his gaze impassively. A shiver passed down his spine. He was convinced now that they were the eyes of a mass murderer.

"I'd like Mark here to meet the witness," said Webb, ushering them away from the prisoner.

"Sure," said the uniformed man. "I'll take you to the waiting room."

The reporter's heart once again began to pound and he could feel his palms becoming clammy. As the door opened, Edwards almost took refuge behind the gangling frame of his friend.

"This is your anonymous caller, Mark," said Webb knowingly.

For a moment there was utter silence, punctured only by a bubble of trapped air escaping to the surface of a bottled water fountain in the far corner of the room. "Good God," muttered the reporter. "It's unbelievable."

"Hello, Mr Edwards," rasped the old man. "I recognize you from your photograph in the newspaper."

"I'm surprised," said the reporter sheepishly. "It was a lousy picture."

Edwards took the old man's outstretched hand tamely. Its skin had all the consistency of a ready-to-cook broiler.

"Why do you blush, Mr Edwards? I forgive you. As soon as I saw that monster I was glad that things had turned out this way. Now that he is behind bars I can relax a little. God bless you, Mr Edwards."

The reporter stared at the man who, in a sense, he had betrayed. The beady brown eyes bore no hint of malice and yet conveyed a sense of deep hurt. The pallid face showed evidence of several scars. The nose was thin and straight. In fact, the whole was an amalgam of what he had variously imagined it to be during the period leading up to this moment. And yet, put a wig on this man and he could pass for Henry Sonntag.

Edwards found his voice at last. "It's just uncanny. You look so much like the man you just identified."

"It is impossible for any man to recognize himself in others," the witness said calmly. "But what you say does not surprise me. You see, Schreiber thought he had murdered me. Gentlemen, I believe that monster, whatever he now calls himself, stole my identity. Hans Schreiber is pretending to be me and now I am here to haunt him."

"Are you really sure?" asked the reporter.

"Anyone who was in a concentration camp knew the face of his persecutor-in-chief. He knew every muscle. The features are etched into his mind, into his memory and into his heart. I remember Schreiber's face better than I remember my own mother's."

"I am sure there is much you now want to relate, sir," said Webb kindly. "But a good start would be your name."

The old man looked at them wanly, his eyes suddenly rheumy and dull. He sighed deeply. "My name is Herschel Soferman."

CHAPTER TEN

MILLIONAIRE BONDS DEALER CHARGED
WITH SWASTIKA MURDERS

by Mark Edwards

Financial wizard Henry Sonntag has been arrested and charged with the murders of software magnate Howard Plant and taxi driver Joe Hyams. Sonntag, 73, of Chigwell, Essex, will appear at Redbridge Magistrates Court tomorrow.

Sonntag was Mr Plant's close adviser on all matters relating to the financial futures market.

The accused came to England as a refugee from Germany after the Second World War. He achieved multi-millionaire status after backing the pound's demise on Black Wednesday.

Howard Plant, one of Britain's richest men, was found dead in the grounds of his home ...

"Doesn't tell us much," opined Dieter Müller, folding the newspaper in half and placing it on the table. He removed his horn-rims and picked up his glass of ice-cold Holsten, downing the half-pint in two gulps. A rivulet of lager dribbled into his grey goatee.

"The *sub judice* law is pretty strict here, Dieter," said Edwards. He had already filled Müller in on the identity of the anonymous caller. "The remand hearing will also have to be a re-hash."

"I love your English pubs," said the German, changing the subject. "Such atmosphere."

"Yes, it's because the smoke gets in your eyes," laughed Danielle nervously. This was the first time she had met the man who had been such a great help to her lover. Müller was probably just an affable professor, but he was so clearly Teutonic that she felt a certain discomfort. She was fully prepared to accept that children could not be held responsible for the sins of their fathers, but this did not mean she could feel comfortable around pukka Germans.

"Here comes Jim with the next round," said Edwards as the portly Pottage juggled with a further pint of Holsten, two whisky macs and a gin and tonic for the lady. "Easy, Jim, easy."

"When I retire from Fleet Street," the West Countryman drawled, "I want to buy a pub in Devon."

"Knowing you, Jim, you'll be too pickled to run it," quipped Edwards.

"There's an old saying in the Rhineland," Müller chipped in. "Let the hen distribute the cornseed and only one chicken will get fat."

Pottage guffawed and almost knocked over the drinks. "I bet you just made that up," he said.

"I did, actually," said Müller in impeccable Received English. "Rather clever, don't you think?" He picked up the paper and stroked his goatee, his smile turning quickly to a frown. "What's going to happen between now and the trial, Mark?"

"It could all take six months or more, Dieter. Apparently the Crown Prosecution Service will be trying to find another witness to back up our man Soferman. From what I hear, the file will be passed to Scotland Yard's war crimes unit."

"But Henry Sonntag isn't being charged with being a war criminal, Mark," said Danielle defensively.

"No, darling, but that's not to say they won't try to pin it on him at a later date."

"So what will the war crimes unit do?" asked Müller.

"Oh, I'm surprised you don't know about Detective Chief Superintendent Eddie Barnard and his crew, Dieter," replied the reporter. "They'll probably contact foreign governments and ask them to appeal for witnesses. They're already building cases against a number of other war criminals who found refuge in this country."

"Of course, of course, my friend," Müller blushed. "It's just that in practical terms I believe they will achieve very little."

"What do you mean?" asked Danielle.

"I mean that so many years have passed that surely no witness can be regarded as reliable. Look at the Demjanjuk fiasco."

"You mean the odds are that Soferman is fingering the wrong man," said Danielle, grabbing hold of straws on behalf of Sonntag.

"Perhaps," said Müller, "but we must always keep uppermost in our minds the fact that Henry Sonntag is being charged with the murders of Plant and Hyams and those murders alone. It is only the modus operandi of the crime and this Soferman character which are raising the spectre of a Nazi past."

"The evidence looks pretty conclusive," said Edwards. "Apparently they found a whole arsenal of SS weapons in his home, including a dagger like the one found near Plant's body."

"*Meine Ehre heisst Treue*," said the professor. "Loyalty is my Honour. That's the SS motto. It's inscribed on every dagger. Do you want to hear the SS oath of allegiance?"

"Why not?" said Danielle, intrigued. Her voice carried just the faintest hint of sarcasm.

"I'll say it in English, although it sounds much more powerful in German. It goes like this: 'I swear to thee, Adolf Hitler, as Führer and Chancellor of the German Reich, loyalty and bravery. I vow to thee and to the superiors whom thou shalt appoint obedience unto death, so help me God.'"

"Notice they always include God in it somewhere," said

Danielle. "The godless always claim God is on their side."

"Pretty good old English, Dieter, old man," chimed in Pottage, in an attempt to keep the conversation light-hearted.

"*Danke*. I just love Shakespeare."

"I'd like to know more about the SS," said Edwards. "I don't want to assume anyone's guilt just yet. Let's concentrate on a man named Hans Schreiber. I'd like to know more about what his military background might be."

"*Bitte*. I should think he was a member of a Totenkopf unit. They were called that because of the skull and crossbones insignia on their collars and caps. It affirmed a special willingness to die for the cause. They were formed to guard the concentration camps."

"Not much chance of dying for the cause in one of those," said Danielle, tilting her head to her right, her voice now heavy with sarcasm. If the professor was upset by Danielle's attitude he did not show it. He knew he was the expert among them and he was there primarily to relate facts rather than express opinion. "To begin with," he continued, "most of the inmates were Communists. But Jews soon began to follow, along with gypsies, homosexuals, petty criminals and dissenters of all types. As the net was cast wider, there was a need for more camps. Dachau was followed quickly by Buchenwald and Sachsenhausen, then Belsen, Mauthausen and Theresienstadt. The number eventually grew to twenty main camps with sixty-five satellites. Most of them were in Poland. Of course, Auschwitz was the biggest and most infamous."

"What sort of men guarded the camps, Dieter?" asked Edwards, impressed with his friend's expertise.

"They were a mixture, really. Of course, the camps attracted their fair share of sadists. But once the war got under way, there was a constant interchange of personnel between the fighting formations and the concentration camp guards. Men no longer considered fit for front-line duty because of wounds or ill-health were regularly transferred to camp guard duties. Their places would be taken by younger and fitter men from the camps."

"So Schreiber might have found his way to the Russian front?" suggested Edwards.

"Not if he was clever. SS officers did all they could to stay in the camp system, especially when things started going seriously wrong. By late 1943 an intelligent man could see the writing on the wall."

"What happened to these guards at the end of the war?" asked Danielle.

Müller re-lit his pipe before answering. "Many SS soldiers stripped their uniforms of identifying insignia to avoid the persecution they knew they would suffer when taken prisoner. The Totenkopf had less that one thousand men and a few tanks left at war's end. They surrendered to the Americans near Linz on 9 May 1945. Most of the division's officers and men were handed back to the Russians. I don't think any of them would have survived."

"They didn't deserve to," said Danielle contemptuously.

"Anyway," Müller carried straight on, "I think our man Schreiber must have, as you English say, done a runner long before that."

"What about Odessa?" asked Pottage. Having read Frederick Forsyth's book and seen the film, it was about the only contribution he felt he could make to the discussion.

The professor smiled at his ruddy-faced companion. "Oh, I think Schreiber was too small a fish to have been assisted by the Odessa network. It was largely run from Madrid with Franco's tacit approval. It used millions of pounds sterling from plundered Jewish bank accounts and sales of stolen works of art. Odessa's aims were to get known wanted war criminals to places of safety beyond normal legal reach. It provided funds for legal assistance for SS men brought to trial and then helped establish them in commerce and politics in post-war Germany. It also provided a sort of social security net for those of the lower ranks who had given earlier service and had fallen on hard times. Schreiber might have fallen into this category."

Danielle stared coldly at the German. "Tell me, Herr Müller ..."

"Dieter, *bitte*."

"Tell me, Dieter, as a German, do you believe old Nazis should be brought to justice?"

"Ahem," coughed Pottage, "I think I must be going. This is all getting a bit too cerebral for me, m'hearties." The rotund reporter downed the last drop of his whisky, twiddled his bow-tie apologetically and bade them an unsteady farewell.

"Sure you'll be all right, Jim?" Edwards called after him.

"Abso-bloody-lutely, dear boy."

While her companions smiled, Danielle kept her eyes fixed on the German. She wanted to know what made the "innocent" generation tick.

Müller returned her gaze with steel-blue eyes. "Look," he said gravely, "I have dedicated my life to the cause of knowledge of this era. For many people the war was the most vivid experience of their lives. But the passage of time can be helpful to the defence. I mean, it is credible for a defendant to say, 'I simply don't remember the details.'"

"You haven't answered my question, Dieter," Danielle pressed. "I am speaking to you as one who firmly believes that the sins of the fathers should not be visited upon the sons. I understand you were born after the war so you should not feel under any threat."

The professor shifted uncomfortably in his chair but quickly regained his composure. "Look, my dear, because of the 1991 Act, old Nazis living here can be punished. Therefore it is immaterial what I believe, but I shall try to explain my position to you nevertheless."

Edwards leaned forward in his chair. He glanced at Danielle. Her emerald eyes sparkled with an eagerness that he shared. They both wanted to know what made the "new" Germans tick.

"Every man is a product of his time," Müller continued. "Except for a few isolated incidents, the Germany of today is not the Germany of yesterday. There was a frenzy in Hitler's day. Even those who would never have lifted a finger against another human being believed in him. He lifted Germany from its post-First World War depression and created a strong and vibrant economy. Do you agree?"

Now it was the turn of the English pair to shift uncomfortably. Müller was beginning to sound like an apologist for the Third Reich.

"That may be so," said Edwards, "but the price was too high."

"Precisely," the professor smiled. "Hitler failed to hold the moral high ground. And that leads us back to the call today to prosecute old Nazis. The question is whether to do so holds the moral high ground."

"I would argue that it does," said Danielle firmly.

"Out of revenge?" asked Müller with raised eyebrows.

"Oh, you mean the eye-for-an-eye canard that's always levelled against us," she replied swiftly. "No, not revenge, Dieter. Justice."

"Ach, so," the professor sighed. "Justice." His steely blue eyes met hers square-on. "Justice cannot be done to the dead, and when people talk about justice to the dead they mean retribution for the wrong which has been done to them. Retribution and justice are two very different things. Indeed, would justice be served by trundling a few of these dotards into the dock and then have them stumble out again into prison? Most of them would be acquitted through lack of evidence anyway. Justice should not be about trials which are show trials or fiascos. The difficulties of survivor testimony are painfully obvious, especially over identification. I return to the trials of Demjanjuk and the rest. It is pathetic to see old and infirm people in the dock or the witness box, disputing with agonized emotion about who is speaking to whom. I am not saying that war crimes should be forgiven. I just do not think we will be better off by purging a few criminals who already have one foot in the grave."

Danielle's eyes widened and her nostrils flared. Müller's views were no different to those she had heard from many leading lights of the British establishment. The Holocaust cast a shadow over everyone, guilty and innocent alike. How convenient if it were simply swept under the carpet.

"As a Jew," she said passionately, "I must believe that the murderers of Jews should be brought to justice."

"Even Henry Sonntag?" asked Müller, his eyes narrowing.

"I believe that Sonntag is innocent. However, if it is proven that he is guilty, then the full weight of the law should be imposed."

"Guilty of what? Murdering a fellow Jew over money, being the Butcher of the Small Fortress, or both?"

"I think we should stick strictly to the general issue of Nazi war criminals," Edwards interceded. He could sense that the argument was about to overheat.

"Yes, let's," said Danielle, her voice once again heavy with sarcasm. "And let's get back to the moral high ground. The Nazis murdered not only Jews but non-Jews as well. This goes right to the crux of what society is all about. No society that condones murder can survive. How can we let these criminals live out their lives in tranquillity? You might as well say to the prospective murderers of today: 'Anything goes, boys. Go ahead – you might get away with it.'"

"What if a prosecution proves unsuccessful?" the German asked, seemingly unfazed by Danielle's conviction.

"Even an unsuccessful prosecution is better than leaving them alone," she replied. "No government should countenance the murder of innocent men, women and children. Governments must protect the lives of their citizens or they are not worthy of the name."

"Bravo, Fräulein Green," beamed Dieter Müller. "I applaud your tenacity even if I do not agree with your views." The German then extracted a loaded briar from the hip pocket of his brown tweed jacket and spent the next few seconds lighting up. The caramel aroma of Clan soon dominated the atmosphere around them. "It's my round, I believe," he said, rising. "Same again?"

Edwards looked at Danielle with eyes that begged an opinion of their companion. He himself felt a little out of his depth. Both sides had made valid points, and yet he knew he would take Danielle's if push came to shove.

"Well?" he asked eagerly as the German chatted with the barman a few feet away.

"In a way I'm glad his views are opposed to mine," she said. "I don't think I could stand a German who sided with me completely. It would smack of condescension."

"He's pretty genned up, you know. He's a university professor back in Deutschland. Is there anything else you'd like to ask him?"

"Sure. Plenty. I'd like to know how Jews or Nazis or both managed to get into this country after the war. I'd like to know all about the neo-fascism that is rising once more in his country. I want to give your friend the professor the third degree."

"Well, here's your chance. He's coming back."

"I decided to try a Guinness," said Müller affably as he downloaded their drinks. "It's so very different from other beers. Not very popular in Germany, I'm afraid. There people like to ..."

"Conform."

"Well ..." Müller drew nervously on his pipe but kept his gaze locked firmly on his female interrogator. "I wasn't going to say so, but yes, I suppose you are right."

The prickly tension between the pair was tangible, and Edwards felt Danielle was going a little over the top. "Ahem," he coughed, "as you both know, I spent a couple of summers in Germany as a student. It was a great place then. You know, it was in the middle of the *Wirtschaftswunder* – that's the economic miracle, darling – and there was this amazing buzz about everything."

"Where were you staying?" asked the professor.

"With an exchange family in Düsseldorf."

"Ah," sighed Müller, "what a joy to stroll down the Königsallee on a summer's day and drink in Germany's post-war achievements."

"I'd never seen such wealth in what is after all only a provincial city," said Edwards.

"Yes," beamed Müller with pride, "and to think that ninety per cent of it was destroyed in the war. The Ruhr is our industrial heartland and it came in for a battering."

"So did Coventry," said Danielle, eager to puncture the German's pride. "First."

For a moment the professor's steely look threatened to overcome the bonhomie with which he had parried her thrusts. "Of course, my dear," he replied, his voice taut and defensive, "I fully understand that he who sows the wind shall reap the whirlwind."

"Look," interjected Edwards with a glance that told Danielle she was out of order, "we're all on the same side now and we might as well concentrate on the matter in hand. I'd like to know more about how someone like Sonntag, assuming he is what the police and Soferman say he is, could have come to this country."

"Hmm," said Müller, his voice softening now that his expertise and not his opinions were being call upon, "I'm sure I can spread some light there." He took another sip of Guinness and licked the froth from his thin lips. "You must understand, my friends, that at the end of the war Europe was awash with millions of refugees. In the ruins of Germany there were also slave and forced labourers, liberated prisoners of war and ethnic Germans who had fled the Red Army. Of course, there were also Jews, although before you say it, my dear, there were not so many left."

A flash in Danielle's emerald eyes told both men that he had pre-empted her.

"For everyone in Germany," he continued, the sadness in his voice palpable, "it was year zero. Broken streets filled with broken people. Wives looked for husbands, parents searched for their children, brothers and sisters tried to find each other. Some were lucky, but for many more there was only grief. These people ebbed and flowed like the tide. And over all this the armies of the Western allies and the international relief agencies tried to impose order on the chaos and help millions of people whose lives had been shattered. I don't think any of us can imagine what it must have been like."

Edwards, visibly moved by his companion's words, swallowed hard. "Is it possible, Dieter, that an SS officer could have come to this country soon after the war?"

"From my research, I would say that it was far easier for an SS man to reach Britain than a Jew. In fact, while Germans could rightly be accused of racism before and during the war, it was the British who were the racists after it."

Edwards and Danielle glanced at one another. Both were perplexed and not a little concerned. They remained silent as Müller paused to re-light his pipe, confident in the knowledge

169

that he now commanded their undivided attention.

"You see," he went on, "mixed in amongst the mass of displaced persons were thousands posing as victims of the Nazis, including many of their supporters in captured lands who withdrew into the Reich with the retreating German forces. Screening was zealous at the beginning, but the Allies were soon overwhelmed by the sheer numbers involved."

"How did they screen them?" asked Danielle, now hooked by Müller's total command of his subject.

"Ah, my dear, it was all, as you say, so hit and miss. Those members of the Waffen-SS that were rounded up were checked for their blood-group tattooed under the left arm. This was unique to the Waffen-SS and it was looked for by investigators at the most preliminary stage of screening. Shortly after the end of the war it was common to see long lines of half-naked German soldiers with their left arms raised, filing past the tables where the screeners sat."

"So the real Hans Schreiber might have been caught this way?" said Danielle.

"In theory, yes. In practice, no. If we assume ..." – here Müller paused for effect – "if we assume that Schreiber did not surrender or was not captured, then he would never have had to lift his arm."

"So if Henry Sonntag is really Hans Schreiber, he would have the tell-tale markings under his arm," said Danielle excitedly. "That should be easy enough to prove."

Müller nodded his head sagely. "One can safely assume that if he has the markings under his arm, then he was a member of the SS."

"That's it, then," said Edwards. "Either the prosecution or the defence has to make him strip."

"And if he hasn't got the tattoo, then he isn't Hans Schreiber," Danielle stated categorically.

Müller raised his hand in caution. "One thing my research

has taught me is that nothing is ever black or white. Some SS men went to extraordinary lengths to have the markings removed. It might take a microscope to detect anything. Also, I would say that from the million men who joined the Waffen-SS it stands to reason that some might have avoided the procedure altogether. Statistics, you know."

"Anyway," said Edwards, "we don't know what procedural rights the police have in checking out Sonntag. They tend to go by the book just in case the charge might get thrown out on a technicality."

"What about the Jews?" asked Danielle. "You spoke about British racism."

The professor took another gulp of Guinness. Lecturing to the uninformed was always thirsty work. He glanced over his shoulder at a grandmother clock perched high on the pub's flecked wallpaper. It would soon be closing time and he was eager to impart the story of British culpability and duplicity.

"You see, my dear," he said quietly, thankful that most of the other revellers had gone home, "there were thousands of Holocaust survivors in the British zone clamouring to be taken out of Germany. They were often in the same Displaced Persons camps as their SS persecutors. Another irony was that while thousands of Balts who sympathized with and worked for the SS were allowed into Britain, Jews were consistently excluded from all labour recruitment schemes."

"But why?" asked Edwards, feeling the first flush of shame that his nation could be party to such injustice.

Müller laughed. "Ah, the wonderful British. So two-faced and so proud of it."

"What do you mean?" asked Danielle, the dichotomy that struck every British Jew beginning to stab at her. Jew first, British second. British first, Jew second. Would the defences of the latter be breached?

"Well," continued the German, "the Home Secretary of the

day cited the shortage of housing, clothing and jobs for not allowing any large-scale immigration. And, of course, a lot of the survivors were sick and elderly and would be a burden. But that wasn't the real reason, Fräulein Green."

Danielle felt a creeping apprehension as the professor paused to re-light his pipe for what seemed the umpteenth time.

"No, the real reason, my friends, was that the Labour government was worried that the admission of Jewish refugees might provoke strong reactions from certain sections of public opinion. In other words," and here Müller's sardonic grin broadened further, "they were worried about risking a wave of anti-Semitic feeling amongst their own people. Ironic, no?"

Edwards tried to stretch his collar with the forefinger of a hand gone moist. He did not possess the knowledge to counter that of his German friend and, anyway, he believed him. He glanced once again at Danielle.

"It sounds par for the course," she said simply. "How many victims did Britain accept after the war?"

"A few hundred."

"That means ..."

Danielle cut her lover short. "That means that if Henry Sonntag is pretending to be a Jew then he was one of them. He told me he came over here as a refugee soon after the war but didn't go into too much detail."

"Oh, I did not know that you had met Henry Sonntag."

"Sorry, Dieter," said Edwards quickly. "I forgot to tell you."

The German paused, trying hard to suppress his irritability. "I think you had better tell me. You cannot expect my input to be of, shall we say, complete value unless I have all the facts."

"He's right, Dani. Go ahead." Danielle hesitated although, in essence, she knew the German was right. They needed him, if only to give another perspective to the complexities of the case. She took a deep breath and then related most of

172

Sonntag's story, missing out the tale of his financial success, which she did not deem pertinent.

Müller sat through the whole thing impassively. He kept his pipe, which now contained only ash, firmly clenched between his teeth. After she had finished speaking, he withdrew the briar and emptied its contents into a glass ashtray.

"Very interesting," he said at last. "More for what Herr Sonntag did not say than for what he did. He mentioned some incidents in the Small Fortress which were truly horrific. The gladiatorial contests, prisoners made to eat faeces, the terrible overcrowding. And yet he never mentioned Hans Schreiber. After all, he must have come across him."

"Yes," said Edwards, "Dani and I also discussed that. But then maybe he didn't want to mention names."

"The very mention of Schreiber's name might have meant putting a label to the thousands of devils going through his mind," said Danielle. "Anyway, Schreiber might not have done anything to him personally. He spoke to me about the Small Fortress in almost a detached manner. As if he were a disinterested observer. I think I was all the more shocked for that."

"I'm trying to arrange for Dani to visit him in jail," said Edwards. "He'll probably be remanded to Brixton."

"How fascinating," said Müller. "I don't expect Sonntag to express contrition, but you might ask him why he never mentioned Schreiber to you."

"There was another thing," she said. "Following the report of the first murder – by the way, Joe Hyams was my uncle – Sonntag telephoned me and pleaded with me not to publish the article. He said I would never understand but that he would explain later."

"Even more fascinating, my dear," beamed the professor. "There is, as you British say, more to this than meets the eye. *Der mutmassliche Täter* sounds as if he has much to hide."

"Alleged perpetrator," translated Edwards.

"And what about your man, Soferman?" asked the professor. "You are hoping to interview him, *ja*?"

"Yes, although not for publication."

"I would be interested to hear what he has to say. I would like to meet him also, but I doubt very much that he would agree to that."

"I think you're probably right, Dieter. I wouldn't even like to raise the matter with him. He's been through enough traumas as it is."

"So, my friend, just keep me informed. Don't forget, I also want you to get me into the trial."

"I told you it probably won't be for months yet. But the remand hearing will be at Barkingside tomorrow. Eleven o'clock at the courthouse in Cranbrook Road. Meet me there at ten-thirty."

"*Danke*. It is very kind of you." The German then turned his attention to Danielle. "I would appreciate your taking me into your full confidence. I have been frank with you and, sometimes, frankness can be rather off-putting. Please remember, my sole aim has been, and always will be, to search for the truth, however unpleasant it might be. That is my job as an historian." There followed a pregnant silence during which the two journalists considered their companion's plea. The German kept his eyes firmly on Danielle, for he knew his efforts were already appreciated by the Englishman.

"Time, gentlemen, please," the landlord bellowed. They had been so engrossed that they had failed to hear the call for last orders.

Danielle fingered her empty glass nervously. Contrition did not come easily, but she did feel that she had been too harsh on the German. "Dieter," she said, her lips pursed, "I should like to apologize for my rudeness earlier on. It was boorish of me. I'm sure we would appreciate your input on this case and, for our part, we will keep you up to date with developments. I should also like to compliment you on your erudition and your excellent command of English."

"Thank you, my dear. My knowledge of English I owe to an excellent college in London. My knowledge of all things appertaining to the rise and fall of Nazism I owe to my father."

"He must be a fine man," said Edwards.

"*Ja*, a fine man," replied Müller wistfully. "You know," he said, changing the subject and looking squarely at Danielle, "believe me when I say that if Henry Sonntag is proven to be the killer and, therefore, Hans Schreiber, no one will be happier than I to see him rot for the rest of his life."

Danielle returned his gaze levelly. "Dieter, I concur completely. If he is proven guilty."

"There is another thing that perhaps we should all bear in mind," said Müller. "It can be best illustrated by an old folk legend. I don't know from where, but that is less important than its message." The professor paused to make sure his audience was paying full attention. "There was a king who owned a mirror which reflected not the person's face, but his personality. One day he offered a reward to anyone who could look into it for one whole minute without turning away. No one could."

"Does that mean a guilty man will somehow always reveal his guilt?" asked Edwards.

"You might think so," replied Müller. "But some people make sure the mirror is permanently covered."

"What do you mean?" asked Danielle.

"I mean that no ex-kapo is going to tell you that he survived the death camps by being a kapo. Just as no Nazi war criminal is going to admit that he murdered people. They will have invented their own cover story and will have repeated it so often that they come to believe it themselves. The truth will be buried so deep that they will no longer recognize it."

Danielle was just about to comment when the landlord cut her short.

"Time, gentlemen, please."

The following morning the two journalists were already sitting in Danielle's car in the court car park by ten-fifteen. She had slept at Edwards' flat. Although they had made love, she had not felt fully relaxed. She could not make up her mind about Müller, and her dreams had revolved around his tale of a devastated Germany, Sonntag's plight, and her own doubts about the veracity of everything he had told her.

"Penny for your thoughts," said Edwards, noting her faraway stare.

"I think you can guess," she replied resignedly. "The circus is about to begin and I've a distinct feeling I may be taken for one of the clowns."

Edwards caressed her short blonde hair. "I think Sonntag's in for a hard time, darling – at the real trial, I mean. This is just the remand. Perfunctory, really."

"You wouldn't think so by the menagerie round the front. Our colleagues are really making fools of themselves. God knows what kind of stampede there'll be when he arrives."

She had hardly finished speaking when the Black Maria carrying Henry Sonntag roared into the compound. The driver did not have time to apply the handbrake before the vehicle was swamped by press photographers. A bevy of blue uniforms sought to keep their ward unmolested as Henry Sonntag, covered by a blanket, was hustled into the court building.

"Not very edifying, is it?" said Danielle, opening her car door. "Come on, let's go."

The pair walked briskly along the path that circumnavigated

the reasonably modern building, its slate-grey corrugated concrete walls matching the leaden skies. They swept into Redbridge Magistrates Court, a stone's throw from the nick in Barkingside, and headed straight for Court 3. The benches were full of journalists. It was clear that few members of the public would have the chance to witness the proceedings. There was just not enough space.

The room was buzzing, the Clerk of the Court having to call for order several times as the three sitting magistrates dealt as quickly as possible with a series of unfortunates accused of relatively minor offences. Everyone was waiting impatiently for the big one.

The Chairman of the Bench was an owlish man in his sixties with bushy eyebrows, a hooked nose and thin lips. Murder cases did not come along frequently and he was damned if he wasn't going to play to the gallery. He was still preening himself as the gaunt and imposing figure of Sir John Tilson, QC, Henry Sonntag's barrister, entered the courtroom accompanied by a pair of juniors eager to get a slice of the action, however minimal. It was not usual for Tilson, one of the biggest wigs in criminal law, to dignify a magistrates' court with his presence. However, this was a high-profile case. Furthermore, his client was very, very rich. Tilson's fees no doubt reflected the fact that Henry Sonntag was getting the best that money could buy.

The tall barrister gave a perfunctory nod to his opposite number. Nigel Blomberg was a good eight inches smaller and sported a paunch. Seemingly genial, he nevertheless possessed a paper-shredder of a mind which gave no quarter. For those who knew them, and Mark Edwards had seen them both in action on numerous occasions, Tilson v. Blomberg was like a Spurs v. Arsenal derby – passion, commitment and no shortage of skill. Henry Sonntag was the current football and the odds were vastly in favour of him being booted into jail for the rest of his life.

His eyes glazed, the reporter was staring at the square plastic light-covers in the false ceiling when Danielle's elbow in his ribs prompted him to shift his attention to the entrance door to their right. He followed the line of heads seeking to catch a glimpse of the accused as he was brought into the courtroom. Because of the room's configuration, Sonntag was standing in front of the journalists, facing away from them and towards the Bench. There was a buzz of frustration, which subsided only when the chairman called for order.

The Clerk of the Court cleared his throat. "Is your name Henry Sonntag?" he asked with a self-importance to match the proceedings.

"It is," replied the yellowy-white head in front of the gallery. The voice was firm and determined. It carried the same conviction when affirming that the details of his address were correct and that he was represented by Sir John Tilson.

"You may be seated," said the Clerk, who then read out the charges slowly and deliberately. The man in the navy blue suit sat rigidly throughout the reading.

The counsel for the prosecution rose sharply, almost before the clerk had finished reading the charges. "Sir, this is an allegation of murder in which inquiries continue. We would respectfully ask for a remand in custody for a further week at which time we will be able to inform the court when this case will be ready to be committed for trial."

The chairman looked across at the defence counsel. "Do you wish to say anything and is there an application for bail?"

Sir John rose, extending himself impressively to his full height. "Recognizing the gravity of the charges, there is no application for bail. May I inform the court that my client strenuously denies both of the charges."

"Thank you very much, Sir John. This case is adjourned until seven days from today. The defendant will be remanded in custody."

With this the courtroom broke into a babble. The remand hearing was all over in less than three minutes and whatever happened in court between now and the opening of the trial would be pure scene-setting.

As Henry Sonntag turned to be led away his eyes alighted on those of the only female journalist present. She nodded in acknowledgement. The man's small brown eyes lingered for a few more seconds before a tug on his arm broke the spell. Danielle Green saw no guilt in those eyes, only the look of a man in torment.

CHAPTER ELEVEN

War Crimes Unit
Metropolitan Police
New Scotland Yard
London, SW1

The Ambassador
The Czech Republic
26 Kensington Palace Gardens
W8 4QY

Dear Sir

The Metropolitan Police presents its compliments to the Honourable Ambassador for the Czech Republic.

As you are no doubt aware, since the War Crimes Act introduced into law by the British Government in 1991, it is now possible to prosecute suspected Nazi war criminals residing in the United Kingdom.

We wish to bring to your notice that a man who goes by the name of Henry Sonntag is currently on remand accused of the recent murder of two British Jews. Following our investigations, we have reason to believe that this man "Sonntag" may, in fact, be Hans Schreiber, an SS Obersturmführer who has been labelled the "Beast of the Small Fortress" of Theresienstadt (Terezin).

We should be grateful if you would pass this request, and the accompanying recent police photographs of the accused, to the Ministry of the Interior and other relevant bodies to instigate investigations into this matter with a view to discovering the whereabouts in your country of any survivors of the Small Fortress who might be able to identify the said Schreiber.

Similar correspondence is being sent to the ambassadors of all countries which might have had some of their citizens incarcerated in the Small Fortress.

I should like to thank you in advance for your assistance in this matter.

I am, sir,
Your obedient servant
        Detective Chief Superintendent Edward Barnard

"Come in. Come in, my friend."

Mark Edwards, trepidation tugging at his nerve-ends, prepared to cross the threshold of the ordinary terraced house in Belvedere Road, Leyton. He'd read somewhere that the district, part of the London Borough of Waltham Forest, once boasted the highest percentage of elderly people per head of population in the country. For some reason he thought of a comment Danielle had once made that the ambition of elderly Jews in the United States was to retire to sun-soaked Miami. Jews in Leyton, east London, however, seemed destined to live and die under grey skies and in abject yet dignified mediocrity. Leyton was a working-class town and Herschel Soferman was nothing if not working-class.

"Thanks, Herschel. Where shall I hang my coat?"

"Here," said Soferman, taking the navy blue gabardine, "I'll hang it over the banister. Used to make these, you know."

"Oh, really," said Edwards, surprised, although he could not think why.

"Yes, yes. I used to be a tailor in Savile Row. A Jewish firm took me in and trained me when I arrived here as a refugee after the war. I'm afraid they went *mechulah* – er, I'm sorry, bust – soon after I retired six or seven years ago. Please come into the lounge. I'll just put the kettle on."

Edwards entered the lounge. It was a through-room which only astonished by its uniform drabness. The wallpaper tried vainly to promote its whiteness but was mostly overcome by an expanse of grubby grey. The leaf-green Dralon suite had seen better days. The whole place had a mustiness about it and cried out for a woman's touch.

The reporter crossed to an old-fashioned fireplace that boasted a miserable two-bar electric heater. Its feeble efforts did little to warm the room sufficiently to make it comfortable. It was clear that Herschel Soferman was not overly flush. The exact opposite, in fact, of Henry Sonntag. Edwards looked up at the mantelpiece. It bore a seven-branched candlestick similar to those he had seen in the homes of Danielle's parents and her late uncle. A menorah, he believed she had called it. Next to it was a fading framed photograph of smiling newlyweds. The man, sporting a fine head of blond hair, was obviously Herschel Soferman in his prime. The young woman in the picture had a horsey face but kind eyes.

"My darling wife," came a voice from behind him. Its tone bore all the sadness of a love lost prematurely. "She died seven years ago. Lung cancer."

"I'm sorry, Herschel," said Edwards, turning round.

The old man, standing gingerly with a cup of tea in either hand, nodded. "Hetty was a fine woman," he sighed. "She helped me pick up the pieces after the war. I don't think I could have survived without her."

"Here, let me help you," said Edwards, moving swiftly across the room to relieve his host of the cups. "Where shall I put them?"

"Oh, on the coffee table. Just pull in your armchair a little closer. Then you will be all right."

The reporter sat down and watched his host sink carefully into the deep Dralon. Apart from his baldness, the likeness to Sonntag was remarkable. The hair around the sides and back of Soferman's head was the same yellowy white. Both had angular chins, narrow noses and beady brown eyes. There were some differences. Soferman's lips were more fleshy than

Sonntag's, the cheekbones slightly higher.

"You're staring at me, Mr Edwards, because you see him in me."

Edwards blushed. "I'm sorry, Herschel. Please forgive me." The reporter swallowed hard. "I seem to keep saying that, don't I?"

"Everything is nonsense, my friend. The only thing that matters is the truth."

"Did you and Hetty have any children, Herschel?"

Soferman's rheumy eyes glazed. "No. Unfortunately, we couldn't."

Edwards changed tack speedily. "How did you get on with Detective Inspector Webb?"

"He interviewed me for a total of six hours. It was really repetitive and he concentrated only on my time in Theresienstadt. I was exhausted by the end. I am no chicken, you know."

Edwards smiled. "I promise I won't put you through the third degree. We can't publish anything now anyway. We can only report the ˙trial. You know, Sonntag's counsel will probably give you a roasting."

Soferman looked at his guest squarely. "The truth, Mr Edwards, fears no man."

"Good for you."

"Now what do you want me to do?" asked Soferman, eager to oblige the younger man.

"Look, Herschel, I don't really want this to be an interview in the real sense of the word. It's not a grilling. As I told you on the phone, I'd like to write a book about this whole thing once the trial's over. I've brought along a tape recorder and I think the best thing is if you just relate your life story in your own words. I won't interrupt even if I have questions. I'll go over the tape in my own time and we'll get together again to clarify anything that needs clearing up."

"Of course, I agree, my friend, even though it may cause me some pain. But I have just one request."

"I'll do my best."

"You told me your girlfriend is going to visit Sonntag – I just can't get used to that name – to visit Schreiber in prison. I would like to know if he says anything about me. You know, it must have come as a real shock to him to discover that I am alive."

"What do you mean?"

"Be patient, Mr Edwards. I shall tell you everything. But first promise me you will tell me."

Edwards shrugged. "I don't see any problem with that ... if he says anything."

"Good. Then let us proceed."

For the next few hours of a quiet Sunday afternoon Mark Edwards listened to the amazing life story of Herschel Soferman. The only interruptions were for cups of tea, calls of nature and the switching of cassettes. The reporter was amazed by his host's grasp of English. It seemed every German he met spoke the Queen's English better than most of her native-born subjects.

Later that evening, Edwards replayed the tapes to Danielle in her Docklands apartment. Both had been embroiled in the case sufficiently to have their own favourite. Now Danielle would hear another side of the story. The tapes were dated and bore the simple label "Herschel Soferman's Story".

"I was born in the Charlottenburg district of Berlin. Anyway, that's what they told me. It's just north of the Kurfürstendamm – you know Berlin, so maybe you know that

area. It was a residential area then and it's the same now, I think, although I haven't been back there since I was forcibly removed in the winter of '43. I will not suffer anything that is German. I will not drive a German car, I will not own a German television set or any other thing that originates in that damn country. Tfhh [Spitting sound].

"I don't remember my father. Apparently he was killed in a car crash when I was four. I was sent to the local Jewish orphanage. It was bombed by the Allies later in the war. No matter. I doubt whether anyone apart from me survived. I have never tried to search for lost friends. Maybe I am frightened to meet them. To dredge up the past. That is why I keep myself to myself. I do not want to re-live the past. [Laughs] But now I am having to, no? [Clears throat] I was unhappy there – in the orphanage – although everyone was very kind. I vaguely remember my mother. [Sighs] I remember her black hair and black eyes. But that is all. The orphanage was my mother and father. I stayed there until I was fifteen. I drifted around a bit and then got a job as a presser in a sweatshop. I was strong for my age. And those irons were surely heavy [Laughs]. In the evenings I studied. Yes, Mr Edwards, I read Schiller and Kant. Goethe, too. I spent all my money on books. Yet [Sighs] I became a tailor. No ambition, my friend. No ambition. Schreiber robbed me of my ambition. I should have gone to Palestine before it was too late. But as German Jews we were so [Pause] German. A German Zionist was someone who paid a second Zionist to send a third to Palestine. Funny, no? [Laughs] You see, we were Germans. We spoke the German language. It was our mother tongue in the truest sense of the word. Language means almost more than blood. We did not know any Fatherland other than Germany and we loved the country as one loves one's Fatherland. But I will never visit that land again and I will never consciously speak its language. I think I told you this before.

"Anyway, where were we? Ah, yes, I was working as a presser. I was a bit of a loner really, although I did have one friend. Avraham was his name. He worked the presses by day and studied the Torah by night. He had payers, you know, side-curls, and looked a pukka Jew. [Sighs] That was his downfall. I'll never forget Kristallnacht. It means Night of Broken Glass. I was sixteen at the time and it was my first job. Goldberg was a bit of a slave-driver. There were about fifty of us working in his factory. We were on the night shift that night. November the ninth, 1938. I'll never forget it.

"Look, Mr Edwards, you've got to understand that up until that year there had been a lot of decrees and things but not a lot of violence. They started by stealing Jewish property. We had a couple of Jews of Polish origin and they were forcibly deported. They were nice guys. One of them, Mietek, taught me Polish. I learnt basic Polish in six weeks. Can you believe that? I had this tremendous knack for learning languages. I taught myself English, too. I listened to the BBC all the time. English is my favourite language. It is so rich.

"Anyway, it all started because my namesake, some young Jew named Herschel Grynszpan, assassinated the Secretary of the German embassy in Paris. That was all the excuse the Nazis needed for a pogrom. There we were, slaving away at our presses, when the front doorbell rings. It was enough to wake the dead, that bell. It had to be what with the noise of the presses and sewing machines. Anyway, we opened the door and there was this Jew standing there. White as a sheet, he was. He was shaking all over. He asked for Goldberg. Said we should all get home as quickly as possible. Said Nazi gangs were running amok in the streets. He said synagogues everywhere were burning. Can you imagine? The stranger then ran off into the night. No one waited for Goldberg to decide anything. Everyone clamoured to get home to their parents or their wives and children. All except Avraham and

me, that is. We were both orphans with no families to go home to. Goldberg let us share a room at the back of the workshop. He had taken pity on us. He worked us hard but he was fair.

"Anyway, Goldberg himself turned up a few minutes later. He was also shaking. 'I've got to lock up, boys,' he said. He told us to keep to our little room at the back. 'Don't venture out into the streets, boys,' he said. 'Don't act like heroes. Wait till it all blows over.' So Goldberg went home and there was just me and Avraham. Alone and frightened in our little back room. We played cards, drank tea and ate a few sandwiches. The usual routine, really. It was our little den and I suppose it gave us a false sense of security.*

"[Breathes deeply] *Then came the banging on the front door of the workshops. They rang the doorbell again and again. The sound went right through us. Then the banging got louder. We knew they must have been using a sledgehammer. There was the terrible noise of splintering wood and shattering glass. Avraham was shaking and wide-eyed with fright. I'll never forget his eyes* [pause]. *Then we heard their voices. Venomous, they were. 'Juden Raus,' they screamed. They were getting more agitated because the place was empty. We heard them smashing up the workshop. We knew we must hide because there was no escape. The only way out was past the thugs. There was a small trapdoor in the floor but there was only space for one. Instinctively I dived into it. I pulled the trapdoor to and then suddenly all was silence. Then I heard a familiar squeak. It was our clothes cupboard door. The only problem was, if I heard it, then so did the Nazis. Suddenly I heard the door to our room smashed open and the clump of jackboots above my head. Within seconds they had discovered Avraham. I'll never forget their curses and his pleas for mercy.*

"[Pause] *There were terrible screams that seemed to go on for ever. Then I heard the jackboots disappear and then silence. It must have been a further ten minutes before I ventured out of my hiding place. I had to heave with all my might because something was holding the trapdoor shut. Eventually I managed to get the door open and haul myself out. [Breathes deeply] It was terrible. I had never seen a human being reduced to something unrecognizable. There was blood everywhere. My friend Avraham was dead and it could so easily have been me. I feel guilty for it even until this day. [Whistle in background] There goes the kettle. Let me make you a cup of tea, Mr Edwards."*

Click.

"Well, what do you think so far?"

Dani stared at the tape recorder. "It's pretty powerful stuff," she said. "He certainly tells a good story. Funny, though ..."

"Yes?"

"There is a point of coincidence in his story and Henry Sonntag's."

"What's that?"

"They were both born and brought up in the Charlottenburg district of Berlin. Strange, that."

"Hmm." Edwards grimaced. "Maybe. Maybe not. Remember, Soferman claims Sonntag stole his identity. Anyway, if I recall correctly, it all becomes clearer later on. Let me make a cup of tea and then I'll switch it back on."

"Where was I? Oh, yes. Poor Avraham. He was one of a hundred Jews murdered on that night, you know. Hundreds of synagogues were destroyed and thousands of shops and offices were looted. Imagine. I had to sit with his body the whole night until Goldberg came back the following morning. Sometimes, when I consider what happened to me afterwards, I wish I had

been in his place. But I think it was from that moment that I knew I would survive; that I would live to bear witness against these monsters.

"From that day on it was a hand-to-mouth existence. I found another room and moved from job to job. Eventually, the pressure on Jewish businesses became so intense that I went back to the orphanage to help look after the younger children. It didn't pay anything, but at least I had a roof over my head and food to eat. However, with all the hardships it's ironic that we German Jews were relatively better off than Jews elsewhere in Europe. The Jews in the east, mainly Poland, suffered first. With all the madness going on around us, Berlin was relatively a safe haven.

"But it couldn't last, Mr Edwards. Eventually our turn came. By this time I was assistant director at the orphanage. The director, Otto Zimmerman, relied on me to look after the acquisition of food and clothing for the children. There were about fifty at the beginning. But by early '43 the numbers had swollen to almost double. Other orphanages were opening up all over the place because of the numbers of parents who had been rounded up by the Gestapo. It was pitiful to see the new arrivals. They were so frightened. Each sad face mirrored my own. I knew what they were going through. That's why they could relate to me.

"Then came the inevitable. It was November. I remember, it was windy and wet and the morning air was cold enough to chill. There came this persistent ringing at the front doorbell. It reminded me of that terrible time on Kristallnacht. Somehow something told me that our time was up. I was the one who opened the door. About fifty men stormed into the house, pushing me aside roughly. Some of them wore long black coats with the collars turned up. They were the Gestapo. The others were a mixture of soldiers and police. "Don't harm the children. Please don't harm the children," Zimmerman pleaded.

"They will not be harmed as long as you follow orders," said one of the men in black coats. He was a small, weedy man and I couldn't help smiling to myself that this was supposed to be an example of the master race. Anyway, to cut a long story short, we had half an hour to get all the children's belongings together. Their fearful cries resounded throughout the building. I tried to calm them down but some of them were inconsolable. Fear was gnawing away at me, too. On the one hand I wanted to run away and on the other I knew I must help the little ones. I stayed, of course. But in the eventuality it was only until we got to the station. I was all set to board the train with them – by the way, it wasn't a cattle-car like they used to transport the Polish Jews – when the weedy man pushed me to one side with his riding whip. 'You stay here,' he said in his squeaky voice. 'You'll be taking another train.' He then sent me to join a group of young men in a waiting-room which had been cordoned off. [Pause] I never saw Zimmerman and the children again. I can only presume that they were transported directly to one of the death camps [sound of rattling china and tea being slurped].

"Anyway, there I was with these other guys. We thought we were being singled out to be shot. In the event we were put on the next train. We didn't know where we were going at first. Then, when the sun came out, we could tell by its position that we were headed more or less due south. We were relieved. Anything was better than the east. There were rumours that anyone going east would never return.

"We ended up in Bohemia, in a place called Terezin, not far from Prague. Ah, Prague. The most beautiful city in Europe, you know. I only got to know it after I escaped from Theresienstadt. I went back there to visit some old friends during Dubcek's Prague Spring. A magical city. It has a very famous Jewish Quarter. Hitler did not want to destroy it

*because he wanted to turn it into a museum of an extinct
people.* [Pause] *Now, where was I? Yes, Theresienstadt. It had
been an old fortress town and was now turned into a transit
ghetto for Jews on their way to the death camps. We didn't
fully realize they were death camps at the time, of course. The
whole place buzzed with rumours. I'd never seen so many Jews
crammed together in one place. It was a real tower of Babel.*

"*It's funny, you know, when you reach a place like that you
find out that the most important thing in life is not money or
jewellery or things like that. I mean, the most important thing
was food. If you had enough food to eat and could avoid the
transports to the east then life was tolerable. Fortunately I met
up with a guy called Oskar Springer* [Pause] *from Frankfurt.
He was a little man with pointed ears and big bright eyes. He
became like a brother to me. He helped me to survive those
first terrible weeks when any newcomer was at a
disadvantage. He helped get me on the detail that collected all
the belongings from the new arrivals. As long as all the
valuables were collected, the Germans turned a blind eye to
the food we used to scavenge. Unfortunately, one day our luck
ran out. That was when we got sent to the Small Fortress. It
already had a terrible reputation. Everyone said that no Jew
ever left it alive. I'd already heard about Hans Schreiber, the
Beast, and now I was going to meet him* [Pause]*.*

"*No words can truly describe the awfulness of that place or
the bestiality of Hans Schreiber, the* mumser*. From almost the
start he picked me out. I remember Oskar telling me that we
looked alike. I didn't think anything of it then. Only recently.*
[Pause] *We were on top of one of the fortified walls,
supposedly to carry out some repair work. Suddenly there was
an explosion and the rampart gave way. Because we were on
top we survived with a few cuts and bruises. Some of those at
the bottom were less fortunate. They were buried alive. But it's
what came after that sticks in my mind. For some reason*

Schreiber said he liked me. He said that Berliners should stick together. He said that because of my blond hair I did not look like a typical Yid. 'But you're Yid enough for me,' he said. [Pause] I've never forgotten those words but they did not have any relevance until the murders. You must also remember that he collected everyone's identity papers on arrival. It made it easier for him to steal someone's identity.

"Anyway, where was I? Oh, yes. Schreiber then led me through a courtyard and into a small room. There was a horse-trough there with a hosepipe leading into it. The water made me feel very thirsty. He made me look inside the trough. At the bottom were two blocks of ice. I'll never forget the smell of lavender that always surrounded him. It was a fetish with him. The next thing he did makes me physically sick to this day. He had an elderly Jew brought in and made him strip. A guard then picked the old man up and heaved him into the trough. The man was weak and Schreiber held him down under the water with his whip until he drowned. [Pause] He then made me drink from the trough. [Lengthy pause] Then this monster began saying again how much he liked me. I was like putty in his hands. I felt numb and yet I remember telling him all about myself. I actually revealed almost every detail of my life to him. Can you imagine, standing there in a room with a drowned man talking about my life history with his murderer? [Pause] But it got worse, Mr Edwards, it got worse._

"I became Hans Schreiber's favourite in a game that he loved playing. He would arrange gladiatorial contests in which Jew would be pitted against Jew in a fight to the death. He would even photograph us. It was his favourite hobby. [Pause] In order to live I killed four of my own people. Four [sobbing sounds]. Four."

Click.

Edwards shut off the tape. He looked at Danielle. Her eyes were glistening. A single tear made a slow and meandering tour of her cheek before entering the corner of her mouth.

"I turned off the tape at that stage because he was inconsolable. He was crying so bitterly I was at a loss as to what to do. I poured him another cup of tea and after a while he seemed to calm down."

"I don't know what to say," Danielle sighed. "Sonntag never told me any of this, except in general terms. He didn't mention Schreiber, but he did mention a lot of barbaric things that were done in the Small Fortress – shootings, stabbings and the like. He said Jews were ordered to eat pig-shit ..."

"Wait, darling, Soferman comes to that."

"Mark, you have to remember that the interview was mainly about a refugee's success story. My emphasis was always going to be on the economic side of it."

"I understand, darling, I understand. You can raise these issues with Sonntag when you visit him, although I hardly think he'll co-operate. Anyway, I'll fast-forward it a bit and you can listen to the rest. It's utterly enthralling."

"Oh dear, Mark ..."

"Yes?"

"There is another thing. When I went to visit Sonntag there was a very strong smell of lavender about the place."

Edwards ran his fingers through his blond hair. "That just about settles it."

"Switch the tape back on," she said abruptly. She was now beginning to have serious doubts about Henry Sonntag.

"I'm sorry, Mr Edwards. I will try now to be more composed. These revelations are not easy for me. Is it switched on? Good. I told Inspector Webb about the contests, but I did

not tell him I had participated in them. In fact, I told him I had not. I'm sure you understand. I wanted to reveal all only after the trial. Schreiber's counsel would try to paint as black a picture of me as he could. I'm sure you agree. [Pause] And so, my friend, I was forced to take part in these terrible contests. Schreiber always made sure my opponents were smaller, weaker or less mobile than I. Oh, I forgot. You remember my best friend, Springer? He more or less drowned himself in a ditch after Schreiber made him eat pig's faeces. He could not take it any more. And who could blame him [Pause].

"Schreiber eventually tired of sporting with me. He put me on a work detail. We were led out to some woods. There was a trench with some shovels sticking out from mounds of earth at the top. We were told to line up at the lip of the trench. We knew the trench was full of bodies by the stench. You could smell it a hundred metres away. We were told to begin shovelling earth on the bodies. I had a gut feeling that we were next. As Schreiber ordered the machine-guns to open fire I dived into the pit. Fortunately I was knocked unconscious by a body falling on top of me, otherwise I would have gagged on the stench and given away that I was still alive. When I came to, there was no one around, but I could hear the voices of the guards getting closer. I hauled myself out of the ditch and hid in the bushes. They then lined up another row of prisoners, executed them and then covered the bodies with quicklime.

"I waited in the bushes until Schreiber and his men finished their work. You can imagine how I felt. Alone, wearing prison clothes and completely penniless. Yet I was free, Mr Edwards. Free. Only one who has suffered like me can appreciate what it is to be truly free. But what to do next? The Germans were to the west and the Russians to the east. Of course, for me the Russians were the lesser of two evils. But I decided to head south towards Prague. I knew my only hope of survival was dependent on me finding one good man. I knew I could not *survive alone and without help. Czechoslovakia was the home of the Good Soldier Schweik. [Laughs] Any country that could produce a character like him couldn't be all that bad, eh? Anyway, I was much more likely to come across a Czech who would help a Jew rather than a German, that was for sure.*

"It was already dark when I reached the outskirts of a town called Melnik, about twenty kilometres north of Prague. I was hungry and cold. I had to do something. You know, I once knew a man who made every decision on the throw of a die. He didn't care, that man. An Australian. Bush hat and all. 'Okay,' he said to me in London soon after the war, 'three or more I go to Hong Kong. One to three I go to Rio.' He then tossed the die in the air and it came down on two. The next day he flew out to Rio. You see, he had plenty of money and he had a choice. But he still preferred to let that choice be decided by something other than his own will. Mr Edwards, I had no money and I had no real choice. But what I had was willpower. Sure, I would be dependent on the kindness of a stranger, but some sixth sense told me that I would survive. Now that I was free I felt I possessed a will that could be betrayed by no man.

"Anyway, it was now or never. I didn't have a mirror to tell me how I looked. I must have smelled terribly but my nose had already got used to it.

"My heart was in my mouth when I knocked on that door. The farmer opened it. He was so broad he took up practically the whole doorway. He immediately brought his hand up to his face and made a choking noise. I babbled something in Polish and then German. A lot of Czechs speak either or both languages. He didn't say anything. He just grabbed me and pulled me roughly inside. Pushing past his wife, he took me straight to a room at the rear of the farmhouse. It was a bathroom. 'You see those clothes hanging there,' he said in German, 'have a bath and then wear them.' Mr Edwards, never in my life have I enjoyed a bath as much as that one. I *just lay there for ages. For all I knew, the farmer could have been calling in the Nazis. I didn't care. I just scrubbed and scrubbed. I felt as though I was scrubbing my body clean of Hans Schreiber.*

"[Laughs] *I must have been a real sight. The clothes were obviously the farmer's. He was wide and small and I was tall and thin. You can imagine. I looked totally ridiculous standing there. Pavel and Sophie Novak burst out laughing. It was then that I knew my luck was still holding out. I owe the Novaks everything, Mr Edwards. I visited them in '68. [Sighs] They're dead now, of course. Anyway, they treated me like the son they had lost in the early days of the war. The farmhouse was remote and I spent an idyllic summer there helping out with the harvest. I grew stronger and stronger. I had not eaten so well in years. [Sighs] But all good things must come to an end.*

"*By May 1945 the whole region was in chaos. Bohemia was full of every type of outlawed army. There were SS units recruited from disaffected Soviets and the army of Andrey Vlasov. God knows how many times he had changed sides during the war. They were all running away westward rather than fall into the hands of the Russians. To this day I don't know why I gave up my safe haven for a life of uncertainty. It all happened in the first week of May. There was a knock on the door. Pavel asked me to open it. There were three soldiers standing there. They were pretty messed up. Not wounded or anything, just dirty and grimy. They tried a selection of languages with us, including Polish. They asked for food and we gave them some bread and soup. I noticed their uniforms did not have any insignia or lapels. They'd been torn off. I asked them who they were and where they were going. 'We've had enough,' said the tallest of the three. 'If the Germans think we're going to fight the Russians on their behalf they can go fuck themselves.' [Laughs] Yes, that's what he said. Zbigniew, his name was. Zbiggy later became a good friend. He said he* and his men – they were anti-Stalin Russians – were deserting and heading west. They said they'd heard the Americans were about to reach Pilsen and they were going there to surrender. As I said, you can call it fate if you like, but something told me that I should join these men. I was too young to really understand what I was doing. I suppose if I had been older I might have hesitated. You know, the older you get, the more set in your ways you get.

"Pavel and Sophie were dumbstruck when I told them what I planned to do. They warned me of the dangers and that I would be much safer if I stayed with them. It was a tearful parting, I can tell you. [Pause] They were the kindest people I had ever met, Mr Edwards. I cherish their memory to this day. [Sigh] But I was driven by this need to go west. I did not want to stay on a farm for the rest of my life. The Novaks gave us enough food to last us a week and the four of us set out for the American lines. When I think about it today, I must have been mad. There were Germans, Russians, Lithuanians, Latvians, a whole tangle of people heading in the same direction. Some who were former enemies now became friends. Nobody cared any more. There were outbreaks of fighting here and there but we skirted round those. After five days we reached the Americans. We just walked into town and gave ourselves up.

"I realized that I couldn't stay with Zbiggy and the other Vlasov men. They told me their greatest fear was that they might be handed back to the Red Army. Zbiggy said he would kill himself before he'd allow that to happen. Well, I can tell you I didn't want to be categorized as a Russian traitor. Then I did something that will make you laugh, Mr Edwards. I asked to see the commander of our DP camp. He was one of those big American types. You know, John Wayne. I told him that I was a Jew who had escaped from Theresienstadt and had fought with the Czech resistance. 'You don't look like a Jew to me, blondie,' he laughed. I was desperate, Mr Edwards. I had *to convince him. So, you know what I did? I dropped my trousers. [Laughs] Yes, right there in front of him, I pulled out my penis. Thank God, he had a sense of humour. He stood there for a few seconds and then nearly fell off the chair. 'Put it away, Hymie,' he said after he'd calmed down. He then looked me straight in the eye. 'What other languages do you speak besides English?' he asked me. When I told him, he wrote something on a US Army letterhead, signed it and handed it to me. It was my lifeline, Mr Edwards. Colonel John Towers had given me back my identity. The letter said I was attached to the US Army as an interpreter and was to help in the interrogation of prisoners. I knew then for certain that I would survive the war. It was all over quicker than I thought. I worked in five different DP camps. I enjoyed helping to weed out the Nazis. You see, the Americans were faced with an incredible collection of potential POWs. Many of them were disguised as civilians and displaced persons of all nationalities. To make sense of the stories they were told, they would have needed literally thousands of highly trained investigators fluent in many foreign languages. There weren't that many of us around and we were greatly overworked. The Americans also changed. At first they were good to us, especially those who had liberated the death camps, and were very harsh on the Germans. But these troops were soon replaced by occupation personnel. They hadn't seen the camps. They had a different attitude towards the Germans. These were the Ugly Americans. They felt more sympathy towards the Germans than towards us. It was disgusting. They were only interested in making a fast buck on the black market.*

"Anyway, about six months after the end of the war I was posted to Berlin. The city was in a shambles. I went to look for the orphanage but the whole street didn't exist any more. I was sad for that, but not for the hell the Berliners had gone through. Never did a people deserve it more. I then realized *that the letter from the colonel was my only means of identification. I suppose I was stateless. I certainly did not want to call myself German again.*

"It was then that fate took another turn. My commanding officer in the American zone told me I was being seconded to the British who were apparently in desperate need of a multi-linguist with experience in DP work. I worked diligently for the British for the next six months and made good friends with my commanding officer, Colonel Colin Blakemore. It was he who helped me get the right papers to be one of the few Jews the British allowed into the UK after the war. I'm thirsty. Let me go make another cup of tea and I'll tell you about the rest of my life. A lot less eventful ... I'm glad to say."

Click.

"Well, darling, that's the guts of it," said Edwards. "The rest of the time he spent telling me about his wife and his life as a tailor. Pretty ordinary, really. You know, I was there for more than two hours."

Danielle stared silently at the tape recorder for a few seconds. She felt stupid and cheated. She had supported a man who was clearly a mass murderer. The weight of evidence against Henry Sonntag was already overwhelming, and Herschel Soferman's moving testimony would have a devastating effect on any jury. She recalled the all-pervading scent of lavender when she had visited Sonntag at his home. It all made sense now. Sonntag had told an awful tale but it had not contained this kind of personal detail. As far as the war years were concerned, it had more or less been third-party.

"The lying bastard," she hissed through gritted teeth.

"Who, Soferman?" gasped Edwards.

"No, Henry Sonntag."

"Look," said Edwards, relieved, "I won't say I told you so."

"You have every reason to. I feel so damn stupid. Your friend Müller must think I'm as naive as hell."

Edwards rose from his armchair and moved across the room. He knelt in front of her and took her pale slender hands in his. Gently, he kissed them. "Darling, I love you," he said softly. "We all make mistakes."

"What shall I do?" she asked, withdrawing her hands and running them through his hair.

"About what?"

She breathed deeply. "About going to see Sonntag in prison."

"Hmm, well, I don't think it's worth it now." Danielle was about to concur, but then hesitated. In a way, Sonntag had betrayed her. Why shouldn't she face him with that betrayal. "I still want to see him, Mark," she said firmly.

"Look, I don't think you should, Dani. You might lose your temper and that'll be the last time I get any help from Brixton's finest."

"I promise I won't make a scene, Mark. I just want to see the look in his eyes."

Mark Edwards knew that his lover would not rest until she had confronted Sonntag. "Okay," he sighed. "Just play it cool."

CHAPTER TWELVE

It was almost four weeks later when Danielle Green, with a little help from a very close friend, managed to get permission to visit Henry Sonntag in Brixton prison. Four weeks in which she had wrestled with herself over whether it was even necessary. Mark had delved deeper into the story and psyche of Herschel Soferman in preparation for the book he was planning to write after the trial. She too had visited Soferman at his home. His sincerity was plain. True, Henry Sonntag's story had also been convincing and moving. Yet for all its coherence, it now seemed full of holes. In retrospect, she felt that a certain coldness had emanated from the man whose cause she had supported. She had half wished that he would decline her request. But he had intimated that he would be pleased to see her.

Thus it was with heavy heart and not a little trepidation that Danielle, a letter of permission from the prison governor in her hand, entered the portals of one of Britain's most depressing institutions. She had done a little research on the place. Built in the early part of the nineteenth century in south-west London, the prison was still a nightmare both for the incarcerated and their guards. Brixton was for ever overcrowded and now housed six hundred prisoners in a space designed for five hundred. But its worst aspect was that it was used extensively to house prisoners on remand. Many an innocent man had spent months cooped up in an environment totally unsuitable for the purpose. English law was predicated on the basic tenet that an accused was presumed innocent until proven guilty. And yet any man awaiting trial in Brixton might assume that the law had conspired to punish him pre-emptively.

"Pretty grim here, isn't it," she said to the burly prison

officer accompanying her to the top-security D-wing of the complex.

"You can say that again, miss. We've got some hard cases here, though. Your man's a Category A."

"What does that mean?"

"Well, whenever he has to be moved he gets an armed escort. Can't be too careful with Category As, you know."

"At seventy-odd I shouldn't think he'd prove very dangerous."

"Ah, but he might have powerful friends who would want to spring him."

Danielle half smiled. Henry Sonntag was probably about the most friendless man in the world right now.

"Anyway," the man went on, "he'll be happy enough in D-wing."

"In what way?"

"He'll have a cell all to himself. He won't have to put up with all the scroungers looking for a touch. He's wealthy, ain't he? Most of the plump chickens prefer to be on their own."

The prison officer led her into a small room with mournful beige walls. In the centre was a grey table, its tubular legs bolted to the floor. She was invited to sit on a regulation plastic seat on the near side of the table.

"I'll be leaving you now, miss. One of my colleagues will stay in attendance during your visit."

"How long have I got, Officer?"

"We usually give you fifteen minutes, miss. But it's not like the other wings. We've got a bit of leeway here."

"Thanks."

The officer nodded and left the room. Almost at the same moment the door at the far end opened and Henry Sonntag, his face as pallid as his grey prison garb, was led in. He gave her a cursory nod and shuffled forward to take his seat opposite her. He looked so different now. Maybe it was the drab clothes. His manner portrayed total dejection. The yellowy-white hair was still perfectly groomed, but the lines on Sonntag's face seemed deeper. The man before her seemed to have aged ten years. He did bear a resemblance to Soferman, but she thought this had been exaggerated somewhat by others.

"Hello, my dear," he smiled weakly. "I'm glad they gave you permission to see me."

"Why?"

"What do you mean?"

Danielle realized she had to control her antagonism. She was not there simply to berate the man. She wanted his explanation. "I mean, we only met once. I'm hardly what you might call a close friend."

"Yes, Danielle, but I told you more than I ever told anyone before."

"That's fine, as long as we can assume that what you told me was the truth."

"It was the truth."

Danielle looked long and hard into the beady brown eyes. "After all that's happened, you can hardly expect me to believe that."

Sonntag swallowed and then stared back at her with a passion born either of self-righteousness or indignation. "Danielle," he said slowly, "I want you to believe me. I swear to you that I did not murder those two men."

"That's a bit hard to swallow considering the evidence."

"Look, there is an explanation for everything."

"I'm sure there is," she said with biting sarcasm.

"Ach ..." He threw up his arms in exasperation, "*Es ist zum Heulen, Verrücktwerden, Aus-der-Haut-Fahren.*"

"I'm sorry, I don't know what you mean."

Sonntag ran his spindly fingers through his hair. "I apologize, Danielle. I said that I feel my head is going to burst. I know how everything must seem to you. It's my lawyer, you see. He says I must not say anything to anyone until the trial."

"Okay, so don't tell me why you were all set to fly to Rio soon after Plant's murder. It was a business trip. Just tell me why your house was so full of Nazi memorabilia."

Sonntag looked up at the high grey ceiling for a few seconds and then stared squarely at his inquisitor. "I collected all those things in order to focus my hate."

"On what?"

"On him."

"On who?"

"On Hans Schreiber."

"But you are Hans Schreiber." There, she had said it.

"Who says I am?"

"You know who. Herschel Soferman."

"Herschel Soferman is dead, my dear."

"Herschel Soferman is not dead. I have met him and you know that he is going to give evidence against you."

"Damn my lawyer. I know Herschel Soferman is dead because ..."

"Because what?"

"Because I AM HERSCHEL SOFERMAN!"

As Danielle sat transfixed by both Sonntag's words and his vehemence, the prison officer moved swiftly to place a restraining hand on his ward's shoulder. "Calm down, Mr Sonntag, or we'll have to terminate this visit."

"It's okay, sir," beseeched the elderly man. "Please, a few minutes more."

"Another minute and you'll have to leave, miss."

"Th-Thank you officer," she stammered, trying hard to regain her composure. "I won't be much longer." She turned back to Sonntag and leaned towards him. "I don't understand," she whispered.

"Herschel Soferman died in Theresienstadt because that's where his spirit died. When I escaped from there I used another name."

"Then who is the man calling himself Herschel Soferman?" Danielle asked disingenuously.

"He, my dear, can only be one man. Hans Schreiber."

Straelen, 9 November 1938

"But, Father, it was a Jew-pig that assassinated our diplomat in Paris," protested Hans Schreiber. "We must take revenge."

Dr Wolfgang Schreiber looked wearily at his son. Resplendent in his SA brownshirt with its swastika armband, the boy was so proud of himself. In fact, Schreiber Senior had never seen him so happy. "I'd rather you didn't mix with that rabble, son," he sighed, knowing that his plea would fall on deaf ears.

"They're not a rabble, Father," Hans protested. "They are only carrying out the express wishes of our glorious Führer. What can be wrong in that?"

"Look, my boy, we live only a few kilometres from the Dutch border. This is not Berlin or Bavaria. In general, people around here are pretty tolerant."

"I am seventeen, Father, and I'm old enough to realize who has been responsible for all the troubles of Germany since the war. It's all the fault of the Jews. Why would all those laws have been introduced if it hadn't been their fault?"

Wolfgang Schreiber was well acquainted with the Nuremberg Laws passed three years earlier. They sought to determine the purity of German blood and were especially harsh on the Jews. He was against the Nazis and their laws, but the whole country seemed to have been whipped into a fervour by Hitler and his henchmen. The youth, especially, had been intoxicated by the uniforms, the banners, the parades.

"Oh, let him go," said Frau Inge Schreiber, entering the kitchen. "Boys will be boys. Anyway, the Jews deserve a lesson, don't they?"

Schreiber Senior swivelled to face his wife. She was truly beautiful: tall, graceful and with the Nordic features so beloved of their nation's leader. She was the perfect country doctor's wife. He was so besotted with her he could forgive her everything, including her politics. The good doctor was just about to reply when a motor vehicle began to hoot urgently outside.

"It's Franz and Helmut and the rest of the boys," exclaimed Hans excitedly. "I'll see you later."

"Take care," Inge Schreiber called after him.

Her husband watched their son dash out of the front door. Dr Wolfgang Schreiber knew he was a weak father. He also knew that the boy had to be protected from himself.

"Don't worry, Mum," Hans called back. "I'm just going to knock a few heads together."

The young man hauled himself aboard the open-top tender. It was adorned with red, white and black swastika flags. "Here, make room for me, boys," he cried. There must have been about fifteen of them crowded onto the back of the small lorry. "*Juden Raus, Juden Raus*," they taunted as the vehicle lurched forward. By the time they were travelling along Kuhstrasse they had broken into the rousing choruses of the "Horst Wessel" song.

There were only four Jewish families in Straelen at the time, and they had the addresses of each. The brownshirts approached the first house just as the streetlights came on. A light drizzle had begun to fall, but it failed to dampen their enthusiasm. "*Juden Raus*," they chanted again, but none of the youths was sufficiently emboldened to leave the vehicle. Instead, they satisfied themselves with throwing bricks through windows.

It was only when they had reached the home of the Mendels on the aptly renamed Adolf Hitlerstrasse that the mood turned more nasty. Both Mendel brothers, Oskar and Eduard, happened to be tinkering with their car.

"Come on, let's get them," screamed Hans. "Let's teach these Jew bastards a lesson."

The brownshirts leapt from the tender before the brothers could haul themselves out from under their car. Although both in their early thirties and no weaklings, the two Jews were no match for their attackers, who were armed with truncheons and sticks. They were pummelled into a bloody pulp.

After a few minutes, the fascists tired of their sport. "Let's drive to Krefeld," suggested one. "There's a synagogue there. We can make a bonfire."

It was more than three hours later when Hans Schreiber arrived home. His face was blackened by soot and his uniform covered in grime and bloodstains. Tired but elated, he told his parents excitedly about the night's events, revelling in every detail.

"There's one other thing, Father," he said finally.

Wolfgang Schreiber raised his eyebrows in abject resignation. What else could there be to wreck his day?

"As soon as I'm eighteen, I'm going to enlist in the SS."

The good doctor looked into his son's stern eyes. He knew then that nothing would prevent Hans from doing whatever he wished. He knew that he would have to compromise his own principles in order to protect his son; and that, in order to do so, he too would have to join that loathsome organization.

London

Mark Edwards was slipping into the peaceful oblivion that always followed the tenderest of lovemaking. He was thankful to have had a diversion from the endless discussions they had

had about Henry Sonntag and Herschel Soferman. He had regarded Sonntag's revelation as almost inevitable given the untenable situation the man now found himself in. Soferman too had expressed little surprise. "What did you expect?" the old man had shrugged. Edwards had debated with Danielle, pointing out that the evidence against Sonntag was far too weighty to be undermined by what most people would regard as a cheap ploy.

He shifted position once again, feeling subconsciously for the warmth of her body. The fact that flesh did not meet flesh would not necessarily have woken him. But there was a sound. A sobbing sound. Someone, somewhere was crying. He awoke with a start and turned towards her. She was sitting up, her bloodshot eyes staring straight ahead. Tears were streaming down her delicate pale cheeks.

"What is it, darling?" he said with mounting concern. He moved across the bed and put his right arm around her, cradling her head to his chest. He stroked the layers of satin around her temple. "Please, Dani, tell me," he said soothingly. "Don't keep it inside."

"I can't help it, Mark," she sniffed. "I was suddenly overcome."

"By what?"

"Please don't think I'm being silly."

"Of course I won't, Dani. I love you."

"I am crying for my people." She sniffed again. "I'm crying for all those millions who died. For all those children. For all the children who were never born because of men like Hans Schreiber. Oh, darling," she sobbed bitterly, "I'm so confused. I know you don't believe Sonntag's claims. When he said Soferman was really Schreiber, my whole world turned upside down. I no longer know what to believe."

"It's up to the lawyers now, Dani," said Edwards, kissing her delicately on the cheek and on the eyelid, savouring the saltiness of her tears. A lump formed in his throat. It was only now that he realized how much the strain of these extraordinary events had taken its toll of her emotions. She had always played hard when it came to dealing with people like Sonntag, Soferman, even Dieter Müller. Sure, she had supported the financier and she was bound to feel betrayed. Yet she had managed to portray a kind of controlled aloofness throughout. After his own interviews with Soferman, he truly believed he was beginning to understand what it meant to be a Jew.

"Maybe we could take a holiday together," he counselled. "We've both got some weeks owing."

"Yes, Mark," she replied, wiping her eyes. "There are two places I want so much to visit." She hesitated, unsure of his reaction. "I want to visit Prague, to see Theresienstadt for myself. I also want to visit a place I should already have been to. Jerusalem."

Edwards was momentarily nonplussed. These were the very places he thought she would have wanted to avoid. "Are you sure?" he asked gingerly.

"I'm sure. I know what you're thinking, but in a way I think it will help me exorcize this thing. This whole affair has made me feel that I ought to be more of a Jew; that I ought to try to understand more about what my people have suffered. I don't think I can get any closer if I don't visit Theresienstadt and Yad Vashem."

"That's the memorial in Jerusalem, isn't it?"

"Yes."

"When shall we go?"

Danielle reached up and kissed him gently on the lips. "I can go alone if you don't feel like coming."

"I go where you go, Dani."

"I love you," she said simply.

"Tell me that again on the Temple Mount."

CHAPTER THIRTEEN

It was almost four months later when Edwards and Danielle finally got around to booking their holiday. Pressure of work and the chief crime reporter's continuing fascination with Herschel Soferman conspired to prevent swifter action. Webb, fully satisfied that he had caught the right man, had confided to the reporter that he had released only part of the contents of the killer's note to the press. It had also apparently contained the cryptic reference "C-street 33". Sonntag, unsurprisingly, had told the policeman that this meant nothing to him. Soferman too had expressed ignorance. In Edwards' mind it represented only a minor irritant. Dani, unfortunately, did not get another chance to quiz Sonntag. Sir John Tilson, his barrister, had forbidden the accused to be visited by anyone unless first vetted by himself. Needless to say, journalists had been bottom of the lawyer's list of priorities.

Dieter Müller, meanwhile, had become like a friend of the family. Danielle admitted having been won over by his sincerity even if she did not agree with some of his views. The only black cloud had been the sudden demise of Jim Pottage. Almost fittingly it had been on 1 April. Booze and gluttony had conspired to make the inevitable heart attack massive. The only solace was that Gentleman Jim had gone the way he would have wished, with a pint in his hand at the Elephant. Although Pottage had been somewhat irreligious, his friends had decided to hold a small memorial service in the journalists" church of St Bride's in Fleet Street. Edwards was surprised by the number of coppers who had turned up. It was testimony to the esteem in which Pottage had been held by London's finest.

The sudden death of the jovial West Countryman had been

the only blot on a period in which the mutual regard the two journalists had for one another had deepened and matured. Sleeping together had been superseded by living together. The experiment was clearly working, although neither of them had broached the question of marriage.

"That's it, then," beamed Edwards, slamming down the phone in his lounge. "It's springtime in Prague ..."

"And springtime in the Holy Land," Danielle called from the kitchen.

"It's going to be a hectic couple of weeks," he said, joining her.

"I know Prague's a beautiful city and all that, Mark, but I'm glad we'll be spending most of the time in Israel. I'm glad we'll be there for Holocaust Memorial Day. Then we can let our hair down a few days later during the Independence Day celebrations."

"Sounds great to me," he enthused, coming up behind her. Placing his arms around her midriff, he nestled his face into the pit between her neck and shoulder. "There's just one snag."

"What's that?"

"What happens if we get a trial date for then?"

Danielle stopped chopping the salad and turned towards him. "That's the only thing that will put a spanner in the works." Her eyes then narrowed in determination. "Otherwise, neither my editor nor your bloody news editor is going to upset our plans. Not even if they get on bended knee."

"That'll be the day," he laughed, "Nick Logan pleading with me. Do me a favour."

"Mark," she laughed. "I do believe you're picking up Jewish expressions."

"Not surprising, is it, my little girl. My *medeleh*."

"It's pronounced *maideleh*."

"Well, you don't expect me to learn Yiddish overnight," he said with mock hurt.

211

"What do you mean, overnight?" she retorted, pecking him on the tip of his nose. "We've been going together long enough."

"It's funny you should say that, but ..."

At that moment the mobile phone rang.

"There you go," he said. "Talk of the devil. That's bound to be Logan." He retrieved the mobile from the dining-room table. "No, Nick, I'm not available tonight, I ..."

"Hello," came an unfamiliar voice, "who is that? I want to speak to Mark Edwards, please."

"Edwards speaking."

"Mr Edwards, good evening. You don't know me. My name is Sam Cohen. I'm the chairman of Ilford Synagogue. I must see you urgently."

"Look, I ..."

"It's about Henry Sonntag, Mr Edwards."

"What about him?"

"I believe he's innocent."

"Well, you must be the only person who does, Mr Cohen."

"Please, Mr Edwards. I know you are very closely connected with this case. I would like to meet you. You know Luigi's Restaurant?"

"In Beehive Lane?"

"Yes, opposite the synagogue. Can you meet me there in an hour?"

"This is all a bit rushed, isn't it, Mr Cohen?"

"Please, Mr Edwards. Money is no object."

"All right, in an hour." The reporter switched off his mobile, asking himself what money had to do with it.

"What was all that about?" Danielle called out.

"Forget about making supper," he said. "I'm inviting you to Luigi's. Some guy wants to meet me there to discuss Henry Sonntag. He believes the man's innocent and said something about money being no object. I don't know what he meant, but

I don't want to be compromised in any way. Put your glad rags on."

This time the BT phone rang.

"Oh, no. Here we go again. The bane of my life ... Hello, Edwards."

"Hi, Mark. It's Bob."

"Okay, mate, no need to gloat. My putting'll be much better next time."

"Will you forget about golf for just one minute. I've got a bit of news for you."

"Fire away."

"Apparently the War Crimes Unit have come up with another witness. Some Polish priest claims he was tortured by Schreiber. The Crown Prosecution Service has been informed."

"Thanks, Bob. Any word on when the case might be?"

"Not yet, mate. But the way things are going I shouldn't be surprised if it'll be soon."

"As long as it doesn't start between the last week in April and the first week in May."

"Why's that?"

"The good lady and myself are taking off on a long overdue holiday."

"A pre-honeymoon honeymoon, eh?"

"From your mouth to God's ears. See you, mate."

Edwards gazed at the dead phone in his hand. Dammit, he really did want to marry the girl. He had almost chosen the wrong time to propose a few moments earlier. Timing. It was all down to timing.

"Webb, I presume," Danielle smiled.

"Right."

"Well, what has he got to say for himself?"

"Oh, apparently the prosecution have got another witness. A Polish priest who remembers Schreiber from the war."

"The more the merrier." She now wanted, perhaps needed, the full weight of the law to be brought to bear on Henry Sonntag.

Thus it was with a degree of cynicism that the two journalists entered Luigi's, a three-minute drive from the flat. It was midweek and relatively early. There was only one customer: a squat, balding man in his early fifties.

"Ah, Mr Edwards," the man said, rising. "I recognize you from your photograph. Here, I have one of your by-lined stories." Cohen produced a yellowing copy of the edition that had carried the story of Plant's murder. He held out his hand, at the same time casting a quizzical look in the direction of Danielle.

"May I introduce you to my colleague, Danielle Green," said Edwards, shaking the man's outstretched hand. "We've been working on this story together."

"Please, be my guests, sit down," Cohen gestured. "I must say, young lady, your face looks extremely familiar. Haven't I seen you in *shul*?"

"Only on Rosh Hashanah. I'm Stanley Green's daughter."

"Ah, Stanley," enthused the older man. "Know him well."

"You will know then that his brother-in-law was Joe Hyams."

"Of course, of course. On your mother's side. I'm very sorry, Miss Green. It's been a terrible business. The whole community is still in shock."

"Can I help you, Signor Cohen," the waiter asked.

"Please, order what you like, you two. I can recommend the lasagne."

"We've just eaten, thanks, Mr Cohen," Edwards lied, "but a lager will do nicely, thanks."

"Diet Coke," said Danielle, glancing up at the waiter.

"I'll have another Pernod, please, Silvio," said Cohen.

"*Prego,*" said the waiter, a tinge of disappointment in his voice. These were recessionary times.

After the waiter had sidled away, Edwards turned to his host. "How can I help you, Mr Cohen?"

"Call me Sam. Everyone does."

"What's your interest in Henry Sonntag, Sam?"

"Look, first of all he was a member of our congregation. Okay, he didn't attend services that often. But when he did, Mark – may I call you Mark? – when he did, it was like royalty arriving." Cohen could see his two guests were puzzled. "You see, the majority of our members are cab drivers and minor businessmen. But we do have a few who struck oil and moved out to Chigwell. They still retain an affection for our *shul*. We're orthodox, you know, not reform. Anyway, these few prime movers, or *gunser machers*, as we call them, had a lot to be thankful to Henry Sonntag for. He made them even richer."

"I take it you're one of the *machers*," Danielle interrupted baldly.

"Quite so," said Cohen, unruffled. "I don't like the term myself, but I suppose if I am one, I ought to admit to it." He shrugged his shoulders again in a gesture of resignation.

Edwards was warming to his host. The man had none of the pretensions of new money. "I think I can guess what you're trying to say, Sam. With Sonntag out of the way, some people are not going to coin it like they used to."

Cohen cleared his throat nervously. "Look, all that's true, Mark. But my friends and I also happen to believe that Henry Sonntag's innocent."

"If you'll pardon the expression, Sam," said Edwards, "I think you're pissing in the wind."

"I know," Cohen sighed. "But somehow or other my friends and I wanted to make an effort. If we could prove Henry wasn't this Schreiber monster, then the case against him might collapse."

215

"The case against him is still pretty conclusive, though, even if he isn't Schreiber," said Edwards.

"Look, firstly, Jews don't kill other Jews. And even if one did, would he do it in this manner? It just doesn't make sense. Anybody in their right mind would smell a rat. No, it all rests on whether Henry is really Schreiber."

"I still don't understand how Mark can help you," said Danielle, aware that Cohen was repeating the sentiments she had expressed months ago.

"Okay, I'll come to the point. Frankly, we've been stitched up. As soon as Henry was arrested, we contacted a private investigator. He came recommended, but all the mumser has succeeded in doing is ripping us off. It's cost us thousands and he hasn't come up with anything worthwhile. Frankly, I think he made up all the rubbish he's been feeding us."

"Like what?" asked Edwards.

"Like Hans Schreiber died on the Russian Front in 1944."

"Well?" asked Danielle.

"Well, it's one thing saying something like that and another proving it. We need proof. Anyway, this investigator chap said he had found a man who could provide the evidence, but that the man wanted ten thousand dollars. Like schmuks, we paid up."

"Where's the investigator now?" asked Danielle.

"In hell, I hope. He's disappeared. I tried ringing his office, but they said he'd moved and hadn't left a forwarding address."

"That's unfortunate, Sam," said Edwards, "but where do I come in?"

"You're chief crime reporter on the *Standard*. If you don't know a reliable private investigator, then who does?"

"Don't you think it's a bit late for that?" asked Danielle. "The trial may start very soon."

"Look, I said money was no object, and I meant it. Only

we've got to have someone reliable." Cohen looked beseechingly at Edwards.

The reporter tinkered with his beer glass for a few seconds. "Sam," he said, "I think you'll be wasting your money, but I know a good man. You need someone who speaks German fluently. I do, but I'm not a private eye. Let me speak to this guy. He may be willing to take the case on. Give me your phone number and I'll contact you within the next few days."

"Thanks, Mark. I really appreciate it. Now let me order some food. Even if you've already eaten, you can still find some room for a little pasta, no?" He turned to Danielle. "Don't tell the *shul* elders," he winked. "They'd kill me if they knew I was eating *treyfe*."

"Your secret is safe with me, Sam," she smiled. "But if you're going to be a naughty boy and eat non-kosher, you shouldn't do it on the doorstep of your synagogue."

"Are you kidding?" beamed Cohen. "And miss out on the best lasagne in town?"

A week elapsed before Mark Edwards managed to make contact with Bill Brown. The private eye had been involved in infidelity surveillance, the least favourite of his occupational pursuits.

"It beats me why the buggers bother, Mark," said the detective, welcoming the reporter to his office off the Strand. "I mean, they usually end up paying me a lot of money to confirm what they already know. There's no stigma attached to divorce nowadays. Anyway, enough of my problems. How can I help you, old buddy?"

Edwards smiled. Brown was a character, a gumshoe from the old school. Creeping towards his fifties, he was about the best private eye around. His work was thorough and methodical, an attribute no doubt passed on by his late father, an ex-German prisoner of war named Ludwig Braun, a Dornier navigator whose plane had been shot down during a night raid on London. After the war, Braun had decided to stay in England after meeting and marrying a local girl. He had changed his name to Brown shortly before his eldest son William was born in 1947. Brown Senior had insisted on speaking mainly German to his three children. He even taught them to read and write fluently. He had forecast the *Wirtschaftswunder* and that new business opportunities would open up for anybody who was bilingual. Ludwig had been more than a little disappointed when Bill had joined the local constabulary in their home town of Bury St Edmunds in Suffolk. He had progressed to detective and fifteen years ago had branched out on his own. "At least I'm in business for myself," he had told his father. Ludwig had died in 1991 still unable to fathom a son who dealt in other people's dirty washing and had never married to provide him with grandchildren.

"Bill," the reporter began, "you must have heard about the Henry Sonntag case."

"Sure. Guilty as hell, so my sources tell me."

"Maybe. But there's a guy with a lot of money who wants you to prove that this Sonntag fellow is not the Nazi war criminal Hans Schreiber."

Brown laughed. "I usually get paid to prove the opposite."

"What do you mean?"

"Well, I can't go into detail, but, as you know, there are still a few suspected war criminals at large in the UK. I've been employed to keep a watching brief on some of them."

"Who by?"

"Mark, you should know better than that."

"Sorry, mate. But on this one you'll have the guy's full permission to keep me completely informed on every development. I'm going to write a book on this whole affair once it's finally over. His name's Sam Cohen and here's his phone number."

"You know what this means, don't you?" said Brown, rising and pouring out two cupfuls of cold liquid from a bottled water dispenser. "It means I'll have to leave everything else and travel to Germany. I'm talking big bucks here."

"As I said, Bill, money's no object to this guy."

"Excellent!" Brown rubbed his hands. "I fancy a trip back to the _Heimat_."

"Come on, you're as British as they come."

"Yeah, but I still have an affection for my old man's birthplace. It's a little village about fifty miles south of Berlin. Nice place. I'll try and visit it again while I'm there. Especially as it's an all-expenses-paid trip."

Edwards smiled. He could not help thinking how much Brown reminded him of good old Jim Pottage. They both had country accents, although the investigator's East Anglian twang was less pronounced. The man before him was also much slimmer, younger and more fit than Pottage had been. However, both men had a predilection for bow-ties.

"Look, Bill, my girlfriend and I are going on holiday next week. Here, I've written down the dates. If anything interesting happens before then, keep me informed. You've got my address and my phone numbers."

"What if something crops up while you're away?"

"Just post the info to my home. Danielle and I don't want to be disturbed. We really need this break."

"Hmm, Danielle ..." Brown beamed. "What's she like?"

"You lay off her, you old dog. You confirmed bachelors are all the same."

"Ah well," the detective sighed, "I suppose I'll have to settle for the professional fräuleins while I'm away. All the fun and none of the responsibility."

"If you can tear yourself away from them for a while, where do you think you'll start?"

"Berlin Documentation Centre, I suppose. That's where they keep all the SS records."

"Oh, there's just one other thing," said the reporter. "There's a good friend of mine, a guy named Dieter Müller. He's genned up on this business even more than me. He's a professor over here researching a thesis on the Holocaust. Here's his number. *Auf ihn ist Verlass*."

"Totally?"

"Yes, you can rely on Müller totally."

Münster, January 1940

"Send in the next one, please, Nurse."

Dr Wolfgang Schreiber admired the hour-glass figure of his assistant as she left the room to collect the next raw recruit for induction into the SS. The woman was nothing if not efficient. Prussian to the core.

The good doctor had achieved the dubious distinction of being the man responsible for making sure that only the finest specimens of young German manhood joined Adolf Hitler's élite. Other doctors had regarded this task as mundane and boring, having very little to do with medicine and much to do with paperwork. But at forty-one years of age, the position represented to Dr Wolfgang Schreiber the pinnacle of his achievement.

Indeed, that he was induction medical officer at the SS base in Westphalia's historic capital was by no means fortuitous. The good doctor had inveigled his way into the job, thankful that the competition was weak and disorganized. All things considered, his need had been greater than theirs.

And now the physician was about to reach the climax of his

ambition. The file in front of him bore a familiar name. Even the nurse had commented that the new recruit was his namesake. Schreiber was a common name in Bavaria, though less so in North Rhein-Westphalia. However, unknown to his nurse, and anyone else for that matter, this recruit was far closer to Wolfgang Schreiber than a mere namesake. This recruit was his son.

Hans Schreiber entered the room shivering, naked apart from a pair of black silky shorts. Despite the cold, he stood smartly to attention. They had rehearsed the scene over and over.

"Name?!" barked Schreiber Senior.

"Schreiber, Hans, Herr Doktor."

The physician ticked the appropriate box. "Age?!"

"Eighteen, Herr Doktor."

They then went through the ritual of ascertaining date of birth, address, occupation, medical history and other salient facts which were already on the sheet in front of the doctor but needed to be tallied with the response of each recruit.

Wolfgang Schreiber then used his stethoscope to ensure that Hitler's finest suffered from no heart or chest ailment. The recruit before him was A1. Nevertheless, the good doctor downgraded the boy's profile and wrote "Asthmatic. Non-combat duties advised." The boy had desperately wanted a combat division, and it had taken all his powers of persuasion to make clear that this would not have been in his best interests because of a certain physical impediment. Damned Hitler had made such a big thing about it. God knew, it would be hard enough for the boy to hide his manhood. At least being in a non-combat unit might give him half a chance. With any luck he might even be stationed close to home with a clerk's job.

"Oh, Nurse?"

"*Jawohl*, Herr Doktor."

"Be kind enough to bring me some papers I left on the table in my office. They're in a red folder. Don't worry, I'll finish with this one."

"*Jawohl*, Herr Doktor," repeated the nurse, and wheeled away in disappointment. If the truth be known, she hated missing any short-arm inspections and the tattooing. For she despised men and to see them embarrassed and in pain gave her no little pleasure.

"Give it two minutes, Hans, and then get out of here."

"But, Father, what about the tattoo?"

"Forget the tattoo. Where you'll be posted they'll never need to know your blood group."

"But ..."

"Trust me, Hans."

Schreiber Junior looked hard into his father's blue eyes. He was about to protest further, but the memory of an incident in a school shower stilled his tongue.

"Thank you, Father," said the boy dully.

"God bless and keep you, my son. Write as often as you can."

"I will, Father."

And with that, Hans and Wolfgang Schreiber parted company.

The good doctor was not to know that the next time he would see his son would be at the end of the most devastating war in history, and that their meeting would prove cathartic for both of them.

222

CHAPTER FOURTEEN

This is the way to Theresienstadt
which thousands have wearily walked.
Each one of the thousands has suffered
the same injustice, from the first to the last.
They marched along, with their heads to the ground,
the Star of David pinned to their breasts,
their tired feet sore and covered with dust,
their tortured souls torn with pain and unrest.
Harassed by orders, their wound-stricken hands
carried their heavy burdens.
O endless road in the summer heat
that burned in thirsty throats.

This is the road to Theresienstadt,
drenched with the blood of our hearts,
where greybeards, dying from agony,
dropped down to the stony path.
It is paved with the horrors and misery
where rivers of tears have shed
by children crying and women weeping
in utter helplessness and dread.
Here old men stumbled with empty looks
and followed meekly the flock.
So many of them will never go back
in the hope of a merciful grave.
This, too, is the road on which hurriedly rolled
the unceasing trucks that carried away
the aching loads of those destined to die.

This is the road to Theresienstadt,
plastered with suffering and pain.
And he who has seen it once in his life
will never forget it again.

Danielle read and re-read the haunting lines of Ilse Weber's poem. They may have lost something in translation, but the words were still strong enough to convey the utter hopelessness of those who had travelled the road to Theresienstadt.

She closed the guidebook and gripped Mark's arm tightly as they continued their tour of the main fortress. It was all so different from the capital city in which they had spent an idyllic weekend. Herschel Soferman had been right. Prague was indeed a magic city, a jewel in the crown of Europe. The Jewish Quarter, especially, had been fascinating, with its synagogues and the overcrowded cemetery where the gravestones leaned higgledy-piggledy in all directions. Hitler had spared the Quarter in order that it could serve as a memorial to the extinction of the Jews. Well, she thought, here was one Jew who was alive to testify to his failure. She and Edwards had alighted from their bus from Prague at the Florenc terminal which was directly outside the Small Fortress, the primary purpose of their visit. But she had insisted they save the venue of Hans Schreiber's nefarious deeds until last.

They listened intently to an English-speaking guide as he described the history of Terezin and how, shortly after Heydrich came to power in Prague in September 1941, the old fortified town had been turned into a transit ghetto, primarily for Jews from Bohemia and Moravia.

"About seventy-six thousand Czech Jews were penned together in accommodation fit only for seven thousand," the guide continued. "In the course of time, forty-two thousand prisoners from Germany, more than fifteen thousand from Austria, a thousand from Hungary, nearly five thousand from Holland and five hundred from Denmark were added. Even though Terezin was only a transit station on the way to the terrible extermination camps of the East, more than thirty-three thousand prisoners died here from maltreatment and disease, nearly a quarter of all people sent here. Out of that number, more than fifteen thousand died from exhaustion and starvation."

"Come on, Mark, I've had enough." The sheer numbers were depressing.

She led him out of the Ghetto Museum and back across the river Ohre. Fortunately, it had turned into a fine spring day. It had been raining when they had left Prague two hours earlier. The sixty-kilometre journey north had taken an hour, and during that time the heavy clouds had begun to disperse.

They approached the ochre walls of the Small Fortress. With each step Danielle felt she was retracing the path of Herschel Soferman. She could not handle the guide's statistics of Jews dying in their thousands. It was much easier to comprehend the agony of one man. The agony of a man she had met. The agony that that man would shortly re-live in an English court of law.

"Are you thinking what I'm thinking?" Edwards asked.

"Probably," she sighed. "It's hard not to think of Herschel Soferman in this place."

"Look!" he exclaimed, pointing to the words daubed across the entrance to their left. "*Arbeit Macht Frei.*"

"The great calumny," she said. "There aren't many Jews who don't shudder at those words. It's on all the gates to the death camps. 'Work Brings Freedom.'"

"People believed it when they went in."

"Yes," she sighed. "The Germans were such masters of

deception, although I suppose there was an element of self-deception on the part of my people. I mean, who would believe that human beings could be capable of such atrocities?"

They walked through the main arch and turned into a building that housed the washrooms. They were in exemplary condition, just as they were when they were built for the Red Cross inspectors invited to witness the model village the Nazis had constructed for the Jews.

They also visited the main exhibition which was housed in the smart eighteenth-century mansion set in the prison gardens. The building was used to house the camp kommandant, his family and fellow SS officers. One of them would have been Hans Schreiber.

"I want to be outside, Mark," she pleaded. "I want to breathe fresh air." Edwards led her back into the main courtyard, and it was there that she noticed the far wall of the compound.

"Look," she said. "That wall looks a bit odd."

As they neared it, the couple could see that the wall was full of holes of varying sizes. It was clear that this was where men had been lined up and shot. She moved her fingers in and around the crevices. How different this wall was to the one they would soon be visiting. One was a monument to man's perfidy and the other to his piety. Danielle shivered as she removed her fingers from the bullet-holes. "Hug me, Mark," she gasped. "Hug me."

Four hundred miles due north-west from Prague, as the crow flies, Bill Brown was gunning his hired red Porsche 911 towards the sleepy North Rhine town of Straelen. He counselled himself that his benefactor had urged repeatedly that money was no obstacle, and there were few cars more expensive to hire than this German mean machine. He had hired it for a month, but was now thinking, with some regret, that he might not need to see out the full term.

He had always wanted to thrash a Porsche along the best motorways in the world with their unrestricted speed limits. That was the reason why he had forgone plane or train and settled for the hundreds of miles of *Autobahnen* from Berlin. He had decided to travel at night to take advantage of the light traffic, stopping a few times to take well-earned refreshment. Driving at a steady one hundred and fifty miles an hour for long stretches was more exhausting than he would have believed. He thought he knew now what the drivers at Le Mans went through. God, but it was so exhilarating.

The private investigator also had the feeling that he was on to something after two weeks of concerted effort. The Berlin Centre, run by the United States government, had provided some useful information. According to its director, others had also been showing great interest in the SS man. The director had not elaborated, but Brown guessed it must have been Scotland Yard's War Crimes Unit. Nevertheless, the private eye had good reason to believe that they had simply requested files on all the Hans Schreibers in the SS. There were only three officers listed and only one had tallied with what he knew about the case. He was sure, however, that the police had certainly not trodden the same path as himself. No one had done that. He had a gut feeling that he was on the verge of a breakthrough.

The only minus so far had been an abortive interview with a man purporting to have been a member of Odessa. Refusing to part with any money, Brown had been warned by the man that he was playing with fire. Before walking out in a huff, the man had intimated that something "serious" might happen should the investigator take matters further. Brown had originally dismissed the man as a crank. Now he was not so sure.

The cold light of dawn was just beginning to dispel the darkness as Brown neared the outskirts of his destination. A light drizzle had begun to fall. He opened his window a little to let in the fresh country air. It reeked of *Heimat*. How he wished his father could have savoured this moment. The private detective dropped a gear as he neared a crossroads. His attention was caught suddenly by a flash of yellow by the roadside. He looked behind him. It was just what he needed. He drew to a halt. He should have posted the stuff in Berlin but had never got round to it. He looked down at the white A4-sized envelope on the passenger seat. Lying on top of it was his favourite bow-tie, the crimson one with white spots. He might as well make himself look respectable even this early in the morning. He got out of the Porsche and walked back along the road, inhaling deeply the sweet nectar of the dawn. He crossed the road and shoved the envelope into the postbox. By tomorrow he hoped to have more to satisfy those who wished to know more about Obersturmführer Hans Schreiber.

In the distance another car was travelling at high speed. If the vehicle had been using headlights, then Bill Brown might have spotted it while checking in his internal mirror that his bow-tie was in place. However, he was not to know that the car had been stolen, that its lights had been extinguished deliberately, or that its gathering momentum was primed to ensure his demise.

As Bill Brown crossed the road to return to his vehicle, the only thing not broken by the force of the impact was the Velcro strap securing his favourite bow-tie. The detective was also spared the indignity of knowing that his killer had then removed all means of identification from his broken and bloody person and had even had the audacity to drive away from the scene in the hired red Porsche.

In another land, a people whose very nationhood had been gained as a direct result of the shame of Germany went about their business unaware of the hit-and-run death there of one William Franz Brown.

Should the German police have had the slightest inkling that the victim was a British private detective involved in the Sonntag case, the news would have naturally made headlines in Israel, headlines that might have alerted two of the many tourists enjoying its indisputable attractions.

But for Mark Edwards and Danielle Green, the tribulations of the case had become but a distant memory as they frolicked in the waters of the Mediterranean, relaxed in the spas of ancient Tiberias, and enjoyed the myriad antiquities of Galilee.

For Danielle, Israel was everything she had dreamed it would be. An old-new land and an old-new people so vibrant that every waking minute was filled with an unsurpassed kaleidoscope of experiences. Edwards, too, had expressed his awe at the achievements of a state that had not yet celebrated its fiftieth birthday.

"They're a brash lot," he told Danielle as they boarded the bus to Jerusalem at Tel Aviv's bustling central bus station, "but who can blame them? After five wars, it's a bloody miracle they're here at all."

"We're supposed to be a stiff-necked people, darling."

"Don't I know it."

The air-conditioned bus was full with the usual collection of faces from every conceivable part of the world. Fine-featured blacks from Ethiopia, red-bearded Hassidim, olive-skinned Yemenites, and the ubiquitous soldiers, accompanied by their M-16 Armalite and Galil rifles. Like all tourists, Mark and Danielle had been alarmed at first by the weapons, but then grew accustomed to the sight. In fact, it gave them a sense of security.

"Well, here we go," said Edwards as the bus pulled away, "we're off to the Holy of Holies."

"I feel a bit strange," said Danielle. "I'm thrilled but apprehensive."

"Why?"

"I'm worried about how I'll react at Yad Vashem."

"We can just visit the Wall, if you like."

Danielle sighed. Both were shrines to Jewish suffering, but she knew that the Holocaust Memorial was more of a magnet to her than the Western Wall. It might have been different if she had not become so embroiled in the Sonntag case.

The couple did not converse much as the bus wound its way up the foothills, leaving behind the drab and sandy central plain and entering another world, a world of pine trees and piety, of amity and light. Above all, it was the light that impressed them. Brilliant in its intensity, it reflected off the rocky landscape and the famous Jerusalem stone of the capital's buildings.

The extraordinary scenery and the groan of the vehicle as it laboured towards the pinnacle of the City of Peace conspired to prevent them from revealing the thoughts that were dominating their minds. Both realized inwardly that there could be but one logical conclusion to their partnership, and yet they had fought shy of raising the issue of marriage. Their path had been smoothed by the fact that Danielle's parents had accepted Edwards fully and unconditionally. And yet the gentile knew that there would always be a barrier, even if it was only gossamer-thin. Danielle, for her part, believed wholly that each person should be accepted on his or her merits, and yet the gremlin that was religion, tradition and culture created a nagging doubt.

"A shekel for your thoughts," he said suddenly.

Before she had time to answer, the bus swerved into the

bustling central bus station. An extraordinary thing happened as they alighted. Air-raid sirens began wailing, not to warn of impending attack but as a lamentation for the millions who had perished. Traffic ground to a halt, the drivers leaving their vehicles to stand to attention alongside pedestrians. To Edwards and Danielle it seemed the whole world had come to a halt. They were to experience the same thing on Remembrance Day for Israel's war dead, the day before pent-up emotions exploded in the riotous Independence Day celebrations.

They took a taxi to the Holocaust Memorial, set in a garden like so many other edifices dedicated to the anguish of Man. Wrapped up in their own emotions, they entered the Tent of Remembrance, there to encounter the famous adjoining squares of basalt bearing the names of twenty-two death camps in Hebrew and English. The flame of remembrance seemed to flicker and wane for a moment, as if its memories were too painful to bear. The place was all numbers, thought Edwards. Six million. How could anyone come to terms with the magnitude of such a crime? Even more moving was the Room of Names, where two million epitaphs bore silent testimony to those who had perished. They learned that the names of the remaining four million must go unrecorded because the communities from which they came had been expunged totally from the earth.

Holding hands, they walked from one silent representation of hell to another. Behind the sixty-five-foot-tall Pillar of Heroism stood the inaptly named Garden of Children. It was, in fact, an artificial cave. Entering the sudden blackness from the brilliance of the noon sun, they were forced to grip the handrail while passing before a panoply of thousands of pinpricks of light. More numbers, thought Edwards. One and a half million children murdered. It was a planetarium of evil. Recorded voices began calling out the names of the dead children, sending a chill through him. He was not yet a parent, yet he felt the same sense of loss.

Danielle had hardly spoken by the time they had finished their tour of Yad Vashem and were weaving their way through the *shuk* leading to the Western Wall. She waved aside the pleas of the Arab vendors and hurried down the steps of the Via Dolorosa. It was only when they had entered the huge open area leading to the Wall that she began to open up.

"I know you've been trying to get me to talk about it, Mark," she said, turning to face him at the entrance to the praying area. "I just don't feel like it. I was very moved, but Theresienstadt was more immediate. It had a greater impact."

"You don't have to say any more, darling. I felt the same."

"Look, it's packed today," she exclaimed, pointing to the hundreds of people, including many Hassidim, swaying backwards and forwards from the waist in pious fervour.

"What are they doing?" he asked.

"They're *dovening*. You remember. The *shiva*."

"Oh, yes."

"Anyway, we've got to separate now. Take a paper *kippa* from that man and put it on your head. You've got your pen and piece of paper, haven't you?"

Edwards watched her wrap a silk scarf over her head and then turn away to walk elegantly towards the women's section. Aware of the religious edict, she had chosen a plain blue cotton dress which covered her shoulders and upper arms. God, she was beautiful, he thought.

The gentile donned the black paper skull-cap and headed towards the milling throng. He tried hard to be the polite Englishman, but in the end had to push and shove to reach the Wall. His first instinct was to touch the sacred stones. He was surprised how cool they were, and how ordinary they looked. And yet he knew that if the stones could speak, they would relate the history of mankind, its good and its evil. In a way, the Wall was alive with words. In seemingly every crevice within hand's reach were little folded pieces of paper bearing messages of peace and hope.

Edwards withdrew the small scrap of paper from his pocket and began scribbling. He then folded it tightly, kissed it and reached to his right towards a crevice that seemed less crowded than most. He rammed the wad into it with his thumb. He then did something that he had not planned. He leaned against the stone nearest to him and kissed it. In that one moment he felt his whole body tingle. It was as if a certain kind of piety had been born within him, a strange feeling of belonging.

Danielle was already waiting for him by the time he reached the main fence about fifty yards from the Wall. "Well," she said expectantly, "wasn't it incredibly moving?"

"Yes," he said quietly, "it was the most moving moment for me so far."

"I know I shouldn't ask, but what did you write in your note?" Her emerald eyes danced with the desire to know.

Edwards took a deep breath. It was now or never. This had to be the moment and this had to be the place. He took hold of her slender hands and gripped them nervously. "I begged God to grant peace on all Israel and protect His daughter, Danielle, and ..."

"Yes?" she pleaded earnestly.

"That He make her my wife."

She stared at him, her eyes suddenly misty. Then they began to glisten as the tears welled. "Oh, darling." She hugged him. "Oh, darling, I love you. I will be proud to be your wife."

They were both suddenly aware that this was the wrong place to show such overt affection. He held her gently at arm's length. "Danielle, there's something else."

She looked at him quizzically. What else could there be?

"I've been thinking about this a lot. I want to convert."

"Oh, Mark, you don't have to. Really. Our children will be Jewish anyway because it runs through the mother's side."

"I want to, Dani," he said passionately. "I want to as much as I want you."

"It's a tough procedure," she cautioned. "The rabbis will make sure you end up being more Jew than Jew before they'll accept you."

"I don't care how hard it will be. I want to join the club." He put his hand quickly to his lips. "Perhaps I shouldn't have said that."

Danielle laughed. "I suppose it is a kind of club, only don't tell the rabbis that." She hugged him again. The last seeds of doubt had been dispelled. She was not marrying out. He was marrying in.

Events began to move swiftly as soon as the lovers, tanned and happy, returned to London. The English capital was grey, chilly and morose compared with the warmth and vitality that had erupted the previous day in Israel. Tel Aviv had throbbed with excitement as its citizens flooded the streets for the Independence Day celebrations. Mark and Danielle had thrilled to the fireworks display and folk dancing in the huge City Hall square. They had blown whistles, buzzed buzzers and joyfully participated in pummelling themselves and others with the ubiquitous plastic squeaky hammers. It had truly been an orgy of fun to round off what had been the most extraordinary holiday either of them had experienced.

"Ah, well, back to reality," said Edwards as he opened the door of his flat. He pushed aside the post with his foot in order to get their luggage inside. "Looks like I've been pretty popular while we've been away."

"Bills, probably," said Danielle.

"Put the kettle on, darling," he said, scooping up the letters. There were about ten, large and small. He took them over to the dining-room table and sat down. "Bill, bill, bill," he rattled off without bothering to open them. "Ah, Bill." In his hand he now held a large, bulky A4 envelope bearing German stamps. He knew it could only be from William Brown, Esquire.

"There's one here from Bill Brown," he called out in eager anticipation. "Where's my letter-opener, darling? I saw you with it last." He did not want to risk tearing any of the contents.

"Here it is," said Danielle, entering the dining room. "I wonder what he has to say."

"We'll soon find out," he said, taking the knife from her and opening the envelope carefully. He extracted a sheaf of papers. They appeared to be the complete SS records of one Hans Schreiber.

"What do they say?" she asked.

"It's all in German. It'll take me a while to go through them."

"Isn't there anything from your friend?"

Edwards shuffled the papers. Yes, there it was. A handwritten letter from Brown. He read it aloud.

"Dear Mark, I hope you enjoyed your holiday and weren't too naughty!

"As you can see from the enclosed documents, I am following up a possible lead. According to those records, an officer named Schreiber was declared missing in action, presumed killed, on the Russian Front in 1944! I assume both the prosecution and the defence have already procured this material. If this turns out to be the man himself, then it's safe to assume that the defence will claim Schreiber is dead and the prosecution that he is alive and is Henry Sonntag. By the way, there were only documents on three SS men named Hans Schreiber. This one was the only man who had been posted to

Theresienstadt.

"Anyway, I wanted to do more checks and made contact with a guy who said he had been a leading member of Odessa. I thought he was a bit of a charlatan. He gave me one item of information: that Schreiber had lived with a woman after the war in Berlin and that the couple had had a son named Franz. Anyway, I thought this character was stringing me a line. When I declined to give him any money, he threatened me and walked out in a huff. I think that might have been a mistake on my part. But it didn't matter, because what happened after that made up for it.

"I checked and found out that there was a couple named Hans and Gertrude Schreiber who lived in the Charlottenburg area of Berlin in 1946. I had to grease a few palms to find out that they had indeed had a son and that his name was Franz. Anyway, to cut a long story short, I discovered that the boy had been placed into care at the age of four. He had a series of foster parents, the last being Herr Fritz Brandt and his wife Inge. They live in Düsseldorf. Flat C, Ost-strasse 12. Telephone 26 36 27. I'm due to see them the day after tomorrow. Meanwhile, I thought I'd try out a long-shot. One of the early foster parents said they thought Hans Schreiber's father was named Wolfgang and that he lived in a small town called Straelen on the Dutch border. I should think he must be dead by now. But I'm on my way there to check it out before I go on to Düsseldorf. Best regards, Bill."

"Wow!" exclaimed Danielle. "That's some letter."

Edwards ran his fingers through his hair. "You're dead right it is. If Brown can find Schreiber's son, then we have a ball-game. All we have to do is match up the DNA with Henry Sonntag's and it will prove conclusively whether or not Sonntag is Schreiber. Wow is right. God bless you, Bill Brown."

"It looks like a whole library," said Danielle, returning his attention to the photostats. "What do they say?"

"God, there must be dozens of sheets here," he said, leafing through the documents. For the next twenty minutes, Edwards punctuated his concentration with exclamations of disbelief.

"Tell me, Mark," she pleaded. "For God's sake, tell me."

"This is fantastic, Dani. The whole record of Hans Schreiber. The whole shebang. You won't believe some of this stuff. There's a complete signed typed biography of the man. How he was born in Berlin and how his family moved to Straelen when he was four."

"That ties in with what Brown said in his letter."

"There's more," Edwards enthused. "Much more. Apparently, he had to go through all this paraphernalia because he had to ask permission to get engaged. He says he intended to get engaged in May 1944. He must have been on leave or something when he met this girl. Let's see, what's her name? Er, Gertrude Haas ... from Berlin. There's a family tree for both of them going back to the eighteenth century."

"Probably wanted to make sure there wasn't any Jewish blood," she said sarcastically.

"Spot on, Dani. There's even a pageful of excuses as to why some of the details are missing. But the most fascinating thing here is this medical report from when he first entered the SS. Look at this stuff. Those crazy Krauts were mad for detail. There's a checklist for skin colour, eye colour, hair colour, even the shape of the hair, for God's sake. It concludes that our friend Schreiber was, quote, Nordic with a little mixture, but still within the Aryan concept, unquote."

The reporter shuffled the papers excitedly. "Just look at this, Dani," he said. "The doctor even had to ask him whether he bed-wet, what age he learned to talk, walk and speak."

"What does that word say?" she said, pointing to the top of the page.

Edwards burst out laughing. "*Geschlechtsorgane*. Trust you

to pick out the word for genitals."

"Well?" She smiled demurely.

"Normal, whatever that means."

"Probably uncircumcised."

"Hmm, you're probably right. But he wasn't completely A1."

"What do you mean?"

"The boy Schreiber suffered from asthma."

"Mark, I don't know how you can understand that doctor's scrawl."

"It's not easy, believe me."

"Is that his signature? At least I can read that."

"Jesus!"

"What is it, Mark?"

"I hadn't noticed it before. I don't know how Bill missed it. It's signed Obersturmführer Dr Wolfgang Schreiber." He shuffled through the papers again. "Yes, here it is. In the family tree."

"Maybe it's not his father, but a man with the same name."

"Hmm. Maybe. Dani, look at this." She peered over his shoulder. "It's a list of his postings and his promotions. He got sent to Theresienstadt in 1941. As Bill said, he finally wound up on the Russian Front and was reported missing, presumed killed in action."

She picked up the white envelope. "Shall I throw it away?" Before receiving a reply, she checked instinctively to see if it was empty. "Hey, you missed another folio ... Oh, Mark," she gasped.

There before them was a photostat of three photographs of a young SS officer resplendent in his new uniform. "He doesn't look like Sonntag. It's not him."

Edwards scratched his head. "Remember, Schreiber stole Soferman's identity. He must have had plastic surgery."

"It's not him and you know it, Mark."

"You know what that means, Dani. It means this information is useless both for the defence and the prosecution. The defence will make great play of producing paperwork on all the Schreibers and proving that none was the defendant. The prosecution will of course say that this is irrelevant and that the files must have been lost. It'll be a stalemate. And they already know it."

"What do you think, Mark?"

"I smell a rat. There are too many coincidences here. Look, there were only a few Hans Schreibers in all the records at the Documentation Centre ... and only one who served at Theresienstadt. This one. I just don't understand it."

The crime reporter's consternation was relieved temporarily by the ringing of his telephone. It was Bob Webb.

"Hi, Mark. When did you get back?"

"A few minutes ago, Bob. I ..." He was about to relate the developments, but thought better of it. It was premature to involve the police. "We had a great time, Bob. Magic."

"How's Danielle?"

"Fine. She sends her love. By the way ..."

"Yes, mate."

"We're getting married."

"Great!" enthused Webb. "It's about time you made an honest woman of her."

"There's something else, Bob."

"Fire away."

"We want you to be best man."

"Honoured, dear friend. Honoured. When's it going to be?"

"Sometime after the trial."

"Talking about the trial, mate, I've got some news for you. The date's just been fixed. It's next Monday."

For a moment the reporter's head spun. It was only four days away. "Bloody hell, that's a bit quick, isn't it? They usually give plenty of notice on a public-interest trial."

"Apparently both sides are ready to roll."

"Thanks, Bob. See you in court."

Edwards replaced the receiver and turned to Danielle. "It's next Monday. The trial's next bloody Monday."

"What are we going to do?"

"What can we do? We can only rely on Brown to come up with something before then. The way he's going that could be a distinct possibility."

"How long do you think the trial will last, Mark?"

"That's anyone's guess. We mustn't panic. There's still plenty of time."

"What about Cohen?"

"You're right," he said, grabbing the phone and ringing the man's home number. It was already late at night.

"Sam here," came the tired response.

"Sam, it's Mark Edwards. How are you?"

"Oh, hello, Mark." The voice was suddenly enthusiastic. "How was Israel? Great country, isn't it?"

"Listen, Sam. Have you heard from Bill Brown?"

"Yes. I got a short note from him this morning. He just said he was making good progress."

"Sam, I've just heard the trial is starting on Monday."

"Jesus," exclaimed Cohen. "What the hell are we going to do?"

"Listen, Sam, I know that Brown is on to something. We'll just have to be patient. And there's another thing ..."

"Yes?"

"The information could go either way."

"What do you mean?"

"It could prove that Henry Sonntag is Hans Schreiber."

"And ..."

"It could prove that he isn't."

"Fifty-fifty, Mark. I'm a gambling man. I'll settle for those odds."

240

CHAPTER FIFTEEN

THE CENTRAL CRIMINAL COURT
Court Number One
Before Mr Justice Pilkington
The Crown vs. Henry Sonntag

A little westwards of St Martin's Church, slightly lower down Ludgate Hill, runs a street called Old Bailey. It is this otherwise nondescript street which gives its name to probably the most famous court in the world. Faced with Portland stone, the building that houses the Central Criminal Court is grimly suited to the dispensation of justice. Built just after the turn of the century, it centres around a dome surmounted by a twelve-foot-high gilded figure of Justice, her eyes unbandaged, her outstretched arms holding the sword and scales.

Perched above the massive segmental pediment of the main entrance are the sculptured figures of Truth, Justice and the Recording Angel. Inside, under the dome and at the head of a marble staircase, is a central hall. The lunettes of the dome were painted with murals symbolizing the meting out of Justice, the Mosaic Law and English Law as represented by the regal figure of King Alfred. In the hall stands a remarkable collection of sculptures, including those of monarchs, such as Charles I, who faced the ultimate cruelty of Justice. That the Old Bailey now stands on the site of the notorious Newgate Prison can perhaps be seen as progress. The prison, once a medieval gateway, was an appalling place where violent felons and others were incarcerated. It was no respecter of wealth or position.

On production of their press passes, Mark Edwards,

Danielle Green and Dieter Müller had undergone the usual security checks before being allowed in through the main entrance. Along with barristers, clerks, court workers and witnesses, they were made to enter a perspex cylinder, half of which closed behind them. The other half opened only when the pressure pad on which they were standing had registered their weight.

"Beam me up, Scottie," Edwards had mouthed as Danielle waited for him to gain entrance. A police officer had then instructed them to pass through a metal-detector before they were body-searched.

Given the all-clear, they made their way to No. 1 Court, the venue for all the great murder trials of the century. Edwards had been there on many occasions, but for Green and Müller it was a new experience. The court was still empty and it was this fact, perhaps, which made it all the more imposing. The veneered oak edifice was indeed huge compared to other courts.

"We'll be sitting here," said Edwards, "in front of the jury and facing the barristers. Personally, I think it's a lousy position, but ours is not to reason why. In line with the jury, at the end there, to the right of the judge's dais, is the witness box. The thing with the canopy and the microphone. That big raised area is the dock. So, when we take our seats, the dock will be on our right, the jury behind us, the witness box, judge and Clerk of the Court on our left and the barristers facing us. Frankly, I think they get a better all-round view up there." He pointed to the gallery where relatives and friends of the accused and members of the public would soon throng.

"Not room for many people up there, is there?" said Müller.

"About twenty-six," Edwards replied. "Thirty at a pinch. It's usually first come, first served."

"My parents and Auntie Becky won't be among them, though," said Danielle. "They've decided to let me be their representative."

Almost before she had finished speaking, their attention was distracted by the sight of Nigel Blomberg and his assistant, Brian Jones, sweeping into court. Wigged and gowned, the counsel for the prosecution looked purposeful and determined. Within minutes Blomberg's adversary, Sir John Tilson, had arrived with his entourage. Then came the rest of the press, who also took up many overflow benches. When most were seated, Henry Sonntag was led into the court and up the short flight of steps to the dock, which was about forty feet from the judge's dais. A court officer sat a few feet from the defendant and on his right. A tremendous hubbub erupted as the public gallery began to fill.

Danielle stared at Henry Sonntag. The accused was dressed in a charcoal-grey suit and subdued blue tie. He sat motionless, eyes seemingly fixed on the judge's dais. She thought he looked extremely aristocratic. However hard she tried, she still suffered ambivalent feelings towards the man.

Mr Justice Pilkington, an elfin-faced man of advanced years, was still in his chambers, toying with the ermine collar on his scarlet robe. He loved murder trials. Lurking behind his somewhat benign countenance was the steel that had made his reputation. The appendage "hanging judge" in a land without capital punishment was indeed an accolade that struck fear into most defence counsels. But the judge knew that Sir John Tilson, QC, was not one of them. Henry Sonntag's counsel was unfazed by the reputations of others and was about as good a representative as the defendant could hope for.

The courtroom buzzed again as ushers delivered seating instructions to latecomers. Some seasoned court reporters were making a spectacle of themselves by vying with each another for the best places.

With the court packed to the rafters, attention was diverted to the members of the jury filing in. Eight men, four women.

One of the men was West Indian and one of the women was of Asian appearance. Otherwise the jurors bore the usual attributes of the English: pale and stodgy complexions with a tendency towards obesity.

"Silence! Silence! Please be upstanding," bellowed the court usher, a tall man with a thin moustache.

There was much shuffling of feet and the usual nervous coughing and spluttering as Mr Justice Peregrine Pilkington entered from a door leading directly to the judge's dais. He nodded sagely. Those for whom the court tended to be a familiar habitat responded by bowing to their learned arbiter. Pilkington turned towards the jury. He had already told both counsel that he would ask its members whether any of them had lost relatives in a concentration camp.

He pointed out that he would not want any of them to suffer undue hardship because of revelations that might be made in the case. One glance at the jury told Danielle that he needn't have bothered. There wasn't a Jewish face among them.

The jury were duly sworn in.

The counsel for the prosecution rose sharply. Adjusting his wig, he shuffled a few papers and then paused deliberately until there was complete silence in the courtroom. The opportunity for histrionics was non-existent, for he was obliged by protocol to remain standing in one position. In an English court the voice and the power of the word was everything. He had been taking lessons in sound-bites, although he believed these were more suitable for television than a courtroom.

Blomberg had read many books and countless newspaper articles on the Holocaust since being appointed to the case. He felt confident that his opening speech would condition the jury to accept the prosecution's case. The barrister oozed confidence. After all, he was a Jew himself. And he was a Jew who believed with all his heart that Henry Sonntag should be incarcerated for the rest of his wretched life.

Thus, in stentorian tones and with a degree of self-righteousness, did Nigel Blomberg present his opening speech. He began by outlining the charges against Henry Sonntag. The court was hushed as he delineated the terrible crimes perpetrated against Joe Hyams and Howard Plant.

"Members of the jury," he continued, "the prosecution invite you to consider each charge separately, and you must bring in verdicts relating to each allegation separately. In order to convict any defendant of any charge, you must be sure of his guilt. We submit that in this case you can be so sure."

Blomberg paused to allow the legal gobbledygook to sink in. He then proceeded to forestall any defence argument about trying both cases at once.

"The prosecution say, members of the jury, that you are entitled to look at the circumstances of one death and find in these circumstances support for the allegations that they make in the other. In other words, that when you consider the murder of Howard Plant, the circumstances of that killing are so strikingly similar to the killing of Joseph Hyams that you can be sure, beyond reasonable doubt, that the same man committed both murders."

Again Blomberg hesitated. He hated spelling it out chapter and verse. It bored him. He could not wait for the fireworks that he knew would erupt when he reached his main theme.

"And who is that man?"

All eyes looked towards Henry Sonntag. The defendant sat rigid in the dock, his features as impassive as a rockface.

"A good question, members of the jury, as you will soon be made aware. That man was the man whom the manservant of Plant heard making the death threat; that was the man whose suitcase was packed as if he were ready to make a hasty retreat; that was the man whose home was full of Nazi memorabilia, including SS daggers; that was the man who called himself Henry Sonntag. We say, in this particular case, however, that he is not. That he is indeed somebody else."

A murmur ran around the courtroom.

"Order," shouted the judge. "Order. I demand that there be silence in this court."

The disturbance subsided quickly. So far, so good, thought the counsel for the prosecution.

"Therefore," he continued, "in the evidence that we propose to call before you, we intend to show three things: one, that he was the man that murdered Plant; two, that the man who murdered Plant must be the same man as the man who murdered the taxi driver; and three, that that man is a man not named Sonntag but, for reasons best known to himself and which will become fully apparent to you, a man who chooses to live under a subterfuge. The subterfuge of calling himself Henry Sonntag when, in fact, he is a Nazi war criminal named Hans Schreiber."

"Order. Order," cried Mr Justice Pilkington as uproar broke out in the public gallery among those who had not been privy to all the machinations of the case. "I shall have order."

It was a full minute before order was restored. Blomberg, having decided to sit down, rose sharply on a glance from the judge. Now would follow the most electrifying part of his speech, a speech that he had practised thoroughly. "May it please you, my Lord," he said, acknowledging the judge's request to continue. He then turned to the jurors. "Members of the jury, upon you is the onus of deciding the guilt or innocence of the man who stands accused before you of two of the most bestial crimes in the annals of homicide in this country. Indeed, as I have stated, the manner in which the victims were murdered conjures up the worst excesses of Nazism. Remember the Nazis, members of the jury?" If not, he was about to enlighten them.

Blomberg waited for heads to nod. He knew that at least

three-quarters of the jury had been born after the war. He just hoped they had learned something about the Holocaust, or had at least seen *Schindler's List*.

"It is worth considering", he continued, "that never since the dawn of history had the world witnessed such a campaign of extermination as that perpetrated by the Nazis in the Second World War. This was not an explosion of religious fanaticism; not a wave of pogroms, the work of incited mobs running amok or led by a ringleader; not the riots of a soldiery gone wild or drunk with victory and wine; not the fear-wrought psychosis of revolution or civil war which rises and subsides like a whirlwind. It was none of these."

Blomberg had practised his speech and the timing of its pauses to perfection. He counted off five seconds in his mind before continuing.

"No, members of the jury, this time an entire nation was handed over by a so-called legitimate government to murderers organized by the authorities and trained to hunt and kill, with one single provision, that everyone, an entire people, be murdered – men and women, old and young, healthy and sick, everyone, without any chance of even one of those condemned to extermination escaping his fate."

The counsel for the prosecution paused again to ascertain the effect his words were having upon his audience. There were a few stifled coughs from the gallery, but the jury remained rapt.

"After they had suffered hunger, torture, degradation and humiliation inflicted on them by their tormentors to break them down, to rob them of the last shred of human dignity, and to deprive them of any strength to resist and perhaps of any desire to live, the victims were seized by the agencies of the state and brought from the four corners of Hitler's Europe to the death camps, there to be killed, individually or in groups, by the murderers' bullets over graves dug by the victims themselves, or in slaughterhouses constructed especially for human beings. For the condemned there was no judge to whom to appeal for a redress of injustice; no government from which to ask protection and punishment for the murderers; no neighbour on whose gate to knock and ask for shelter; no God to whom to pray for mercy.

"It is in all this that this last campaign of extermination differs from all the other massacres, mass killings and bloodshed perpetrated throughout history, such as the annihilation of defeated tribes in ancient times, the slaughter of conquered peoples by the Mongols, the wars of religion of the sixteenth and seventeenth centuries, the Chmielnicki pogrom of 1648, the massacres of Greeks and Armenians at the hands of the Turks at various times, even the more recent massacres in Bosnia."

Blomberg allowed a few seconds for his compacted history lesson to sink in. The silence was music to his ears. He then continued, the power of his baritone voice rising inexorably as he sought to press home the enormity of the Nazi crime.

"The Holocaust visited on the Jews is different from all these earlier massacres in its conscious and explicit planning, in its systematic execution, in the absence of any emotional element in the remorselessly applied decision to exterminate everyone, but everyone; to the exclusion of any possibility that someone, when his turn came to be liquidated, might escape his fate by surrendering, by joining the victors and collaborating with them, by converting to the victors" faith, or by selling himself into slavery in order to save his life.

"The prosecution shall seek to prove, ladies and gentlemen of the jury, that on two nights in November last, the most brutal excesses of the Nazi era were visited upon two Jews, by the defendant, a man ostensibly living as a Jew. However, we shall seek to prove that the defendant is indeed an impostor; that he is a man who has lived a lie for nigh on fifty years and that, in a racist frenzy, he carried out these brutal killings in the same fashion in which he dispatched his victims in the notorious Small Fortress of the Nazi camp at Theresienstadt. In the course of this trial in which he stands accused of two murders in the United Kingdom, we shall seek to prove that the defendant is indeed the so-called Beast of the Small Fortress, an SS officer who has the blood of many more men on his hands. In order to do this, we shall bring forward two witnesses who suffered at the hands of this man. Indeed, we shall seek to prove that the identity of one of them, a man strikingly similar in physical appearance to him, was stolen by the defendant in order that he could create a cover for himself as the Nazi empire crumbled. What better surety for survival at war's end than to pretend to be a Jewish victim? Even to the extent of having plastic surgery in order to resemble that victim, a man, members of the jury, a man whom he had believed he had executed. During the course of this trial, we shall seek to prove that not only did the man who calls himself Henry Sonntag murder Mr Hyams and Mr Plant, but that the man before you has the blood of many other Jews on his hands."

This time as Blomberg paused a buzz began to fill the courtroom, almost imperceptibly at first, and then gaining momentum as reporters and visitors in the gallery comprehended the full weight of his speech. "Nazi bastard! Rot in hell, Sonntag!" and other heated curses rained down from the gallery.

"Order. Order in court," bellowed Mr Justice Pilkington, pounding his gavel in staccato bursts. "The court will be silent," he roared above the din. "A further outburst like this and I shall have the court cleared. Order. Order."

This time it took a full three minutes for order to be restored and for Blomberg to conclude his opening address. The prosecuting counsel was now in full flow. A steely stare from

Sir John informed him that his adversary was just as determined.

Meanwhile, throughout the mayhem, Danielle had kept her gaze firmly on the man in the dock. Henry Sonntag had remained impassive, a still and lonely sentinel surrounded by a sea of bobbing heads.

"What the hell's happening with Brown?" asked Edwards as he sat in the Old Bailey cafeteria with Danielle and Dieter Müller at the end of the second day of a trial that was riveting the nation. "He's got to come up with something soon."

"Maybe he doesn't know the trial's started and is taking his time," suggested Danielle.

"His German is as good as mine," said Müller. "I can't believe he would cut himself off completely. The German newspapers are full of it. I've been keeping a close watch myself. Look, I bought yesterday's edition of *Die Welt* today." The professor removed the newspaper from his briefcase and showed it to them. The trial had made front-page headlines.

"I just can't understand it," said Edwards. "Look, Dieter, I told you that he was on the verge of a breakthrough. He was on his way to Straelen and then to Düsseldorf. He must have got the information he wanted by now."

"I agree," said Müller. "But sometimes things don't go to plan. He might have been on what you English term a wild-goose chase."

"And what about that Odessa man?" said Danielle. "Maybe he's got something to do with it." She frowned in concern. "Oh, Mark, I don't want to jump to any conclusions."

"Look," the crime reporter said, "don't think it hasn't crossed my mind."

"What are we going to do?" asked the professor. "Perhaps

we should inform the police?"

"I've thought of that, Dieter," replied Edwards. "If we're worrying prematurely, we might put a spoke in it for Bill. The last thing he'd want is the German police chasing after him. Anyway, let's analyse the situation. Bob Webb and the poofy manservant, what's his name ...?"

"Bates," said Danielle.

"Yeah, right. Well, they've given their evidence. The defence made a big play about the note and that nobody seemed to know what it meant and also the fact that the murder weapon, the gun, has never been found."

"But they found the knife," she said.

"Yes, but it was clean of fingerprints. Listen, they'll try anything to get their man off. It's only natural. So far, it's been a plain, old-fashioned murder trial. The evidence was straightforward and damning. For those of us in the know, the question of identity is more fascinating."

"So what do you propose to do, *Kamerad*?"

Edwards looked squarely at his friend. "Soferman's on tomorrow. And then this Polish priest character. Their testimonies might take a couple of days. I've got a feeling that this is when the real fireworks are going to start. And that's not even counting if and when Sonntag is called to the stand."

"So?" shrugged Müller.

"So if I haven't heard from Brown by tomorrow evening, I'll go to the police."

"Are you sure we should wait that long, Mark?" said the professor. "You are getting me worried now. Perhaps he's been attacked by *ein verrücktes Huhn*."

"A nutcase," Edwards translated.

"One more day, then," said Danielle.

"Okay, *Kameraden*, I must be going. I'll see you two tomorrow morning."

"Goodbye, Dieter," the journalists chimed in unison. They

watched the professor lope out of the cafeteria.

"It must be hard for him," said Danielle.

"What do you mean?"

"I mean that it must be tough being a German with all this going on." She glanced down at the table. "Hey, he left his newspaper behind."

"Don't worry. It'll give me something to read last thing at night."

"After having sex with me, I wouldn't have thought you'd have the strength to read," she jibed.

The following day, the tension in Court No. 1 was palpable, especially among those privy to the knowledge that a certain Herschel Soferman was being called to give evidence.

"How do you think he'll cope?" Danielle whispered to Müller as the usher requested the court to rise.

"It depends who you mean," replied the professor. "Soferman or Sonntag?"

It was true, she thought. The ordeal would probably be traumatic for both men. She leaned against Edwards. Just the touch of his body gave her comfort.

"I call Herschel Soferman," boomed Nigel Blomberg.

The court was hushed as Soferman entered from the rear door. He passed the dock without looking at Henry Sonntag and shuffled towards the witness box. He rose the couple of steps to the lectern, stood beneath the canopy and faced the court.

For a few seconds the tension in the air between the two men was like waiting for the first flash of lightning of a summer storm. Suddenly, and for the first time since the start of the trial, Henry Sonntag lost his ice-cool composure. Rising to his feet, he gripped the rail in front of him until his knuckles blanched. The accompanying officer moved to restrain him. "*Hochstapler! Lügner! Mörder!*" he bellowed. "*Nazi Schwein.*"

"The defendant will restrain himself," shouted Mr Justice Pilkington as tumult broke out in the gallery. "Order. Order."

"What did he say?" buzzed the reporters. "What did he say?"

"He said, 'Impostor, liar and murderer'," Edwards shouted above the din to those nearest him. "The other phrase you understood."

"I shall have order," warned the judge as the cacophony subsided. "I must warn the defendant that one more outburst like that and I shall have him removed."

Sir John Tilson glared at his client. Sonntag had been made fully aware of the tactics the defence would employ and the outburst was detrimental to his own interests.

Henry Sonntag took his counsel's hint and resumed his seat, his scowl re-directed at the witness.

Herschel Soferman's bloodless face stared at his adversary in abject horror. The witness began to break into a cold sweat.

"You may proceed, Mr Blomberg."

"Thank you, M'Lord," said the counsel for the prosecution, and waited for the usher to ask the necessary questions of Soferman.

"What religion are you?"

"Jewish," Soferman croaked.

All eyes turned to Henry Sonntag. He glared at the witness, but remained silent.

Herschel Soferman placed a skull-cap on his head and took the oath on the Old Testament.

"Now then, Mr Soferman," began Blomberg, "please tell us your name."

Soferman duly responded, the fear in his voice manifest.

"Mr Soferman," continued Blomberg, "I want to take you

back to a time of your life you'd probably rather forget; the days of the Second World War. First, tell us briefly about your background."

Herschel Soferman, already fully briefed by counsel, spent the next fifteen minutes relating his experiences in the orphanage, the raid on Kristallnacht, and generally what it was like to be a Jew in Berlin at that time. Danielle noted that the witness grew more and more relaxed as his narrative unfolded. Her own brief had been to write a colour piece on the trial. Her newspaper had two other specialist reporters covering the verbatim aspects.

"Thank you, Mr Soferman," interrupted Blomberg. "Now there came a time when you arrived in Theresienstadt and the notorious Small Fortress there. Please tell us about that."

The court listened agog as the witness told the story of how he had been rounded up in Berlin and transported to the transit camp north of Prague. Even Edwards and Danielle, who knew the story backwards, were once more entranced by the tale. But this did not prevent them from seeing how skilfully Blomberg was guiding his star witness.

"Now, Mr Soferman," he said cajolingly, "does any particular Nazi in the Small Fortress stand out in your mind?"

Herschel Soferman then launched into a diatribe about Hans Schreiber's terrible misdemeanours, punctuated intermittently by gasps from the gallery. Even hard-bitten court reporters looked aghast at Henry Sonntag. The defendant disappointed them by maintaining a steely repose.

"I think this is a good time to adjourn for lunch," interposed Judge Pilkington when it appeared that the witness had concluded.

"The court will rise," the usher responded.

The cafeteria buzzed with the excited chatter of those wrapped up in the only case of the day worth covering. Reporters covering other trials eyed their colleagues enviously.

"What a morning," enthused Danielle. "Sonntag's outburst was extraordinary. You could feel his hatred for Soferman."

"The poor man was as white as a sheet," said Dieter Müller, wiping some errant mashed potato from his goatee. "I felt sorry for him. But I think I'm going to feel more sorry for him later on."

"What do you mean?"

"Well, I know Sir John would not have welcomed his client's outburst, but it must mean he's got something up his sleeve. I think he is preparing to challenge Soferman on the identity issue. I think we are in for some fireworks, young lady."

"How do you think the jury's reacting?"

"On the evidence so far, I think they can have only one opinion, especially as they would not have had Sonntag's outburst translated. Mr Sonntag is as guilty as hell as far as they are ..."

The professor was interrupted by the arrival of Mark Edwards. "Phew!" the journalist whistled. "I'm famished. What's on the menu?"

"Typical English rubbish," laughed Müller.

"How's it going, darling?" Danielle asked Edwards.

"You don't know how lucky you are, Dani, working on a Sunday paper. All that time to construct your masterpieces. Meanwhile, I'm slaving away in tandem with John Tibbs in order to make sure that the public of this great metropolis are kept abreast of this incredible case. Yes," he added with mock pride, "we on the *London Evening Standard* report the news as it happens."

"As long as it's not after four-thirty or something," laughed Danielle.

"She's right, Dieter. Everything after that is a dead duck, I'm afraid. Strictly for the morning papers. Anyway, let's eat."

Within fifteen minutes, Edwards had gobbled a pallid steak pie and chips and joined his two companions for the resumption of the trial.

The break appeared to have had minimal effect on the repose of the two protagonists. Henry Sonntag once again sat bolt upright in the dock and his eyes did not appear to follow the shuffling figure of Herschel Soferman as he passed him on the way to the witness box.

"Thank you, Mr Soferman," said Nigel Blomberg, QC, once the old man had safely negotiated his way to the microphone. "Now you were relating to us the nefarious deeds of a man named Hans Schreiber. What did this Hans Schreiber look like when you saw him some fifty years ago?"

The witness's eyes glazed as he replied. "He was blond, about six feet tall and had small brown eyes. I can never forget those eyes."

"Do you remember anything particular about his methods of killing?"

"Yes. After he had finished toying with his victims, especially those who participated in the contests, he would shoot them through the nape of the neck ... and then carve a swastika on their foreheads."

"Did you manage to see the kind of knife he used to carry?"

"Yes. It was an SS dagger. It had the SS motto engraved on it. Loyalty is my honour."

"Was there anything else on the knife?"

"Yes. The initials 'HS'."

"I ask you to look at exhibit one, sir, the knife. Do you recognize it?"

"Yes. It is identical to the one he used to carry."

"Now, Mr Soferman, I am going to ask you to look at these photographs of the bodies of Mr Hyams and Mr Plant. I appreciate that these may cause you some consternation, but do you recognize anything about them?" Blomberg passed the photographs to the court usher who in turn handed them to the witness.

Herschel Soferman stared at the photos for what seemed an eternity. Finally, he croaked, "They are the same methods as used by Hans Schreiber."

The counsel for the prosecution, noting the effect that all this was having upon the jury, then reminded the witness of his visit to the identity suite at Tottenham police station.

"Did you pick out someone at that parade?"

"Yes, I did."

"As far as you were concerned, who was the man you picked out?"

"Hans Schreiber."

"And is that man, the man that you say is Hans Schreiber, in this court today?"

"Yes, sir. It is him," rasped Soferman, pointing a wavering finger at the dock. "He is the butcher. He is Hans Schreiber." The witness then burst into uncontrollable sobbing.

Once more the court broke into uproar. Reporters scurried to and fro, especially those working for evening papers and wire services. Judge Pilkington was forced once more to vent his spleen.

Henry Sonntag sat through the mayhem, a sardonic smile on his lips. There would be no more outbursts from him.

"Do you feel well enough to continue, sir?" the judge asked kindly once order had been restored.

"Yes, I am fine now," Soferman replied, wiping his rheumy eyes. Danielle thought the man looked completely spent.

"You may continue, Mr Blomberg," said the judge.

"Thank you, M'Lord, I just have one last question of this witness." He turned to Soferman. "Now, Mr Soferman, after the war did you still have your identity card or papers?"

"No, sir."

"What happened to them?"

"They were taken from me by Hans Schreiber after I had told him everything about myself and my family."

"Do you recall anything in particular that he said to you at that time?"

"Yes, I will never forget those words. He said, 'You may not look like a typical Yid, but you're Yid enough for me.'"

"What did you understand him to mean by that remark?"

"Nothing at the time. It was only recently that I realized it meant he was planning to steal my identity."

Sir John Tilson jumped quickly to his feet. "We object, my Lord. This is calling for conjecture on the part of the witness."

Judge Pilkington pondered for a few seconds. "I agree with your objection, Sir John. The jury will disregard the witness's last statement."

"Thank you, Mr Soferman," said the prosecuting counsel, and sat down.

The gaunt figure of Sir John rose, more slowly. This was the moment for him to begin his ploy. In the circumstances, it was all he had. He cleared his throat.

"If it please you, M'Lord ... Mr Soferman, is it fair to say that you hate Nazis and anybody you think might be a Nazi? In fact, that you hate everything German or that might be German?"

"Yes, I do," replied Soferman vehemently.

Tilson smiled wanly. "Don't you think this clouds your judgement, Mr Soferman?"

"No, I do not."

"I remind you, sir, about the awful horrors that you say you lived through during the Second World War. You said you had been subjected to unspeakable barbarity and described those events vividly. You said you had witnessed contests arranged by this Hans Schreiber in which Jew was pitted against Jew in gladiatorial fights to the death."

"Y-Yes," stammered Soferman.

Edwards and Danielle were not the only ones in court to know that this was a moment of truth for Herschel Soferman. The man had said that the reporter was the only person he had told about his own participation in those contests. The two journalists realized that it might seriously affect Soferman's credibility if he too were shown to be a murderer. They also knew that it was one thing to withhold facts when not asked, but quite another to lie under oath. A lie, however understandable in the circumstances, might undermine the jury's faith in him. But there was also the question of whether Henry Sonntag had told his counsel about these contests. By claiming that he himself was the real Soferman, then it was odds-on he had. The outcome rested on Tilson's next question.

"Would you say that the mind of anyone witnessing these contests might be affected by what they had seen?"

"Y-Yes," Soferman stuttered again. "I mean ..."

"Yes, Mr Soferman?"

"It's possible."

"Did you, yourself, participate in these contests, Mr Soferman?"

The court was hushed. Herschel Soferman appeared stunned. He tried to speak but no words would come.

"I ask you once more, Mr Soferman, did you yourself participate in these contests?"

Blomberg was on his feet. "My Lord, the learned counsel for the defence is subjecting the witness to undue stress."

Mr Justice Pilkington did not agree. "The witness may answer the question."

"N-No," stuttered Soferman.

"Did you not kill four men with your own hands, Mr Soferman?"

"Y-Yes ... I mean, no. Oh, my God, yes." The man began

sobbing quietly.

Tilson was aware that he was playing a dangerous game and that the whole ploy might backfire on him by making the jury more sympathetic to the witness. It was enough to have forced the man to admit that he too had blood on his hands. It was time to be more gentle. "I put it to you, Mr Soferman, that participation in those terrible contests would have tested the sanity of any man."

The counsel for the prosecution jumped to his feet again. "We object, my Lord. Is my learned friend suggesting that this witness is insane? If he is, then let him say so clearly."

"My observation was a general one, my Lord."

"Please make your point, Sir John," said Mr Justice Pilkington testily.

"Thank you, my Lord ... Furthermore, Mr Soferman, the terrible experience of being left for dead in such appalling circumstances, the difficulties you faced after making your escape, and even those encountered while establishing yourself in a foreign country would be enough to affect any human being for the rest of his life, would they not?"

"Yes, I suppose so," replied Soferman, visibly shaken, but regaining some of his composure.

"I would put it to you, Mr Soferman," Sir John continued, "that your mind has been tormented for fifty years and I am afraid your judgement has become warped."

"That is not true," the witness rasped. "My mind is clear." He then pointed again at the defendant and yelled, his voice a mixture of hurt and bitterness. "It is his mind that is warped."

"The witness will restrict himself to answering the questions," Judge Pilkington interceded.

"Thank you, M'Lord," said Sir John. "Now, Mr Soferman, may I ask you if you have changed your appearance in fifty years, taking into account, of course, the ageing process?

"No."

"Does the defendant look as he did fifty years ago?"

"Yes. He is much older. But it is the same man."

"Do you agree there is a remarkable similarity between the two of you?"

Here it comes, thought Edwards. The fat was now about to hit the fire.

"So people tell me," replied Soferman, and then as an afterthought, "Anyway, that's probably why he stole my identity."

"Indeed, Mr Soferman, your positions could be reversed."

"I don't know what you mean."

The court was rapt. Even the nervous coughing in the gallery had ceased.

"I mean that with the positions reversed, you would be in the dock and he in the witness box. Because that's the truth of the matter, isn't it, Mr Soferman? By your own admission, you have killed four men. Yet we maintain that it was not you who participated in those contests, but you who ordered them. You are in fact Hans Schreiber and Henry Sonntag is the real Herschel Soferman."

"No, no," screamed Soferman. "That's a terrible lie, a terrible lie."

Suddenly there was pandemonium, with Tilson bellowing above the din, "You know all about the horrors of Theresienstadt, Mr Soferman, because you inflicted them."

"Order. Order."

Blomberg was on his feet, banging his fist on his lectern in unison with the thumping of the judge's gavel. He was incensed by Tilson's allegations.

"Order. Order," shouted Pilkington. "I order the public gallery to be cleared."

It took a full ten minutes before Nigel Blomberg, QC, was given the opportunity to respond.

"M'Lord," he began self-righteously, "these have been

monstrous suggestions never made before today and quite unsustainable. They are mere speculation of the worst type and we object."

Mr Justice Pilkington turned to the defence counsel. "Sir John, I hope you can make good these horrendous suggestions, the like of which I have never heard in a lifetime at the bar and on the bench."

"I hear your Lordship's comments, but at the moment I am making these suggestions upon instructions from my client and I await the witness's answer."

"I believe the witness has already answered, Sir John," said the judge, "and I propose to adjourn until tomorrow morning."

"It's a lie," sobbed Soferman as the ushers moved to clear the court. "It's a lie."

CHAPTER SIXTEEN

Mark Edwards had suffered a fitful night, his mind racked by the incredible scenes in court and indecision about what to do regarding Bill Brown. He glanced at his watch. It was already seven-thirty. The sun shone weakly through a chink in his bedroom curtains. He glanced at the slumbering form of his lover. Danielle had never met the private eye and he could not therefore expect her to show the same level of concern.

He switched on the lamp at his side, his hand accidentally sweeping from the bedside table the newspaper he had begun reading the previous night. He leaned over and picked it up. As anticipated, *Die Welt* was indeed full of reports and opinions about the trial. He flicked through the pages until, suddenly, his eye was caught by a two-paragraph filler at the bottom of page five.

STRAELEN – Police are appealing for help in the identification of a man whose body was found in the middle of a main road leading into this small town on the Dutch border. They believe the hit-and-run victim was probably a tourist.

A police spokesman said it was "strange" that no documents were found on the man, whom they described as blond and in his mid-forties. The spokesman said the man wore English-made clothes, including a bow-tie, and "may have been returning from a party somewhere early in the morning."

Edwards went cold. He knew he should not jump to conclusions. It might have been anyone. But it wasn't anyone. No one other than Bill Brown would be seen dead wearing a bow-tie in the early hours of the morning. He grimaced at his own black humour.

The reporter left his bed quietly, put on his dressing gown, and made for the small escritoire in the lounge. He opened the hinged top and withdrew a large brown envelope. He extracted three photographs with "Copyright, Mail on Sunday" on the back of them. Bill Brown had had the same copies. Edwards did not know whether he would need the photographs of Henry Sonntag, but he knew now what he must do.

"I call Pastor Stanislaw Warsinski," proclaimed Nigel Blomberg, QC.

The court was hushed as the tall and stooping figure of the Polish priest came forward to take the stand. Wearing cassock and dog-collar, the bespectacled cleric brought an air of godliness to a trial imbued with tales of the Devil.

"My Lord, this witness has excellent command of English and we feel it unnecessary to call for an interpreter." On the judge's nod, Blomberg turned once again to the man in black to complete the formalities. "On which Bible do you wish to be sworn?"

"I am Roman Catholic." The English was heavily accented.

The prosecuting counsel called for the Douai version of the New Testament. He then ascertained that Pastor Warsinski was born in Warsaw and still lived there, and that he had been transported to Theresienstadt at the end of 1941.

"Did there come a time when you were sent to the Small Fortress at Terezin?"

"Yes."

The man of God then described the horrors of life in the Small Fortress, his story being similar in parts to that of Herschel Soferman. He had not witnessed the gladiatorial contests personally but had spoken to people who had.

"Does any particular Nazi stand out in your memory?"

"Yes."

"What was his name?"

"Obersturmführer Hans Schreiber."

"What impressed you about this man, Hans Schreiber?"

"He was a sadist. The man was so evil that he shook my faith in God."

"Could you elaborate, please, Pastor."

"If anyone upset him he would first taunt them, then make them kneel, then ..." The old priest hesitated, as if the memory was indeed continuing to shake his faith in the Almighty "... he would shoot them through the back of the head in cold blood."

"Did he do anything after this, sir?"

"Yes, but only if they were Jews. He would carve a swastika into their foreheads."

"You saw this with your own eyes?"

"Yes."

"Did this Hans Schreiber do anything to you personally?"

"Yes. He swore at me. He called me a Polish papist swine and then struck me across the face with his riding stick. But it was the Jews who suffered most."

"Did you think you could ever forget his face?"

"No. It was the face of pure evil."

"Now, Pastor, did you attend an identification parade at Brixton?"

"Yes."

"Did you pick somebody out there?"

"Yes. The man I knew as Schreiber."

Blomberg turned to the judge. "For the record, my Lord, that man is Henry Sonntag, the defendant ... thank you, Pastor Warsinski."

As Blomberg sat down, Mr Justice Pilkington turned to the prosecuting counsel's adversary. "Any questions, Sir John?"

"Yes, my Lord," Sir John Tilson announced wearily, as if he

were being overwhelmed by the prosecution. Nothing, however, was farther from the truth. He shuffled a few papers until he felt he commanded the jury's full attention.

"Sir," he said, turning to face the witness, "would you say that your experiences in the Small Fortress were the worst of your life? In fact, would you say the six-month period in which you were there seemed like years of mental and physical torture?"

"Yes, I suppose so."

"Would you say that your mind became tortured by this inhumanity and that, from time to time, became confused because of the strain?"

"Yes, but I will never forget my experiences or the man who inflicted such terrible tortures upon so many of God's innocents. I think God would forgive me for calling that man a beast."

"Your being a man of the cloth, sir, makes your oath to tell the whole truth all the more sacred, does it not?"

"Yes. I swear that I am telling the truth."

"You would not wittingly lie?"

"I don't understand."

"You would not lie consciously."

"I think not."

"Sir, I would ask you to look at the man third from the left in the front row of seats at the back of the court. Can you see him?"

All eyes turned to Herschel Soferman. The old man cringed. Like everyone else, he had not expected this ploy from Tilson.

"I'm afraid I cannot see him too well," said the pastor, visibly irritated.

"My Lord, I beg the court's indulgence and would request that the witness be allowed to step closer to the man in question."

"We object, my Lord," boomed Blomberg. "The previous

witness is not on trial here."

Mr Justice Pilkington considered the matter for a few seconds before pronouncing, "You may proceed, Sir John."

The court usher led the priest to within two feet of Soferman, now ashen-faced and sweating profusely.

"Now, sir, could not the man you are facing be Hans Schreiber?"

The pastor peered at Herschel Soferman, instinctively adjusting his plain round spectacles. His voice betrayed his confusion. "Y-Yes ... I suppose it could."

"Thank you, sir," said Sir John as a buzz once more filled the courtroom. "We have no further questions of this witness, my Lord."

Nigel Blomberg sprang to his feet once again. In the circumstances there was only one course open to him to minimize the damage. His own turn would come if Tilson chose to put Sonntag on the stand. "I close the case for the prosecution," he said testily.

Edwards disembarked from the Lufthansa jet at Düsseldorf's Rhine-Ruhr airport knowing that he had two choices. He could take the easiest option and head for the Brandt family address or he could travel the thirty-five miles north-west to Straelen. There was no contest. He owed it to Bill Brown to get to that small town as soon as possible.

He hired a 3 Series BMW and headed west along the A52. He could not help but acknowledge that he felt a certain nostalgia for the country, especially for Düsseldorf, which had been his base during his summer student exchange. It was a country that made it very easy for the visitor. Everything was orderly and efficient, and yet the Germans were also extremely hospitable. If you left an item of clothing in a hotel bedroom, it would be forwarded rapidly. If your car broke down on an *autobahn*, a patrol car would arrive quickly with free help. Most educated people spoke English but would let you try out your German, without being intolerant about it like the French. Danielle had feared that the new larger Germany would return to the nationalist arrogance of the past. He himself believed that the new Germans now looked to the European Community as a substitute for their old destructive nationalism. Of course there was racism, a certain animus against foreigners, but he believed that this was just as prevalent in other western European countries. There were still a few sentimental old SS veterans, but these were dying out fast.

He turned onto the motorway heading north. The roads were a revelation. London's M25 was but a distant bad dream. He was convinced that the Germans made the best roads in the world. But if they made good engineers they also possessed traits that infuriated him. Being a legalistic people, they devised rules and laws for all kinds of minor things which would be better left alone. They hated to break the law, or to see someone else breaking it. It seemed to offend against their profound need for *Ordnung*. In England, people did not hesitate to cross the road when there was no traffic. Not so in Germany. They would wait sheepishly for the pedestrian traffic light to turn green. And the Germans also liked to mind your own business for you. Once he had walked down Königsallee with a shoelace undone. No fewer than seven people had warned him to do it up, not because they were concerned with his safety, but because it looked out of place. *Ordnung muss sein.*

By the time Edwards had finished his musings, he was passing the sign announcing his destination. At first sight, Straelen looked a delightful town. Lying between the Rhine and the Maas, it struck him as an ideal location for the oft-repeated Patrick McGoohan television series, *The Prisoner*. Pastel plaster decorated the old town-houses and the cobbled central square had a timeless quality about it.

He approached one of the townsfolk and was directed to the local police station. He had decided that it would be necessary only to say that he'd read about the accident in the newspaper and thought it might be his friend.

"Why didn't you go to the police in England?" asked the sergeant in charge of the case. It was his first major incident since being posted to Straelen. He tried to decipher the Englishman's press card. A typical country bumpkin, thought Edwards. Too much Bratwurst.

"I wasn't sure, Sergeant. Anyway, I had to come to Düsseldorf on a story. I just arrived this morning. Here's my ticket."

"A friend of his, you say? Well, if it is him, I'm sorry. It's not a pretty sight. He's been patched up a bit, but the car hit him with such force that it broke nearly every bone in his body." As an afterthought, the policeman added, "His face is pretty unmarked, though."

Edwards followed the sergeant to the mortuary, his stomach knotted and his heart pounding. They entered the cold room. The body, enveloped in a grey sheet, was still lying on the slab. The German slowly uncovered the face.

The policeman was right. Bill Brown was completely unmarked around the face. Just below the chin, Edwards could see the beginning of the massive bruising which he knew must cover the rest of the body. "It's him," he said dully.

"Okay," said the policeman, replacing the sheet, "let's have a statement."

More than an hour elapsed before the Englishman was allowed to leave the station. He had asked the policeman about Wolfgang Schreiber. The officer first checked the telephone directory. There were three Schreibers but no doctor and no

Wolfgang. "It's probably ex-directory. I can't check the electoral register for you because of our stupid data protection laws," he said, "but I can do the next best thing." The man had then simply directed the reporter to the one person in town who he was sure would know.

Edwards drove the short distance to the town archivist's office in Kuhstrasse. The policeman had assured him that there was nothing that Peter Schmidt did not know about the town or its inhabitants.

"I call my client, Henry Sonntag."

Once again the tension in the court sharpened as all eyes swivelled to the man in the dock. The defendant strode the thirty feet to the witness box steely-eyed and with an upright bearing that signalled either innocence or arrogance. There were a few gasps from the gallery as he placed a *kippa* on his head and took the oath on the Old Testament.

"Please tell us your name," said Sir John.

"Henry Sonntag."

"Is that the name you were born with?"

"No. I was born Herschel Soferman. At least, that's what they told me in the orphanage in which I was brought up."

"Why did you change your name?"

"I changed it because Herschel Soferman died in the Small Fortress."

"You do not mean this literally?"

"No. I mean spiritually. His spirit was destroyed by Hans Schreiber. Henry Sonntag seemed as good a name as any to choose. Nobody seemed to care much after the war and all the records were destroyed anyway."

"Tell us, Mr Sonntag, did you kill either Howard Plant or the taxi driver, Joe Hyams?"

"No, sir. But I know who did. I will never forget the hallmarks of the butcher Hans Schreiber. I am not that man."

"Now, Mr Sonntag, please tell us about your life, starting at the outset of the Second World War."

The court sat transfixed as Henry Sonntag's story covered the same ground and described the same experiences as Herschel Soferman's. It digressed only after the escape from Theresienstadt. The defendant told a complex and compelling tale of fighting with Polish partisans, fleeing the Red Army, and reaching Berlin by an incredibly circuitous route. He too had gained employment as a translator and interrogator of suspected war criminals for British Intelligence. He too had a story that it would be difficult to prove, or disprove.

"Ah, Herr Edwards, you rang me from the police station. Welcome to Straelen. Ours is a beautiful town, no?"

Edwards shook hands with Peter Schmidt, a lean and bookish man in his early forties.

"Please, Herr Edwards, be seated. I will prepare a cup of coffee for us both."

The reporter looked around the small, well-lit ground-floor office. It was spotless and orderly, apart from some heavy books lying open on a pinewood table in the centre of the room. He stood up and moved closer to them. They were in old German script and must have dated back hundreds of years.

"You know, Herr Edwards," Schmidt called out, "Straelen was first mentioned in a certified document more than nine hundred years ago. In 1064, to be exact. Napoleon sojourned here also ... and we won the national medal for town design in 1979."

"You must be very proud, Herr Schmidt."

"I am, sir," said his host, entering the office with a cup of coffee in each hand. "This is a fine town and it has fine citizens."

"It's about one of them that I want to ask you. You see, my grandfather was German ..."

"Now I know why you speak such good German, Herr Edwards."

"Thank you. I suppose I owe him and my mother a lot in that respect."

"Milk and sugar?" asked the German.

"Just milk, please."

The archivist poured the milk. "Please continue, Herr Edwards."

"My grandfather – he died ten years ago – had a good friend who came from this town. A doctor by the name of Wolfgang Schreiber."

"Really! How fascinating. It's a shame your grandfather passed away."

"Why?"

"Old Wolfgang is still alive and kicking at ninety-five, Herr Edwards. And what's more, he still has all his faculties. A wonderful old gentleman."

It was on returning for the afternoon session that Nigel Blomberg, QC, began the task of trying to wear down Henry Sonntag. Tilson had made great play of the fact that Sonntag did not bear the tell-tale SS tattoo under his left arm or a scar in its place. His younger adversary had countered this by arguing that statistics dictated that at least some among the huge total of SS men were likely to have avoided the tattoo. Twenty minutes into the cross-examination, however, Blomberg was still far from achieving his goal.

"Now let us put to one side for the moment your true identity. You had every reason to murder Howard Plant, didn't you, Mr Sonntag? After all, the man was going to dispense with your services and owed you a lot of money in commission. You don't pretend that Hans Schreiber would have had any reason to kill Plant, do you?"

Sonntag looked squarely at the prosecuting counsel. "The man who murdered Howard Plant hated all Jews, rich or poor, and was determined to wipe them out."

"But why particularly Plant?"

"You said yourself it wasn't just Plant. Why should I kill a taxi driver?"

"Because you yourself said that the man who murdered them was a Jew-hater, and we maintain that that man is Hans Schreiber. We maintain that you are Hans Schreiber."

"That's a lie," Sonntag hissed.

Blomberg changed tack.

"I refer back to the police evidence and the notes left by the murderer. Tell me, Mr Sonntag, does 'C-street 33' mean anything to you?"

"No, sir."

"But an SS dagger does, doesn't it, Mr Sonntag?"

"I don't know what you mean."

"I am referring to the dagger found near the body of Plant. The one with the initials HS inscribed on it. HS for Hans Schreiber."

"I don't know anything about that dagger. The last time I saw a dagger like that, it was being used by Hans Schreiber ... by the man who now calls himself Herschel Soferman."

Blomberg was not about to let his quarry escape so easily. "But there are plenty of other SS daggers that you do know about, aren't there, Mr Sonntag? In your home was found a collection of Nazi memorabilia the like of which would be coveted by any Nazi-lover. I'm sure you would agree that we usually surround ourselves in our homes with things that we love. Yet you surround yourself with photos and news clippings of Terezin, and with the uniforms and weapons of the very people you say persecuted you. Do you not find that strange, sir?"

Sonntag was unfazed. "Of course it is strange. But only in that it helped me focus my hate and loathing. That room and its contents reminded me of the hell that I lived through, and yet its very presence helped me lead a more or less normal life."

Blomberg continued to drive home his attack. "I suggest that there is no doubt that you are the real Hans Schreiber. But let us take for a moment your idea that you are Soferman. Are you capable of killing?"

"No, sir."

"But Soferman was, wasn't he? In the Small Fortress, he had to kill in order to live. So even if you were Soferman, you could still have committed the murders of Plant and Hyams."

"I killed to live," replied Sonntag through pursed lips, "not to murder. It was self-defence. I could never murder."

"Finally, Mr Sonntag, let us consider what you were doing at the time of your arrest. You were preparing to flee the country, weren't you, Mr Sonntag?"

"No, I was not. I had already planned that business trip months before. I have clients in South America."

Nigel Blomberg tried a few more ploys to break Henry Sonntag, but all were fielded by the defendant with the same cool reserve. The man would not be drawn or brow-beaten.

Sir John Tilson then proceeded to call a series of character witnesses on Henry Sonntag's behalf, including Samuel Cohen. They testified as to the philanthropic nature of the defendant; that Henry Sonntag gave freely and extensively to both Jewish and non-Jewish charities.

Mark Edwards stood outside the small town-house in Annastrasse in some trepidation. Affixed to the wall next to the mahogany door was a nameplate informing all that this was the home of Dr Wolfgang Schreiber. He could not imagine that any visitors the good doctor might have would be patients. It was unlikely he would still be practising however much he coveted his title.

The journalist was troubled by the knowledge that it would be necessary to impart to a frail old man the fact that his son was standing trial for murder in a distant land. Whatever crimes Hans Schreiber had committed could not be levelled against his father, if this was indeed his father.

He rang the ornate brass doorbell twice.

The door was opened only slightly. "*Ja?*" came a woman's voice. The accent was Bavarian.

"I beg your pardon, madam," said Edwards, using the most polite form of German address. "Does the honourable Dr Wolfgang Schreiber live here?"

The woman, noting the foreign accent and the good manners, opened the door a fraction wider. Edwards could see the white of a nurse's uniform.

"I'm very sorry to bother you, but I've come a very long way to see the good doctor. I've come from London."

"Who is that, Hilde?" came a rasping voice from within.

"I don't know, Dr Schreiber," she replied. "A minute, please, Herr Doktor." She opened the door fully and faced the reporter. "Can you say who you are and why you are here," she said sternly.

Edwards' mind raced. The nurse was a formidable-looking battleaxe in her mid-fifties. A real blonde Brunnhilde. Like any good reporter, he was trained first to get his foot in the door. "Please tell him my grandfather was German and knew him before the war."

"Wait here," said the battleaxe.

Edwards was prepared to force an entry should her answer have been negative. A few seconds later she was back.

"You may come in. But please keep it brief. He is a very old man and must not be subjected to too much excitement."

"I assure you I will, madam," said Edwards, and crossed the threshold.

"Wait in the hall, please. I will just prepare him."

The first thing Edwards noticed was that the house had that sort of mustiness that one always associates with the elderly. The second was the ticking sounds that seemed to emanate from every room. Suddenly the gongs of the grandfather clock opposite him sounded. They were followed quickly by more highly pitched chimes and bells. Edwards glanced at his watch automatically and then smiled to himself at his foolishness. It was already five in the evening.

"Clocks," said the nurse on her return. "He loves clocks. Not that he can hear them very well. You may go in now."

Edwards followed the heavily starched uniform as it swished along a short corridor and into a room to his right. Dr Wolfgang Schreiber was sitting in a wheelchair silhouetted against a pair of large french doors. He was facing the garden.

"Lavender's going to do well this summer," he said. "I've had three more bushes planted."

As soon as the old man had finished speaking, the reporter sensed the heady scent of lavender in the room. It was all around. Soferman had mentioned how much Hans Schreiber loved lavender and Danielle had said that Sonntag's house had stunk of it, even though he had later claimed that it was to focus his hate. No, this was too much of a coincidence. The man before him had to be Hans Schreiber's father.

"Good evening, Herr Doktor," said Edwards warmly.

"Please, sit down young man," the old man gestured,

swivelling round to face him.

As Edwards' eyes adjusted to the light, he could see that the man before him was truly ancient. His skin was pallid and blotchy and wiry tufts of hair sprouted from his nose and ears. He wore a hearing aid and thick-lensed spectacles. There was little overt resemblance to Henry Sonntag.

"Now what's this I hear? Your grandfather was an acquaintance of mine?"

"Yes. Ludwig Braun." It was the first name that came to mind.

"You'll have to speak up, young man. I'm afraid I'm half deaf. And these glasses are just for show. I'm almost totally blind as well. I can see only shadows. I don't remember any Ludwig Braun, though. You're from England, you say."

Edwards, realizing that the photographs of Henry Sonntag he carried were totally useless, raised his voice by several decibels. "Yes, my grandfather was a German prisoner of war. He used to mention that you were his family doctor and how good you were. I told him before he died that if I ever visited Straelen, I'd look you up. Frankly, I didn't believe you'd still be alive."

"Hmm, I did have a few Braun families on my list, but I don't remember any Ludwig."

Edwards realized that the conversation was going nowhere. It was best to come to the point sooner rather than later. He could not bring himself to play games with the old man.

"There's another reason why I'm here, Herr Doktor."

The old man's ancient features took on an odd expression, as if he knew he was about to be faced with an unpalatable truth.

"If you have seen or heard the media you will know that there is a major court case going on in London at this moment."

"I told you, I am blind and I cannot hear well," said the

doctor defensively. "What is this court case?"

Edwards took a deep breath. "My name is Mark Edwards. I am an English journalist. There's a man named Henry Sonntag who is on trial for murdering two Jews in London. The prosecution is claiming that this man is really Hans Schreiber, who was an SS officer at Theresienstadt. I believe that he is your son. The problem is that Sonntag claims that the main prosecution witness against him is in fact the real Hans Schreiber. I'm afraid it's very complicated."

Wolfgang Schreiber remained silent for what seemed an eternity. "Go on," he said simply.

"I have checked all the records and they seem to point conclusively to the fact that Hans Schreiber is your son." Edwards' heart was in his mouth as he prepared to state the true purpose of his visit. "I know how difficult this must be for you. But if we can check your DNA against that of the two men, it will prove conclusively who is your son and may save an innocent man from being punished."

Once again there was a long silence before Wolfgang Schreiber replied.

"I have no son, Herr Edwards," the old man rasped. "My son was killed on the Russian front. He is dead. He no longer exists. You understand?"

"But ..."

"Nurse! Nurse!"

"Please go, sir," ordered the battleaxe as she scurried into the room. "Can't you see you're upsetting him? He's a very old man."

Mark Edwards, nonplussed, allowed himself to be shown the door without objecting. There was simply nothing he could do. He could not force a man of ninety-five to co-operate. The only avenue now left open to him was the Brandt family in Düsseldorf.

Danielle Green had never felt so alone. The events of the third day of the trial had been testing enough. The fact that she had not had the familiar figure of Dieter Müller next to her was like losing a confidant when she needed one most.

By six o'clock that morning, her lover had already left their flat for Heathrow with instructions to inform his office that he was suffering from a severe bout of flu. He had assured her that Nick Logan would find plenty of people willing to replace him. She had expressed her trepidation, but Mark had been determined to check out the newspaper story. "I owe it to Bill Brown." He had been adamant that the police should not yet be called in.

She could not get back to sleep and for the next two hours had sat up in bed worrying about him. Finally, unable to bear it any longer, she had telephoned the only other person in whom she felt she could confide. But after she had told him about Mark, the professor had said that he was suffering from a stomach bug himself and might have to miss the day's proceedings. He had blamed the illness on the Old Bailey's cottage pie.

Müller had missed perhaps the most fascinating day in court yet, as Henry Sonntag parried all attempts to faze him. The closing speeches by Blomberg and Tilson, though, had been predictable. The former had played on the fact that only Sonntag had had the motive to kill Plant, that he had been identified positively as Schreiber, and that his defence that he was Soferman had been a scurrilous lie, a "red herring" to deflect the truth. Sir John, for his part, had made great play of the fact that everything in the case seemed to cut both ways; that no one could be sure who was Schreiber and who was Soferman; that both looked alike, spoke alike and professed a loathing for all things German. Tilson's last words rang in her ears: "The law dictates that where there is doubt, there must be acquittal." She glanced at her watch as she sat by the telephone. It was already seven in the evening and Mark had not rung. She watched the television like an automaton, unable to concentrate even on the leading item on the Channel Four news.

"In another sensational day in the Old Bailey trial of ..." the newsreader began. The only factor that focused her mind was the artist's impressions of the main characters in the trial. Soferman and Sonntag looked more alike in the drawing than they did in real life.

The phone rang.

Danielle jumped. She stared at it in shock before picking up the receiver. "Hello," she said apprehensively.

"Hello, darling," came the reply, setting her heart thumping.

"Oh, Mark, I've been so worried."

"Everything's okay with me, Dani. Don't worry. As long as you're okay. I heard all about the trial on the news here."

"Yes. I think the judge will begin his summing up tomorrow. By the way, where are you?"

"I'm in a public telephone box right now, but I'm staying in a hotel in Straelen, a small bed and breakfast. I phoned the Brandts and they've agreed to see me at eleven o'clock tomorrow morning. Düsseldorf's only about forty miles away. I told them I was a colleague of Bill Brown ..." He hesitated. "He's dead, Dani. My hunch was right."

"Who could have done such a terrible thing?"

"It may have just been an accident," he said unconvincingly. In his heart, he was sure it was the work of Odessa or some right-wing fascist group.

"Oh, Mark. Please be careful."

"I will, Dani. Don't worry." It was understandable that she should be afraid. He was scared himself. He tried to hide the fear in his voice as he told her about his meeting with old

Schreiber. "He's convinced his son died on the Russian front. I just don't believe him. I don't know why. Maybe it was the tone of his voice."

"Please ring me as often as you can, Mark."

"Of course I will. Listen, Dani, I forgot. Take my pager into court with you tomorrow. It's on the middle shelf of the bookcase."

She glanced up at the small rectangular miracle of the modern age. The device was ideal for a court reporter. It alerted its carrier by flashing a tiny red light and vibrating before delivering a short message on the liquid crystal display.

"I see it."

"Don't forget."

"Okay."

"I love you."

Danielle sighed heavily. "I love you too, with all my heart."

It was only after he had rung off that she realized that he had not given her his hotel telephone number. And that she had not told him about Dieter Müller.

The following morning, Edwards checked out of his hotel at seven o'clock. He was eager to reach Düsseldorf. He had decided to forgo breakfast in Straelen and have it instead in an old haunt he used to frequent in the plutocratic Land capital. The small bistro just off the Königsallee had always been open for early birds. He hoped it was still there.

He glanced down at the map by his side. It looked fairly straightforward. He would take the country lane that would lead him to the main drag. He swung the black BMW into the lane, which was barely wide enough for two vehicles. The road was empty and he would have enjoyed hurling the car at speed through the cut in the countryside. But the German police were nothing if not efficient and he did not want to risk being stopped for reckless driving.

He thought about the Düsseldorf he had known six years earlier. To some, the town held little charm. But he believed this was probably attributable more to envy than to aesthetics. The plain fact was that a city that had almost been destroyed totally had picked itself up by its bootstraps to become the epitome of the Economic Miracle. In his student days, everything in Düsseldorf had breathed money. This was hardly surprising, considering that it had become second only to Frankfurt as a centre of international banking and finance. He had enjoyed the buzz of a place where in smart society people were judged by their money and how well they flaunted it. But Düsseldorf was also the birthplace of Heinrich Heine, and it could afford to promote the arts like almost no other city. Continuing to drive steadily through the country lanes, the reporter reminisced on his visits to the opera and the theatre and the unrivalled joy of the Grosses Schützenfest, the hugely popular rifleman's festival held every July along the banks of the Rhine. He had gone there with the Hartmanns, the family with whom he had spent two idyllic summers. He knew he should pay them a visit.

Edwards was so engrossed in his own thoughts that he did not notice the red coupé that had been following him for the last mile. Suddenly it started to hoot urgently, seeking to overtake. Well, thought Edwards, if the guy wanted to kill himself, it was up to him. He had already lowered his passenger window to allow more of the fresh morning air into the car. Now he pressed the button to lower his own in order to wave the guy past. He baulked at the sudden gust of cold air. "Go on, you bugger," he muttered. "Pass me, then."

He took his foot off the accelerator and waved frantically, but the red car, a Toyota Celica, did not shoot past him as he expected.

"Here, hold on, mate," he muttered as he tried to keep his eyes on the road ahead and at the same time confront the driver who had pulled alongside him. It was only then he noticed that the other man was wearing a balaclava. His first thought was that, although the morning was fresh, it wasn't that fresh.

"Pillock," Edwards shouted at the man through the open window. "Fucking overtake me, then."

Suddenly he saw the gun levelled at his head. In the next split second there was a flash as a bullet whizzed past his eyes and through the open passenger window.

"Jesus Christ!" he screamed, his first instinct being to slam on his brakes. The Toyota shot past him. There was the pungent smell of burnt rubber as it screeched to a halt at an angle that effectively blocked the road.

Mark Edwards sat rooted in his car seat as the hooded man climbed out of the red car and, gun in hand, walked purposefully towards him. The inertia brought on by abject fear was leaving him a sitting target. He was still sitting motionless when the assassin aimed his weapon.

Suddenly the instinct for survival returned. He slammed into reverse and, gearbox screaming in protest, began careering back along the lane. The engine whined with the overload of revs, the din masking the sound of several rounds which the attacker had loosed at his receding prey. Edwards did not look to check whether the man was shooting, or doing anything else for that matter. His only concern was to continue reversing at top speed until he could find a gap to back into and turn around.

He must have covered at least a quarter of a mile before he sighted an entrance to a farm track on what was now his right. As he swung into it and came to a halt to change into first, he noticed that the red car was copying his manoeuvre. Edwards didn't know which road would lead to civilization. All he was interested in was getting the hell out of there.

He accelerated up through the gears faster than he had ever done before. But a grand prix driver he was not. His pursuer may have been a lousy shot, but he was already gaining.

"Bastard!" screamed Edwards as the adrenalin pumped through his veins. He negotiated the bends with all the expertise he could muster, yet still the Toyota gained.

He slammed into third and then down into second as he fought to negotiate a double chicane. A quick glance in his mirror confirmed his worst fears. The Toyota was right on his back bumper. "Jesus!"

The BMW shrieked as he put his foot to the floor, once more creating a precious gap between pursued and pursuer. But then his heart plummeted. He appeared to be in a cul-de-sac.

"Oh, shit!" he screamed, slamming on the brakes. The G-forces sent his stomach into his mouth.

The driver of the red Toyota, also seemingly unaware of the topography of the area, did not react with a response commensurate with the circumstances. His car swerved first to the left and then to the right before hitting the lip of a ditch and hurtling into the trunk of a giant oak.

Edwards sat motionless for a few minutes as his addled brain tried to make sense of what had just taken place. Beads of sweat dripped from the tip of his nose onto his dry lips. He stared ahead, unappreciative of the idyllic country scene facing him: blue sky above, cows grazing in the meadow, their concentration suspended only temporarily by the follies of human beings. Had this gunman killed Brown? Why was somebody so interested in preventing them from knowing more about Hans Schreiber? Why was old man Schreiber so reticent? Was Henry Sonntag manipulating events from behind bars? There were a thousand questions. And he did not have the answers.

He climbed groggily from his car, checking that there was no damage to the vehicle. Miraculously, the BMW had escaped without a scratch. He peered at the twisted heap of the Toyota. It resembled a crushed beetle. His first instinct was to get the hell out. Then curiosity took over. He walked the ten yards between him and his adversary with more than a little trepidation. The man might be alive and ready to gun him down.

On closer inspection, Edwards could see that no one could have survived this wreck. The whole front of the car had caved in, smashing the windscreen. The driver was slumped over the hideously twisted steering wheel. Blood had oozed in patches over a wide area of the balaclava. The reporter placed two fingers under the base of the woollen helmet and felt for the pulse in the man's neck. There was none. He then cupped the man's shattered head in his hands and slowly shifted him back into his seat. Carefully, he raised the balaclava to just above the hairline.

Despite the mess of blood and broken bone, he could make out that the dead man was young, probably in his early twenties, and that his head was shaven. It was then that he noticed the tattoo on the man's uncovered right arm which confirmed him as a neo-Nazi. It read *"Die Juden sind unser Unglück"*, the Jews are our Misfortune – a favourite slogan of Der Stürmer.

Beneath the words was a swastika.

CHAPTER SEVENTEEN

While Mark Edwards was driving urgently towards Düsseldorf, others connected directly with the trial of Henry Sonntag in the United Kingdom were still asleep. London was one hour behind the Continent.

In deepest Hampshire, the haunt of stockbrokers, financiers and judges, Mr Justice Pilkington's sleep was peaceful. He had worked all evening on his summation and was satisfied that the jury would be advised correctly. True, the case had been extremely emotional. Yet most murder trials were. Passions had run high, yet no more than in other racist trials on which he had adjudicated. However, the differences in the Sonntag case had been the modus operandi of the killer and the extraordinary claims made by the defence. Despite the latter, the good judge believed there could be only one verdict.

A few miles further west, Sir John Tilson, QC, was sleeping fitfully. He had clutched at straws, trying to introduce an element of doubt into the jury's mind. His client's early outburst had not helped and Sir John had had to admit that the evidence against him was substantial. He had been worried about Sonntag testifying, fearing that the man would be hoisted by his own petard. Instead, Sonntag had performed admirably. The barrister felt that they had succeeded in sowing an element of doubt in the minds of the jury, if not the judge.

In Thaxted, rural Essex, some two hundred miles to the north-east, the counsel for the prosecution was enjoying the satisfying slumber of one confident of success. The Crown would demonstrate once again its ability to protect its subjects from those who would do them harm. There were many who saw Nigel Blomberg, QC, as a future Lord Chief Justice, none more so than Nigel Blomberg himself. The Sonntag affair was the sort of case on which reputations were made.

Meanwhile, in a small terraced house in Balham, south London, a man at the opposite end of the court spectrum was already awake and drinking a welcome mug of hot chocolate. Fred Higgins was an early riser; always had been. It was usually the case with ex-servicemen. Following his national service, spent fighting slant-eyed rebels in Malaya, the logical progression for Higgins was to join the police force. This he had done, serving with distinction for nigh on thirty years. On retirement from the Met, Higgins had applied for a post as attendant at the most famous criminal court in the world. Now several years in the job, he thought he had seen them all – the murderers, the robbers, the rapists. But the Sonntag case was the first in which he could recall having to clear the public gallery.

The man in the white shirt and scarlet shoulder-flashes had often had to admonish errant family members of accused or victim. Usually a stern word and a finger-wagging had achieved the necessary. However, he had never experienced emotions running as high as they were in the current trial in No. 1 Court.

As Fred Higgins sipped his hot chocolate, he prayed that the coming day would not see a repeat of those scenes.

Mark Edwards drove down Königsallee, delighting in the bustle of the city's most fashionable boulevard. People were already sitting in many of the pavement cafés. The hard-faced matrons of Düsseldorf would soon be parading in their finery outside the many fashion and jewellery stores. That the recession now meant that many of them could not afford to enter the stores was immaterial. To be seen was the thing.

The Englishman turned left into Graf Adolf Strasse, past

Berliner Allee and left into Ost-strasse. He pulled up outside number 12. The block looked pretty functional. It was obvious that it had been built since the war.

When he rang the doorbell of Flat C, he was praying that this might be the lead he needed to unravel the conundrum that had begun to obsess him.

"Welcome, Herr Edwards."

The man who opened the door was fat and balding. Aged about sixty-five, he had a round face with a thin clipped moustache and wore old-fashioned circular spectacles.

"Thank you," said Edwards. "Herr Brandt I presume."

"Yes, Oskar Brandt," the man smiled. "Do come in. My wife is just making some coffee. Would you like some?"

"Thank you, Herr Brandt, that would be nice," said Edwards, relieved that his host had greeted him so warmly.

The next few minutes were spent exchanging pleasantries, before Brandt raised the inevitable question. "Now, Herr Brown was saying something about the fact that our Franz's real father lives in England and wants to make contact with his son."

"Yes, that's right," the Englishman lied. "Our client, Hans Schreiber, realizes that this is an unusual request after all these years. But he is terminally ill and wishes to see his only son before he dies."

A puzzled frown crossed Brandt's face. "Oh, I'm sorry. I will try to be as much help as possible, but that may not be very much."

"What do you mean?" asked Edwards as Frau Brandt, a plump and kindly matron, brought them their coffee. She eyed her husband enquiringly.

"I mean I think you made a wasted journey, Herr Edwards," said his host. "The surname of Franz when we got him at the age of eight was Vimmer, not Schreiber."

"I don't understand." It was all Edwards could think of to

say. Then he remembered Brown's letter. There had to be some explanation, but at this point he had no idea what it might be. The only thing he could do was pursue the matter. It was still his only lead.

"Look," he said cajolingly, "there's probably some simple explanation for all this. Tell me more about Franz anyway."

"We hardly see Franz any more, Herr Edwards," said Frau Brandt. "He last turned up about nine months ago."

"Can you tell me something about him?" said Edwards. "I believe he had been fostered since an early age and that you were his final foster parents?"

"Oh dear," sighed Herr Brandt in obvious discomfort. "I'm afraid Franz was a very disruptive child. He was intelligent but he was traumatized by his experiences in early childhood. He was extremely moody. Very friendly one moment and very aggressive the next. I'm afraid to say ..." The old man looked at his wife.

She sighed deeply. "You might as well tell him, Oskar."

"Franz left our home at sixteen, Herr Edwards," said Oskar Brandt. "He usually visits us once a year for a few hours. The last time he came was about nine months ago. I don't think his real father would want to meet him."

"Why not?" The Englishman was intrigued.

"Franz has peculiar views ..."

"We're Christian Democrats, you see," interrupted Frau Brandt.

"Perhaps we were not strict enough," said her husband. "Franz mixed with the local riff-raff. He came to hold strong fascist views and his opinions became even more hardened after reunification. I'm afraid the boy always idealized his real father while hating his mother for abandoning him. Franz believed his father was a hero for Führer and Fatherland who had died alongside Hitler in the bunker. I think maybe you should not tell his father this."

There was only one thought racing through Mark Edwards' mind: Like grandfather, like father, like son. "Do you have any photographs of Franz?"

"Only these," said Frau Brandt, extracting a small photo album from the drawer of an old oak dresser. "I'm afraid they're not very good. They're only from when he was a child."

Edwards flicked through the album. The photographs must have been taken with an old box camera. They were very fuzzy and gave no clue as to the man's present appearance. "What does he look like now?"

Herr Brandt shrugged. "Tall. Thin. Clean-shaven. Pretty ordinary-looking, really."

Edwards rubbed his chin in disappointment. "Thank you, Herr and Frau Brandt. You have been a great help. Here's my telephone number in London. If Franz should make contact again, kindly ask him to call me."

Oskar Brandt lifted himself wearily from his chair. He looked firstly at his wife and then at his guest. "There is one other thing, Herr Edwards. I don't know whether it will help you. When you mentioned that his real father was terminally ill, it rather threw me."

"What do you mean?"

"It is all rather sad," said Frau Brandt.

"It happened about a year ago," Oskar Brandt continued. "An elderly lady claiming to be Franz's mother came looking for him. We were a bit hesitant with you before because, you see, she too said she was suffering from a terminal illness and that she wanted to see her son before she died."

"What was her name?" asked Edwards. It had to be the Gertrude Bill Brown had mentioned in his letter.

"She said her name was Gertrude Vimmer. She said her husband, Fritz, had recently died. She said she had nobody else in the world apart from her son. She gave us a sealed package and then asked if she could write a letter to her son. It must have been a long letter. It took her a full half-hour to write and she seemed distressed. She sealed the envelope and asked us to give both to Franz when he next visited, which we did, of course. He turned up three months afterwards. It was very sad. He went as white as a sheet when he read the letter. He didn't say another word. Just took the package and left."

"Did Frau Vimmer leave an address?" asked Edwards, trying to unscramble his brain.

"Yes, here it is," said Frau Brandt, flicking through her phone book. "We tried telephoning her after Franz came round, but her number was out of order. Now where is it?"

Edwards gripped the side of the dresser until his knuckles blanched.

"Yes, here it is ... Berlin. Charlottenstrasse 33."

"Hold on there," bellowed Fred Higgins. "Don't all push and shove. First come, first served." The court attendant had never seen anything like it. At least one eager beaver had been outside the entrance to No. 1's gallery since the early hours. The trial that seemed to have caught the whole world's imagination was causing a nightmare for one Frederick Arthur Higgins. He was thankful at least that there were no family members of the accused or the victims staking their claim to prime positions. Indeed, the only person who had had special permission to enter before anyone else was the man whom he had seen giving evidence during the trial, the one they said resembled the defendant. The man had said that the view had been too restricted for him downstairs. Well, thought Higgins, he now had the best seat in the house. Front row in the gallery. It was surprising how those old codgers bounded up the stairs when it came to the end of a trial.

Some twenty feet below, and opposite the gallery, Danielle Green sat fidgeting nervously with her pager. Mark had caught her on her car phone as she was driving into town and had explained breathlessly how he was following up a hot lead which necessitated flying to Berlin. He had assured her that he was safe and that there was nothing for her to worry about. He had warned her not to mention a word to anyone. But she was worried. She had recognized a hesitancy in his voice which told her he was hiding something.

Danielle had telephoned Dieter Müller earlier from home to ask how he was feeling. The professor had told her that his illness had been diagnosed as a severe form of gastro-enteritis. He said that however desperate he was to see the conclusion of the trial, the bug had laid him out completely.

As the dénouement of the trial approached, the chief feature writer of the *Mail on Sunday* had never felt so alone.

Never had Mark Edwards wished a flight to be over more quickly than the one he took from Düsseldorf to Berlin's Tegel airport. In a little over an hour he was in a taxi headed for the Charlottenburg district near by. The adrenalin began pumping as he neared his destination. He was hoping against hope that Gertrude Vimmer was still alive; that she knew the whereabouts of her son; that she or he might be able to clear up the mystery of the address in the killer's note, C-street 33.

"Here it is," said the driver, pulling up outside a small town-house. "Number 33."

The reporter's pulse raced. There was a "for sale" notice outside the property. He paid the driver and walked up to the green-painted front door. He rang three times and then peered through the letter-box. It was clear that the place was empty. Then something caught his eye. He noticed the next-door neighbour peeping out from behind a curtain. Anything was worth trying now, he thought.

The curtain returned quickly to its normal position as Edwards approached the house. He rang twice before an old woman's voice cackled from behind the door. "What do you want?"

"I'm looking for Frau Gertrude Vimmer," he shouted back. "It's very urgent."

The wait seemed interminable before the door creaked open. A frail old lady stood before him, her wispy white hair unkempt and her face a map of wrinkles. "It won't help any more if it's urgent, young man," the woman said in a surprisingly firm voice. "Frau Vimmer is dead. She died about ten months ago."

Edwards knew he was staring failure in the face. "Can you tell me something about her, madam. You see, I'm a lawyer representing a distant relative who wanted to make contact with her."

The old lady hesitated. She looked him up and down. The man seemed personable enough, and a lonely widow needed company occasionally. "You'd better come in," she said. "But I can't talk for too long. I have to go out."

"That's fine. Just a few minutes will do. My name is Mark Edwards and, as you can tell by my accent, I'm from England."

She led him into the morning room. There was a strong smell of cinnamon which reminded Edwards of the biscuits Danielle's mother loved to bake. He sat in a chair opposite the old lady.

"You know," she said, "you're the second man coming round here talking about being a relative or something."

"What do you mean?"

"Well, shortly after Gertrude died, there was this chap who came knocking on my door. Said he was her son. I looked at him hard. And you know something, I think it may have been him."

Edwards realized that the woman had obviously recognized Franz. "What did he look like, Frau ...?"

"Haas."

She then proceeded to give a description which matched that given by the Brandts.

"Did he leave a contact address or telephone number?" Edwards' heart began to quicken.

"No, he just said it didn't matter any more. He knew what he had to do. The way he said it was a bit eerie. 'I know what I have to do,' he said."

The Englishman sighed deeply. He was so near, and yet so far. "Tell me, Fräu Haas, did you know his mother well?"

"Did I know her well?" she replied wistfully. "Gertrude was my best friend. We were neighbours ever since I was a newlywed just after the war. She was living with a man. A terrible man ... maybe I shouldn't be telling you all this."

"No, please go on. Please, Fräu Haas."

"He was a real Nazi, that one. An SS man. He used to beat her up something rotten. I hated him. Thank God, he left her after only a few months. Thank God, she eventually married again and led a reasonably happy life. Then, last year, Herr Vimmer died and she got the cancer. It was all over in weeks. The pair of them."

"What was the name of the first man she lived with?" the reporter asked, his mind racing.

"Schreiber. Hans Schreiber. And I hope he comes to a sticky end. If he's still alive."

"But I was told Gertrude and Hans were married."

"Yes, that's what everyone thought. You know, it was a bit of a stigma then to be living with someone. You'd have thought people would have had enough on their minds with all the devastation."

"What happened to her son, Fräu Haas?"

"Oh, he came along about nine months after Schreiber left. It was such a pity."

"What do you mean?"

"Poor Fritz Vimmer just couldn't take to the boy. He was a good man, but he couldn't accept another man's son. It was one of the reasons they didn't get married. Not until she agreed to put Dieter into care and ..."

"Dieter?"

"Yes. His first name was Franz but she always called him by his second, Dieter."

Edwards suddenly felt his whole body begin to tingle. "What was Gertrude's maiden name, Fräu Haas?"

"Müller. Why?"

"Jesus Christ," he gasped.

"What's wrong, Herr Edwards? You look as though you've seen a ghost."

Edwards knew he had to act quickly. He withdrew a hundred-mark note from his wallet and thrust it into the old lady's hand. "Thank you, Fräu Haas. May I use your telephone?"

"Of course," she said, "but ..."

"No, you keep it," he said. "How do I reach directory enquiries?"

Within less than a minute, Mark Edwards was through to the Faculty of History at Heidelberg University.

"No, we don't have any professor by the name of Dieter Müller here," the Dean told him tetchily. "The only Dieter Müller I've heard of is a guy who pretends to be a professor. He's a right-wing revisionist involved in neo-Nazi activities. The man's a maniac."

At the Old Bailey, Mr Justice Pilkington was already well into his summing up.

"... The prosecution have said that Henry Sonntag is Hans Schreiber. That is part of the evidence; it is not the offence. He is not charged with being Schreiber. He is charged with murder ..."

Danielle suddenly felt the vibrations of her pager. Her heart skipped a beat as she realized it had to be Mark. She unclipped the device from the belt of her grey striped suit and read the simple message. "Ring Berlin 66 22 53 immediately."

The court ushers hated any toing-and-froing during a judge's summing up. Fortunately, she was at the edge of the reporter's bench and was able to slip away without causing too much bother. Already armed with a bunch of phone cards, her fingers trembled as she dialled the number.

"Hello, Dani."

"Hello, dar ..."

"Now listen, Dani," he cut in. "Listen to me carefully. Where's Müller?"

"I-I don't know," she stammered. "I rang his home this morning and he told me he was too ill to attend court. Why? What's happened?"

"Dani, you're not going to believe this, but Dieter Müller is Hans Schreiber's son."

"What!"

"Listen. He's also a rabid neo-Nazi over here. He's crazy. I'm sure he's behind Brown's murder. He also tried to have me murdered – for God's sake don't worry, I'm okay – but I just don't know why he's done all this. There's a lot more, but I can't go into detail. Nothing makes any sense yet."

"What shall I do, Mark?" She fought to control the trembling in her voice.

"Get hold of Webb. Tell him all this. Tell him to find Müller. Whatever he does, he must find Müller."

"What shall I do after that?"

"Stay in court. Carry on as usual. I'm flying back right away, but I don't think I'll make it before the end of the session."

"Please be careful, Mark." Danielle could feel her heart pounding.

"Don't worry. I love you. 'Bye."

Within ten minutes, Danielle Green was back in her seat in court, shuddering slightly at the thought that the place next to her had once been occupied by Dieter Müller. She had given Bob Webb a description and he had assured her that he would put out an all-points and that the first port of call would be Müller's home.

As Mr Justice Pilkington droned on, she noticed a number of uniformed police officers taking up positions at the rear of the court.

"And so, members of the jury," the judge continued, "it is incumbent upon you ..."

Both Nigel Blomberg and Sir John Tilson were doodling when it happened. Each had done his respective job to the best of his ability. Each was now awaiting the verdict with equanimity, for their emotions could hardly be compared with those of the main players. Both realized that some you won and some you lost; that that was the nature of the game.

Opposite the two Queen's Counsels, Danielle Green and the court reporters tapped their pencils irritably. The judge's summing up always took an age and most of it was a recounting of what had gone before. They just wanted the verdict.

The only person paying undivided attention to Mr Justice Pilkington's summation was the lady on his right, the court stenographer. After all, it was her job not to miss a word.

Herschel Soferman was leaning on the protective bar in front of him in the first row of the gallery, trying to catch any hint that the judge was advising the jury to find Henry Sonntag guilty. He cocked his head, at the same time staring at his adversary who was sitting below, about thirty feet away. Soferman had just apologized to the brown-haired man sitting next to him for obscuring his view.

The defendant, as usual, was sitting erect in his chair and listening to the judge with stoical indifference.

Gallery attendant Fred Higgins, mindful of the hour, was preparing himself mentally to handle the rush for the exit once the judge had asked the jury to consider its verdict. He did not believe the twelve good folk would be out all that long.

Suddenly, the tall, brown-haired man next to Soferman was on his feet.

"ENOUGH!" he bellowed. "COWARDS! COWARDS!"

"Look out! He's got a gun!" screamed a woman juror.

In that same instant, all Fred Higgins could think of was how stupid it was that the Old Bailey did not employ the same security methods at the public gallery entrance as it did at the main entrance. No tubes and no metal-detectors. A farce.

Before the good judge could call for order, or the worthy counsels crane their necks to see what was happening above and behind them, the brown-haired man had levelled his weapon at the man in the dock.

Henry Sonntag did not move. Maybe he did not have time to move, or maybe he just welcomed the end to his torment.

The first shot hit the defendant in the temple. The second pierced his right ventricle and exited his left. Henry Sonntag was dead before he reached the floor.

By now the screams of those in the gallery were hysterical, people clambering over each other in an effort to escape. All except the brown-haired man, Herschel Soferman and Fred

Higgins.

Higgins, his military and police training now making him act instinctively, tried to forge his way through the mob to reach the gunman.

Herschel Soferman, either through cowardice or trauma, had curled into a whimpering ball at the feet of the brown-haired man, who lowered the gun slowly to the old man's head. He did not hesitate before blowing Herschel Soferman's brains out.

"You bastard!" screamed Higgins as he lunged at the killer. "You can't do that in my court."

The attendant grappled with the man, who coolly thrust his knee into the ex-policeman's groin. As Fred Higgins lay winded on the floor of his beloved gallery, his adversary raised the barrel of the pistol and placed it carefully into his own mouth. The force of the exploding bullet lifted him clear off his feet, over the protective barrier and down onto the floor below, narrowly missing the prostrate and trembling personages of the Queen's Counsels and their assistants.

His bones broken by the impact, the attacker's body lay askew. Some might even have imagined that the twisted figure resembled a swastika.

The smell of cordite hung in the air.

While others were simply sitting or lying around in shock, Danielle Green was making her way gingerly towards the attacker's body. She forced herself to look at it. Despite the blood, brains and bone fragments, she recognized the shaven face below the dyed and matted hair, and the unseeing steel-blue eyes that stared up at her.

CHAPTER EIGHTEEN

The first senior police officer to arrive at the scene of the carnage was also the first to discover the two letters in Dieter Müller's breast pocket which explained his motives and the killings of Joe Hyams, Howard Plant and Bill Brown.

News about the finding of the letters was soon leaked. With the media clamouring for their contents to be made known, Scotland Yard decided to bow to the pressure the day after the unprecedented events at the Old Bailey. The ensuing press release made the front pages from Berlin to Buenos Aires, from Tel Aviv to Tokyo. Part of the release carried the verbatim contents of the letters. The first, written in German, was signed "Your mother, Gertrude". The second, typewritten in English, was signed "Franz Dieter Müller". It was dated the day of his death and, therefore, must have been written that fateful morning.

Dear Dieter

I do not know where to begin. It is so very hard for me to put into words the desperation that I have felt all these years. Now that I have only a very short time to live I feel that I cannot die without at least letting you know the reasons why I had you placed into care all those years ago. My only hope is that you have had a good life. I hope you receive this letter before I die and that you can visit me, although I am frightened for the effect that this might have on you.

I began searching for you about a year ago. It was a long process. I won't bore you with it. There were many obstacles put in my way. I was an old woman who didn't have the right connections. Anyway, eventually I found out that your last foster parents were the Brandts in Düsseldorf. They seem very nice people. They told me that you idealized your real father. I feel that you must know the truth about him. He was not the glorious soldier you imagined. His name was Hans Schreiber. He was an Obersturmführer in the SS.

We pretended to be married but weren't really. It was just after the war. There was devastation everywhere in Berlin. I was so desperate that I needed the comfort of a man. Hans Schreiber was nice to me at first. But then he turned into a brute, Dieter. He was a drunken bully. He used to beat me up. He would tell me he would treat me the same way as he treated the Jews in Theresienstadt. You would not believe what he did there and I cannot bring myself to tell you, even now.

After a couple of months he came home drunk again and told me he thought the Allies were on to him. He said he had a master plan. He said he would pretend to be a Jew and try to reach England as a refugee. He laughed at the irony of it. I told him he was mad, but I was relieved that he was leaving me.

Anyway, your father left and I was alone again and pregnant. Then I met this man named Fritz Vimmer. He was a good man. He tried to make a go of it when you were born. But he just couldn't father another man's son. Of course, I never told him who your real father was. I held out until you were almost four, but the rows were becoming more frequent. Eventually, I weakened and agreed to have you placed into care. Times were hard. We hardly had anything to eat. I thought you would be better off with another family, a family that would give you love from all sides.

I wasn't sure I should tell you about your father. But Germany has changed now and it is wrong to glorify the past. I am going to give you one thing Hans Schreiber left behind. I always kept it. It is his SS dagger. My fondest wish is that you will bury this and with it the past.

Oh, Dieter. I am so sorry. Can you ever forgive me?

Your mother Gertrude

TO WHOM IT MAY CONCERN

If you are reading this letter, then it can only mean that I am dead.

I explain my actions as a glorification of my leader and saviour, Adolf Hitler, and as a response to the sullying of His eternal name by my father.

You will find accompanying this note a letter from my mother which must be read in context with my own.

My father, who will also be dead by the time you read this, was a man who betrayed all the principles as delineated by our most glorious Führer. This man, instead of fighting to the death to save the blessed Third Reich, slunk from the scene of our temporary defeat like a weasel. This man, whom I can barely bring myself to call my father, not only ran away, but adopted the identity of the very people he had so expertly and correctly murdered. This man, in order to save his own skin, actually became a member of that damned race. No words can express my horror at his perfidy.

Upon receiving the letter and his knife from my mother, I decided to attempt to find my father with the express purpose of killing him, but not without first confronting him with his crime, not against me, but against the whole German people.

To this end, I decided to come to England. I knew it was, as the English say, a long-shot. I decided the best way to flush him out was to murder a Jew. Who would care anyway? I murdered the taxi driver, believing the police would publish the note I left by the body in full. Only one man would know the meaning of C-Street 33, and his curiosity would bring him there on the appropriate date. But the police did not publish the full note. Only "For you – Hans Schreiber". I knew then that I must kill again. That it must be some prominent Jew-boy. A very rich one. Someone that would make them take notice.

Imagine my surprise when Henry Sonntag was arrested for the murders I had committed. I mean, I knew I had killed Plant. At first I did not believe all the things that were said about Sonntag. I did not believe that he could be my father. And yet the testimony of Herschel Soferman made sense. I decided I would kill my father in court. And yet I was confused. Sonntag claimed that Soferman was really my father. I knew then that I must kill them both.

I knew that the British private investigator, Brown, was on my trail and arranged to have him murdered. I also arranged the murder of Mark Edwards. I apologize to his family. I liked him. I am happy you are reading this, because it means I have succeeded in my aim. Traitors to the Fatherland must die. I must die, also, but as a true German patriot. LOYALTY IS MY HONOUR.

Franz Dieter Müller

"It was the grand gesture," said Bob Webb, opening his arms wide and almost knocking his pint off the bar counter.

"But why did he do it when he did?" said Edwards.

"Either he just snapped or he realized the game was up when the court began to fill with uniformed bobbies," suggested Danielle.

"You know something?"

Webb and Danielle looked enquiringly at the reporter.

"I kind of feel sorry for him."

"How can you say that, mate?" said Webb. "The guy nearly had you bumped off. Besides, he murdered four other innocent people."

"Three innocent people," said Danielle quickly. "Schreiber was hardly innocent."

"The point remains," said Edwards sadly, "now that we know that Sonntag didn't murder Joe Hyams and Plant, it must leave open to doubt the identity of the real Schreiber. Sonntag or Soferman. Even the court didn't get a chance to decide that." The reporter had not mentioned Dr Wolfgang Schreiber to his police friend, or to his editor for that matter. As far as everyone was concerned, he had gone to Straelen only to check out Bill Brown. There was no point in involving the doctor. The old man had denied that his son was alive, anyway. The SS file's photos were clearly of somebody else. Maybe it was just fortuitous that the names coincided. Anyway, perhaps there was another way that could prove who the real Hans Schreiber was.

"What about the funerals of the two men, Bob?" asked Danielle. "I hear they'll both be buried in a Jewish cemetery. They're both fully paid up for Waltham Abbey."

"Ironic, isn't it?" said the detective. "But there's not much that anyone can do about it. In England, you're innocent until proven guilty. There've been noises from the Jewish Board of Deputies. I mean, they're in a right state. They realize they might be burying a Nazi in their back garden."

Edwards stroked his chin thoughtfully. "There's one way we could clear the matter up, Bob."

"How?" asked the policeman, his steel-grey eyes widening.

"A DNA test."

"Shit. I hadn't thought of that ... but there's no precedent. We can't ask for a DNA test if we haven't got a reason. And as Müller's dead, we haven't got a reason."

"Bob," said Danielle, leaning towards the big man excitedly, "look into my eyes and tell me you can't do anything."

Webb looked into Danielle's emerald-green gaze. "God, but you're a lucky bastard, Edwards."

"Well ...?"

"Look," replied the policeman, "we'll have blood samples from the autopsies of each of them."

"Well ...?"

Webb shrugged. "Oh well, who needs to go through all the red tape. Peter Baker at the Met's lab in Lambeth is an old mate of mine. Leave it to Uncle Bob."

Sam Cohen welcomed Edwards and Danielle into his palatial home in the heart of Chigwell. Sam, a middle-aged Essex Boy, was proud of the fact that he had made it from a tenement in Hackney to live among the new money. True, some of his neighbours were a little suspect. They included more than a few shady businessmen and the odd East End wide boy who was clever enough not to need to escape to Spain's Costa del Crime.

"My daughter, Stephanie." He pointed proudly at a photograph of an attractive young woman wearing the black robes and mortar-board of a new graduate. "Got a first in law. She's a barrister now."

"Obviously Daddy's favourite," said Danielle.

"A real *bubbeleh*," beamed Cohen.

The businessman then introduced them to his wife, a smart-eyed blonde who scurried to and fro keeping them well stocked with coffee and cheesecake. Obviously a *balabusta*, thought Danielle.

The three then discussed the machinations of the incident that had captured the imagination of the world, especially the Jewish world.

"Extraordinary business." Cohen scratched his balding head. "That Müller chap was a complete *meshiggenah*. I read your piece in the *Standard* today. I couldn't believe he'd taken you in like that."

"That's usually the way with psychopaths, Sam. The clever ones are so hard to spot."

"And you almost copped it too, Mark, like poor old Bill Brown. I feel a bit responsible."

"Don't worry, Sam," said Edwards. "As far as Bill's concerned, it went with the territory. And I'm a crime reporter, remember."

The older man's smile of relief quickly turned to a frown of concern. "Look, maybe I shouldn't ask you for help again, but

I wonder if any of your police friends can help speed up the release of the bodies? I mean, by Jewish law, they should have been buried already. The *hevreh kedishah* are going mad."

"Burial authorities," translated Danielle.

The little man carried on. "They don't care which one may or may not be Schreiber. They say that in order to safeguard the integrity of whoever was the real Jew, both must be buried with all haste."

"Hang on a little longer, Sam," said Edwards. "I think the police'll be finished with their autopsies soon."

At that precise moment, in a building on the south bank of the River Thames, two forensic scientists from the Metropolitan Police Service were about to draw the final conclusions from their DNA testing on the blood of Henry Sonntag, Herschel Soferman and Dieter Müller.

Peter Baker, the deputy director of the laboratory, had spent the last week extracting and then analysing the genetic profiles of all three men. Firstly he had extracted the double-stranded DNA from the nuclei of the different blood cells and then, with the help of an enzyme, had chopped them into pieces of varying lengths. The DNA mixture was then placed at one end of a slab of jelly-like material with a positive electrode at the other. Baker had watched with his usual fascination as the negatively charged DNA was pulled towards the electrode, with the smaller pieces moving faster than the larger ones.

The beetle-browed scientist had then used chemicals to divide the famous double helix into single strands before mixing in a radioactive probe of small, identical pieces of synthetic DNA. The probe matched up with the opposite sequences on certain of the human DNA pieces and binded to them. Thanks to the latest development in the field, the whole process now took only a week.

He scrutinized the photographic film which recorded the position of the pieces to which the radioactive probes had attached. The pattern of bands was unique to each individual.

"Hey, Robin," he called to his colleague, "we've got a match."

The man named Robin then did a second test. "Here, look. There's another one here."

"Bloody hell!" exclaimed Baker. "That's confirmed it, then."

The forensic scientist grabbed his phone. His fingers trembled as he dialled Bob Webb's number.

"Hello, Bob. Listen, mate, are you sitting comfortably?"

"Don't fuck me about, Peter," growled Webb. "Get on with it."

"Our results show that Müller was in no way related to either of the other two."

"You're joking."

"There's something else, Bob. I couldn't believe it myself when I saw it."

"Well, go on then, you bugger," snapped Webb.

"There can be no doubt about it, Bob. Henry Sonntag and Herschel Soferman were brothers."

CHAPTER NINETEEN

Mark Edwards was already familiar with the territory. He plied the hired car, another of his favourite black BMWs, through the quiet streets of Straelen, turning finally into Annastrasse.

There was only one course of action that he could take after Webb had given him the results of the DNA test. The only possible explanation for the fact that Dieter Müller was not the son of either Sonntag or Soferman was that his mother had been made pregnant by someone else but believed the baby was Schreiber's. "She probably got pissed one night and never even realized it," was the policeman's opinion.

This explanation may have cleared up one question. But the undeniable truth that the adversaries in court were indeed brothers had posed many more. Only one man might reasonably be expected to supply some, if not all, of the answers.

"Now are you sure you want to come in, Dani?" the reporter asked, pulling up outside the home of Dr Wolfgang Schreiber. "I may have to use a little rough stuff with his nurse."

Danielle Green nodded. She was fully prepared for any eventuality. She had decided to forgo the funerals of Henry Sonntag and Herschel Soferman in order to be with her future husband. The old doctor *must* talk.

Edwards rang the doorbell with steely determination.

This time Schreiber's nurse opened the door wide. Her face bore a scowl, but before Edwards could say anything she bade them enter and led them into the room with the french doors. The old man was once again peering at his garden with unseeing eyes.

"Your guest has arrived, Herr Doktor," the Amazon said

with undisguised displeasure.

"Come in, Herr Edwards," said the old man, gesturing in welcome. "I have been expecting you. Please be seated." Wolfgang Schreiber then made staccato sniffing noises. "I smell a woman's perfume."

Edwards, astounded by the reception, could only stammer his reply. "Y-Yes, my colleague, Fräulein Danielle Green, is accompanying me."

"Hilde, I heard the kettle whistling. Please bring us some coffee."

"*Jawohl*, Herr Doktor."

"You mustn't mind her," said Schreiber apologetically. "It can't be easy looking after an old codger like me."

Edwards looked at Danielle, shaking his head in disbelief.

"I knew you would be back, Herr Edwards." The old man sighed deeply. "You see, I heard the news. Of course, I followed the case all along. But now that he is dead, I can at last open my heart. I have carried the pain for too many years."

"I don't understand, sir," said the Englishman.

"I will try to explain, but it may take a long time."

"Go at your own pace, sir. I will try not to interrupt you."

"Thank you, Herr Edwards. You see, I know that there is still some doubt about who the real Hans Schreiber was. Frankly, to me it doesn't matter any more. He is dead. That is all that matters."

The old man cleared his throat. His voice was rasping but the words were fully coherent. "You see, it all began in Berlin in 1922. That was the year Hans was born. He was my brother's boy. My older brother, Josef. It all started when my brother brought home a girlfriend. He was besotted with her. He started to fall more and more in love with her. It was inevitable that they would get married, but there was one problem." The old man hesitated as the nurse brought in their coffee. Edwards watched the old battleaxe pour. She added sugar and milk to the old man's drink but left the guests to fend for themselves.

"As I was saying ..." Schreiber brought the spout of his safety mug gingerly to his lips and took a few sips. "There was this problem, although it did not carry the same stigma as later. You see, Rachel Jakobs was a Jewess."

There was a stony silence, punctuated only by the ticking of the clocks.

My God, thought Edwards, that made Hans Schreiber a Jew. Both under Jewish law and the Nuremberg Laws.

Although Danielle could pick up only a few words, she could see that Edwards was transfixed by the man's story. She felt his body tense suddenly.

"Carry on, Herr Doktor," Edwards said quietly. He could feel his heart pounding.

"My parents were against it. Even if you discount the religious aspect, Rachel was an orphan and did not have any money. Josef was headstrong, but he did make one concession. They lived together as man and wife, but did not actually get married." The old man hesitated. Lifting his glasses, he wiped a tear from his misty, unseeing eyes. "The accident happened almost four years later. I had just got married to a local girl here – we met at university – and was just starting out in practice. Anyway, poor Josef was killed in a car crash. By that time they had had two children, Hans and Helmut, one after the other. Hans was the elder. Poor Rachel was devastated. She could not cope. She asked me to take one of the children. I took Hans. She was in Berlin and I was here in Straelen. So far away. Suddenly, I heard from my parents that she had run away with a man, a Jew, and had taken Helmut with her. My parents did not try very hard to find her. As I told you, they were against the marriage in the first place."

"So you brought up Hans," said Edwards flatly.

"Yes. It was only at the end of the war that I realized I had taken the more capricious of the two children ... but I am jumping. Let me go back to those early years. My wife and I could not have any children and we loved him as dearly as any real parents. But he was never a happy boy." For the next half-hour Mark Edwards sat enthralled by the story of the young Hans Schreiber: how the boy had been taunted at school because he was circumcized; how he had joined the SA and had participated in the terrible events of Kristallnacht; how he had pleaded to join the SS.

"What could I do, Herr Edwards? He was all we had. You see, I hated the Nazis and all that they stood for. I was a doctor. I was a man dedicated to the well-being of others. But I was weak with my adopted son. I gave him everything he wanted. Now he wanted to join the SS. But I knew that he would never be able to serve because I knew the truth. He never knew what he was then, Herr Edwards."

The reporter's ears pricked at the word "then" but he remained silent.

The doctor continued. "I told him that he would have a hard time because of his circumcision. He always believed that he'd had to have the operation because of an illness. 'You're a doctor,' he used to say, 'can't you do something about it?'" Well," the old man sighed again, "I did what I could. I used every trick in the book to become the SS medical officer in charge of recruitment at Münster."

"You altered the files, didn't you, Herr Doktor?" said the Englishman, and then added quickly, "I'm sorry. Please continue."

"Yes. You are right. I had all the relevant papers and I altered them to suit my purpose. I knew an expert forger and he helped me. I paid him quite a lot of money. When the records went back to the SS central register, all details about his mother had been expunged. I only agreed to help Hans if he would join a non-combat unit. He was A1, but I put down in his records that he suffered from asthma so that he could never be transferred to a combat force. Finally, I swapped Hans's photographs for those of some other soldier. I still don't understand why I did that. Something told me we would all pay dearly for Hitler's madness. I didn't see Hans again until the end of the war."

Something told Edwards that the conclusion of this fantastic story was about to be revealed. He could see that the old man was shaking. The reporter suddenly felt guilty for putting him through all this.

"Please, Herr Doktor," he said kindly. "If you would rather rest a little ..."

"No," rasped the old man. "No. I must tell it all. I must."

Edwards gripped Danielle's hand. She squeezed back. She did not know what the old man was saying but she could see that he was suffering.

"As I said," Schreiber continued, "the next time I saw Hans was soon after the end of the war. I was so pleased to see him. So happy that he had survived. And then ..."

Tears welled in the Englishman's eyes as he watched the old man struggle with his emotions.

"... and then he boasted to me about Theresienstadt, about how he had killed Jews and how he now planned to pretend to be a Jew in order to escape the Allies."

The old man wilted in his wheelchair, tears streaming down his gnarled face.

"Please, go on, Herr Doktor," said Edwards hoarsely. He looked at Danielle and shook his head slowly. The concern in her face mirrored his own.

"I told him, Herr Edwards ..." The doctor winced. "And when I told him, I knew then that I had lost him for ever. I was glad to lose him for ever. I told my adopted son who had become this animal ... I told him that he was a Jew."

EPILOGUE

The following day, Mark Edwards and Danielle Green drew up at the Jewish cemetery at Waltham Abbey. The sun was spreading its warmth over the serene Essex countryside. The dawn chorus itself seemed to have extended into late morning as if the birds were determined to mark this day as a new beginning.

The journalists had been moved by the extraordinary story of the blind old doctor. But there were still many questions left unanswered. Questions that no one could now answer. Did Hans Schreiber ever feel contrition for his awful deeds? Did the revelation that he was a Jew cause him crises of conscience, or did it simply make his subterfuge an easier game to play? How did Helmut become Herschel? Did his mother get married again, to a man named Soferman? And if so, what happened to them? The questions could go on for ever. But the biggest question of all would never be answered. Who had been the real Hans Schreiber?

The couple parked their car and walked silently, hand in hand, the few yards to the main office. Edwards donned his skull-cap before asking the sexton the whereabouts of the graves of Herschel Soferman and Henry Sonntag.

"Block G, Row L, numbers 112 and 113," came the reply.

"What do you mean?" said Edwards incredulously. "Does that mean they're buried next to one another?"

"Yes." The man shrugged. "That's the way they came in. One straight after the other. Neither was married and needed a double plot and neither of them had any families to object, so ..."

The pair thanked the sexton and continued to walk for a further hundred yards before they came upon the two fresh mounds. They were unmarked apart from small sticks bearing their respective numbers. According to Jewish tradition, headstones would only be set some months later.

"Mark, we don't know which grave belongs to whom," said Danielle with concern.

"Does it really matter, darling?" the reporter said, extracting a slip of paper from his pocket. "They were brothers who were born Jews and have been buried as Jews."

She stared at the fresh earth and sighed. "This is going to make a helluva book. Have you thought of a title yet?"

"There can only be one title, Dani. He took it to the grave with him: *Schreiber's Secret*."

Then in halting Hebrew, the gentile read aloud the *Mourner's Kaddish* that Danielle had transliterated for him.

"Yitgadal, ve'Yitkadash, Shemai Raba..."